COLLIDE

The Bringer of Darkness series
Book One

Taara Petts

To my Mum,

Without the support and
encouragement,

This book would not have been
possible.

All my love, and gratitude - goes to
you.

Thank you for always being there.

Prologue

*S*he perched on the hilltop; gazing down at the once life filled city – which was ruined, burned and had the faint aroma of rotten corpses. Her hair billowed in rhythm to the ashes – that had now consumed the sky.

Cautiously, he stepped towards her; hoping that he wouldn't frighten her, but she knew he was there – she always knew. "Do you remember what this place was like?" She asked; her voice cold and empty – eyes not once leaving the smoking city.

"Barely. Though, I never really liked the city. Too crowded and full of . . . humans," he replied, as he followed her stare.

"I do. It's strange, the fire never seems to go out – I never intended for that to happen. Still, I like it," she snickered and snaked her tongue out to glide along her lips.

He walked closer to her; his footsteps crunching on the untouched snowy surface, until they had fallen in line with hers. How long had she been here?

Her eyes darted to her left – where he approached from; her lip lifted in a sadistic grin. "You know, I always thought blood looked better on the snow," she teased – purposely trying to get under his skin. Her eyes trailed up to the white flakes, that had now entwined with the ashes. "So, I'm assuming you are here to convince me to come back with you? If that does not work, I guess you will drag me back?" A wryly grin spread along her lips.

He chuckled slightly – his brows narrowed.

"Afraid so, are you going to play nicely?"

"Play nicely?" She teased in a dark tone, "when do I ever-"

Before she could finish, his hand whipped up and struck her to the ground with the hilt of his sword. Black powder burst in her face - drifting into her nostrils and down her throat; she dropped to the floor and left out one pain filled gasp. He was reluctant to go to her; he had done this before, and it didn't end well . . . for him. However, he had never used the powder then - it was a new thing they had created.

"That was easier than last time," he finally said to himself. He straightened out his coat and placed his hand over her eyes; he nodded after he was satisfied, she was fully out. "I'll have to congratulate Mara, her little substance worked."

Two men in long draped clothing and faces covered with black cloth, carefully carried her into a dark carriage - the four black stallions shook their manes, as they waited impatiently. "I will make my own way there. Take her to Evander. No stops whatsoever, do you understand?" They nodded immediately and struck the horses into action. As they left, he walked up the hill and stared to the empty city. "What have you done Crow?"

⌣

She lay curled up on the bed, she looked so different than he remembered - smaller in a way. Her hair was black, dry and matted - like a stray dog. Her nails long, pointed, dark and looking more like claws with each shift. Her lips and all her veins - which had spread around her face, were the deepest purple he'd ever seen. Her eyes: however, he found it hard to look into them and when he did - it was harder to look away. An icy blue, but completely empty of emotion.

Everything was just . . . gone. It broke part of him to see her like this, yet he had felt partially responsible. She had slaughtered so many - she had tasted blood and found she liked it and if he couldn't save her, then he would have to destroy her - no matter how hard it would be.

"I know you're awake," he announced, as he slouched against the wall. She didn't raise her head or shift in his direction, but she let out a quiet hiss before she responded.

"Why have you brought me here Dacre?"

"To keep you safe." A vicious snarl rolled off her tongue and her head suddenly sprung up. She rose to her feet – the slender black bodice gown she wore, was once the most elegant – envied by everyone who saw it, but now the lace was torn and muddy.

"To keep me safe?" She mimicked with a spit.

"Yes. To protect you, we are not your enemies Crow, regardless of what you think."

"Protect me from what?" He didn't answer; his eyes darted away then back to her. "Oh, I get it now," she continued – a smirk pulling at the corner of her mouth. "Protect me from myself," she laughed maliciously; her sickening tongue trailing along her lips.

"Have you seen what you are becoming? You destroyed an entire city Crow! Killed men, women, CHILDREN!" He snarled. His fists clenched so hard – the knuckles turned white.

"Enough!" She hissed. "Is this your attempt at trying to appeal to my 'human' side?' To spark my humanity?" She scoffed and rolled her eyes.

"You are not you anymore. You are not who you used to be."

"Who did I used to be?" She snapped, Dacre growled and marched towards her; he grasped onto her arm and placed his other hand on the back of her neck. He pulled her before a tall mirror – that was holding on for its life on a rusted bent nail.

"Look at yourself, is this really who you want to be!" He barked. She battled out his grip and whirled around to face him. "Can you see how it is changing you?"

"Why did you come back Dacre? Did you think you could miraculously change me? Bring back that small, weak girl?" She raised her brow, her hand running down his chest. "Bring me back to you? You'd be better off killing me." She teased with a snicker; he pushed her back. "However, I wasn't the one who left, it was you who vanished, you were out of this. You didn't want to know. You can't stop this; it has already begun!"

"I can try," he spoke softly, but felt the tight knot of worry tighten in his stomach. It was risky, openly talking to Crow like this. She didn't like it when someone didn't agree with her – it made her angry and that's when things got destroyed.

"What makes you think that I won't kill you? Do you think you are untouchable? That I can't bring myself to harm you?" She trailed a sharp fingernail along his cheek – a threatening gesture.

9

"I know you wouldn't," he took a step closer; his face inches from hers. Crow sneered and laughed humourlessly.

"Isn't that what Markus and Elizabeth thought? Yes, they thought it to the very last moment, right before I pushed their own swords into their hearts. Evander also thought he could change my mind, didn't work out well for him either."

"The darkness is contaminating you – taking over. You didn't manage to kill Evander and I think it's because you didn't want to." She cocked her head to one side – her eyes widened slightly.

"More tricks? Evander is dead, I left him gargling on his own blood."

"And I saved him – was just in time too. Crow, the darkness is taking over at an alarming speed, but I promise you I will destroy it!"

As if his words had flipped a switch – black swallowed her eyes. A cluster of grey mist materialized around her, circling around her like tentacles. With a sneer she threw out her hands, the mist hissed and shot into his chest– burning into his flesh. Pain sizzled in his veins as his body was hauled back – crashing into the wall, blood splattered from his mouth.

"Listen to me," he began as he forced himself to stand; his hands raised – pleading with her. "You need to regain control. Try to fight it." She snapped her sharp teeth and waved a hand in dismissal. Dacre shot up; his back colliding roughly into the ceiling, before dropping to the floor.

"You're a fool Dacre. The darkness cannot take over your body, you must invite it – become one with it."

"Y-You wanted this?" He asked through blood filled coughs. She laughed bitterly.

"How naïve you all are." She leaned down and lifted his chin up; her eyes burrowing into his, "I am the Darkness." She leaned into him and gently pressed her lips to his, she flicked her wrist and smirked as she heard the bones in his neck snap.

Elegantly stepping over his body; she walked over to the door – locked, of course it was. How silly of them to think that a flimsy door could contain her. The door shrieked and cried from its hinges, before crumbling into dust before her.

"HOLD!" A man with cropped hair and an overgrown beard hollered – fury fuelled his face. Evander's jaw clenched as he aimed his pistol at her, the men that flanked him following his movement.

A grin ghosted across Crow's face. "You aren't dead after all. I guess I'll have to try harder next time," she raised her brow – teasing. "Are you going to shoot me, Evander?" Crow asked in an amused tone.

"Stop where you are Crow. I don't want to hurt you," he warned. "I've never wanted to hurt you." She smirked as she saw the torment in his eyes; he hated doing this.

"Dacre will not be happy if you do." She laughed and fluttered her eyes. "Even he couldn't bring himself to kill me, I had him quivering under my touch – old habits die hard I guess."

"Where is he?" Evander asked – overlooking her remark.

"Don't worry, he's just . . . sleeping," she chuckled again and bit her lip.

"What did you do to him?"

"What will you do for me if I tell you?" She taunted.

"I'm not playing your wicked games! What have you done to him?" He ordered with a growl.

"I know a game we can play; it's called cat and mouse. I will be the cat and all of you can be the mice. Ready. Set. Go."

Crow brought her hands up towards him; she winked, before a blaze of black fire burst out like a tornado. Evander quickly dove to cover, the other guards around her began firing rapidly and an array of bullets flew forward – like bees defending the hive. Crow tossed her hands out – stopping every bullet until their weapons ran dry. She growled lowly, "One thing I never told you Evander," she called to him. "Human weapons don't work." Her hands twisted around – the bullets turning with her. Evander's eyes widened, and he placed his gun on the floor and raised his hand in surrender – she had already killed too many of his men.

"Crow, look at me. Don't do this," Evander begged.

"They fired at me first," she snapped. "So, why shouldn't I? It's only fair. I never did understand why you'd insist on recruiting human soldiers – they die so easily."

"Crow, please. This is not who you are, who we are." He flashed her beseeching eyes and took a few daring steps closer to her. "It's always been us. Me, you and Dacre. This isn't who we are."

"You know; you and Dacre are so convinced that you know who I am, more than I do. You've always made choices about me, but never included me. Said you knew what was best for me. When in fact, you have no idea, at all. This is what's best for me, and I choose this." She uncurled her fingers.

"NO!" Evander cried.

Crow could only smile as the last man dropped; she clapped her hands in excitement and laughed as she spun around playfully. Her face suddenly darkened as she turned to face Evander – her head tilted to the side. "What will it take to kill you? Bullets don't work, burning doesn't work...perhaps this will." She hovered her hand in his direction once more; her fingers began to curl into her palms.

Suddenly, Evander released a bloodcurdling shriek as unbearable pain soured through him; his back arched and he collapsed to the ground – blood choking from his mouth, nose and ears.

A quick obscure figure zoomed past her and knocked her aside. "That's enough Crow!" Dacre called; he pounced forward, pinning her hands above her head. "This is over," he growled; he pulled a vial out – ripping the lid with his teeth and forced it down her throat – covering her mouth so she couldn't spit it up. She tossed and kicked, praying for air, but her blood began to still; she could feel it turning to ice in her veins – the dancing of her heart began to come to an end and her eyelids felt like a tone weight as they closed.

Dacre sighed and ran his hand down her cheek, "I'm sorry," he whispered before scooping her up in his arms. "Evander?" Dacre called out.

Evander was breathing hard, he winced as he stood up and nodded once to Dacre – wiping the blood from his face. "I'll live, but we should go. Now."

"They're here? Already?" Dacre asked – somewhat worried.

"Not yet, but they will be. If they get her, we might as well slit our own throats."

"Mara-" Dacre began, but Evander shook his head – cutting him off.

"Mara, will not help us a second time. We are lucky she did this for us." They both looked down at Crow; all the darkness slowly began to drain away – finally returning her to her natural state.

"Evander, that wasn't her who killed your men." Evander scoffed.

"Spare me the speech Dacre, I know fine well what makes her like this. What do we do with her?"

"Keep her frozen. When it's time, we'll wake her. No matter how long we have to wait."

Chapter One

"When life gives you lemons, you make lemonade. However, they don't tell you what to do when that lemonade becomes bitter. Everything then changes."

I was always one of those people that enjoyed their own company a little too much. I enjoyed it so much, that I didn't talk to anyone else – not in school or college. I always felt like something was different about me – I know, typical cliché teen. It wasn't in a big-headed kind of way – but, almost like I could feel my life going down an already planned out path. Whether that was a good thing or bad thing, I didn't know.

I didn't really care that I was by myself, everyone around me always seemed to be trying to outdo one another and would do childish things just to fit in. I was never much of a people person anyway – I knew what I liked, did things to please myself and no one else. Don't get me wrong, I had friends and I had done the whole, 'popular', thing, it wasn't really my piece of cake.

"Well, well, well. What a surprise to see you here." A familiar voice sang sarcastically – cutting into my deep thought. "Always by yourself. Budge along Narrdie." I couldn't help but smile. Audric Slater, my best friend, and the only other company I didn't mind.

"I was enjoying the peace and quiet, of course it always gets ruined by you," I teased. Audric laughed.

Audric was extremely attractive, muscular, toned and stood tall at 6 feet. He had a perfect golden tan and dark chocolate, cropped hair – with shaven sides. His jaw line was angled to the point it could cut glass and an early morning shadow tickled at his chin. Audric always ended up having people swoon over him, except me – to me Audric was like a brother.

"Did I startle you?" He asked in his deep yet amused tone.

"Not even a little, try harder next time." He chuckled as he sat down beside me. Audric had an unusual colour of jade eyes, which only stood out more in the sun; he bit into a protein bar as he tossed me another.

"Reading?" He quizzed as he leaned back and took a swig of his water to wash down his snack.

"Not today, I finished the book you gave me, I worked out the ending before I was even halfway through it. I was just thinking and enjoying the sun."

"Anything in particular? And you could do with more sun, your skin is like a piece of paper." He pressed on, I shrugged and pulled a daisy from the ground and began pulling it apart – petal by petal.

"Nothing important."

"But still something?"

"Suppose. I've been feeling like something is about to happen with me, like I'm not in control of my own life; like there's already a plan. One that I won't be able to back out from, sometimes I find myself in random places and can't even remember how I got there. What do you think?"

"I think you aren't going to know what's hit you," he blurted – his eyes darkening slightly.

"What do you mean by that?" I asked, he scowled and opened his mouth as if he was going to say something but was interrupted by the bell. He jumped to his feet and rubbed the back of his neck, "Nothing. I'll bring you two books next time. Now, hurry up. Don't wanna be late for Professor Viktor." He began to lightly jog off – throwing his hand back in a wave.

Audric pulled a no show as I sat at my desk; my essay sprawled across the table. I was pissed, he'd left me to do our reading in front of all the students and three tutors. Recreating old historical poems, was something that I was utterly disastrous at - Audric seemed to have a strange talent for it and most of this was his work anyway.

Without Audric being here, I was left with a room full of eyes – all waiting for me to mess up. Which was very likely. I never tried to befriend any of them either – that probably made it worse.

Just as expected, a wave of stuttering, losing my place and bright red cheeks – all came into effect as I stood in front of everyone. By the time the bell went, I was in desperate need of some cheesy chips and some type of neon-coloured energy drink. After stumbling over my words countless times and having the room snicker at me; I decided that Audric was going to suffer for leaving me.

All I wanted now, was to grab my food and sit on the grass patch under the big oak tree and text Audric how much I hated him. Of course, nothing was ever that simple in a typical young adult life.

I darted around the tables, glancing at students after students piling inside. The food hall was always so crowded, I'm surprised they had any food left. I gave a quick smile to the woman behind the checkout as I paid for my food; she always looked so fed up – who could blame her? Gliding around the tables as fast as I could, I suddenly felt something hard stop me in my tracks. My foot collided with someone's leg and my whole body tumbled forward – my cheesy chips mushing against my white t-shirt. I cursed under my breath. "Fucking hell!" I heard an angry sneer reach into my ears. Alaska Fletcher – the type of girl who thought she was everything at school and carried it over to college as well. She had long blonde hair, sharp fake pink nails and wore clothes that really should have stayed in the bedroom. "You idiot! You got your greasy chips on my shoes!" I swallowed my urge to laugh as I glanced down and saw the sparkling white heeled boots – now brightly stained with soggy yellow cheese.

"Excuse me? You're the one who put your foot out!" It took everything in me, not to slam her head on the table - over and over. Alaska scoffed and stood – she brought her face close to mine. I grimaced as the smell of her tangy overpowered perfume surrounded me – so much I thought I could taste it.

"I think you should say sorry. These shoes were expensive, not that you'd know anything about that." She laughed bitterly. I shook my head and rolled my eyes; I wasn't in any mood to play this back and forwards game.

"Apologise to you? Here's a bright idea, don't stick your tacky boots out – keep them under the fucking table." She scowled and took a threatening step towards me – I didn't flinch. I wasn't scared of her, not one bit. Instead, I laughed sarcastically and followed her movement, if she wanted to have a fight – I was more than happy to oblige. "Make a move, I dare you."

"Now, now ladies why don't we calm down. Alaska, could you kindly move out of Narrdie's way? I think we're done here." Alaska's eyes flared with shock and outrage as Audric came to my side and glared down at her. She made a quick gesture of running her hand through her hair like a brush and batted her eyelids at him.

Bile rose in my throat.

"Well, Narrdie-" She began – Audric held up his hand and cut her off.

"I asked you to move out the way, I won't ask again." His voice cut into her cruelly; she swallowed hard and immediately stepped aside – her eyes wild with embarrassment.

I didn't stop to curl under the big oak tree, and I didn't stop when Audric bellowed my name for the fifth time. Instead, I marched straight towards the back gate – I wanted to go home.

Audric was quick on my heels. "Narrdie! Wow, slow down, smiler. Talk to me," he shouted. I ignored him. Audric gently snared his hand under my arm and pulled me to stop; he playfully spun me around to face him. "Are you angry with me?" He asked in an amused tone. My eyes narrowed into a scowl as he covered his snicker.

"I don't need you to fight my battles or come to my rescue Audric. I'm not a child."

"I wasn't fighting your battles. I was just calming things down – you know before it turned bad... for Alaska." He smiled slightly, flashing me his pearly white teeth. "Come on, moody," he tugged on my sleeve playfully. "You know you can't stay mad at me." It was true. In all the years, I had known him, I was never able to hold a grudge against him, especially when he gave me his usual crooked grin.

"Fine, you're off the hook, but I'm still going home. I swear I'm going to lose my mind in this place. I didn't even want to come to this college." I didn't. I wanted to do the cliché thing for someone my age and go travelling – my parents flipped when

I told them and basically dragged me here. "I'll see you tomorrow. You owe me for our poem reading, I fucked it all up. I'm thinking a Mocha and a donut on you this Saturday and not a boring plain donut – I want three kinds of chocolate!"

Audric suddenly snatched my wrist before I could turn away from him – his face turned hard. "Audric? What are you doing?" His grip was tight, and I could feel the pain begin to burn where his fingers were – I winced.

"Don't move," he began; his voice was low. "Don't make a sound – trust me." His voice was dark – frightening. My heartbeat begin to pace rapidly – it was like someone was playing drums in my ears.

Audric's face seemed to change; his expression was unlike any I'd ever seen before. His eyes shifted from his unusual shade of jade to black – the veins around the sockets began to darken. I wanted to pull away – to run screaming for help, but he held on too tightly and I could feel my entire body begin to tremble. I had never seen this before, was I dreaming? Had Alaska knocked me out and I was imagining all of this? Either way – this wasn't the Audric I knew.

"You're hurting me." My voice was shakier than I wanted it to be.

"Wait," he hissed in a voice that sent shivers up my spine; his eyes looked past me and remained fixed on whatever he was looking at. If this was his idea of a joke – I wasn't laughing.

Several minutes passed before Audric began to move like a normal person again. He glanced at me – his eyes back to his usual jade with no weird veins. A shiver went down my spine as he surveyed me, I felt horrified, what had just happened?

"You alright?" His voice was soft as his fingers gently uncurled from my wrist. I immediately jumped back and spun around – trying to see what he was looking at, but there was . . . nothing.

"What was that?"

"What was what?" He repeated blankly – his eyes lifting-up in a fake puzzled expression.

Anger bubbled.

"Don't Audric, don't you dare do that and pretend nothing just happened!" I barked; I was desperately trying to hold back the ball of emotion that began to push its way to the surface – a scream bubbled in my throat; my fist clenched with the threat of hitting him and my eyes misted with frustrated tears.

"I'll explain later," his voice was stern and that meant the conversation was over. I frowned, I wanted to know, and I wanted to know now. He shook his head; his eyes begging me to leave it alone. Reluctantly, I nodded. "Thank you," he said in a relieved voice and ran a hand through his hair. He gently kissed my wrist that was still red raw and smiled sheepishly at me, before he quickly sped out the back gate without another word.

That was the last I saw of Audric that month.

*T*hank God, this year was almost up, no more college and nothing but summer – no commitments. Maybe this time my parents would agree to me travelling during the holidays – doubtful. I just had to get through todays lectures and then I could spend the entire holidays, without having to even pick up a pen. Just get through today.

However, the first lecture was English and unfortunately for me – it was another poem reading today...a poem I had completely neglected to write and after last time, I didn't think anyone would mind if I didn't show up. A double period break sounded ideal, the sun was out, and everyone was inside – a perfect time to read my book. Maybe if I kept skipping lectures, they'd have no choice but to expel me from the college – fingers crossed.

Just as I arranged myself in a comfy spot and opened-up my book at Chapter Seven, a nervous voice reached my ears.

"Narrdie." I knew that voice and I was still mad at that voice. I snapped my book shut with a grunt, (would I ever be able to read in peace again?) I looked up to Audric – this time I didn't try to hide the anger and hurt I felt. Audric half smiled; his hands were tucked into his pockets, he almost looked like he was ready to bolt. "You still mad?" He asked in a forced playful tone – trying to lighten the mood.

"What do you want?" I snapped.

"Listen, if only you could see it from my point of view-" He trailed off.

"Your point of view? What is your point of view? Does it mean you're going to tell me what the hell happened last month?" I knew the answer before I had even asked the question – my voice was hoarse. I felt like diving on him and beating him to death with the spine of my book, but I would never do that... to the book.

"No. At least not yet. Maybe saying, 'my point of view' was the wrong thing. I can't tell you what's going on. Me coming here and hoping everything would be done and forgotten is well . . . bullshit," he admitted – his eyes dropped from mine. I snorted. "Narrdie, listen-" he began – waving his hands up. I held up my hand to stop him.

"The way I see it, you freaked out and had a psychotic break, you hurt my wrist – even though I begged you to let go. If that wasn't bad enough, you left me on my own, without any kind of explanation. Then you come here, and try making a joke, I would have expected it from anyone else – but not you." He flinched back slightly; hurt – good, I wanted to hurt him.

"Can you please just hear me out?"

"No."

He studied me for a few heartbeats. "No?" He repeated, somewhat shocked.

"No. Leave me alone, I can't be fucked with all your fumbling excuses," I flung my book back open, lifting it high on my knees – just enough to cover my face.

"Narrdie," he begged once more. I pulled my headphones on over my ears and played my music at full blast – I wouldn't even been able to hear air raid sirens. I forced myself to bop along to the music and ignored every attempt he made at getting my attention.

Finally, he tucked his hands back into his pockets and walked off.

Deep down I wanted him to come back and demand we sort this out – but he didn't.

Chapter Two

A shouting match had broken out between my mum and dad, they argued quite a lot, but this one sounded like it was going to get violent – again. It wasn't long until I heard the smashing and clanking of cups and plates being thrown around – I was surprised we had any left. I slowly closed the front door behind me; I didn't want them to know I was home; they would just turn their resentment for each other towards me. A small whimper reached my ears as I tiptoed towards the stairs. Freddie - my Golden Retriever was cowering behind the two-seater sofa; his tail tucked between his legs – eyes looking all dopey and timid. "Freddie, come, that's a good boy."

I'd found Freddie two years ago; he was only a small pup – the runt of the litter. Even so, the minute I saw him, I knew he was mine. He'd been thrown into the pouring rain and was howling; it broke my heart to see that no one would help him; I'd taken him home that very night, wrapped up in my jacket – from then on, he'd always stayed loyal and by my side. My adorable fur-baby.

Freddie immediately ran to join me at the bottom of the stairs – his tail waggling; he nudged my hand – daring me to race him up the stairs. It was the same routine we had every night and as always Freddie would win, even when my dad stood on his paw – he'd still beaten me to my room. He wasted no time once we reached my room – diving onto the bed and rubbing his face all over my blanket – my bed was more than likely going to be covered in hairs – as was everything else I owned. Still, could you really be classed as a dog owner if you didn't leave the house covered in hair?

I locked my door, not wanting any of the loud confrontation downstairs to spill into my room, if I kept myself to myself – so would they. A weird mutual agreement we all had. He barked in excitement; it was like I hadn't seen him in years. "Shush your mush! Go to sleep you goof," I stroked him behind the ears and under the chin, before kissing him on the head; he yawned and stretched out across half the mattress, occasionally pawing at the sheets. My eyelids felt heavy; too heavy for me to even attempt to keep them open – if I was tired, then why argue with it? I threw my bag towards my wardrobe and flopped onto the bed beside him, not bothering to take off my shoes or my jacket – that took way too much effort, more than I had. I just lay there – drifting off into a nice cosy sleep.

I jerked up, my heart beating a panicked rhythm, Freddie's bark had entered my dream and scared me – it took me a few moments to shake off the grogginess. Groaning, I rubbed my eyes and looked over to him; his ears back, tail up and crouched low – his eyes staring out the window as a grumble sounded in his throat. "Freddie! Quiet, you'll wake mum and dad!" I hissed as I checked the time – 2:45am. I paused for a second and listened – still arguing. What on earth could cause a row to go on this long? "What are you barking at?" I frowned and forced myself out of bed – taking a second to steady my dizzy self, before groggily heading to my window and flinging open my curtains. "Is it that bloody squirrel again? I've told you, don't let him coax you into..." It wasn't the tormenting grey squirrel at all – it was Audric. Standing in the middle of the road, a handful of pebbles in one hand and a playful wave in the other – signalling me down with a cheesy grin. *This boy. He was persistent, I'd give him that.*

I raised my brow; if I went downstairs now my dad was sure to kill me and then Audric afterwards ... I guess it was going to have to be the window. Cool night air shocked me, shaking my body awake, it was bitter, and the frost licked at my nose. I leaned over the banister and glared down at him, had he any idea how late it was and how much trouble I could get in for this? The banister rocked slightly but I was too pissed to acknowledge it – Audric's eyes widened.

"It's late you know! I have neighbours and you think pelting rocks on my window is an acceptable thing to do at nearly three in the morning?" I growled.

"Be careful! That's gonna snap!"

"I'll be fine, what are you-" Freddie's yelp startled me again; my grip on the banister faltered and the bracket snapped. I gasped as my whole body hurled forwards over the edge and towards the ground – I screamed.

I waited for the pain of my body hitting the ground to come, waiting for the burning of broken bones and the wetness of blood to spread around me – but it never did. Instead, I was cradled in Audric's arms and being carried towards the empty park bench.

He gently placed me down and kneeled in front of me, "are you alright?" He asked; his voice was concerned yet hid a hint of amusement. His smile desperately twitched at the corner of his mouth before increasing into a wide grin – a grin that I grudgingly returned.

"I'm okay," I replied, a little breathless.

"Any injuries?"

"Just my arm – its cut," the amusement in his eyes drifted slightly as he took my arm into his hands and examined the slash.

"Hmm ... it's not too deep, you'll be okay. I'll sort it out." His playful smirk widened, I rolled my eyes and gently nudged his arm. "That was a hell of a scream, I'm surprised you didn't wake your whole street up. You always scream so... girly?"

"Shut up, I've heard you scream higher than me when I put that worm in your hair! Thank you for coming to my rescue ... again," he nodded to me and winked.

"Anytime."

Audric froze; his forehead creased into an unpleasant line; he glanced over his shoulder – eyes turning black again and this time I knew that what I was seeing was real. I wanted an explanation, but my gut warned me not to start quizzing him right this second – something wasn't right. I could feel it, it was a sort of shift in the air, like it was afraid to cast a breeze – even the trees and night birds faded into silence.

"Audric?" I was careful to keep my voice low.

"We're not alone. Don't move and stay behind me. Say nothing," he warned. I nodded, my heart jittering in my chest. Audric stood protectively in front of me, every part of his body tensed up and he seemed to grow taller – his muscles swelled, he looked...powerful. Immediately my heart began to bray against my chest; my hands trembling as I tucked them under my legs.

A tall man in a long black trench coat and a hood covering his face – strolled out of the dark trees, hidden in darkness, I could tell he was of equal build to Audric. I could vaguely see a golden handle of what looked like a sword or dagger hanging from his belt, it wasn't hard to miss as the park lamps made the green gems on it twinkle – a gun resting on the other side of his belt. The moment I saw them, utter terror seeped into me – who was this man? Why would someone need to carry weapons like this – especially in this town? "Oh my god," I managed to whisper; my voice slowly escaping me. Audric flashed me a dark look – a warning not to make another sound. It was hard to contain the scream that bubbled in my throat and the urge my legs felt, wanting to run.

"Greetings, young Watcher. Peace be upon you." The man spoke; his voice eerie – the kind of voice that would make you run screaming if you came across it in a dark alley. The man bowed, and Audric mimicked him – not once moving his gaze.

"Greetings to you, stranger," Audric replied - meeting the man's chilling voice with his own. The man took another step closer; the light struck his face and my jaw dropped open.

He was alluring and frightening, the very image of him made me feel like I wanted to stand up and go to him – I had to clutch onto the bench to restrain myself. His skin was sickeningly pale, it was almost on the verge of grey; I could see every single dark purple vein on his body. His hair fell just below his ears; it was glossy and black, as the light hit, I could faintly see the strands of red blended into the ends. His eyes were as dark as the night itself. He petrified me and yet, he interested me at the same time. I held my breath for a second.

He was a perfectly pictured nightmare.

"May I enquire about your name?" Audric asked in an extremely polite yet cautious tone.

"My name is too complicated for your tongue; however, you may call me Egregious. I find that name... fitting," the man sneered - Audric stiffened.

"Egregious. What is your business here?" He questioned – all attempt at politeness had gone. "Isn't it a bit too soon for your kind to be here?"

"I would have thought that you would already know my business, or do you often see Shades hovering around human parks? This one specifically." Egregious mocked, a cruel smirk pulled his mouth up, "still, young Watcher, you persist to insult my intelligence." Audric's jaw tightened and his fists slowly clenched - his knuckles turned white.

"Surely friend, I do not understand what you mean," he said with gritted teeth.

"Do you really think I can't see your human friend?" Egregious laughed then glanced behind Audric, "please Watcher, allow me to meet the human?" Audric didn't turn to speak or look at me but gestured me forward with a flick of his wrist.

"It's alright," Audric finally said when I remained sitting. I gulped; took a breath then slowly stood and stepped to the side – just enough so that he could see me. Audric's hand stretched out in front of me, warning me not to go any further. The man's eyes locked with mine – surveying me thoroughly and no matter how much I tried, I couldn't break contact.

"Ah, there she is. Interesting," he burst loudly – I jumped slightly. "Hello young female."

"H-Hi." I swiftly replied, my voice barely a whisper – I wasn't sure how much Audric wanted me to say to him and my throat had gone bone dry – my mind felt like a puddle.

"May I know your name?" I looked at Audric for confirmation, he tilted his head and nodded once.

"Narrdie." A grin ghosted his face.

"What a beautiful name, Narrdie. You do seem to look a lot like her . . ." He trailed off then looked me up and down slowly; his tongue snaked out and licked his lips.

"Like who?" I asked, Audric hissed – time to shut up again.

"I don't think your Watcher would like me to tell." There it was again, the name 'Watcher'.

"Why do you call him Watcher?" I asked timidly, flinching when a grumble came out of Audric. The man snickered for a few seconds; his eyes gleaming with excitement. Audric went still.

"He hasn't told you anything has he?" He taunted, "Yet he has been protecting you for so long. Come now Watcher, that hardly seems fair. You're not giving her a chance." Audric snarled; his hand forcefully pushed me back, as he took a threatening step forward.

"What do you want Shade?" Audric's voice was fierce – direct.

"Collect and deliver." All the delight in the Shade's voice dropped – his hand dropped beside the hilt of his sword.

"Collect what?" Audric asked sternly, as if he already knew.

"Her. She is to come with me. Stand aside and live, move against me and die. It's time to pick a side Watcher," he answered in a murderous voice. Audric snarled as he leapt forward at Egregious – who smirked and copied the movement.

Everything happened so fast – too fast for me to keep up, faster than anyone or anything I'd ever laid my eyes on.

They slammed into each other, the sound like the clashing of boulders and thunder, Audric had latched onto Egregious; the Shade hadn't even managed to knock a hair on Audric's head. Audric ceased him roughly and threw him across the park with a tremendous force, crashing him through not one, not two but three trees – which groaned and splintered. I had never seen anything like it in real life – it was the sort of thing you'd see in superhero movies.

Audric suddenly appeared beside me and signalled for me to jump on his back, my brow raised, he rolled his eyes. "I can run faster that you can," he explained in a rush – reluctantly I obeyed.

He wasn't lying, he was fast; he dashed towards the road and away from my house; he ran so fast I felt like the world had started to play in slow motion, the mud barely had a chance to crumble under his foot. The breeze hit hard against my skin, it was bitter cold and stung my chapped lips. I wanted to get the hell out of there, but like any person would – I looked back, expecting to see the Shade crumpled up on the ground. Terror hit me like a punch to the gut.

He wasn't crumped under the trees; he wasn't groaning in pain; he was on his feet – unharmed; his eyes wide and crazy. He swung a crossbow – that was strapped to his back, into his hands and a pernicious grin spread wide on his face.

"We're not finished here!"

"AUDRIC!" I warned with a shriek.

The black arrow tore through the air, the sound whooshed past me, making my ears ring; it grazed across my arm and punctured straight through Audric's chest. He let out a pain filled gasp; his blood spitting out.

I dropped from his back and tumbled hard to the ground, flecks of mud and tiny stones sticking to my open cuts like glue. Audric lay unconscious – bleeding vigorously from his chest and back; his eyes closed and breathing slowing. A searing pain burned into my thigh, as I tried to go to him - a piece of smashed glass had gouged itself into my stomach and a small pool of my own blood began to stain my jeans and pool around me. I whimpered as shaking hands gripped around the glass – the sharp edges biting into my fingers, with a pained cry I tore it from me. *Mistake.*

The Shade confidently glided towards us with a sickening smile; he fixed his crossbow onto his back and hummed as he loomed above Audric. Audric groaned and forced himself to his feet – he wobbled; his face paler than I had ever seen, his breath coming out in wheezes and blood soaking into his shirt. The Shade's colourless brow lifted, and he shook his head. "How disappointing you must be to your kind, a Watcher fallen by a poison arrow. You should have known – remembered that we never go anywhere without them, you've gotten too comfortable playing your mortal role. Tragic," the Shade taunted. His eyes gleamed with pleasure; he tilted his head and turned his hand anti-clockwise – Audric's back heaved, and a bloodcurdling screech bellowed from him, I heard a snap – like strips being torn from a sheet.

"Stop it!" I begged, "Whatever you're doing to him, just stop and leave him alone!" Ignoring the burning in my stomach, I moved to Audric again, the consuming agony in my stomach tightened and my arms gave up on me, I glanced behind – the trail of my blood was thick.

The Shade flicked his hand and Audric hurtled across the grass – like he was nothing more than a ball of paper. I stared, a mixture of bewilderment and horror peaked at me, I had never witnessed something like this, it was magic – power. Actual creatures with abilities that you would only see on TV or read in books, never in a million years did I think such things like the Shade even existed. If that was real . . . what other horrifying things were there? I dared not to think – at least not now. The Shade closed the space between us and squatted down in front of me; he flipped me over onto my back and ran his finger down my cheek – I shuddered as his cold touch. "Narrdie, if only they told you, you might have lasted longer. You have no idea how important you are – were. My orders are to bring you back but killing you would be so much more rewarding. By the time I got here the Watcher had already deceived his kin and cut you down. That would work, it has happened before."

"Why are you doing this? I'm not who you think I am," my voice quivered. He laughed – as slimy as a hyena's. He glanced down to the dagger tucked into his boot – his eyebrows wiggled at me. With all the effort I had left, I kicked my leg out, knocking him off his legs. I wasn't going to just lie down and submit. The Shade groaned his annoyance and shook his head, before pressing his foot down lightly over my wound. I froze instantly – sucking the air through my teeth.

"You're being very rude Narrdie, we're in the middle of a discussion and you're not paying attention. Very rude indeed," he hissed and dug his heel in hard, I groaned and clutched onto my scream – hurting me was entertaining to him, he could press down all he wanted – he would not have my scream. "Does it hurt?" He quizzed in a playful voice, "are you afraid to die? I bet you haven't even thought about it before," he scoffed in aggravation when I didn't answer; lifting his boot; he hammered down harder – ripping the wound wider, black spots burst behind my eyes. My nails dug into the soggy grass, the mud pushing its way underneath. "I asked you a question!" My eyes shot up; I spat up hitting his cheek and gritted my teeth.

"No!" I growled, "I'm not afraid." He wiped his face; his eyes flaring with outrage. A tight hand snapped to my throat as he pulled me closer to him; his teeth were sharp and his tongue long and pointy like a snake.

"You're going to regret that."

I looked at Audric, for what I believed was the last time – Egregious was going to kill me. I was going to be murdered in this park, not far from my house. If I was to die, I prayed that Audric would live, that my death would give him a chance to run – find somewhere safe and far away from Egregious. *Let me not die in vain.*

The sight of Audric, caused relief to wash over me like a wave on a hot beach. He was alive. He was better than alive; he was on his feet – his eyes were aflame. "Audric," I whispered.

"Let her go!" Audric snarled, the black arrow was clutched so hard in his hand, it snapped and crumbled to the grass.

"Audric," the Shade said – irritated. "Welcome back. Narrdie and I were just getting acquainted." The Shade stood and roughly dragged me up with him; slowly he pulled out the gemstone knife and held it against the base of my throat. I didn't even have to look at him to know he had a mocking smirk sprawled along his lips. *Theatrical pig.*

Audric's eyes widened furiously, he stepped forward with a low growl and crouched ready to run at us. "Easy Watcher, one wrong move and she dies, I'll be sure to make it hurt," Egregious warned and pulled the knife closer, he was the only thing that kept me from curling up on the ground. "Don't do anything you'll regret; you know what happens if you harm her. You'll have both sides coming for you," Audric cautioned – venom spilling out of his voice. The Shade laughed then cocked his head to the side, his wet tongue sliding along his lips. "I'm warning you," Audric hissed. "You hurt her; I will tear you apart." Egregious laughed and pressed his body against mine; he held my face with his right hand – the knife in the other. His slimy tongue trailed up my cheek, sending shivers down my spine. Never so much in my life had I wanted to take a wired brush to my own skin.

"She tastes lovely," he teased and flashed Audric a leer. Audric's jaw clenched as the Shade began to move his hand across my chest – advancing down to my stomach. The veins spread around Audric's face; the whites of his eyes turned a murky yellow. He licked my neck, chuckling darkly onto my skin, I felt his blade tiptoe closer, until finally resting inches from my wound – I breathed in. He snickered, then with a brutal force – jammed the knife into my stomach.

The pain was unbearable – like a hot iron burning me over and over, with a mixture of salt and lemon juice rubbed in. However, despite everything I still refused to scream – no matter how much I wanted to; I'd rip out my own voice box just to prevent it. "Having fun yet?" He whispered in my ear. I couldn't respond, the words seemed to evaporate from my mouth, and everything started to fade in and out; the forest began to fade in my eyes.

"Egregious!" Someone called, their voice both bored and annoyed. Audric frowned and narrowed his eyes at the new person, deciphering whether or not this person was here to kill us or help us. "That's enough." The Shade went ridged and he gulped suddenly; immediately he pulled the knife out – I could feel his body shaking.

"My Lord?" His voice quivered.

"I do believe, that Narrdie feels quite uncomfortable in your presence. Let her be," the man said; tone sharp – demanding. The Shade grumbled and sniffed my hair again; his fingers lightly brushing my skin – he leaned his head away with a sigh and took a step back. The strength holding me up vanished and my legs felt like they had just been kicked from underneath me. I collapsed to the ground and pressed my hand over my wound – I needed to stop as much of the blood as I could before I passed out, however I was so weak my hands began to go limp. The grass was soaked in crimson.

"Shame. I was enjoying myself. Narrdie, I'm afraid we'll have to continue another time," he teased in a sarcastic, saddened voice before licking his lips at me – his hand snaked out to stroke my hair once more.

"Egregious!" The other man bellowed viciously – making the whole park shake. "Leave. You are wasting my time."

"My Lord." Egregious bowed to him; his body suddenly began to vibrate and shimmer. Just like a play in a pantomime – he vanished, leaving behind a small burst of smoke. The other man remained hidden behind trees; his face masked in shadow. Whoever he was, I was thankful he was here, regardless of his intentions.

"My apologies, Lady Narrdie. Egregious is not very polite at times; he lacks proper manners. This was only meant to be a warning – he seems to have taken it too far."

"What kind of warning is it when Shades attack innocent humans?" Audric hissed, taking a threatening step forward – the anger close to erupting.

"Innocent?" The man repeated with a cynical laugh. "She is far from it! You know the things she has done! The things she will do again! Take this warning back with you Watcher, prepare. You do not have long left." Audric's face hardened, and his eyes kept darting towards me with worry. "The darkness is inside her and we both can feel it; it calls to those hiding in the shadows, and we call back to it. She may not remember now, but it will not take long for it to return and this time – you won't be able to block it." He glanced at me with dangerous eyes and I could feel something unpleasant begin to consume the park.

It felt like smoke seeping into my body and suffocating my lungs.

"Audric," I winced. I couldn't see – everything was going hazy, and the temperature seemed to drop to the point where my teeth were chattering. Audric's eyes darted from the man to me, he flashed a pleading look to him; his jaw unclenched.

"She'll die," Audric warned him. "If I don't help her, she's dead. What use is she to you then?" The man breathed out, as though he was tired by this whole night. He nodded, and half bowed.

"Until we meet again, Watcher."

The second the man vanished, Audric was by my side – his hands cupping my face; he clenched his jaw and carefully lifted me into his arms – holding me tight against him. "I've got you." I winced and hissed through my teeth from the pain, even though my body fought to shut down – my mind crowded with questions. Each step he took, sent a wave of pain rippling throughout my body, I whimpered, my head weakly dropped onto his shoulder. "Sorry. I'll try and be gently, just stay awake for me. I'm so sorry Narrdie, I should have prepared better for this." I could barely understand him, my withering heartbeat was all that reached my ears.

"C-Cold," my voice jittered.

"I know darling, hold on," his begged.

Wheels skidding along the tarmac burned my eardrums – the smell of worn-down rubber staining my nose, a black car pulled up on the curb and Audric let out a breath of relief, "thank the mother." The passenger door swung wide as he made a beeline towards it – panting. "How'd you know?" He asked as he gently lay me in the back seat and buckled a seatbelt around me – pausing afterwards to stroke my cheek, he pulled a blanket out and gently tucked it around me – not caring about the blood that began to spread over the wool.

My eyelids felt like dead weight, they dropped themselves closed and my body responded with it, my limps turned too heavy for me to lift, my legs felt non-existent – even breathing seemed like a chore.

"Bayona," a woman replied. "Do you want to stand around talking or are you going to get in? Whatever you decide – hurry it up." Her tone was harsh, and a low growl lingered behind it. "Audric?" She called her voice suddenly sounding alarmed.

"Shit, Narrdie? Open your eyes for me," Audric begged – voice panicked. I tried to speak and tell him I was just tired, but I couldn't – it was too much.

Then – I couldn't hear anything. Everything went black.

Chapter Three

I felt like I was flying. Warm welcoming clouds, wrapped around me – soothing my sore skin, until it felt as soft as a kitten, curling me up so that nothing could possibly harm me again, I wanted to stay here. Reality began to dawn on me, and realisation hit, these weren't clouds, but . . . pillows and blankets – swarming around me. My fingers eagerly brushed the soothing material, it felt so exhausting to even lift my hand – my whole body was aching and screaming. Was I dead?

Muffled voices echoed, the type of chatter you'd hear in a dream or in the background of a phone call. One voice I knew, I'd recognise it no matter what – Audric and it dawned on me that the other voice must have been the woman from the park.

The park. It had been real, it wasn't a strange nightmare like I hoped, which meant that Egregious was real...and still out there – waiting. Cold fingers brushed my cheek soothingly and my heart fluttered – I was almost sure it was Audric, the tenderness of his touch caused a lump to form in my throat. "Astrid?"

"I told you not to go to her, I told you it was too dangerous – but did you listen?" The woman scoffed, "you should have backed off and let us deal with it. Do you know she could have died because of your childish game?" The woman spat towards him. "Look at her, she barely survived." Her voice turned tender as she approached me, I could feel her fingers take hold of my wrist, her touch gentle and light as a feather.

"Is she gonna be alright?" Audric asked, ignoring everything she had just said – his fingers finding my cheek again.

"She's resting, and her injuries have healed well. So yes, she will be fine – as long as you let her rest," she assured him, the sound of her hand slapping his away. "You'll wake her up," she cursed.

"Thank you, Astrid," Audric said as he breathed out in relief. "I know this was hard for you to do."

"Don't ever make me do it again. It is not hard to do Audric – it's just painful. She needs her rest now; she will be very confused and scared when she wakes. Best not to crowd her," the woman suggested – the anger in her had faded.

"I'll stay with her," he decided.

"You will do no such thing." A loud, vicious snarl stung my ears, another followed quickly in response– they sounded like feral animals, my heart began to perform somersaults in my chest.

"Why can't I stay with her?" Audric snapped hotly.

"You watch your tone with me," the woman warned. "Mitchell wants to speak with you."

"You told him?" Audric's voice quivered slightly, and I could feel the tension go thick in the air.

"Of course, I did. What did you expect? That you could hide her here – in his house, without him knowing? I thought even you, were smarter than that Audric. We best hurry, he's not a patient man."

Finally, my eyes found the strength to tear open – a burst of light hit them, and a sharp uncomfortable sting flooded in. I expected to feel the horrific pain in my stomach, feel it tear open and bleed – but there was nothing, no hot iron, no sharp pain, not even a dull ache. "What the-?" It was gone. The gaping wound had closed, healed completely – it was still red and sore to the touch, but there was barely even a scar. Had I been in a coma for a week? A month?

My legs were stiff as I tried to move them and after giving them a few moments to wake up, cringing at the awkward feeling of the pins and needles – my toes were finally wiggling. Slowly, I rose to my feet, hoping that they wouldn't turn to jelly under me. I'd only peer my head around the door and make sure they were gone – I wasn't ready to see them just yet.

$\smile$

*C*uriosity had gotten the better of me.

I slid to a stop just around the corner of the hallway, wincing slightly at my tired limbs, they had come to a pause outside of a glossy dark oaked door. I could faintly see the engraved images of wolves, howling and jumping around with each other, the pups piling on top of what I believed to be their mother. The detail was amazing – even from where I was standing, I could tell how much craftsmanship had gone into it; a name was carved in the centre, 'Gartentis' in a concise elegant print.

Pulling my gaze from the beautiful door, as much as I wanted to scrutinize every detail of it – my eyes landed on the woman.

She was equally as beautiful as the Shade, more in fact – a lot more. Her skin was pale like the Shade, except her skin seemed to have a white glow to it and even I could tell it was softer than his. Her hair was the same colour as an eggplant, with long elegant curls trailing down her back, neat tight plaits had been fashioned around her head like a crown, all held together by a golden clasp with a black stone in the middle. The woman was slender with perfectly toned arms and subtle curves, a jawline to die for and perfect plumped lips. She wore a white summer dress with embroidered silver leaves and spirals – it complimented her body perfectly. Her eyes reminded me of the sea at night – dark with a hint of danger and like the sea, you didn't know what dangers lurked beneath it.

"Well?" She asked Audric; he didn't answer. She shook her head and mumbled, "Coward," before lightly tapping.

"Come in," a bold voice called – he was pissed. The woman held open the door then signalled Audric in before her – she gave him a comforting and encouraging nod, before lightly pushing him forward. Once they were both inside and the door safely shut, I tip toed closer and placed my ear against the smooth wood.

"Mitchell, you need to understand-"

"Quiet Audric. This is not a small incident you can just trick your way out of! This is probably one of the most reckless and idiotic things you have ever done. How dare you disobey my orders and bring her here. It's too soon. Not only that, but what you asked of Astrid – caused her pain."

"I had no choice! They'd found her at the college and then came for her at her own house. You know what could have happened if they got there before me. It would have all been over, all the work we've done would have been for nothing." Audric's voice was tight – holding back his full temper.

"I would have sorted it; we would have figured something out. You broke the rules of the Watchers. You intervened, before the date was ready. What will I tell the Order when they realise what has happened?" A sound like a fist slamming onto a table – made me jump.

"They said nothing when you took in Astrid and Bayona."

"That was entirely different circumstances," Mitchell snapped aggressively. "You know that."

"Mitchell. Sweetheart please, hear him out," the woman begged in a tender voice.

"Quiet please Astrid." All anger instantly dropped when he answered her, replaced with love and kindness. Which disappeared the second he focused back onto Audric, "I should rip out your spine for this. You've pushed us months back, possibly even years. We aren't prepared – the Order will demand action for this." My immediate reaction was to grab the door handle, I didn't want Audric getting into serious trouble – even if I didn't know what was going on. Why punish someone for saving another's life? Nothing was making sense anymore. "I don't think I can protect you on this one, they could slot and strip you." The woman gasped.

"They sent a Sivv," Audric announced his tone solemn.

"Go on," Mitchell urged, the fierceness in his voice dwindled slightly.

"It came to the school, in broad daylight – for all to see. A Sivv Mitchell, think about what could have happened. Then a Shade in a public park, not caring to keep anything hidden, he openly attacked – anyone could have walked by or peered out their window. They don't care about being hidden anymore. What was I meant to do? Take a seat and watch it happen?" Audric snorted sarcastically. "That Shade wasn't planning on taking her, it wanted to kill her."

"Kill her?" Astrid breathed. "He must have been acting out alone, the main goal was to always keep her alive."

"It isn't uncommon for a Sivv to stay close to humans. However, a Shade? They don't do the little jobs themselves. Are you sure it was a Shade?"

"He called himself Egregious." My body shuddered at his name, the hairs on the back of my neck stood – almost like I could feel his breath.

"I've heard of him. He used to be a follower of . . ."

Two small fingers lightly tap my shoulder – a girl. I didn't notice anything about her – all I could focus on was the deep black, scabby empty sockets where her eyes should have been and the scream that bubbled in my throat and out of my mouth.

I tucked my legs into my chest and wrapped my arms around myself the second I got back into the room, my breathing was rushed – my heart thundering and my eyes filled. Maybe I had fallen out my window, cracked my skull open and died right there – maybe this was my own weird hell.

Within seconds, footsteps raced up the stairs after me – only adding to the panic that shot through me, their mumbled voices, getting louder and louder. Audric slowly walked in with his hands raised and his casual crooked smile, "Narrdie?"

"Where am I? Who are you people?" I could barely get the question out, my voice bounced so much. He leaned down to touch my shaking hands and I immediately jerked it away – almost like it was a shark about to bite me.

"It's only me, I'm not going to hurt you."

"I don't know you," I breathed. He wasn't the Audric I knew, the one who used to bring me different books and feed me protein bars, he wasn't the friend I'd known most my life – he was a stranger. Genuine shock tattooed Audric's face – it was almost laughable. What did he expect?

"You're afraid of me," it wasn't a question, but I answered him.

"Yes." His eyes glassed over, and his face turned hard; he nodded once and glanced over his shoulder to the eggplant haired woman; his jaw clenched.

"Astrid?" She stepped into the doorframe, her eyes assessing the silent question he'd just asked – signing, she nodded.

"Okay," she told him as she gently brushed her hand along his shoulder. Audric didn't look back as he left the room – I didn't care. I was more concerned about Astrid heading towards me – a comforting smile graced her lips. I backed up as much as I could, pulling the blanket around me – as if it would save me from her. "Everything is alright, no one wants to harm you. You're only tired, you should close your eyes."

"I'm only tired," I repeated automatically, my voice locked in a trance like state. Hypnotism, that's what this was, I wasn't sleepy, and I definitely did not want to close my eyes – especially around these people. Yet, I couldn't fight it, no matter how much my insides screamed at me to stay awake. – I couldn't.

I was trapped here, a prisoner – forced to stay, forced to sleep. Audric, the one person I thought I could trust the most, was the one who was holding me captive. A gut-wrenching pain hit my stomach, betrayal – the type that made your world crumble, made food taste like ash, bile rise in your throat and hurt pin your heart. How long had he been planning this? Lying to me for all these years.

"Hello?" I called as someone rapped the door with their nails, the sound both gentle and eerie. I pulled my knees back into my chest, my hands gripping the bedsheets tightly – nowhere to run. The young girl that I had ran away from, popped her head in the doorway – blacked out large sunglasses, hiding her sockets.

She smiled sweetly; her straight black hair falling from her shoulder and covering most of her face. On second glance, she didn't seem as scary; she had on the cosiest looking pale pink turtlenecked jumper, tight black jeans and an assortment of beaded bracelets with strange symbols. She was barefoot, and I noticed spiralled patterns tattooed along each of her toes. She followed my glance, a chuckle escaped her lips, she wiggled her feet as she spoke. "I don't like shoes, never have. Hello Narrdie. If you wish to sleep more, I can come back?" She had a slight hint of French in her accent, it sounded angelic, like music in the distance – beckoning you to come and find its source.

"No. Erm . . . It's alright, y-you can stay." I flinched slightly as she bowed her head to me and plonked on the bottom of my bed – crossing her legs. She had faded markings around her face, neck and hands, beautiful swirls, patterns and symbols – the type you'd see on Nordic ruins and creepy old books, which were probably cursed.

"I scared you before and for that I am sorry, I was concerned when I checked on you and saw you were not in your bed. I should have put my glasses on and warned you about my eyes before you saw them, but I just wanted to find you and make sure you weren't hurt." I frowned and surveyed her slightly, something she had said confused me – a lot. I knew it would probably come off as extremely rude, but before I could stop myself, my mouth was already speaking.

"You saw that I wasn't in bed? How?" I expected her to be insulted and storm out, but thankfully she smiled pleasantly.

"I may not have eyes, but I can still see," she answered – thinking that was all the explanation needed. I stared blankly at her.

"I don't understand," I admitted sheepishly, she opened her mouth to explain but Audric's voice cut in. My eyes lowered from him, I found myself recoiling closer to the wall – a movement he didn't fail to notice.

"Bayona, no," he warned her. "Not yet."

"Then when?" She half bit back.

"When Mitchell decides, go take it up with him. Can I speak to Narrdie...alone please?" I shifted, even though I was still weary of this girl, I wanted her to stay. I bit my tongue, to stop myself from pleading with her – I didn't want him here.

"Certainly," she said shortly. She smiled sweetly to me, then creased her brow unpleasantly at Audric before leaving us alone together. Audric didn't move any closer than the door, didn't speak after the girl left and wouldn't even look at me. I may not have wanted him here, but just standing there with his arms folded – pissed me off.

"Did you come here just to ignore me, Audric?" I snapped.

"No, I just don't know what to say," he admitted.

"I want to go home."

"I know."

"But I can't, can I?" My voice trembled, Audric clenched his jaw and shook his head. "Why? What's going on? Tell me." He breathed out hard and ran a hand through his hair.

"I'm not sure you can handle it, at least not all at once. I know that doesn't make any sense, but one day it will."

"Fine then," I growled. "Let me leave." Audric immediately took a step closer to the door – ready to stop me if I tried. "Are you seriously doing this?"

"Narrdie, I'm sorry but you can't leave here." Hot burning rage boiled in my blood.

"Why? Why are you doing this? Are you going to kill me?" I ask softly, my voice trembling; my eyes filling up. Audric's eyes widened, he shot forward – making me flinch back – and took my face into his hands.

"Of course not, Narrdie I would never hurt you. Never ever. It's just...too dangerous."

"What's too dangerous?" I rose; shoving him back; my hands clenched into tight balls at my sides.

"I can't tell you."

"Why not?" I took a step closer, my eyes flicked to the open door, if it came down to it, I'd happily knock him on his ass and step over him to leave here.

"Don't Narrdie," he warned sternly.

"Audric, that's enough." A tall man barked. He was dressed casual, black trousers and a blue shirt, I knew straight away that he was related to Audric; he just looked like an older angrier version of him. Caramel wavy cropped hair – cleaned shaved and very muscular arms. He swept past Audric, took my hand and lightly kissed my knuckles; his dark amber eyes met mine, as he smiled and cleared his throat. "Forgive me for not coming sooner, I had a few things to... correct," he threw a displeased look towards Audric. "It took longer than I thought it would. My name is Mitchell. It is an honour to meet you, Narrdie Moon. I have heard so much about you. I apologise that we've had to meet like this, it was not the way I wanted all of this to go. I can't tell you everything yet, but for now I will let Audric tell you the basics. Why you're here and who we are, keeping this from you will prove to be no good," he said with a kind smile. He turned to Audric and bowed his head – granting him permission to talk, it was the first time Audric stopped frowning since the park.

"Narrdie, this is gonna be a lot for you to take in, so try and stay with me. At the park with the Shade, you asked him why he called me Watcher," Audric began as he took a seat beside me, his forehead glittered with sweat. "A Watcher is what I am classed as – Mitchell also, it's a bloodline of beings that have been around since... well, an extremely long time. Our job is to clean up and cover incidents that can't be explained. For example, there will be a Watcher cleaning the park, making sure everything is put right, before anyone wakes up, removing any signs of us or the Shade ever being there. Our job is to keep it away from humans, keep it hidden - keep a certain balance in the world and to protect it. I know how this sounds but believe me it's true." He paused and they both looked at me nervously, I nodded letting them know I was keeping up – a pulsing in my head began. "It would be extremely dangerous if humans found out about our world, Shades aren't the scariest things out there."

"Catastrophic even," Mitchell chimed in. "There are human factions that are aware of us, but they don't get involved unless we need them to. They know how bad things would become if the two sides mixed."

"Do you understand?"

I scoffed, "if you told me this any other day, I would have had you committed, but I saw what...Egregious did, the power he had and he didn't even break a sweat doing it. So, trust me I'm believing everything you say." I hated the way the shivers went down my spine when I heard the name, hated how much my voice quivered with fear when I said it.

"I'm sorry to tell you that everything you know - is about to change and I'm so sorry it had to be this way. I wanted to keep you from this as long as I could, I tried." I looked to Audric; my heart strings began to pull inside me.

"So, you were only my friend because things like the Shade wanted me." It wasn't a question, more a realisation I was trying to tell myself. Still, it hurt. It hurt like hell, the one person I loved the most in this world, the person who was always there when I needed him. Now I realised he was only there because he had to be.

"No," Audric began as he lifted my chin, and making me look at him. "No. I was charged with protecting you and then when it was time, I was to be your guide and trainer. Narrdie, I love you so much, you stopped being my charge and you became my best friend and every day I tried to find a way to spare you from this. I prayed that we would realise that it wasn't you they wanted, that we'd all got it wrong and you could live happily and peacefully. Please don't think that I don't care for you because I do. More than anything, more than my own life." Like a wave knocking me over, I felt overwhelming relief hit.

Kidnapped or not, I wrapped my arms around him and hugged him tightly, even after everything, I still loved him.

"Thank you," I whispered in his ear before looking towards Mitchell. "I understand the dangers. The things that Shade could do, if that was released into the world...I don't think humans would stand a chance." I was still a little nervous and my voice still held a sudden shake to it, but even I knew that people couldn't win against Egregious. In less than an hour, the Shade had shredded the park to pieces and almost killed us, the way he'd thrown Audric without even touching him – terrified me. People could never know that powers like that existed. Mitchell was right, it would be devastating.

Audric shared a looked with his brother, a look of uncertainty. I hadn't been very cooperative lately, maybe they thought this was all me pretending so I could run out of here. "Audric, it's okay. Really, it is." I smiled to him, my grin growing wider when I saw the spark in his eyes return; his own smile beginning to tug at the corners of his mouth. "Don't worry, I'm still your friend – no matter how much of an ass you are." Audric snickered and Mitchell covered his own smirk with a cough. "What about the woman in the car and the other girl? Are they Watchers?" Audric swallowed hard and looked to Mitchell.

"My turn?" Mitchell guessed, he pulled the seat from the empty desk and joined us around the bed – breathing out hard before opening his mouth to talk. "No, they aren't Watchers. The woman who brought you here, is Astrid – my wife. The other girl, who . . . sent you screaming back to this room, is Bayona . . . who is rudely eavesdropping behind the door." Bayona suddenly skipped into the room, laughing as she nudged Audric to move along, plonking on the bed and sprawling her legs across Audric's lap – she signalled Mitchell to continue.

"You were just about to talk about me, I wouldn't miss this for the world, it's the best part," she chimed. I was going to like her.

"As you might have figured out, Bayona isn't your normal type of girl. She is rare, exceedingly rare and very, very powerful . . . especially for her age."

"Careful," she warned him playfully.

"You're not human?" I guessed; I was beginning to think that no one was going to be human anymore.

"No, she's a Witch."

"Like in children's fairy tales?" All I knew about Witches was that they were evil, hideous and more than often lived-in houses made of sweets and ate children.

41

"No, she is a Psychic Witch, a Witch belonging to the Pleiades Sisters, she's the eighth sister. Don't worry, I'm sure she'll tell you all about herself in time." Bayona nodded with a bright smile and Mitchell winked at her, they all seemed relieved.

Perhaps they thought I would freak out and start screaming again.

"That's how she can see," I interrupted, it wasn't a question, but he answered anyway.

"Yes. Her Psychic abilities are so strong it makes her able to see, in fact she can see better than all of us. She can even see things before they happen, that's how Astrid was able to find you, sadly by the time the vision came to her, Egregious had already began his attack." Bayona's smile faltered and her head dropped – guilt washed over her. Audric lightly stroked her hand and kissed her on the head, he mumbled something in her ear and the warm, cute smile reappeared on her face.

"The Pleiades? As in the cluster of stars?" She nodded and Audric laughed in bewilderment.

"Wow, you actually can pay attention in college," Audric teased as he lightly shoved me.

"Shut up! So, you're pretty much a star? Amazing! I'm sorry I ran away from you... screaming, it was really rude of me." His hand lightly took hold of mine.

"No need to apologise. Technically I'm not a star yet, when powerful Witches die, they ascend into stars, only if they are worthy and pure of heart."

"Which you are," Audric told her warmly. "And your sisters deserve to have stories written about them, they were some of the most amazing Witches known to all." Bayona smiled and leaned her head on his shoulder.

"What about the other woman, Astrid?" Mitchell sucked in air, sweat forming on his head; he scooted his seat closer to me. Bayona and Audric seemed to stiffen slightly, and that pit of worry seeped into my gut once more.

"Okay," he began. "Astrid. First, just keep in mind that you are completely safe here, with all of us. None of us would ever do anything to harm you, Astrid included. She's a . . . Vampire."

Silence.

I realised that I hadn't moved or spoken in a while, but a kaleidoscope of images about Vampires ripping people apart and drinking their blood, had begun to play in my head like a theatre production. Suddenly, the sweet looking purple haired woman and her warm voice, had changed to a demonic creature waiting to kill me. Audric, Bayona and Mitchell stayed quiet and still – waiting patiently for me to gather myself, I could hear my own heartbeat and a frightening thought raced across my mind – could the Vampire also hear it? A Vampire. Vampires were one of the main things I'd watch in films and read in books, they were always the same – blood thirsty and soulless killers. There's a Vampire downstairs.

"Narrdie? Are you okay?" Audric asked in a concerned voice; his hand lightly tapped mine.

"A Vampire? I certainly know what they do," I rubbed along my neck, it was like I could already feel the sharp fangs digging through my skin.

"Narrdie, Astrid doesn't drink human blood, she doesn't even crave it. She's old enough to block out that part of herself, she's happy feeding on animals. She's in full control, half the time you wouldn't even think she was a Vampire," Audric reassured me with a confident smile.

"This is a lot to take in," I admitted and swallowed a lump in my throat. "A lot to take in, I guess I'll get used to it...in time." I smiled to them all and they all smiled back, Audric looking happiest out of them all. "Where is the Vamp...I mean Astrid." I smiled apologetically.

"She's downstairs, she didn't want to frighten you." Another wave of guilt slammed into me, a vicious predator was hiding downstairs, so it wouldn't scare me and here I was, assuming she'd be a killer.

"I'm sorry, I don't want her to feel like she has to avoid me in her own home. She saved me, didn't she? There wasn't even a scar when I woke up this morn..." I trailed off as a thought crashed into my mind, had it actually been one night? I stood up and looked around for a calendar or a phone, anything that would tell me the date. "What day is it?" I asked as I filtered through a stack of paper on Audric's bedside table.

"Thursday," Audric replied as he slowly tidied up after me – he hated mess.

"Thursday? I've been here almost a week! I have to get home, my parents are going to go off it, they'll be so mad! They've probably called the police!" Without thinking, I darted past Mitchell and fled down the stairs, my feet sounding like a herd of elephants.

"Narrdie! Stop!" Audric called as all three of them were quick on my heels.

My heart skipped a beat as deep purple hair appeared at the bottom of the stairs, Astrid – the Vampire, looked to us with eyes filled with panic and surprise. "Astrid, don't let her leave!" Audric ordered her. She scoffed and rolled her eyes and before I could even blink, she was standing at the door; her speed shocked me and I had to remind myself of what Mitchell had just told me about her; she gave me an apologetic smile. Suddenly, Audric flung me over his shoulder and began to carry me back upstairs, Astrid groaned.

"Audric, bring her into the sitting room for gods' sake and watch her stomach! Animals, all of you! Is this really how we behave and treat guests?" Astrid nagged as she shook her head and ushered everyone to follow. Audric plonked me gently on the sofa and let out a long-exaggerated breath; a wide grin stretched across his face.

"Where did you think you were running off to?" He asked sarcastically.

"Home," I answered blankly.

"You can't go home," Mitchell said softly. "I'm sorry, I really am but, it's too risky. For your own safety, you have to stay here."

"Told you so," Audric added. A lump built in my throat, the type you would feel when you ate something hot too fast. I looked to Audric, whose jaw was clenched and lips pressing into a thin line.

"My family? They could be in danger," I fought against the tears welling up in my eyes, as much as I didn't like them and they didn't like me, it didn't stop them being my parents – even if they didn't want me. Freddie wouldn't understand why I didn't come home, he'd probably think I purposely left him behind, I almost burst into tears right there – thinking about his little face and the cries he'd make.

"If you go home, you're putting them at risk. Mitchell will sort it, they'll be safe. I promise." They'll be safe? For all we knew, my parents were already dead. Egregious could have gone back and slaughtered them; he could have gone back that very night and done it. Before I could even breathe in and flat out refuse to stay, Bayona gasped and let out a pain filled groan.

Her head fell into her hands and her whole body began to shake violently, I held onto the screech that was ready to burst, as I watched blood slowly trickle from the sockets where her eyes would have been. Within a second Astrid was by her side, prying her hands free and gripping them tightly, she leaned her forehead against Bayona. "Bayona, hold onto me." Her voice was stern – ordering. "Take what you need."

"Seeing things that are quite strong, can really take a toll on her – even kill her. That's why Astrid lets her take her strength. Elder Vampires are some of the strongest races know to us," Audric quickly whispered, obviously spotting my confused expression – I nodded my gratitude. I didn't know what she was seeing but it must have been big, the blood from her sockets had become a mask on her face, I could smell the sweat that seeped out her pours; her hands trembling as her nails dug slits into Astrid.

"D-Dacre," her voice was strained. A low growl rumbled in Astrid's voice, Audric went stiff beside me; his knuckles clicked as he clenched his fists.

"Piece of shit," Audric spat. "He's purposely making this hard for her! He could have called instead of using her like this!"

"We don't know that," Mitchell defended, even though he didn't sound convinced either. Whoever this Dacre was; he wasn't really being welcomed with open arms – even sensible Mitchell's nostrils flared every time someone said his name. Mitchell's words popped into my head, "no one here will hurt you," I was beginning to think that this Dacre – wasn't part of that sentence.

"When?" Astrid hissed; her voice sending shudders up my spine.

"Anytime now, he was blocking me out," Bayona said through breaths; she had stopped shaking and smiled her thanks to Astrid. Astrid took a cloth and began to clean the blood from Bayona's face, softly brushing back her hair. "Thank you," Bayona whispered, Astrid gently kissed her on the head and continued to clean the blood.

"Mitchell. He can't know, it's too soon." Audric began frantically, almost pleading with his brother.

"I know, Audric," Mitchell replied as he tapped his chin – pondering what to do.

"You know how he could respond!"

"He's already suspicious," Bayona announced, her voice weak and brittle. "He was wondering why I was watching him."

"Mitchell, what about our room?" Astrid cut in, "he won't smell her there."

"That could work, your scent would be too much for him. Not just a pretty face are you, my love?" Mitchell said as he smiled and winked to his wife, Astrid chuckled softly.

"Dacre isn't human either, is he?" I asked, already knowing the answer.

"No, he's not," Audric replied through clenched teeth, he seemed to really have a hatred for this man.

"Will he hurt me?" Silence. My chest felt like it was going to cave in, fear was slowly snaking its way back. Maybe he was the same as Egregious...maybe he was worse.

Three knocks echoed throughout the house.

Chapter Four

*T*he ocean looked like an art piece in a well-guarded gallery, Astrid's side wall had been completely replaced by a line of windows, overlooking the ocean in all its breath-taking and beautiful glory. The water glittered, like a blanket of tiny little diamonds had been sewn together and laid across it, the setting sun covering water in a golden haze, the skies a mixture of soft pinks and warm oranges.

It was an image that no painter could copy, an image that no photographer could capture and rightly so, it deserved to be free. I had never been invited to Audric's house before and whenever I mentioned it – he'd always find an excuse; I hated him for keeping this view to himself, however right now, I didn't want anyone to disturb me. I almost forgotten what had happened the past few days, like none of it mattered anymore. It was like the ocean was teaching me how to wash it all away, showing me that what happened was nothing more than a pattern drawn into the sand – sooner or later it would smooth over and start again.

However, my beautiful view began to disappear behind the water, sinking into the subtle waves – I wished it could have stayed. Astrid's room was an art form in itself, a four-posted dark wood bed with transparent drapes flowing around it, was arrange neatly – right down to the last crease. The soft lilac cotton duvet, was pulled over the bottom pillows and tucked in and an array of different sized cushions took up most of the space, each one a different shade of purple and lilac. The bed was a spell, calling me to it and I knew that if I was to touch everything on it – it would be like touching a new-born pup. I wasn't disappointed. I ran my fingers along the duvet, feeling the fuzz gently tickling my fingertips; I squeezed the pillows and almost squealed with excitement – duck feathers. The mattress itself, was ready to swallow me up as I sat – pulling me in closer, daring me to lie down.

The rest of her room was neatly organised, with mounds of piles of books, all in pristine condition – not a speck of dust lingering, plants of all shapes and sizes – each one growing healthy and tall. I could tell that she took pride in everything she did, a subtle smile curved at my lips and I found myself laughing at the thought of the scary Vampire, spending hours watering and caring for her things.

I was in that middle place between awake and asleep, when your eyelids are heavy, your body feels like a cloud and it's the comfiest you think you'll ever be. Sadly, it always gets interrupted by something, whether it be a sudden urge for the toilet, a baby crying or in my situation – a shadow materializing in the corner of the room.

The corner of Astrid's room was engulfed in darkness – moving darkness. Mist poured from it, the room seemed to drain of heat and every single hair on my body sprung up – even the warmth of the bed seemed to turn to ice. Sickening laughter filled my ears, as the darkness began to form into a familiar, terrifying figure.

"Narrdie! How I've missed you." I couldn't breathe. I tried to scream, but nothing came out – my throat was dry and my feet felt like they had turned into cement.

"E-Egregious." I could feel my hands itching towards anything heavy, that I could smash him to death with. Weapon. I needed a weapon, my eyes frantically looked around, but there was nothing, Vampires didn't need weapons; they'd use their fangs and super strength. Witches didn't need them – they were the weapons. Watchers didn't need them either – Audric proved that in the park. However, I wasn't any of them; I wasn't powerful, intimidating and I didn't possess super strength. I was a weak, frightened human – with nothing but the bedside lamp. Chilling laughter surrounded me as he followed my eyes; he waggled his finger – as though he was telling off a naughty child.

"Don't be foolish my dear, that will only get you hurt. I see someone has fixed you up. Good, I always like my projects to be in tip top condition before I break them and trust me – you will break." Before I could even take in another breath, he launched himself towards me and slammed me into the wall, Egregious was on me in an instant; his hands pinning my wrists to keep me in place. "Living under the protection of Watchers, a Vampire and a Witch. My, my, your life has changed in a blink of an eye, hasn't it? They really think they can keep you safe? Keep me from you," he laughed sarcastically, his tongue seeping out to lick my cheek. He twisted my arm around and around until suddenly, it popped out its socket.

The shriek that came from me was deafening, Egregious hissed and spun me into Astrid's mirror – shards scattered around me. One shard in particular, was longer and sharper than the others.

If I was to go down, then this time I'd go down fighting. My heart skipped a beat, as I snagged the sharp piece and threw it towards him – bullseye. Egregious hissed through his teeth and stumbled back, his eyes furious as they looked down to the shard, protruding from his stomach. Egregious hunched over; a ripple of snarls rolled off his tongue, as he slowly pulled the shard out, my nose burned as the stench of his gloopy black blood filled the room. Not wasting any time, I inhaled as much air as I could and screamed.

"AUDRIC!"

Egregious roared, both with anger and pain; his eyes flared as he struck his hand out again – grabbing a fistful of my hair. "Stupid girl!" Like a lion with his game – he had me. Pinned down on the bed, he straddled me; his hand pinning my wrists once more. White strands began to sprout from the roots of his hair, black veins shooting down his arm and into his fingers – that sickening smile curling over his razor teeth. I sucked in for air, but it wasn't there; wouldn't even brush pass me. There was only pain, poison in my blood, fire on my skin - razor blades clawing down my throat. I could feel hands around my neck squeezing, choking the life out of me. It felt like someone was ripping out my heart - slowly.

I couldn't cry, couldn't scream – couldn't even move. It felt like everything inside me was dissolving like acid.

The door burst open, and I knew it was him; he'd heard me, he'd heard and came for me – like he always did. I was saved, they had all come to save me. Audric stopped for only a second, frozen in shock; he crouched low, ready to haul Egregious off me, but Mitchell flung his arm out to stop him.

The Shade sighed and lowered his hand; the black veins crawling back up his arm like worms. Air filled my lungs once more, it felt like coming up from a long dive and finally the burning on my skin turned cold. "You all seem to have an act for intruding," Egregious hissed – not an ounce of his usual mocking tone. His attention suddenly snapped to Mitchell; his jaw clenched and unclenched. "It's been a long time," he greeted with a twisted grin.

"Astrid, go to Narrdie," Mitchell ordered her; she nodded and cautiously began to make her way; her eyes were black, and her teeth were long, sharp and ready to shred him apart at a moment's notice. Egregious didn't dare move; he didn't even look in her direction. Astrid's hands reached for me, her eyes not once leaving the Shade, they felt warm on my skin as they gently wrapped around my arm. Cautiously she pulled me from under him, my legs turned to jelly and buckled, she lightly slung my arm over her shoulder and placed her other around my waist.

"Tut, tut, Vampire. I'm not quite finished with her yet," Egregious warned; eyes now following every move she made. Astrid froze with a rumble in her throat; she protectively held me tighter, placing herself between him and me; she exchanged a glare with Mitchell – a silent question, a plea to tear him apart.

"Bayona?"

"I got him," Bayona hissed; her black empty sockets, glowed brightly as she held up her right hand – a crescent moon tattoo in the centre of her palm.

Egregious grumbled; his face straining, "Release me, Witch. We both know you can't keep this up for long." Even trapped and close to being torn limb from limb – he remained a smug prick.

"Mitchell, someone is channelling him." Bayona's voice was strained, her sockets and nose began to bleed rapidly; her hand shaking, it had only been a few seconds and she already looked like she was going to collapse. "Something strong," she whimpered. Audric immediately gripped onto her hand, offering her his strength; but almost instantly he looked exhausted – his skin paled and dark blotches fell under his eyes.

"Stand aside, Mitchell," a growl rumbled from the doorway, the voice radiated strength, authority - rage. A man, who I could only assume had to be Dacre, stepped between Mitchell and Egregious. He looked like a ferocious animal, wild cropped black hair, unkempt beard and illuminating yellow eyes. He was tall and built a lot bigger than Audric and Mitchell, the long-sleeved grey tunic he wore, was covered in rips and holes. He locked eyes with Egregious – whose expression was beginning to falter and change to terror.

"Dacre?" The Shade's voice cracked and suddenly he seemed to shrink as Dacre closed the space between them, Dacre shook his head and breathed out hard.

"Astrid, you can bring Narrdie over now. Bayona, Audric – let go. He's not going anywhere," Dacre's voice was gruffly. The glowing light from Bayona's sockets faded, blood still trickled down her cheeks; she turned to grip onto Audric – practically collapsing in his arms. Audric looked drained himself; his skin was gaunt and grey, heavy bags pulled down his eyes and he looked like he was going to keel over. Still, he scooped Bayona up into his arms and held her frail body tightly. Astrid didn't take her eyes from Egregious as she walked around him, squeezing me close as his head whipped in my direction – she growled with a warning.

"Your Witch is strong, but she is much stronger, and she'll be here soon! She's woken," Egregious wheezed viciously, Dacre growled and gripped the Shade's throat tightly.

"Mitchell, take everyone out," Dacre snarled. It wasn't a request. Mitchell didn't argue, he just nodded.

"Audric, Astrid let's go."

The screeching of Egregious was awful, I didn't know what Dacre was doing to him and I hoped he'd never tell me. Audric caught my eye and stretched his hand out to brush my shoulder. "Narrdie, are you alright?" I nodded but couldn't find any words – all I could focus on was the screeching. "Cover your ears," Audric ordered. I obeyed, pressing my palms over my ears, digging my hands in harder, until all I could here was ringing and buzzing.

Chapter Five

*C*hopping onions with Astrid, was a perfectly human activity and it almost felt like everything was fine – even if my eyes burned and watered with the onion sting. I had spent most of my time here with Astrid, cooking, cleaning, questioning her on her books – even sitting beside her was comforting. I thought she would have been the one I didn't want to be around, but I had really gotten to like her – Bayona too. For a Vampire, Astrid made the best herbal tea I'd ever tasted, it was rich with a mixture of fresh fruit and flowers we'd picked earlier, she'd shown me how to prepare and steam them. Astrid took a big gulp from her own drink – blood. She'd purposely poured it into a tall mug instead of a glass, so that it wouldn't freak me out; even though I knew it wasn't from a human – it still sent shivers coursing through me.

"How long have I been here now?" I asked as I stared into my drink, swirling the cup around in my hands – watching the leaves and flowers dance in the water. I was thinking about my parents and had been all night; I wondered if they were worried that their baby girl had gone missing – or whether they had even noticed. I'd ran away once before, the first time my dad had slapped me, if it wasn't for Audric finding me – I would have been halfway around the world by now.

"Three weeks, more like two for you considering you slept for several days." Astrid frowned as she looked over at me, "are you thinking of your parents?" I nodded. "Don't worry, Audric has texted them from your phone and Mitchell has contacts high in the human world – in case they called the police," she reassured me with a half-hearted smile. "But that's not what the problem is, is it?"

"I need to see them," I said reluctantly.

"I know, sweetheart," she said soothingly as she continued to chop, I wanted to express how I felt more. Explain to her what my relationship was like and had always been like with them, but Bayona skipped into the kitchen with a big grin and her blackened sunglasses on. "Morning Bayona," Astrid chimed.

"Morning Bayona," I copied.

"Bonjour Astrid, bonjour Narrdie. It's going to be a lovely day today, sunshine!"

"Fantastic." Astrid said sarcastically.

"Does the sun burn you up?" I asked her, thinking about all those Vampire novels I'd read. "Mitchell said your bedroom window, blocked the sun rays." Not once had I seen her go outside when the sun was out, she would even read in the sitting room with the large ruby curtains closed. She laughed lightly and placed her hand in the sun that shone down onto the sink; she twisted it round and wiggled her fingers.

"See, no burning." She turned her focus back onto her cooking, scrapping the onions into the pan and mixing it with the diced beef – the smell already making my mouth water. "It just makes my kind uncomfortable, it's like an itch on the bottom of your foot – awkward to scratch and hard to get rid of."

"Garlic?"

"Nope."

"Silver?"

"Guess again."

"Holy land?"

"Like any other land."

"A cross?"

"Just a symbol."

"Aha! Holy water?"

"Wrong again," she chuckled. "It's nothing but a bitter taste." I nodded, finally feeling satisfied – the movies had it way wrong. She paused from cooking and glanced up at me with a playful grin. "You got any more for me?" Before I could answer, Bayona sucked in air; her smile suddenly slumped, and she bit her lip.

"Bayona?"

"Dacre would like to see you, Narrdie," she offered me a sheepish smile. I hadn't seen Dacre since Astrid's room; Mitchell had asked him to keep his distance from me – at least until I had come to terms with everything. The sound of Egregious tortured screams rang in my ears again, my skin prickled with discomfort – I shook off the memory and looked nervously to Astrid. She'd stopped stirring and slammed the spoon in the table, she placed her hand on my shoulder – giving it a gentle squeeze.

"Did he animo you?" She asked shortly, Bayona nodded. "The cheek of him, couldn't just come down here and ask." I could almost hear the snarl in her voice.

"Animo?"

"Sorry Narrdie, I forgot you're new to this. Animo, it's like a psychic link – mind talking, most can do it – even some humans," Astrid explained with an apologetic smile.

"That's so cool."

"Why does he want to see her? Did he have the courtesy to tell you that?"

"Of course, he didn't; he just requests to see her. Mitchell says it's alright for them to meet now."

"Mitchell doesn't know what he's talking about," Audric growled as he stepped into the kitchen; his face frozen and hands clenched into tight fists. "She isn't speaking to him, not alone."

"She has a name and her own voice," I snapped. Audric hadn't really spoken to me since the day Dacre came, Astrid had told me that he felt responsible – ashamed that he hadn't killed Egregious. Audric flashed me a glare of annoyance and I had to bite the inside of my cheek to keep from ripping his head off.

"Fine. Narrdie, you are not speaking to him by yourself, better?" That boy was on thin ice. Very thin ice.

"Why not? What's wrong with me?" Dacre asked as he leaned casually against the kitchen arch, biting into apple; he winked in a mocking manor to Audric. Audric and Dacre's eyes clashed and I could feel a sudden heat of rage swarm around the room – almost choking.

"You shouldn't even be here," Audric spat.

"That is very rude Audric. However, I'm not deeply offended because you, young man – have no authority over me. This is my house after all." I raised my eyebrows in surprise, no one had mentioned that this house didn't belong to Mitchell – I'd just assumed. Dacre's voice was calm and cocky; his eyes were teasing – taunting Audric's anger.

"Audric, don't rise to him," Astrid said, throwing Dacre a look of disgust.

"Don't test me Dacre," Audric warned as he took another step towards him. I rolled my eyes and before I could even stop myself; my mouth opened.

"Would both of you just shut up." They all turned to me; some with amused expressions. "You want to talk so badly, then lead the way, Dacre. Any more of this, I'm bigger scarier than you, talk and I'm walking." Audric turned to stare at me with immense anger on his face; pissed because I'd stepped on his toes.

"This isn't a game Narrdie," Audric snapped. "I'm your Watcher, it's my job to protect you and letting you be alone with him – is not happening."

"Really, because I thought we were playing hide and seek! Yes, you're my Watcher, so you can watch as I go and speak with the person who saved me the other day."

Dacre smirked widely, "oh I like her." He threw his apple in the bin and gesturing me to follow him, but not before he gave Audric a mocking wave goodbye.

"Narrdie-" Audric began and was quickly silenced by Astrid as she began ordering him to peel potatoes. I made a mental note to thank her for that later.

*B*ayona's room was strange, it reminded me of a teenage girl – going through a typical hippie phase. Unusual trinkets, stones and jars that held weird creatures and sloppy liquid, took over every shelf and surface. A green tapestry was pinned high on the farthest wall; full of symbols and images that I didn't understand – each one hand painted. Maroon and crimson fabrics, were draped all around the room, in a messy yet fitting fashion, her bed was full of different sized pillows and cushions and a grey bobbly blanket under them. There wasn't a light in her room, instead groups of candles resting in odd places around the floor, seemed to burn but never go out.

Out of all their rooms, I liked this one the most, it was the type of room that you could spend all day in and just feel all your troubles float away.

Dacre flopped down on a cluster of pillows, that were gathering in the corner of the room and let out a long-exhausted breath; he gestured for me to have a seat beside him – I remained standing. I preferred to stay as far away from him as I could – the closer to the door the better. This was the person that everyone was scared about me meeting, this was the person who caused all that . . . screaming. Dacre chuckled tediously and ran his tongue along his sharp teeth; he crossed his legs together and rested his hands on the back of his head. "Nervous?" He asked in a tickled voice.

"A little," I admitted.

"Good. It's your hearts way of telling you to be alert, you should always pay attention to it – it could save your life. Especially when your Watcher fails to, which he will." I rolled my eyes.

"What do you want?" I cracked, I wanted to get this over and done with and be back with Bayona and Astrid – cooking food.

"I wanted to give you this," he said – his voice turned serious; he reached into his pocket and held out a small purple pouch to me. "It won't bite."

A ring, hidden away in the pouch, was cold as it rested in my hands, it was unusual in its beauty – decorated with a clear rugged stone, which was locked tightly in the middle of two square knots. I looked at it for a moment, admiring the way it still managed to sparkle, even though I could tell it was old and uncared for. "It's real crystal, probably older than me."

"What are you?" I breathed; the words turned cold the moment they left my lips – did I really want to know? "And why give me this?"

"Keep this on you and whenever you're in danger or need me, all you need to do is touch it and I'll know where you are." His yellow stare met my eyes and for a split-second I didn't feel afraid of him – my blood clawed under my skin in a way I'd never felt before.

"What are you?" I asked again, my voice barely a whisper.

"Never take it off. Mitchell was going to call a meeting after we finished talking, we should go – it involves you. Besides, I think Audric will pop a blood vessel if we stay here any longer," he said as he rose and headed out the door. I followed at a short distance.

Everyone was waiting in the sitting room – faces turned sour as Dacre strutted in. I took a seat beside Astrid; where she immediately asked me if I was alright and scanned me over for any injuries. Bayona lifted her feet and sneered as Dacre attempted to sit beside her – for people that lived in his house, they really didn't like him being home. Audric's eyes were full of resentment when I looked over to him; his expression remained solid, but it was clear to see that I had damaged his ego, good – it needed to be knocked down a peg or two.

"I've come to a decision," Mitchell began, pulling us all to attention. "We can't put it off any longer. The sanctuaries have reached out, they know what has happened and they've accepted."

"All of them?" Astrid asked in shock.

"Yes, all who have heard." Astrid breathed out in relief, as Bayona clutched her hands together with happiness – even Audric looked like her wanted to grin. I had no idea what it meant, and no one looked willing to explain it to me either. I could almost hear their answers already – it's not time. "Narrdie, I'm sending you home and what I'm about to ask you is going to be hard. You need to go in and tell them that you're leaving, tell them that you're going to travel the world. Audric told me that, that is what you wanted to do, and you've had countless arguments with your parents about it. Go inside, pack your things and leave." Mitchell crouched down in front of me and gave me an apologetic smile; his expression softened and his hands gently cupped mine. "Can you do that?" I sighed and swallowed the lump back that had formed in my throat, even though they never showed it, they were my parents – my mum and dad. I didn't want to do this, but it was the only way. Audric placed his hand around my shoulder and gave me a gently squeeze, I looked up to him and he smiled slightly and winked to me – looks like I was forgiven.

"I'm gonna have too, when is this happening?" I hated how shaky my voice was; hated that they were all watching me, when I had tears fogging up my eyes.

"Today. We can't afford to waste any more time. While Narrdie is at her home, the rest of us will pack and when she returns – we're gone."

"Gone?" I repeated, no one seemed as shocked as I did – barely even battered an eyelid.

"The Order has been in touch, it's no longer safe here, so we need to relocate." I stood, outraged that they had to leave there home because of me.

"But Egregious is dead."

"Someone was channelling him, which means they know our location," Bayona added; her voice calming.

"No. That's not an option, how can you even think it? No one should have to leave because of me, you've worked so hard on this place. It's your home." My voice had become high pitched, I could feel the tears blurring my vision.

"Narrdie, this is just one of many homes. The Order places us and when that home is targeted, they decided what we do," Mitchell explained. "It's just stuff, it can all be replaced."

"I don't know what the Order is because every time I ask anything – one of you says that it's not time. All I'm hearing is you must move because some Shade and his friend are trying to kill me, for reasons that you won't even tell me. You people don't even know me, yet you are all willing to leave and risk your lives for me. This isn't right," I was pretty sure that only dogs could hear me now.

"Mitchell, can we do this later? Give Narrdie some time to process this?" Audric asked as he slowly began to pull me towards the stairs, Mitchell frowned but Astrid gave him a stern look – which meant he was not allowed to disagree.

"Of course, bear in mind – we need to get this done today." I shrugged out of Audric's hold and ran upstairs, slamming Astrid's bedroom door. Yes, it was a childish thing I was doing, but after these three weeks – I had earned this tantrum.

For once, everyone left me alone; my wailing was probably enough to tell them that I didn't want to be disturbed. I didn't know why I was crying so much, but I needed this, I hadn't cried once since Audric had brought me here. I cried about Bayona's room, about how much time it must have taken her to pin up all the drapes and how long the candles had been burning. I cried about Astrid and how much time she'd spent keeping everything clean and tidy, all the times she'd spent looking out her window – watching that beautiful sunset. Finally, I cried about Audric; he had given up so much for me and I never knew and now I was the reason that they all had to leave.

"I can't make them do this, I won't," I told myself as I sat up and wiped my eyes. "I'll go, then everything will be okay, they can stay here." I headed towards the window and began undoing the old, rusted slacks. Before I could even pull the window open, something fast threw me back hard into the mouth of the pillows.

"It won't work Narrdie," Dacre snorted as he slouched in the doorway; his arms crossed and a smug grin pulling at the corners of his mouth; he pulled out a red apple and bit out a big chunk. "Do you really think that they wouldn't come looking for you? That Audric would just accept you've left?"

"What's with you and Apples?" I growled.

"They're good for you, you should eat them more," he replied as he offered me a bite.

"I'm not putting everyone in danger and forcing them out of their home. All because someone wants me dead," Dacre scoffed; he opened the window and chucked the apple out.

"Firstly, it's my home. And someone doesn't want you dead, a lot of someone's want you dead – there's a big difference. Narrdie, those people downstairs, they aren't being forced out. Did any of them look upset?" I thought back to it, they looked more excited than sad – it was me who was upset.

"No," I answered him.

"No home we have is permanent. When the Order of the Watchers decides it's time to relocate – we relocate. It's been like this from the beginning. Those lot down there are thrilled about leaving, they'll get to see people they haven't seen in decades, this is the life they've been born into."

"They are still going to be in danger with me here. I've made my choice," I grunted and went to storm past him. Dacre rolled his eyes; he gripped my arm tight and pulled me back – gently pushing me back on the bed.

"Where are you going? I haven't finished proving you wrong yet," he growled slightly. "You know we can't just let you leave like that Narrdie."

"Move out my way!" I ordered, shrugging out of his grip and barging past him once more.

"Narrdie, before you go . . ." I turned towards him and that's when I felt the pain slam into my head.

Once again, I was tucked in Astrid's bed; I could feel the soft cotton blanket draped over me and the gentle duck pillows, soothing the ache. My head was throbbing – pulsing, almost like I had a tiny marching band inside; I rubbed my temples and whined. I leaned up and felt hands gently forcing me to lie back down, "easy Narrdie, don't get up to quickly." Mitchell warned as he and Dacre were sitting over me, the smug look remaining on Dacre's face. I was beginning to understand why the others didn't like him.

"Mitchell I . . ." I blinked a few times and glanced to Dacre. Anger bubbled as the realisation slammed into me, "did you hit me?"

"It was the only thing I could do to stop you, either that or break your legs and I'm sure you wouldn't have liked that." He smirked teasingly. "I admit, it wasn't my greatest plan."

"You bastard!"

"I did warn you," Dacre mocked.

"You piece of-"

"Enough," Mitchell snapped. "I am not happy one bit about what he did, it was – excessive. However, stopping you was the right choice. Narrdie, you coming here hasn't put us in danger, this is what we do - what we've always done. If it's not you, it would have been someone else, so you leaving – just adds extra work for us. Once the pain has gone down, would you please come back downstairs, time is not on our side right now. Dacre...out, let's not mention this to the others please Narrdie," Mitchell interrupted before Dacre could say anything – it took everything I had not to throw things at him. I cursed as I could hear him snickering, all the way down the stairs.

"I'll do it," I announced after I took a few gulps of water and the pain pills Mitchell had slipped me; I felt my heart suddenly sink and my hands quivered. Doing this meant I was leaving my life, my normal dull life; I'd probably never go back to college (not that I wanted to anyway) and I had no idea how long it would be until I saw my parents again. Mitchell clapped his hands together and immediately jumped up and started telling us the plan once again; his voice sounded nothing but a faint murmur.

"I will begin packing, along with Astrid and Bayona. Only take what we need, Bayona that means no candles and no drapes." Bayona's lip lifted in a sneer; she flicked her hair and skipped upstairs; Astrid followed – giving Mitchell a peck on the cheek. "Audric, you and Dacre will take Narrdie to her house. This is not up for discussion; we need to get this done quick. Anyone got a problem with that?" Mitchell looked at Audric with a look so savage, it made him flinch back. Even Dacre avoided meeting his eyes; not one of them dared open their mouths to argue – or make a sarcastic remark. "You are both responsible for her – keep her safe."

"Always," Audric automatically responded, flashing me a smile.

"I'll protect her with my life," Dacre chimed sarcastically.

Chapter Six

$\mathcal{T}$he drive to my house was painfully and awkwardly quiet, an unpleasant tension lingered in the stuffy air – Audric and Dacre occasionally turned to flash each other hatred stares. On the other hand, I was too busy trying not to break down; I'd always done exactly what my parents said and now I was going there to do the exact opposite, or so they thought. I fidgeted all the way there, biting my nails right down – one finger even bled. Dacre's bright yellow eyes caught my sight in the mirror; his brows raised.

"Not long now, soon you'll be reunited with your parents," he informed me. I was surprised to see a comforting genuine smile grace his lips.

"Yeah, sure," was all I could say.

"Narrdie, it'll be alright," Audric reassured me. "I promise, at least you'll get to see Freddie." I gasped and leaned up, the last I saw of him was when he was locked in my bedroom – he'd probably starved to death. Audric caught my panic and smiled dismissively, "relax, when I brought you to our home I went back and let him out, he's fine." I let out a long breath and smiled to him.

"Thank you."

I expected my house to fill me with some sort of warmth and nostalgia when I saw it, but instead it was like seeing a stranger – a stranger with a dark look in their eyes. My mind raced with questions, but one bothered me the most – had they missed me? "In you go, we'll wait here," Audric said softly and gestured for me to go in – I didn't move. "Narrdie? Do you need a minute?"

"I thought I'd miss it," I admitted.

"And do you?" Dacre asked; his voice gentle, as though he was talking to a frightened child.

"No, it feels like I've never been here before, it feels...wrong."

"What about your parents? Do you miss them?" I had mentioned them a lot to Astrid, wondering if they'd noticed I was gone – if they were frantically worrying about where I was. However, I hadn't thought of them and if I missed being with them.

"I don't know," I admitted. Dacre reached his hand back and popped open my car door.

"Time to find out."

My hand was shaking when I grasped the brassy handle; I expected to hear the familiar shouting that came with this house, but it had gone from a megaphone of screaming – to an eerie silence. My heart began to skip a beat every other second; I never thought that I would be purposely disobeying them. It felt like I was walking on a frozen lake, scared that at any moment the ice would break, and I'd freeze to death.

Two brown beady little eyes peered around the corner, suddenly a golden blob raced towards and began jumping up at me – desperately trying to lick my face. "Freddie! Hello, my baby, who's my beautiful little boy? I've missed you!" I whispered to him; rubbing my hands all over his head; he whined and waggled his tail – paws tapping on the floor like an Irish dancer,

"Where the fuck, have you been?" My dad roared aggressively as his large hand seized my arm and threw me into the sitting room. My mum sat with a nonchalant expression in the single seater; a cloth in her hand and all the spoons we owned in front of her. "Answer me girl!" He commanded in a fiery rage – my mum flinched.

"I'm nineteen years old dad, I can make my own choices. Why the sudden curiosity in my life?" I snapped back. For a second my parents looked shocked, I had never snapped at my dad like this, if I even gave him a funny look, I'd normally get a thump.

"Watch your mouth, this is my house you're living in!"

"Not anymore! I'm packing my stuff and I'm leaving," I quickly darted past him and stomped up to my room; the lock on my door had been broken clean off its hinges. My brows shot up in shock, sitting in the middle of my bed, were my two bright green suitcases – which had already been packed with everything I wanted. Packing my stuff was never going to be the hard part, getting past my dad without a war breaking out was the part I dreaded the most. I took a moment to compose myself, before awkwardly dragging my bags down the stairs, immediately I headed straight for the door – a strong arm pulled me back.

"You're not going anywhere!" For a split second I thought my dad's eyes had shifted to black, I was frozen – raw panic iced over my veins. The pain from his fingers pulled me back from my thoughts, I shrugged out his hold and pushed him back.

"You can't stop me!"

"You're gonna regret talking to me like that!" He swung his hand back and I knew what was coming; every time I even raised my voice, I'd get a smack. I flinched back and closed my eyes – bracing myself for the familiar sting. "Let go of me!" My dad snarled; Dacre gripped my dad's hand; his long fingernails digging into his arm.

"If you ever try to harm her again, I will kill you. Narrdie, get you stuff and get in the car, now." Dacre and my dad glared at each other; their eyes locked in a battle of submission. Audric appeared beside me; he gently placed his arm around me and picked up my bags.

"Come on," he whispered and swayed me towards the door. "Freddie, come." He called back, Freddie barked happily before sprinting past us and diving in the car – bouncing up and down on the seat.

"Get in the car Narrdie." Dacre repeated, his voice still holding onto his aggression. The front door was already closed by the time I looked back.

"To answer our question Dacre, no I don't miss them."

"You alright?" Audric asked once we were all buckled in.

"Fine. Can we go now?" He nodded and pulled onto the road; I leaned back, cracked open the window and stuck my head out. After tonight I knew I'd never go back there again, even after all of this was sorted and over – I'd never see my parents again. Freddie nudged my hand; then rested his head on my lap, his tail waggling as I traced lazy circles in his fur – as least I had him.

"You wanna talk about it?" Audric offered – Dacre scoffed and rolled his eyes.

"No, but thank you," I gave him a fake smile. "Wake me when we get back," I mumbled as I snuggled down with Freddie.

The car skidded from side to side, I could smell the rubber from the wheels burning and my ears stung from the deafening screeches – my hands tightened around Freddie. Dacre was half leaned out the passenger window, his eyes a brighter yellow than usual; his mouth lifted in a snarl as he rapidly began shooting a gun at a car behind us. "Narrdie, keep your head down!" He barked in a dark voice.

"What's happening?"

"Oh, nothing much, just some people trying to kill us," Dacre snarled sarcastically. He darted back inside to reload his gun, his eyes ablaze with murderous intent.

"Who?"

"Narrdie! Head. Down." Dacre growled – glaring at me until I scooted down in my seat. "Don't make me tell you a third time," he warned, his eyes boring into me.

"Audric, who are they?" I asked, my voice a shaky mess.

"Shade's lackeys, they might as well be sniffer dogs – can track you for miles." He shouted back as he spun the car to the right.

"What do they want?" I could feel the bruises that had started to take colour on my arms, as the car tossed me around. Freddie whined; the poor thing looked like a deer on ice – trying to find a safe place to stand.

"You! They've come for you!" Audric explained in a rush, before forcing the car to swerve to the left. I felt like I was going to throw up everything inside me, I couldn't tell whether it was from Audric's driving or the sudden panic of another creature from the Shade's world. I screamed as a bullet shot through the rear window, buzzing past my ears and hitting the dashboard – ringing lingering painfully in my ears. I felt dizzy – bile rose in my throat; I tried to catch my breath and speak but I couldn't. I had never even seen a gun in person before, let alone had a bullet fly past and miss me by an inch or two.

"That's why, you keep your fucking head down!" Dacre snarled.

"That won't do shit Dacre, you know that," Audric growled as he glanced to Dacre's gun.

"I'm not aiming for them; I'm aiming for their tyres. Why don't you focus on driving!" Even in a time like this, they still couldn't resist bickering.

"They want me?" I could already feel my heart increase so much that I thought at any second, it would give out on me.

"They won't get you!" Dacre snarled, he exchanged a look with Audric; Audric clenched his jaw and nodded. A dark grin spread on Dacre's mouth; he threw his gun to the side and dove out the window with a snarl.

"DACRE! Audric stop!" He sped up. "Audric!"

"He knows what he's doing! He's done this before."

"We can't just-" A sharp bolt of black electric shattered what was left of the back window, I shrieked and curled into Freddie. Audric's head shock back, to check if I were alright; his eyes met mine and for the first time since I'd known him – he looked afraid. I'd always felt safe, even when Egregious had found and attacked... twice, even when I was moments away from death – Audric was always there. This, this was different, I could see it in his eyes; this time he didn't think he'd be able to save me.

Audric was still looking in my direction – double checking that I wasn't hurt; not noticing the person standing in the middle of the road – smiling widely.

"Audric!"

"Oh sh-" He slammed his foot on the brakes and spun the steering wheel desperately, we skidded along the road – for what felt like a lifetime. With one hand gripped onto the handle and the other holding onto Freddie – I held on as tight as I could, it was all I could do to keep from screaming. I felt the car clash, with what I could only guess was a pot whole. The car toppled over, the groaning of the steel scrapping along the concrete – singed my ears. We slid along the ground, glass and gravel jumped to cut my arms and face; my seat belt pulling me tighter and tighter, I thought it was going to cut me in half. Suddenly, a hard thud hit – finally stopping the car, I was thrown forward and felt something solid smack into my head.

I didn't know if I had been knocked out or if my eyes had dropped into my skull and had just been rattling around. I could feel something wet trailing down the side of my check and from the throbbing in my head, I had an idea what it was from. "Narrdie?" I tried to pull myself up, avoiding the shattered glass all around me – but it was no use.

"Narrdie?" Audric called again; his voice was hoarse.

"I'm alright," I replied hastily. "Freddie? Freddie!" I called anxiously, he was nowhere to be seen; he wasn't in the car and I couldn't see him on the road either. I prayed that he was ok, that somehow, he managed to jump out the car before we'd crashed. "Where's Freddie?"

"Narrdie, get out and run," he said through winces.

"I can't, Audric I'm stuck," the seat belt had trapped me to the chair, like a helpless animal stuck in a cage. I pulled against it, ignoring my body's screams of protest, the aches and pains began to make themselves known. "The seat belt . . . I can't get it loose."

"Hold on I'm coming," Audric groaned snapping his own belt; he hissed through his teeth as he forced himself up and began to pull himself around the wheel to get to me. Blood covered half of his face, mud and glass clinging to his cuts, a deep slash bled heavily from his collarbone.

Sharp claws smashed through the window and gripped Audric's shoulder, he yelled out in pain as the claws dug deep into his shoulder – the blood oozing in between its knuckles. I shrieked as the claws wretched him out the window, like a ragdoll. A chilling screech filled the area, making the ruined car shake and groan. I could feel my whole body began to tremble; I had to get free, I had to see what had happened to Audric, I had to find Dacre and Freddie. I pulled at my seatbelt, growling and cursing under my breath. "Come on, let me out, let me out!" I pulled once more and could almost cry with happiness, as the belt suddenly unclicked. Ignoring the pulsing in my head, the aching of my shoulder and the burning in my legs; I gripped onto the outside of the window frame and hauled myself out. Everything hurt, each step felt like I was walking on lava barefoot, but I couldn't stop; I had to keep following the trail of blood. I had to find . . . "Audric."

I'd forgotten how to breathe, I tried to speak but my throat felt like sandpaper. The good news was that I'd found them both, Audric and Dacre – alive. The bad news . . . they weren't alone. Audric and Dacre had been forced to their knees, their hands tied behind their backs, both looking like they'd taken a beating, clear white bone poked out from Dacre's sleeve and one of his eyes was closed and held a deep gash - creating a puddle of blood around his knees.

A man dressed in dusty grey turned to me with a sadistic smirk; he was skinny, almost like a walking skeleton; his skin was a mixture between grey and blue and had dents and purple blotches all over. Even if his appearance didn't make me sick (which it did), the stench of him was enough to create bile rise in my stomach - even from where I was standing. "Look whose here boys," he sang. The men behind him all laughed unpleasantly; they all wore the same dull grey - smelling as equally bad as the other. There was too many, far too many for Audric and Dacre to fight, there had to be at least twelve and the only thing that was going to stop these men, was a nineteen-year-old girl - who had only just been born into this world.

"Narrdie run!" Audric called to me, the man lifted his lip in a growl before swiftly striking him once across the face - blood splattered from Audric's mouth. A low growl escaped my lips; but it wasn't mine, I didn't recognize where it had come from, but it was enough to make the men stumble back slightly. They exchanged a worried glance with each other and adjusted their weapon belts, the main man swallowed hard.

"Let them go!" I warned, my voice for once sounded strong - not an ounce of the usual shakiness.

"Can't do that I'm afraid," he licked his lips with his sharp tongue, which had a number of sickly-looking boils - all looking ready to pop.

"Let them go, I won't ask again," I growled. The man perched his lips and whistled; he glanced up to the sky, a dark laugh rolled of his tongue.

"The night clouds are clearing," he blurted. The man looked to Audric; whose jaw was clenched. "I'm guessing you all forgot what tonight was. The blood moon has risen, go ahead - look up."

Curiosity was going to get me killed one day.

It stung, the second I looked up and those clouds parted - my eyes burned. The Moon, the blood Moon as he called it - hurt. It wasn't like any Moon I used to gaze at, it was dark - sinister as it beamed down on us, the red glow pulling down my strength into a dull ache; I tore my eyes away, rubbing hard as my feet stumbled; my eyes felt like they were on fire. "Feels like you're being buried alive, doesn't it?" The man raised his brow and turned to Audric and Dacre, "is this the first it's happened?

Seems we picked the perfect time to come and get her. Egregious was right, she's awake." He turned back to me with a smirk.

Something flared inside of me, clawing its way to the surface – ripping off my skin. I felt my eyes change, my pupils split, and I could see every little detail. The sweat forming on the man's forehead, the skin flaking away on Audric's deep shoulder gash, the fleck of dust jumping from Dacre's shoulder and into the air. I felt stronger, everything was heightened. My eyes snapped back the man, he looked excited and scared all in one; his eyes looked me up and down and he swallowed hard. Audric's eyes widened slightly; he looked over to Dacre, but Dacre didn't turn to him – he was watching me. There was a longing in his eyes.

"Before we all fly off the handles and judge our opponents too quickly – we should all calm down. You might want to look at this first before you make your next move." He took out a bullet and held it up, twirling it around in his fingers. The bullets were glass but had a sharp silver point at the tip and black gloopy liquid sloshing around inside. "Know this?" He asked casually, I shook my head; feeling my heartbeat slowly begin to increase, Audric had said bullets didn't work on nonhumans – except I was human, and this bullet would kill me. "Well, this isn't any normal type of round. Let me show you," he winked to Dacre as he loaded the cartridge back in. "When this bullet shreds into the flesh and enters the blood, I can make the host of the liquid feel anything I want. We got a bunch of these beautiful things, by someone named Mara." Dacre's eyes widened.

"You lying prick!" Dacre snarled. The man smirked and turned dark eyes to him, he crouched down and tilted his head.

"What? Did you think she was on your side? Fool, have you forgotten what she is? Mara is anyone's . . . for the right price of course." He aimed the gun at Dacre, then smirked as he moved towards Audric – my heart dropped into my stomach. "Just kidding," he grinned with a vicious laugh, before I could even take in another breath, he fired the gun once – right into my chest.

The moment the bullet ripped into me – my knees buckled, I felt the capsule burst open and the liquid rapidly course throughout my veins. "Burn."

A ripple of scorching pain tore into me, with each breath I took – it got worse. All I could do was scream; my hands scratched against the bullet wound, blood staining my fingers and under my nails. It was like the blood in my veins was replaced with fire, burning everything in its path – blistering under my skin.

It stopped. My veins chilled, my skin cooled, I felt the moisture sooth my aching throat, every trace of pain had vanished and the bullet that I felt ripping further into me – had disappeared. I gasped, sucking in every bit of breath I could, feeling like I had been buried alive; my hands were still shaking when I felt the hole where the bullet had entered – expecting the bite as my fingers felt it, but there was none. Hands clapped around me gently and carefully lifted me to my feet, Audric. I looked up to him and he smiled and wiped tears from my cheek, he nodded towards Dacre; he was on his feet – unharmed. "You're safe," Audric soothed in my ear.

The man that had us captive, was now on his knees, black blood dripping from his mouth – cowering and shaking, he timidly looked up. "Tell your men to stand down," the woman ordered in an eerily calm voice.

Beautiful would have been the wrong word to describe her; she was so much more than that. Her olive-green hair was styled into long dreadlocks that trailed down to the floor – the ends changing into leaves of reddish browns and dulled greens. Her eyes were a bright emerald, as they bored down onto him – long black lashes framing them perfectly. Her long earth toned dress was entwined with leaves and flowers and revealed light parts of her flawless sparkling skin. Her long slender nails forcefully dug into the man's neck; thick gloopy black blood streamed down his front. "Do not make me ask again Melphos," she warned.

Melphos nodded – every part of him shaking, one by one his men vanished with panicked looks on their faces. I'd never seen so many men look terrified of one person before, I wiped my mouth to keep from smirking. "Thank you. Apologise to the Lady Narrdie." Hate filled eyes met mine; his jaw clenched and if looks could kill – I'd be nothing but ash on the ground. The woman dug her nails in harder, smiling as he groaned, "I do not like the way you are looking at her. Lose the look or lose the eyes. Now – speak."

"I humbly apologise . . . Lady Narrdie," he politely said as he bowed his head, I hissed lowly – Dacre snickered his approval.

"It'll do. Give your master's a message. The Elemental Sisters refuse their offer, we stay on the side of the Watchers and always will. Your kind upset the balance too much, you taint this land with your very breath. Remove yourself from my sight and pray to the mother, you never cross my path again." She released her hold and without another glance, he scurried away into a cloud of black smoke.

She raised her brows and wiped as much blood as she could from her hand – grimacing at the smell. The woman elegantly strode over to me and placed her non bloodied hand on my cheek, she smiled gently, I could feel the warmth lick at my icy cheeks. "Child, do not fret and please do not be afraid. Are you harmed?" I nodded, not being able to find any words, stunned by her grace. She frowned lightly and moved her hands towards my shoulder – she froze, "May I?" I nodded again, her appearance dumbfounded me; my insides were kicking me, trying to get me to say something - anything.

She placed her hand over the bullet wound, a gently silver light began to glow, it didn't hurt; it was soft and wet – like a puppy licking my hand.

She moved her hand away, uncurled her fingers and revealed the small bullet, it was completely intact with all the liquid swimming inside the glass case. "All better, it needs wrapping up when you return home, but after a few hours, you'll be all healed."

"Thank you," I stuttered. Dacre headed towards us, wide surprise on his face, I looked up to Audric, who had the same expression. Audric sucked in air – ready to speak when a car skidded to a halt a few feet from us – ruffling up dirt and little stones on the road.

Mitchell shot out, followed by Astrid and Bayona; their expressions turning from alarmed to relieved to see we were all safe. Astrid immediately took my face in her hands and smiled lightly, after being satisfied that I wasn't hurt; she turned towards the woman – shock plastered her face.

Bayona didn't stare in shock, she didn't frown with wonder; instead, she dropped to her knees suddenly and placed her tattooed hand in the air, she was breathless when she spoke.

"Bless the Goddess and those before me." Bayona didn't set her blacked out eyes on the woman or even lift her head up; she stayed on the ground – waiting. The glamourous woman smiled widely, her perfect white teeth gleaming; she placed her hand over her heart, before placing it against Bayona's tattooed palm.

"Dear Bayona, ut dea benedicat tibi et sorores coram nobis, docebit vos." I looked to Audric to see if he knew what she'd just said, sadly he shook his head, as did Dacre and Mitchell. "I have heard many things about you, what a very rare creature you are – I had wanted to meet you for a long time, daughter of the stars. We have many things to discuss," Bayona lifted her head up to the woman and smiled in gratitude, it wasn't hard to see the excitement that vented out of her – she practically vibrated. Mitchell stepped forward, a slightly confused but always respectful look upon his face; he bowed.

"Forgive me, my Lady but, what is your name?" He asked, Bayona giggled and shook her head, she skipped to his side and link her arm through his.

"Mitchell, Astrid, Audric, Narrdie...Dacre. Meet the Priestess, Goddess, Elemental Sister – Erenna." Everyone gasped, (except me) and bowed low – Dacre was hesitant and only bowed when Astrid growled his way.

"Please my children, stand."

"How did you know where to find us, Lady Erenna?" Audric asked as he rose.

"Audric! Watcher of Narrdie, I am so pleased to finally meet you; you have done well with protecting and watching Narrdie," Audric blushed slightly. "The Earth heard your call and it came to me. When I heard who had called to me; I couldn't just stand aside and allow it to continue." Erenna set her eyes onto me, as did the others – all waiting.

"Me? My call?" I burst. "I called to you?"

Erenna smiled widely, "you do not know how powerful you are, do you? When you felt the Moon's sting and the fear for your friend's lives, your soul split and searched for help. When the Earth realised that it was you – it found me."

"M- My soul split?" I asked, my voice a little panicked.

"Relax young one, all is well. You still have so much to learn, to realise and to conquer. Mitchell, we must return to your haven, prying eyes and listening ears are all around. Also, you have guests awaiting your arrival."

"What about this place?" I quizzed as I looked around at the Shade's dead men that Dacre had shot and more than likely cut up. The tipped over destroyed car, with broken glass – blood splattered marks on the concrete and the long bloody trail that had come from Audric. It looked like a massacre.

"All shall be fixed before any humans come across this road, I'm sure Mitchell can gather someone to sort this?" Erenna asked as she turned to him with a smile, Mitchell nodded and bowed once to her.

"I have already sent word to the Watchers in the area, the human factions will organise a closure."

"Thank you. I have just one more thing before we leave, Narrdie? Does this belong to you?" She whistled highly, the bushes rusted and a yellow howling dog with big beady eyes, bounded over to me.

"Freddie! Oh, thank god!" I smiled and dropped down to him – nestling my face with his.

Chapter Seven

$\mathcal{E}$renna met us back at the house, which I supposed was my home now – at least until we had packed up and left. Audric raised his brow, as Erenna opened the front door and ushered us into the living room.

"Yeah, because that's the most bizarre thing that's happened today – she's managed to get into your house," I mumbled sarcastically. Audric scowled at me and lightly shoved me. "Watch it, I'm injured!" She cleared her throat, her smile wide and proud as she sucked in air to speak.

"I would like you all to meet, my sisters," Erenna announced the moment we were gathered; she moved aside to reveal three equally mesmerising women – two sat gracefully smiling on the couch, the other was leaned against the wall behind them; her arms crossed and face sour, they looked like an expensive art piece in a posh museum. Erenna swiftly drifted past me; her hand squeezed my shoulder before she set herself down to join them, Astrid signalled us all to sit down with a hiss – thinking we were all being rude by gawking at them. "Sisters," she greeted pleasantly as she bowed her head, they all responded in the same way – reaching out their hands to grasp hers. "It's been so long since we have all been together, I have missed you all."

"As have we. Erenna, why have you summoned us all?" One of the sisters spoke - sounding impatient and irritated.

Her crimson hair reminded me of roses, lightly waving down to her breasts; her amber eyes flicked between us all, I noticed twinges of gold entwined with the amber; her lips, a dulled red as they pressed into a tight line. Her clothes seemed strange for a Goddess – though what did I know about Gods and Goddesses? Still, it wasn't like anything I'd picture one to wear. The maroon cat suit was tight against her, golden spikes sat upon her shoulders – the light bouncing from them, making them shine. A transparent shawl was draped around her waist, fastened with a golden buckle; it flowed down to the floor and trailed behind her – it looked like fire flickering. Her eyes shot back to Erenna; she tapped her finger against her arm – waiting impatiently.

"Manners Fyra," Erenna warned. "I apologise if you were dealing with things Sisters, but I believe this is more important." Erenna gently cupped her hand on my arm and pulled me towards them, giving me an encouraging smile. "This my sisters, is Narrdie Moon." Fyra scoffed. "Look upon her yourselves and tell me what you find, tell me I am wrong." I could feel my palms turning clammy at my sides, I wasn't used to so many people staring at me in the way they did – it felt like I was an Alien, placed in an exhibition for the whole world to come and judge. The worst part, I still didn't understand why my name and who I was, was so shockingly special – no one would tell me yet.

I glanced over my shoulder to Audric and Astrid, Audric had a very strange and confused look on his face – it took a lot of my composure not to laugh. Astrid's eyes met mine; she winked and nodded with a smile – mouthing the words, 'you're alright'.

"Mother of all!" The smaller one gasped, pulling back all our attention. She rose with a hand over her mouth; she was the most unusual looking out of the four, but still as beautiful.

Her eyes stunned me, there was no iris, not whites – just silver. Her hair was broken into three tight plaits – pulled together to form a high ponytail, which still fell to her hips; it was a magnificent blend of silver, grey and white. She wore a dress that resembled a Greek chiton, it was mainly all white silk – except for one piece in the middle, which was a very pale pink. The silk wrapped around lightly over her tiny body – decorated with little diamonds and crystals that occasionally twinkled at me. Shawls dangled from her wrists; the attachment was so small – it looked like it was part of her skin. Her skin was pale, paler than the Shades and Astrid – it was like snow. "It can't be, it is too soon – years too soon, how is this possible? Wenona?" The silver woman asked in pure excitement; her pale pink lips; lifted into a wide smile.

"Aronnia, calm yourself," Erenna gently told her, then turned to face the final Sister. "Wenona, what do you see?"

The last Sister rose, she had a certain look that made me instantly know that she was the oldest out of the four, it wasn't because she had the face of an aged woman; she just seemed to give off a specific authority out of them – carried herself differently. She held my hand in hers then stared into my eyes; my instinct was to look away – but I didn't. Wenona had crimped shoulder length hair with a blocked full fringe and was the colour of sea foam teal, one side had been clipped up with crystal white shells. Her eyes scanned me up and down – resting once again on my eyes. Her eyes were pretty, a subtle mixture of so many different blues, blending together like the sea – I'd lost count. Her clothes were bare, sky-blue meshed fabric draped around her neck and down to cover her breasts; it wrapped around her waist then burst out into an elegant Prussian blue. Silver chains with pearls dotted all over, fastened around her neck, shoulders and down her chest – sparkling in the light and shelled spiralled markings decorated all around her skin. "She is hard to read, there is a block on her – a block that she didn't put on herself. Clearly someone does not want us to pry around inside her; but I do believe that it is truly the child we've all been waiting for."

"I can assure you it is," Dacre spat.

"I did not ask for your input!" Wenona snapped, her head snapping towards him. The room shook slightly and the soft expression she'd given me, was gone and replaced with hatred. She held her stare, the shaking growing more violent.

"Back off!" Bayona hissed to Dacre; Dacre held a murderous look.

"Dacre!" Mitchell ordered, Dacre clenched his jaw and finally dropped his eyes.
The room stilled.

"Sister," Erenna called, pulling her sisters attention back. "The Earth responded to her call," Erenna explained, quickly trying to shift the tension. "It is her." Wenona nodded once then lightly stroked my cheek; she joyfully smiled and turned to her other sisters.

"The Earth confirmed it, as do mine. Fyra, Aronnia, do you deny it? Does yours deny it?" Riddles, why did everything anyone said - sound like riddles. Aronnia shook her head and grinned merrily, her skin glistening like snow as she practically hopped up and down. Fyra lifted her lip in a sneer and let out a light hiss, which seemed to whip at me like a snake. Erenna breathed out hard and clenched her jaw.

"I see nothing, mine are silent," Fyra grumbled.

"I don't believe that, I think you are lying out of spite," Aronnia snapped.

"It's nothing but a human, a human that is wasting all our time. May the Fires of th-" A low snarl filled the room as Wenona whirled on Fyra, cutting off her hate filled words.

"You will hold your tongue, or I will take it. Aronnia, Erenna, please may you go and help our sister to cool down - outside. I would hate for our lovely hosts to witness any more of this rude behaviour." Wenona was terrifying, when she was mad, it was like all the warmth from the room vanished and was replaced by a chilling, sinister cold. This only confirmed that she was the eldest and in charge. "Fyra, do not show your face in this house until you can remember where you placed your manners, the disappointment and shame you have caused is profoundly disgusting. Ut dea dimittet vobis." Wenona didn't take her eyes away from Fyra until she was out of the room, however Fyra had her head firmly looking down - not daring to say another word.

Wenona turned to us, her face calm and relaxed and her voice full of regret. "I apologise greatly for her, she hasn't been woken for quite some time, and it seems she has forgotten how to act in the human world." Astrid smiled sweetly as she stepped forward, bowing to them all before she spoke.

"No need to apologise, most of us tend to lose our way every now and then - some more than others," she through Audric and Dacre a certain look. "Priestess Wenona, is there anything at all I can get you and your sisters?" She offered in her motherly tone, how on earth had I been so frightened about Astrid - it made me wish I could have taken back my first four days, I'd spent them completely avoiding her.

"How very generous of you Madam Elder, however I must decline as I was rather hoping that Lady Narrdie would escort me for a walk in the garden. I am dying to see that lovely water feature you built Mitchell. Narrdie, would you mind escorting me?"

"Of course not," I blurted and jumped up eagerly.

At first the walk was silent, it wasn't an awkward silence which I was thankful for, but as we got closer and closer, I could feel my hands becoming clammy with nerves. "It has been a very confusing time for you, hasn't it?" She asked softly.

"Yes," I admitted and bit my lip slightly. Of course, I was confused, in the past two or three weeks, strange creatures had tried to kill me - me! A nineteen-year-old girl, with crappy parents, a terrible habit of daydreaming and chewed up fingernails. I had gone from all of that, to living with Watchers, Witches, Vampires and whatever the hell Dacre was. Things I never thought existed, now did and they were nothing like the movies. I had been attacked and almost murdered not once, but three times - pain I'd never thought I'd feel, at least not within the same month. All of this happened because I was special in some way, no one had even explained to me why - it was still not the time.

"Is there anything you want to ask? What are you confused about?" She knew exactly what I was going to ask, I could tell in her eyes. Perhaps, she was the one that was going to tell me.

"All of it, all of this! Everything happened fast, so fast, it still doesn't feel real sometimes. One day, I'm planning my next route after college, where I was going to move to a flat or house. Then the next day, my life decided that, that wasn't the plan it was going to have. Now, everyone I seem to meet, already knows me. I'm some special being, who needs protecting from things like the Shade and the men that Erenna stopped. Whenever I ask one of them in there, why this is happening and why I'm so special, all they say is, 'it's not time yet' - why do they get to decide when it's time?" Wenona nodded after each sentence, then once I finished, she gave me a comforting smile and linked my arm with hers. She patted my hand and let out a long breath.

"They are not keeping it from you to spite you Narrdie. Even I know the time isn't right, think of yourself as a cup, being filled with water. You have to time it right, because if you keep pouring - it's going to overflow. Even if you think you can handle it, within a few seconds there's water everywhere. Do you understand what I mean?"

"I do, no one's ever really put it like that, they just say when it's time I'll understand." I half smiled at her, part of me still wanted to demand that someone told me everything, however

I really did understand what she meant. Too much information, especially something like this – could turn someone inside out. "What are you and your sisters? If you don't mind me asking?"

"Of course not, we should have told you there and then. I suppose even we forget that you are new to this. You may ask as many questions as you want Narrdie, as long as it's not too soon – I will answer," she chuckled and squeezed my arm. "I am an Elemental Sister, as are my siblings."

"Yeah, I heard Bayona mention something like that. Elementals, as in the Earth, Water, Air and Fire? Those elements?" She nodded as her smile widened, her body jittering with excitement.

"Yes, we are the guardians of those elements, without us – this world could die. The elements generate from us, gathering strength, energy and growth and when it is time for us four to pass on, we will find the next four descendants and it will keep on going."

"My school religious teacher's head, has just popped somewhere. So, you four are like the big cheese?" She glared down at me in amusement; her eyebrow twitching up slightly.

"Yes, the big cheese. I am the Goddess of Water and the eldest, Erenna is the Goddess of Earth, Fyra the Goddess of Fire and the youngest of us is Aronnia, the Goddess of Air. She may be the youngest, but she is the strongest out of us all – so don't let her sweetness fool you. Together we are the Elemental Goddesses, Priestesses or Witches – we are known by many different names. All races know who we are, however, we've only really shown ourselves to Watchers and Witches."

"Wow, you all must really feel the pressure, to have all that resting on you – seems a lot. So that's why Bayona dropped to her knees when she saw Erenna," it wasn't a question, but Wenona answered anyway.

"Yes, Witches, Warlocks, Mages, Shamans and Mediums do it; they have for thousands of years and will for many more. Out of all the races Witches and Mages are the closest to us, they do it out of respect. Not just to us, they do it to each other – unless they are at war. If we do not recognise them; they would stay on their knees until we did, or until we left," she laughed lightly.

"Palm to palm?" She turned her hand over, showing me the crescent moon tattoo – just like Bayona's one.

"Moon to moon."

"What did Erenna say to her, none of us understood it."

"An ancient language known to all who wield magic, if those words are not spoken, but the moons touch, it means the other recognises you but does not respect you. Shall we sit by the fountain? There's more I would like to tell you."

We walked the rest of the way to the fountain in silence, still linked arm in arm. I didn't expect the fountain to be as big as it was, the concrete was dark – almost black, with lighter flicks. It had three tiers; each one was round with concreter moulded symbols around the outside; the top tier had a tall tower shaped like Lily petals – the water flowing down from it into the base of the fountain. It was the biggest I'd ever seen, more like a pond than a fountain. Wenona dipped her feet into the water and smiled to the little fish, which began to circle around her feet, jumping out of the water – they were like miniature orange dolphins.

"I can't believe Mitchell made this," I glided my hands along the surface of the water, the fish chasing the waves.

"Oh yes, he is very skilled. What was that?" she asked as she leaned her head down towards the water, pulling her hair away from her ear. "How sweet, thank you little ones."

"Did the fish just speak to you?" I asked as I watched the fish swim happily around her.

"Of course, Goddess of Water – that includes everything that lives in it. They said that Mitchell built this for Astrid – it's where he proposed to her." I smiled, picturing the cold faced Mitchell, taking time and care in building this; knowing that one day he'd have to leave it behind.

"Since I've been here, he's always been strict and by the book, it's strange to hear him wanting to do something romantic." Wenona frowned for a moment and took in a breath.

"Go easy with him Narrdie, Mitchell wasn't always the way he is; he is the highest ranking Watcher there is – he's seen and had to do unspeakable things, he's lost so much," she explained gently. Guilt swept over me, I never really took the time to get to know Mitchell, and I'd always class him as a very anal person. A dull person who would never allow himself to have even the slightest bit of fun, I wondered what Astrid had seen in him. "He's a proud man Narrdie."

"Say no more, it'll never leave my lips."

"*M*yself and my sisters used to live in Rome," Wenona began. "Hundreds and hundreds of years ago, it was so beautiful – the most beautiful place we lived. The humans knew who and what we were, so they only thought was to treat us like Queens; they'd bring us flowers, food, gold and silver and all sorts of other trinkets. They even tried to sacrifice a goat in our honour, but Erenna wouldn't have any of it, she ordered him to be set free immediately. She was gifted with extra offerings that week, they feared that they had angered her and begged her forgiveness day and night – of course she agreed.

"Our home there was magnificent, absolutely stunning. We had golden crafted seats, engraved with all kinds of ruins, the softest blankets draped over them – nothing like they make now. Grand paintings of angelic men and women, sculptures of talented warriors and animals decorated over our home – we didn't care much for any of it, but we took it with gratitude. Of course, we added our own touch to make it more to our style.

"An old Witch was living a few miles from the city and heard that we had come, she came as soon as she could; she was speechless at first – shocked. We invited her to stay after learning that she was gravely ill, we wanted to care for her and make her final days the happiest they could be. Nuess was her name, she was such a lovely creature, kind, loyal, brave in the face of danger and no matter how much we told her not to – she still took care of us. On her last day, she wanted to gift us, help us make our home more fitted to us – she always thought it looked too cold and like a showroom. She used the last of her magic to enchant the house, made most of the rooms as big as we wanted – yet it wouldn't affect the outside. She left the room with the thrones as it was, she said it was the showroom that the city wanted; she deemed that when the city people came to visit – it would be held in this room." Tears misted over Wenona's eyes, she swallowed hard before continuing.

"We took her to the highest mountain for her final hours, she wouldn't hear any goodbyes, or final words; she wanted to just be silent and watch over all of Rome. We stayed with her even after she died. Back then Narrdie, we never thought of anyone but us four being family, until we met Nuess." Wenona was looking off into the sky, I wiped my own tears on the back of my hand, I opened my mouth to speak – but only a whimper came out. After a few seconds of swallowing down the lumps in my throat – my voice returned to me.

"She sounded amazing Wenona; she really did."

"Thank you Narrdie," her voice broke.

"What did you do will all that space?" Wenona's smile spread wider, and she laughed lightly.

"This, you may not believe. I created a room with an exquisite waterfall, which fell into a huge pond and never ran dry. I invited many creatures to come live here, fish of all kinds and a family of otters.

"Erenna wrapped her room in vines, filled it with trees, flowers and even had a meadow in there – it was so big, but peaceful. She had her own lovely creatures stay with her, deer's, rabbits and other small rodents, foxes and wolves – none of her creatures ever attacked one another." She clarified, seeing the worry form across my face. "They didn't need to, when they were hungry Erenna would sort it for them. Her room was a place for relaxation, and she welcomed many people to come and see it and I even enjoyed spending many days there. Peaceful.

"Aronnia's room was like a palace in the clouds, filled with birds, so many different kinds; some looking straight out of a fairy-tale." She looked down to me with a playful grin, I laughed lightly.

"What?"

"You won't believe me for this next part," she warned with a giggle. "Aronnia removed the roof in her room, she felt caged in – she always does when she's inside. Dragons, from all over the world would come to check on her – hiding themselves of course." She raised her brow and lifted up my chin, closing my shocked – wide open mouth. I had no words. "Told you so, I'll explain more about them another time. The Dragons were loyal and adored her more than anything, if she was hurt or sad – they'd feel it in the wind and come to her. Many stayed with her, a lot of the smaller ones made a permanent home there. One in particular never left her side, slept beside her, travelled with her and spent days guarding the home while it was under threat. She was no normal Dragon, she was the biggest, strongest and most respected out of the lot – an Elder Dragon. If only you could have seen it Narrdie, it was breath-taking at night; the Moon would rise right over her room and the Stars would shine down brightly – so many stars." I was still speechless after learning that Dragons had existed, picturing them snuggling up with her.

"And Fyra?" Wenona's face hardened slightly; she gulped and took in a long breath, her eyes dropped from me and gazed into the pond.

"Ah, Fyra. She turned dark after Nuess died. Nuess, was never accepted by the humans; they saw her as something evil and tried to force her to leave – every time she visited. Fyra hated them for it, thought they were partly to blame when she got ill, said that everyone turned her away when she came looking for help. She didn't like living with humans anymore; she didn't accept their gifts – their offers, she'd turn to ash. She didn't want any of them near her anymore; she filled her room with fire, so that no mortal could ever enter again." She took a few breaths, as she continued to wiggle her feet around gently.

"The way the city people treat Nuess, is that still the reason she hates humans?" I asked in a soft tone, I didn't want to upset her, but curiosity got the better of me, she looked up and half smiled – it didn't reach her eyes.

"I do not know for sure anymore. She learned that one city was notorious for the torture and brutal murder of all things magic. Countless Witches and Mages were killed, she was so angry – angrier than I'd ever seen her get. She came to us and demanded that we punish them all, she said if they worship us as Gods, then we should show them what happens when you anger the Gods. Of course, we all refused, told her that we were angry about it also, but this wasn't the way. She left that very night, we thought that she was going to release her anger alone, we never imagined that she'd-" Her voice cracked; she closed her eyes and a tear rolled down her cheek once more. I lightly took her hand and gave it a gently squeeze.

"You don't have to tell me, not if it's too hard for you to relive," I assured her. After a moment she looked back to me, her eyes holding the threat of more tears; she stroked my cheek.

"Thank you, child, it is sweet for you to care for my feelings – I will share the rest of the story. I assure you, I'm alright." I nodded, she kept a hold of my hand and it made me happy that she was taking comfort from me. "We didn't hear about it until it was too late, otherwise we would have stopped her. The night she left, she went to that city – the one that had killed all those Witches and Mages. She sat upon the mountain top; she could feel the heat radiating underneath the stone, it felt her rage and called to her. Once she felt it, that was all she needed;

she freed it and allowed the hot liquid to burn everything. Men, women and children turned to statues where they stood, buildings collapsed and crumbled into the sea of flames, they are still there today - it's become an attraction for humans now." I gasped after I realised where she meant, I had learned about it in school, when it was Volcano week in science - I could never get my mini-Volcano to blow.

"Pompeii," I whispered.

"Yes. She pretends that those memories don't hurt her, but we know they do. Not long after it happened, she vanished and went into isolation, told us not to come looking for her - I believe she regretted it the moment she'd done it. We never saw her again for another two hundred years." I couldn't stop my mind from imagining all those poor people, trying to run and hide from Fyra's wrath, clinging onto their loved ones. Not wanting Wenona to read my face I shook off the thought and looked to the little fish - still surrounding her.

"What was she like, before Nuess?"

"She was happy, probably the happiest out of all of us. She laughed; her laugh was contagious, once she started - we all did. She only started to change once we began to interact with humans, she saw them as selfish beings - all with cruel intentions." I scoffed.

"She's not wrong there." Wenona's head shot up as a strong breeze lifted up our hair.

"Aronnia? You may approach dear sister, you are not interrupting us," Wenona called into the air.

White smoke flew towards us and drove itself into the ground, it slowly began to fade away leaving Aronnia standing elegantly. I couldn't help but jump at the sight of it, if it wasn't for Wenona's hand steadying me - I would have fallen into the water. "Wenona, Narrdie," she politely bowed; she was so mesmerising that I couldn't help but stare. Wenona bowed her head in return, her eyes glinting as she tilted her head to Aronnia.

"Aronnia, you must be cautious with your entering, Narrdie was almost a new climbing frame for the fish. What is wrong?"

"Forgive me for intruding on you both, but Fyra has left and the wind is unsettled - we must not stay here for much longer, Erenna is getting warnings from the earth. Wenona, even the birds are retreating, if they could the trees would let themselves be swallowed up. Something is coming." Aronnia replied; she didn't look panicked, but her voice quivered slightly, unlike Aronnia I couldn't feel any difference in the wind. Wenona sighed, closed her eyes and rubbed her temples, I bit my lip; I couldn't help but think that Fyra was particularly aggravated because I was here.

"I'm sorry," I blurted sheepishly, Wenona and Aronnia turned to me with a puzzled gaze.

"What on earth for Narrdie?" She asked.

"Fyra left because of me, I didn't want this, and it already seems like everything is falling apart." To my surprise Aronnia and Wenona laughed softly.

"Fyra is sulking, she doesn't like what is coming, none of us do, but this war has been coming for a long time. Fyra has tried to hide away from it, says it doesn't involve her – but it does, it involves all of us. She'll come around," Aronnia reassured me, Wenona nodded in agreement with her.

"Fyra is hot-headed," she added, we all shared a quiet chuckle, before Wenona cleared her throat and spoke.

"Aronnia, please may you find her and remind her of the oath we all took.
Prepare everyone to leave as soon as possible. We will be along in a short while." Aronnia bowed once to each of us before heading in a fast blur back to the house. Wenona breathed in then smiled as she splashed some water on her face, the droplets immediately sinking into her skin – leaving her cheeks dry.

"What's happening?"

"These next few moments are going to go by fast, the warning that Aronnia and Erenna have received – means that it isn't just a handful of lackeys on the road this time," she warned me. "I am telling you this because, I need you to be ready and do exactly what anyone says. Things will be explained to you very soon, I promise." I gulped and nodded; I took her hand and smiled to her.

"Thank you for telling me about Rome, Nuess and Fyra. I really enjoyed hearing about that part of your life, normally people keep as much as they can from me."

"You are most welcome Narrdie," she brushed my cheek.

Without warning the ground shook ferociously, I gripped onto Wenona to keep myself standing; my heart immediately thundering in my chest. Two large branches from the trees opposite us, bent towards the floor, the branches began to entwine together. After a couple of seconds, branches took the form of a woman. Erenna pulled herself free from the trees and quick stepped towards us, panic plastered in her eyes; she was breathless and her whole body trembled. "Erenna?" Wenona questioned as she quickly closed the distance between them – she gripped her sister's arms to steady her.

"The young Witch Bayona has seen what heads our way," she took herself a moment to catch her breath. "Narrdie must be taken to a safe haven immediately, we must make haste."

"Has she shown you?" Erenna nodded, "show me Sister." They placed their tattooed palms together and closed their eyes. Their bodies began to vibrate violently; their eyes rolling around under their eyelids, when suddenly – their eyes snapped open. Wenona clenched her hands into fists and took a deep breath, her eyes slit, and her face hardened.

"They aren't holding back this time." She looked ready to shred everything apart, but her voice remained calm – a deadly calm.

"Aronnia has already headed out to stall them, they are coming in a mass of numbers – this house will be rubble by the end of the day. We must leave at once," Erenna spoke fast, so fast I had to focus hard to catch every word. Wenona nodded and then took a moment to regain her self-control, the water in the fountain began to slosh and spit violently.

"Erenna, load everyone in their cares. Do they know their next location?"

"Yes, the older Watcher said Lazarus Mountain has reached out, they are already preparing in case we need immediate help."

"Good. Has Fyra returned?" She asked unsurely.

"Yes, she has, she is helping with the packing, if Aronnia doesn't return soon – she will head out to find her. I will go and help also, keep Narrdie close to you." Erenna said as she gave me a shaky smile. Wenona, paused for a second, freezing me in place with her eyes. "Wait," she ordered, as she hastily stepped back to the pond and dove her hands into the water. "I will not let you be abandoned, come to me and hide within." It took me a moment to realise that she was gathering the little fish, I could faintly see them skipping up her arms and vanishing into her skin.

I struggled to keep up with her, occasionally prancing or bursting out into a light jog; she kept glancing over her shoulder to make sure I was still behind her. Erenna hastily headed down the path to meet us; her hair was ruffled, and she had blood speckles staining her gown. She clenched two long blades in her hands, both soaked in blood. "Are you harmed?" Wenona asked as her eyes rested on the blood.

"Not my blood dear sister. Everyone is ready, the cars are packed and are awaiting around the front. Aronnia has returned unharmed and is with the Lady Elder Astrid, they are holding back Seekers and the young Witch Bayona is fending off a young Shade – Dacre is assisting her. We must move now; there are more Shades coming, stronger and more experienced than the young one." Erenna didn't cover the worry on her face as she spoke, cold shivers began to snake up my spine. I had only dealt with one Shade these past weeks, Egregious. He was strong and scary enough, but more like him – possibly stronger, even the Elemental Sisters seemed worried.

"How on earth do they know?" Wenona snarled, they began to head towards the house and suddenly paused when they realised, I wasn't following them. They both turned back to me, with raised eyebrows.

"Astrid and Bayona? Fighting? What about Audric and Mitchell, where are they? Are they fighting to? Can we help them?" Wenona marched over to me and snagged my hand – pulling me along, I tried to tug away but it felt like my hand was trapped in a vice.

"Keep moving Narrdie, the most important thing is to get you to safety! They have all trained for this, they will be alright."

Fyra was waiting by the car; a look upon her face meaning, that she didn't want to stay here for too long. The moment she spotted us; she flung the car door open and ushered me inside. "Hurry! Narrdie buckle yourself and make sure it's secure," she ordered me with a stern look. I didn't want to anger her any more than she seemed, so I moved as fast as I could – she checked the belt once I had strapped myself in. I prayed that my heart would calm itself down, the last thing we needed was for me to end up falling into cardiac arrest. "Hold onto your courage," she told me softly.

Audric was waiting in the car for me, a cut on his face and blood soaking his clothes; he threw his arms around me in a quick hug and breathed out in relief before forcing a smile; I could feel the fear radiating from him.

"Next time, no going off for long talks, especially when we are preparing to leave," he breathed, I nodded and squeezed him tight.

Wenona spoke into the driver's window; the moment Mitchell had jumped in; he impatiently tapped the steering wheel as she spoke - itching to leave. I looked out my window and my heart dropped, clutched in Fyra's arms was Bayona; she carefully buckled her into the passenger seat. Bayona sat completely still with only her fingers twitched - almost like she was typing. I glanced to Audric, who was focusing hard on her; his jaws clenched. "She's stuck," he mumbled through clenched teeth.

"She has been since she took out the young Shade," Mitchell said as he gently felt her head. "Her temperate is normal, she should be alright soon," Mitchell assured us.

"What do you mean stuck?"

"No one was there to help her - give her strength and because of that the visions had trapped her," Audric explained in a rush. "The Shade probably noticed she was watching; it feels like an itch you can't reach - he probably snagged her."

"No," Fyra cut in. "She's locked herself in on purpose, she harvested some of the young Shades power, so she can watch carefully - see if there is going to be any upcoming dangers on the road."

"Drive fast, head towards Lazarus Mountains," Wenona cut in. "We sent word of your arrival, they are standing by in case you need assistance, our Elements will watch out for you while you drive there," she said in a rush. "Aronnia will use the mist to cover you."

"Wait!" I yelled as Mitchell started the engine; he glanced into the rear-view mirror at me with an aggravated look; he clenched his jaw. "What about everyone else?"

"Astrid and Dacre will run close behind you, they are much faster on foot, we will travel by our Elements. All will be well Narrdie Moon. We will see you in due time. Now go." Without another word she tapped the car and turned back towards the house; a long spear materialized in her hand - forming itself from water.

"Mitchell. Go!" Audric ordered. Mitchell slammed his foot down and the car screeched to life, I dug my nails into the leather as I held on, if the Shades didn't kill me - Mitchell's driving would.

Mitchell drove fast for the first few miles - getting us as far from the house as possible. Finally, when he thought it was safe enough, he eased up on the pedal and let out a calming breath.

"You tired?" Audric asked gently; his face had softened, his eyes stained with purple bags, and I could see the exhaustion in his eyes.

"A little," I answered, my eyes felt like weights had been attached to them - I felt like I hadn't slept in days. Audric nodded, raised his arm and gestured for me to lie across him. "You're covered in blood."

"It's dried," I scowled at him. He snickered and rummaged around in one of the duffle bags in the back of the car, eventually pulling out a cotton mustard yellow blanket and draped it across himself - leaving part of it to cover me with. "There, no more blood."

Once I had found a comfy position; I closed my eyes and tried to concentrate on falling asleep.

Chapter Eight

I knew I was still dreaming the moment my eyes set on the raining petals, falling from the brightly bloomed blossom tree. My hands reached out to catch a cluster of the baby pink petals; they were soft to the touch, as was the grass underneath me. The air was fresh and clear, a hint of something sweet, lingered through the breeze – strawberries, my favourites.

I squinted as I sat up, the sun bright in my eyes; the warmth lightly licked my cheeks, as I leaned my face up towards it – I know it was just a dream, but I wished I could stay like this. The smell had gotten stronger, luring me to find it; I didn't have to look far. Sitting in a cute wicker basket was a load of fresh strawberries, big, bright red and looking extremely juicy – my mouth immediately began to water. My hand crept out to take the biggest but pulled back as alarm bells rang in my ears – too many people were trying to kill me, and this would be a perfect way to do it. Who did they belong to?

"Go ahead, they are not poisoned," I heard voice call. I felt a gust of wind blow behind me – almost knocking me over, the wind blew again, and my eyes widened as I realised that it wasn't a blow off wind, but it was someone's breath.

It was the biggest thing I'd ever seen; they had always been written as huge beasts, but this one was different – big, but it wasn't a beast. It was glorious. Its' thunderstorm grey scales, sparkled when the sunlight touched them – bouncing off an array of sharp silver spikes trailing along its' back. The spikes trailed all the way down to her clubbed tail – looking like it could tear down a house with one flick. Her talons razor sharp, looked like they could cut right through me without an effort at all. I wasn't scared. Apart from the spikes and talons, she didn't look dangerous or terrifying, like I expected Dragons to look; she looked more elegant. Her face was round, with two horns on either side of her head – her orange eyes looked sweetly down at me.

"Are you..." I trailed off; I couldn't remember the word that Astrid has used.

"Yes," I heard her angelic voice, speak into my head. *"My mind is in yours, which is how you can hear and understand me, it is called Animo."*

"Right . . . Animo. I knew that... Who are you?" I thought to myself. I released a squeak when she answered me.

"My name is Indra; I am a friend of Priestess Aronnia and I am so pleased to meet you, Narrdie Moon. I have been waiting a long time." Indra placed her right foot forward and slowly bowed her head to me, I couldn't help but smile at her – she was so compelling; she flicked her head to the wicker basket. *"Will you please have a one now?"*

"How do you know my name?" I asked, plucking the biggest strawberry. The minute I bit into it; I could have screaming with happiness – it was the best I had ever tasted – even for a dream. Indra laughed lightly.

"Everyone knows who you are my dear Narrdie. Sadly, I must speak fast as you do not have much time here – you'll be awake soon. I have known what is to come for an awfully long time and my advice to you is simple and may be frightening for you. The moment you are settled at Lazarus Mountain, you need to begin training – combat and to unlock the gifts within you. I know you are full of doubt and believe this is all wrong, that everyone must have the wrong person, but you are wrong Narrdie – in time you'll understand."

"Indra, I don't understand, why this is happening? If everyone wants me to 'understand in time', wouldn't it just be easier to tell me now?" Indra's eyes softened sympathetically, and her mouth lifted in a half smile; she leaned her head down on the grass – closer to me.

"They want you to uncover the truth on your own, you will know when the time is right, as long as you look deep within you. It has to be done this way Narrdie." A smile grew along my lips as I looked into her big eyes, she seemed so friendly and everything she was saying seemed to just calm me.

"Thank you, Indra."

"Time for you to wake up, it was a pleasure to finally meet you, Narrdie Moon."

☾

$\mathcal{W}$e were still on the road when I woke up and opened my eyes, I had decided to keep my dream to myself – at least for now. Audric was flat out against the car door and thankfully Bayona had seemed to come out of her trance and was now sound asleep. Mitchell looked into the rear-view mirror and smiled to me, "she'll be asleep for some time now, she came out of it about an ago. How did you sleep?" "

Really well actually, thanks. Is she ok?" I whispered, not wanting to wake Audric or Bayona.

"She's exhausted, she's been watching them for a good couple of hours, she'll be alright though." He glanced over to her and gently moved her hair out of her face – I smiled.

"How long have I been asleep?"

"Five and a half hours, which I'm glad about – you really needed it." My jaw fell open. Had I really been asleep that long? My dream with Indra seemed to only last five minutes, I rubbed my eyes and yawned.

"Are you not tired Mitchell? I can switch with you, just tell me where to drive," I offered. He smiled and shook his head.

"It's alright, we only have another hour. You can drive?"

"Not legally." He laughed, which made me smile; I had never heard Mitchell laugh before. Mitchell smirked widely and shook his head, he let out a long breath.

"Narrdie, I apologise in advance for this."

"For what?" I asked with a frown.

Before he could answer, my door swung open. "Boo!" Dacre yelled as he burst his head inside and climbed in. I screamed waking everyone up.

"DON'T DO THAT!" I snapped angrily at him, driving my fists into his arm, I scowled towards Mitchell, who raised his fingers in surrender.

"What's wrong? What is it? What's going on?" Bayona burst in a rush, her hand suddenly glowing.

"Nothing Bayona, just Dacre playing pranks. Go back to sleep, you need your rest," Mitchell said gently, pulling her blanket back over her. She mumbled something under her breath, as her eyes closed.

"The fuck is going on?" Audric grumbled out, still half asleep.

Dacre hissed playfully to him. "Language Audric, there are ladies present."

"Prick," he grunted; he turned to check on me and smiled – I winked and gave him the rest of the blanket, within seconds he was asleep again. Dacre lifted his lip in a sneer before leaning over to me and whispering – testing me.

"I see you get scared easily, that's a fun little piece of information."

"Talk to me again on this journey and I'll take Audric's knife and stab you in the throat," I warned. Dacre frowned and quickly nodded – Mitchell burst out laughing once again.

I felt a warm hand brush my cheek, "Narrdie? Wakey-wakey, come on sleepy head – we're here." I opened my eyes, at first everything looked fuzzy and . . . green. With a high-pitched yawn, I ran my hands through my hair; little strands sticking to my skin from sweat – three people stuffed in the back made it very warm. I was desperate for a shower, when the fresh air hit me, it made me realise how much we all smelt – I needed to be clean again. I rubbed my eyes trying to get rid of the fuzziness, but I'd only made it worse.

"Hi," I murmured, still very sleepy.

"Hey," Audric replied with a thick chuckle; he brushed down a piece of my hair that happened to be sticking up. "Your hair is all over the place."

"I wouldn't, it's really greasy," I warned him.

"It doesn't look it, but you'll be able to have a nice hot bath soon, full of bubbles. We all will," he promised with a smile. "Come on, out you get. Here put this on, it's getting cold." He tossed me a thick black coat with a grey fluffy hood and a pair of thermal gloves. "You want a scalf?"

"No this'll be enough, are you sure we're here? Everything's green and leafy, are we sleeping in the woods?" I asked, as all I could see were trees, trees and more trees. He nodded then shifted nervously as he helped me out of the car. "What? We are sleeping here. Where? In the trees?"

"No, it's just we have to go by foot."

"So?" I pressed; I rolled my eyes. "Just tell me."

"Look it's not far, but you have to be blind-folded when going up the mountain, it's the guiders orders," he said in a rush. I stared blankly at him and blinked for several seconds.

"Seriously? Who do they think I'm going to tell? Who would even believe me?" I was way too tired to deal with this; I didn't feel comfortable being blind-folded and having to trust strangers taking us up to this unknown building.

"We're all going to be blind-folded, even Mitchell who has been here many times. It's the Law of Lazarus Mountain – non-negotiable I'm afraid." I breathed out hard, it didn't feel right – but I barely had any energy to argue about it anymore.

"I understand it's their law, but it's just . . . will we be safe?" Before Audric could answer Dacre sniggered and slinked over to us, he tossed an apple up and down in his hands.

"Narrdie, you're such a timid little thing, afraid of everything." His sudden roar of laughter was vicious, it made me flinch. "Who's afraid of the big bad Wolf?" He mocked.

"Back off." Audric cautioned as he clenched his fists, his knuckles cracking.

"She said I couldn't talk to her during the journey – journey's over."

"No, it's not, we still have to go up a mountain," I bit – instantly wishing I hadn't when his lips turned into a wicked grin. I rolled my eyes and shifted away from him.

"Why don't you go and chase a ball or something," Audric growled.

"You don't think she can defend herself? Then come on young Watcher – defend her," Dacre dared. Audric and Dacre stepped to each other; their faces so close their noses were practically touching; I rolled my eyes (an expression I was getting used to doing) and flashed Mitchell a plea.

"Enough both of you!" Mitchell called over, after he nodded to me; his voice was exhausted and irritated. "Instead of acting like children, why don't you both be useful for once and unpack the car. The Monks are ready to guide us and you're taking up everyone's time," he snapped. I snorted and covered my mouth to keep from laughing.

"Monks?" I repeated.

"Yes," Mitchell said blankly.

"Actual Monks?"

"Yes Narrdie."

"Like Monks that wear the long coats?"

"Yes, and they're robes not coats," he corrected.

"Monks who shave their heads?" Mitchell breathed out and turned to face me.

"These Monks don't shave their hair, but they do have the crescent moon tattooed in the middle of their forehead. Any more Monk specifics you want to name before you believe me? Astrid and Bayona have already left and reached the base safely, Audric and I are next, then Narrdie and Dacre. I don't want to hear any arguments – it's their decision. Would either of you like take it up with them?" He asked, looking between Dacre and Audric with a warning glare.

"No way," Audric said with a gulp.

"No," Dacre answered as he looked down.

"Didn't think so."

"You two are scared of the Monks?" I asked with a chuckle.

"These aren't like the Monks you've learnt about in your history or religious class. These Monks are brutal, fast, insanely trained and they don't hesitate. They could kill you before you even had a moment to register, they were there. One minute they are in front of you and the next, you're on the floor with your throat slit and limbs torn off." Audric explained in a shaky voice, I gulped and fidgeted nervously.

"They are some of the best fighters all sanctuaries have, no one has a clue where they were trained," Dacre chimed in.

"They won't tell you? Please don't mention to the Monks the stuff I said before, I'm quite attracted to my limbs." Knowing all this, didn't make me feel any safer; I was just thankful that they were on our side.

"Even if they wanted to tell us – which they don't. They couldn't anyway, they cut out their own tongue so that if they are ever captured – they can't succumb to torture," Dacre explained. He had a bored look upon his face, as he twisted an apple around in his fingers.

"You're going to be the reason I never eat another apple."

I sat waiting with my head in-between my hands on a broken tree stump, I didn't like being left alone with Dacre, he made me feel uneasy. I was exhausted, I was cold, and I was hungry, all of those made me vulnerable to his harassment. I began to pick around the skin around my nails, each time I looked up and caught him staring at me – the hairs on the back of my neck rose. "Nervous?"

"No," I lied; he bit into another apple and slowly began to walk in a circle around me, I rolled my eyes and sneered. "Can you just magically make apples appear?

Do they just fall out of your ass?" I snapped, he laughed – almost choking on a bite.

"I filled a bag," he replied with a mocking grin; he pointed his apple towards me.

"You are nervous."

"No, I'm not."

"Yes, you are. I can smell it on you. It's slowly seeping out of you and dripping down your body, it's alluring. You're timid around me," he paused in front of me and tilted his head.

"Now why is that?"

"Where are the Monks?" I asked, trying to change the subject, his eyes trailed down to my hand and he snickered as his eyes set onto the ring; he snagged my hand.

"You're afraid of me, but you're still wearing that – interesting." He ran his tongue across his glistening teeth, no, not teeth – fangs.

"I don't get you, Dacre. One minute, you're protecting me and making sure I'm safe from dangers, such as Egregious and my dad – then you change. So, what's you game here?" He looked at me with surprise, and I could tell he was choosing what to say carefully – which he always did.

"Perks of the job," he said in an amused tone; he placed the apple back to his lips and bit down.

"Then step back and do your job," I growled.

"You know what I like about you Narrdie?" He asked; he jumped onto the log beside me – resting on his feet. "I like the fire inside you. It doesn't come out much, most of the time, it must be pushed or annoyed, but when it does come out...I can see why you're the one. Pretty soon that fire will come out whenever you want it too." He caught my gaze and held it for a while, I didn't know whether to thank him or smack him; I swallowed hard and nodded to him – he nodded and finally looked away.

"I think I can hear the Monks coming," I announced as I stood up, Dacre's arm snatched mine and pulled me back to the log. He dropped his apple and stood - sniffing the air, a low growl rumbled in his throat. "Dacre? What is it?" I asked as I took a step closer to him; his arm reached around me – keeping me behind him, fear got the better of me and I gripped his wrist.

"There's something wrong in the air," his voice was cold.

"What is it?" I breathed, I felt like someone was watching us. I already knew what he was going to say – it still didn't stop the chills from crawling around me.

"Blood." The moment he confirmed my thoughts; my heart began to race; my palms grew sweaty, I felt like I couldn't breathe. I stumbled back and Dacre gripped my arm once more, "don't move." He sniffed up once more and clenched his jaw. "Whatever it is, it's heading towards us, it's not the Monks." My mind went straight to Audric and the others – were they safe?

"Dacre, whose blood is it?" The moment I asked, I was terrified of what the answer could be – scared that the next words to come out his mouth, would be one of their names.

"The Monks, it must have got them when they were heading back down to lead us." He turned to me, his expression calmed; he held out his hand, "come on Narrdie. I won't let anything hurt you." I took his hand without hesitation, he immediately started marching us up the mountain. "We have to move quickly."

"You and Audric said the Monks were brutal," I said through breaths. "You said they were the best fighters any Sanctuary had."

"Yep."

"Brutal, fast, could slit your throat and remove your limbs – before you would even notice. Right?"

"Yes Narrdie. What's your point?"

"You and Audric didn't even want to fight them. So, if they are that deadly," I pulled him to a stop and made him look at me. "Then what the hell could have killed them? All ten of them?"

"Keep moving Narrdie," he growled as he forcefully tried to pull me along – I snatched my hand free.

"What could have done it Dacre?"

"Many different things!" He snarled and ran his hand over his hair, "there are creatures out here, which are deadlier than you could ever imagine. Mitchell and Audric and the rest of that lot try and keep this from you. You thought Egregious was terrifying? There are things in my world that would make him curl up in a ball – screaming and crying. You, need to get used to this, because it's your world now and we won't always be here to protect you. Now move your fucking legs!" I flinched back from him, my eyes had filled up and were about to overflow; my chest burned. "I said move your legs. It's hunting us and standing here isn't going to help." I expected him to grab my arm and start dragging me again, but instead he offered me his hand.

"It doesn't matter how fast we move; it's going to get us Dacre!" No matter how much I told myself to calm down, I couldn't stop my voice from sounding panicked and I could already feel my knees begin to buckle.

"Look at me, I'm not going to let it get you. This time I am here to protect you, now will you please take my hand?" I nodded shakily and took a deep breath as I gripped his hand. "Don't let go."

"I'm scared," I admitted – tears trickling down my cheeks.

"I know," he said gently, softly pulling me into a quick sprint. "Narrdie, what did I say about that ring again?" Branches whipped at my face, as our walk had turned into a sprint – the wind lashed at my skin with frozen spikes; my teeth clattering together.

"As long as I have it, I can call for you if I'm in danger." He nodded and held onto my hand tightly, not giving me any opportunity to slow down – I didn't want to slow down, I wanted to get out this forest no matter what.

"Good, I need you to listen very carefully. You aren't going to like this, but it's the only thing I can do," he said as he pulled me to a stop behind a wide tree. He glanced around to make sure everything was alright, giving me an apologetic look; he pulled me down onto the floor and pulled his coat around me.

"You're leaving me to fine the Monks, aren't you?" My voice quivered; I tucked my knees into my chest and through my hands around them.

"Yes. I'll be as quick as I can, I need you to stay here. Stay low, stay quiet and stay alert." I clenched my jaw and swallowed hard; I didn't want him to leave me here – like a sitting duck.

"O-Ok," I stuttered. "Dacre, please hurry."

"I will. If someone or something sees you and it's not me. Run, you run, and you don't stop running until one of us finds you, clear?"

I scoffed, "run where?" He gripped my face in his hands and forced me to look at him.

"Narrdie, you just run! Nod if you understand me," he snarled as his yellow eyes stared me down, I swallowed hard and nodded over and over.

Dacre had taken himself into the forest and left me on the ground; he'd warned me be still and as fast as Astrid, if danger came. I cradled myself, tucking my knees into my chest and wrapping my arms around them – trying to keep my bones from clattering from the cold; I had to keep telling myself to breathe – at that moment, I thought I was going to have a panic attack. I was shaking, I couldn't stop shaking; I wasn't sure if it was my body temperature dropping or if I were just utterly petrified. I wasn't cut out for this; I wasn't cut out for anything everyone was expecting me to do – I couldn't fight these things; I couldn't even find the courage to tell my parents that it was me who crashed their car and put the headlight out. Dacre looked worried about this creature...maybe even scared. Perhaps, he'd really ran away – told me to wait here so that he had a longer getaway time, while the creature tor me apart – I wouldn't put it past him.

The snapping of a tree branch, made my insides freeze over, my breath caught in my throat, pins and needles prickled along my skin – even the trees and the icy wind howls, had gone quiet. The branch snapped again, and I bit the inside of my cheek to stop from screaming, the second snap had come from the opposite side. Either it was incredible fast, or there was more than one – I prayed it wasn't the latter. It's feet smacked against the ground violently, loud grumbles bouncing from the trees – it stopped and began sniffing the leaves, I knew that any minute now, it would pick up my scent.

The shrubs groaned as they were forced apart, its pace slowed as it emerged from the foliage and out into the clearing. My breath came in slow raspy bursts as I tilted my head around to look at it; my hands shaking with fear and adrenaline, the moment I saw it – I wished I hadn't.

Especially when it's red eyes, locked with mine.

I had seen my fair share of horror films, spent many nights hiding behind the pillow; cowering when the monster revealed itself and ripped everyone apart. The minute I looked at this thing – I wished I had a pillow. The skin on it was enough to make shivers spiral all around me, it was a matted black and red mess, looking more like leather than fur – parts of it shredding and melting off in the clumps – that looked too much like clotted blood. Its' red eyes widened – the pupil dilating the moment it saw me; it's blistered, grey tongue snaked out and licked along it's yellow, blood-stained teeth. The claws on its feet were long, curling over like a raptor – perfect for dismembering body parts. A piece of brown fabric was stuck on its middle claw, my heart dropped into my gut – it was from one of the Monks robes.

This was the creature that was going to kill me, it was going to tear me apart and probably eat me. Part of me knew that I'd be saved when Egregious and the men on the road attacked, but this time I was fully convinced – I was going to die. I knew I should have ran; I should have ran the second those bushes rustled – the second I heard the twig snap, but my legs had gone numb and no matter how hard I tried to move my fingers and rub the ring to call Dacre – I couldn't, they felt like they had turned to stone. Saliva dripped from its mouth, the leaves sizzled and burned as the gloopy spit landed on them; its mouth widened; I heard the crack of its jaw dislocating. A ripple of rumbles travelled up its throat; it released a deafening screech, forcing the forest to quiver. I squeezed my hands over my ears – pressing as hard as I could, the blood trickling between my fingers and pouring down my cheeks.

The screeching wouldn't stop, it didn't pause for air, didn't stop to swallow – it just kept shrieking. My vision had blurred – the forest going fuzzy, my hands and hair were soaked in the blood, which poured out of my ears like a fountain – my mind felt like a puddle. I couldn't figure out how long I was curled up – silently screaming, I didn't know if it had been seconds, minutes or hours, until Dacre finally showed up.

With two swift movements, he hauled its head from its body and tore out its heart – his hand burning where its blood touched – the screeching instantly stopped, Dacre sneered as he tossed it into a corner; he pulled out a box of matches and set it on fire. His eyes turned dark as they flicked towards me; his lip lifted in a growl. "I'm confused Narrdie, at what part did I say to curl up and wait for it to shred you apart? I'm sure I told you to run," he bit aggressively – gripping my arm and forcing me to my feet. "Look at the state of you, covered in your own blood, I mean can you even hear me?"

"Y-Yes, I can hear you," I breathed.

"Then why didn't you run?" He asked, as he began to pull me along, his fingers biting into my skin.

"I-I couldn't feel my legs," my voice trembled. He paused and dropped my hand, slowly he faced me, and a dark look prowled on his face.

"Couldn't feel your legs? What about now?" He spun his leg round and kicked the back of my knee; I stumbled and fell on my knees, wincing as specks and rocks cut into my palms. "Stand up!" He barked, dragging me up before I even had the chance, he flipped me round and threw me against a tree; his hand shot out and gripped around my throat.

"Dacre!"

"You feel your legs now?" He lifted his lip in a disgusted sneer; his bold yellow eyes turned black and sharp fangs extended from his mouth – his nails growing long as they dug into my neck. My eyes darted around for something to use – just to get him off me and that's when I noticed, a strange bite resting on his shoulder – black puss oozing out of it. That creature had bit him, an infection was spreading around his body and was changing who he was. *Que the zombie outbreak.*

"Let me go Dacre." I kept my voice calm – as calm as my fear would allow and gently placed my hands over his, "let go Dacre." His hands dropped from my throat; he snarled and struck me hard across the face. I felt the sting of his claw, ripping into my cheek; I cried out, feeling the four deep burning lines begin to overflow – my shoulder becoming drenched, as the crimson liquid gushed down. He tilted his head menacingly as he looked to his smothered claws – breathing in the bloody scent. "Dacre," I whimpered, "please stop this."

He groaned as he shook his head and rubbed his eyes, he backed away from me. "Narrdie?" His voice was shaky, he drummed his nails into his head – groaning in pain.

"One of those things bit you Dacre, and it's doing something to you," I told him carefully, cupping my hand over my cheek. He scanned the gashes on my face; his eyes widened.

"Narrdie I . . . you have to run. Your blood smells so tempting to me, you need to go. If I change again..." he leaned his face closer to me, his expression shifted to something frightening; he breathed in deeply. "I can hear your heartbeat; poor Narrdie, you reek of fear – always so frightened." He sniffed the blood on his hands and moaned in pleasure, he slid incredulous eyes to me; his grin going razor sharp. "You should be running." He warned heatedly. "I'm fighting the urge to rip out your throat, drain you dry and then eat the rest." My mouth felt like sandpaper, I couldn't breathe - everything was starting to spin again. *Come on Narrdie, get a grip and go* – I told myself. He gripped the sides of his head again, I took the opportunity and tried to dart past him.

Within seconds he was on me, his hand shot out and blocked my path, a rumble echoed in his throat as he narrowed his eyes to me. "Where are you going?"

"Nowhere," my voice quivered.

"Good girl. That would be very rude, might even make me mad and we wouldn't want that. But it's good that you weren't trying to run away, because if you were... I'd have to break your legs." Dacre leaned into me and traced my cuts with his tongue, instantly, I felt the tingling; I shuddered under him. "You do taste good, Narrdie. Not like other humans, they all have a similar flavour – bitter even." I swallowed hard, other humans? Had Dacre killed and ate people? Perhaps that was why Audric didn't like me being left alone with him, maybe he was the monster they all hated.

"Let me go, Dacre!" I commanded.

"Why won't you be quiet?!" He snarled then turned me around so that my face was pressed up against the bark, mud and bits of the trees clung to my cheek. I felt the sudden sharpness of his fangs shred into my neck, the pain followed quickly after and I screamed out. He held me fiercely, one hand around my arms and waist so that I couldn't struggle and the other across my chest and collar, with each gulp the pain sawed higher. My legs had turned to jelly, my toes had gone numb.

"P-Please, stop," I begged, my voice as faint as a ghost, my voice seemed to only encourage him; his grip tightened and he bit down harder – teeth shredding into more skin.

I thought I had become so weak, that I could no longer feel the pain anymore; the forceful push that pinned me to the tree, had all of a sudden, eased away and I slumped down the mossy floor, it was warm and wet with blood – my blood. Dacre groaned; he retched with pain and crumpled in on himself – shaking violently, his mouth opened to screech but no noise came out; his back arched and his hands locked in place at his sides. I pressed my hand over my neck, to try and stop the bleeding. "Dacre?" I tried to call to him, but my voice was barely a whisper. Something was hurting him, and it wasn't the bite on his shoulder.

A woman, glared down directly over Dacre, she stood tall and held her chin up – exuberating power. It was freezing, but from the amount of clothes she wore – she mustn't have felt it, a long sparkling lilac dress, ran across her breasts – like a tube; her stomach was exposed, showing a crescent moon – cupping her belly button. The dress split at the side of her thigh and trailed to the floor – the ends turning mucky from the mud. She had long black hair, which was clipped up on one side; her cheekbones were bold, and she had a muscular, yet flattering figure. A leafy pattern was painting around her mossy green eyes. She was closely followed by seven men in black armour, two of the men approached and stood on either side of her – spears in their hands.

The woman had her hand outstretched; her hair blew angrily, but there was no wind, she hissed slightly, and her hand began to shake. I'd seen this before, Egregious has done this to Audric – this was torture magic. Dacre shrieked; his whole body convulsed aggressively; blood began to trickle from his nose. "STOP! Stop it now! Leave him!" I winced, my throat felt raw and every movement I made pained. The woman looked to me with a shocked expression and raised eyebrows, but thankfully lowered her hand – her men giving her confused looks. Dacre winced once before lying still, my eyes rested on him – waiting, finally his chest lifted and eased, he was breathing.

"Yorg, Lenis, get rid of the half breed," her voice was fierce and savage.

"No! Don't you touch him!" A blue swirling light surrounded me and Dacre, one of the men lightly raised his spear towards it – approaching slowly. The second the tip of the spear grazed the blue light, a sound like electric bellowed in my ears – followed closely, by a shock that slashed towards him like a whip. The man jerked back, he pulled his glove off and gasped – his hand was slit in several places, bleeding profusely. I had never seen this thing before and was full of curiosity myself, especially as it seemed to be protecting me and Dacre, but now was not the time for my mind to wander. The woman signalled her men to step back, she crouched low, meeting me eye to eye.

"Young girl, this half breed was feeding from you, it is forbidden on these grounds. It has also killed four of my Monks – another grand taboo." I looked her over, noticing the familiar crescent moon on her hand, the same as Bayona.

"Look Witch, I don't care who you are, I don't care about your laws and I don't care what he's done. I am in a lot of pain, I am covered in blood, I've almost died twice tonight – so, forgive me if I don't sound in the mood to have this back and forth, chit chat about who done what. He did not kill those Monks, a creature bit him and made him act this way, and it killed the Monks. He needs to be taken to a man called Mitchell and the people he is with up the mountain, if you take us to them – I will tell you what happened. His name is Dacre, he is…friends with them. So, I would really appreciate it if you could help us, if not then I suggest you leave us alone because weird things seem to happen when I get mad, understand?" I breathed out heavily, shooting pains began to lash my skull, I leaned over and coughed onto the leaves – blood spraying from my mouth.

"My Lady, this girl needs a healer," one of the men warned her. The woman didn't speak, she just stood there blinking and glanced back to her men; she exchanged a look with the two Guards at her side.

"Witch?"

"Nyda," she finally spoke, as she cleared her throat and looked back to me. "My name is Nyda; you don't need to keep that shield up around us, you and the half breed are safe. I give you, my word." I looked around at the blue swirling light, not really sure how to make it go away.

"How do I drop this?" I asked sheepishly, Nyda frowned and blinked several times.

"You don't know how to drop your own shield?"

"I didn't even know this came from me," I admitted.

"Who are you?"

"My name is Narrdie Moon." Nyda's eyes widened slightly, she looked back to her men – their expressions mimicking hers. "You know who I am." It wasn't a question, but she answered anyway.

"Yes, we all know who you are and have been waiting to meet you for a long time. Now, you need to tell yourself, that you are safe, and it should drop. Go ahead," she urged with a kind smile. I swallowed and thought past the pain that I felt, telling myself that everything was ok – they were here to help me. The blue shield flickered, before vanishing in one bright flash; I laughed in amazement – I was going to have to practice that. "Well done. Who waits for you up the mountain? I assume your Watcher is with you?"

"Yes, Audric and Mitchell Slater are my Watchers, I came with a Witch, Bayona and Astrid – a Vampire Elder. The Monks took them all up first. We were with the Elemental Sisters, they are the Guardians of-" Nyda raised her hand and nodded with a slight smile, she seemed to be beaming at something I had said.

"You were separated from your Watcher?" One of the men asked, flashing a worried look to Nyda.

"I know the Elemental Priestess; they arrived earlier. Considering you are still under the care of Watchers; you should not have been separated from them – for that I am sorry, and I will find out why that was arranged. Yorg, Lenis bring the half breed, carefully. I will attend to Lady Narrdie."

"Hybrid," I corrected her.

It didn't take long to get up the mountain, Nyda had healed me as much as she could so that I didn't have to feel discomfort or feel like I was going to pass out. She carried me most of the way, the loss of blood from my neck, had made me too dizzy to stay on my feet, I didn't mind being carried by her; she had an alluring smell like roses, which almost put me to sleep on her shoulder. My whole body was drained, even lifting a finger seemed to completely cripple me.

"Here we are," Nyda announced soothingly, gently placing me onto my feet. Right on que, Audric bolted over to us – the others following close by. He had a wide grin as he pulled me into a strong hug, the grin quickly dropped from his lips, the moment his eyes slunk to the bite and that familiar look of rage returned; his hand cupped my chin, moving my head to the side to examine the claw slashes on my cheek. He looked to Dacre and I knew he'd worked out that the blood all over Dacre's face, had come from my throat, a murderous tint darkened his eyes.

"I'm going to kill him!" He spat as he lunged for Dacre, I jumped forwards and thrust my palm into his chest. I'd only meant to push Audric back a little, but I felt something burst from my hand and into Audric's chest; he yelped as his body flew backwards and landed hard on the ground a few feet away. I swayed, almost falling down – Lenis court my arm and held me until I was steady.

"Thank you Lenis. I can't handle all this fighting, especially, our own people, I'm so tired and I am sick of being in pain and bleeding all the time. Can someone just please, take me somewhere I can sleep?" Audric stood; wiping mud from his clothes, his eyes met mine and the look her gave me meant one thing – betrayal. I swallowed hard and tore my gaze away from him; I felt awful for humiliating him in front of everyone – I'd only meant to keep him back, not throw him. "Mitchell, Dacre got bit by something out there, it killed the Monks. When he came back, he was different, animalistic – I think the bite changed him." Mitchell nodded, his face still holding the surprise and shock from pushing Audric.

"I know. It was a Skinner," he announced. Nyda hissed through her teeth, the two men beside her gripped their spears, until their knuckles turned white.

"Skinners? They do not habitat these grounds, are you sure?" Nyda asked, her voice tight.

"Yes. Bayona, saw them." I looked around, everyone apart from the sisters and Bayona was here. "Can you please bring him inside? I'll take a look at him, Astrid will you assist me, my sweet?" Mitchell requested; he turned to head back inside but not before he gave Audric a disapproving glare.

"Wait," I called – stopping everyone in their tracks. "Where's Bayona?"

"Infirmary," Audric answered coldly. "She's still very weak. The walk up the mountain took it out of her." Astrid growled towards him and signalled him inside with a flick of her head. She smiled to me and reached her hand out.

"Come on Narrdie, I will take you to the infirmary to get some rest," Astrid offered with a wink. I turned Nyda and bowed my head to her.

"Nyda, Yorg, Lenis, thank you for helping me. Please thank the rest of your men for me." All three elegantly bowed.

Chapter Nine

Dacre

*D*acre jerked up, only to be forced back down by straps, restraining his hands and feet to an infirmary bed, each strap was infused with silver – he smirked. "Interesting." He pulled against the straps, after a few moments of tugging; he sank back into the bed and laughed in annoyance, silver – as though that alone was enough to contain him. He head felt like a weight, a weight that brayed and pushed against his skull, each muscle vibrated with ache and fatigue; he pulled once more and felt the sting as the silver singed his skin.

"Don't pull. They tighten if you try and fight them, they just keep going until they break your bones," said a youngish girl as she glided into the room. "Tight, tight, snap!" She sang.

She was a pretty, hair the colour of autumn leaves – tied loosely in a wavy ponytail; she had sun kissed skin and freckles dotting over her cheeks and nose, that made her lavender eyes – seem more hypnotic. Something about the way she gazed around the room, made Dacre think that she wasn't all there – like she was lost in a daydream. "You're a half breed, aren't you? Dacre, right?"

"Hybrid and you are?" He asked, more out of boredom.

"Sharia."

"Well Sharia, where am I?"

"In the isolation infirmary, Lazarus Mountain. It's Nyda's sanctuary," she said as she prodded his restraints with her finger, Dacre raised his brows as he noticed the butterflies painted onto her nails in white varnish – he rolled his eyes.

"Why am I here?" He asked through gritted teeth, her movements were causing them to tighten.

"A pack of Skinners got onto the grounds, killed the Monks and bit you. You then bit Narrdie and almost tore her apart; she almost died." Dacre's head snapped up; he clenched his jaw.

"Narrdie, is she…"

"Alive? Yes, she's recovering well – seems very tired though, been asleep for quite a while." Sharia shrugged her shoulders and twirled a strand of her hair between her fingers. "The scars from where you clawed her face are almost gone and she cut open her hand in her room, apparently she was mad and punched the mirror in the bathroom. Temper, temper, temper." She sang. "You're in a lot of trouble, Audric and the Vampire, I think they want to rip your heart out and the older Watcher is struggling to keep everyone calm. I know you probably want to see her, but you're not aloud and she more than likely doesn't want to see you anyway. I'm surprised you're even allowed to stay here, though they are probably discussing whether you'll be banished or not." Dacre rolled his eyes and leaned his head back.

"You talk too much. If you take a moment to breathe when you speak, you'll probably be able to tell when people want you shut up. Which in this case, is now," he grunted in a hateful tone, she scowled and growled lowly. An unkind smile spread across his face, "you look and act too young to be a Skin-changer, surely you haven't grown into your powers yet?"

"How did you know? And I'm one hundred and twenty-three. I fully ascended two years ago, actually," she spat as she flicked her nails in annoyance. Dacre scoffed; she was definitely too young.

"Hundred and twenty-three . . . still a baby. You still haven't managed to shield your eyes, that's how I knew, seems you haven't learnt much. I've met Skin Changers who could cover their eyes before they even learnt to talk. You must be slow, as well as young." He laughed rudely at her, she hissed; her eyes flared darker. "Now, go bore someone else with your uninteresting chatter."

"Fine." She snarled, her lip quivering; she stormed out and slammed the door behind her. Dacre leaned his head back and closed his eyes – he never did like Skin-changers, but inexperienced ones where the worst.

*D*acre snarled, as her scent seeped into his noise, it was like burn cinnamon – a smell that would linger for hours. He sat up as much as he could, or as much as the straps would allow before they tightened and turned to keep a watchful eye on her. "Why are you here?" He spat.

Fyra gracefully walked around the infirmary and rested herself at the foot of his bed; she wore a ruby Kimono, and her hair was up in a tight bun – held together by a red butterfly pin. Her brow rose playfully. "You seem to have upset the Skin Changer girl, ran out in a most foul mood. She was mumbling that the Hybrid was rude and mean. I think you made her cry." She titled her head, as she looked him up and down.

"What is it you want, Lady Fyra?" He quizzed in an irritated tone; he didn't care for any of the sisters. However, this sister, had a danger to her – one he didn't enjoy.

"Nothing for you interest, I just came to see it for myself." She traced her pointed red nails along the bed frame, tapping lightly, Dacre watched her closely and clenched his jaw.

"See what?"

"Your bite. I am not as easily fooled as those that fill this sanctuary, Dacre. I saw right through you the moment the Witch Nyda brought you here. Do not get me wrong, it was a well thought out plan and it seems to have worked as you will be getting released quite soon." He glared at her and narrowed his eyes.

"If you know, should I be expecting a trial?" She laughed but it lacked humour.

"We all have our little secrets here, plus I do not care enough to get involved. However, I will warn you only once of this," her sharp nail trailed up his leg as she walked closer to him, she dug the tip of her nail under his chin and drew a spot of blood. He hissed through his teeth, urges to release his claws and slash her throat were strong – it was a good thing he couldn't move. "Any harm comes to my sisters, I will slowly destroy you, piece by piece. I'll do it slow, savour your pain and I may even feed you your own flesh – that is how twisted I can be. Do I make myself clear?" She warned him, her tone laced with venom. "Nod, Hybrid." Dacre nodded, a sly smirk pulling at the corners of his mouth. "Good boy."

"There's a lot people don't know about you, isn't there? I don't think even your sisters know; seems we all have our secrets. I do wonder what your game is here," he teased. Fyra tilted her head and held her finger over her lips.

Chapter Ten
Narrdie

*M*y fingers traced the thin scars – which Dacre's claws had caused, they felt bumpy and raised, but thanks to the Healers and Nyda's magic – they were almost too small to see, nothing more than thin white lines. Nyda had warned me that I may be left with these, she swore they'd be no thicker than a sewing needle, but truthfully, I didn't mind them. They helped me look less . . . new to this, that maybe I did belong here, everyone else had their fair share of scars and battle wounds – so why shouldn't I?

We had been here a couple of weeks now, the first week I'd spent in the infirmary – Astrid had scolded me for losing my temper and punching one of the bathroom mirrors, the glass had shredded my knuckles and almost broken my thumb. Audric teased me and said he would teach me how to throw a proper punch, earning himself a scowl from Astrid. The other weeks had given me time to read and train – just like Indra had told me to do, Audric had forgiven me and was over the moon that I wanted him to be my trainer. "It's a Watchers honour to train the one they are watching," he'd basically sang to me – tears glossing his eyes over. I expected him to go easy on me, too slowly build up the training – I was wrong. Each night I'd go to bed with aching bones, screaming muscles and skin dotted with black and blue bruises, I wasn't allowed to use a healer, because Audric wanted me to experience fighting with exhausted limbs.

I had developed a routine here, one that was starting to help make all this seem. . . easier.

Every morning, just as the sun started to rise – I'd come out here, sit on my rugged rock, with a nice hot cup of tea and a soft throw, watching as the sun peeked through the branches and leaves; the glowing rays falling on the forest bed. The part I loved most – watching the water droplets twinkle in the sunlight, like a blanket of glitter. This was one of the only times I had to relax, before the training schedule that Audric created kicked in, I'd have at least an hour and a half before he'd come and find me.

If I wasn't training with Audric, then I was learning the history of this new world with Mitchell and Astrid – Mitchell being the stricter teacher out of the two; he wanted me to be familiar with things like Skinners, Sivvs and Shades. Astrid was opposite, she wanting me to know the different races, sanctuaries and factions. It felt like school, but a school I never wanted to leave – a school that actually cared and taught me things I'd use and need.

"Bonjour Narrdie," Bayona greeted as she skipped over to me, Audric and Mitchell followed her with wide smiles and chuckles.

Bayona had come out of the infirmary a week after me, we had spent our recovery time, eating junk food and listening to her tell funny stories about the others. She had spent her energy to the point of exhaustion, Audric had told me how frightened he was – scared that she would die. The first night in the infirmary I'd stayed awake, cooling her down and wiping away the sweat with a cool cloth. The healers had spent hours each day, pouring energy into her, refiling her magic with their own – even absorbing Astrid's strength to fill her muscles. Bayona plonked down beside me and gave me a tight hug, Audric began jumping around me – pretending to punch me.

"You ready for your next session Moon?" He asked cheerfully. "Bruises all healed up? Ready to make fresh ones?" I rolled my eyes and kicked him lightly in the shin.

"Definitely, what's on the menu today then Mitchell?" I asked as I slid out of my jacket, light green blotches decorated my arms.

"Just shield strengthening today, nothing more, you need to learn to hold the shield without it draining everything you have. Shield strengthening takes a lot out of a person, so I don't want to push you too much – especially when you're still learning." I nodded and turned to face Bayona, she bounced up and down with excitement, shield training was one of her favourite things; she liked to show how many colours she could do. Apparently, each colour represented a different strength, a different element that the shield borrowed the power from.

Audric and Mitchell stood at either side of me, ready to catch me if I suddenly collapsed – which I had done numerous times. Audric flashed me an encouraging wink and cleared his throat. "You girls ready? Right, Narrdie up it goes."

I squeezed my eyes shut and told myself over and over, that I was in danger. My blue orb shot out around me, it always felt heavy – too heavy. I winced, it felt like I was trying to push over a brick wall, the sound of the shield snapping and slashing out was deafening – like thunder in my ears.

"You got this," Audric whispered.

"Now Bayona!" Mitchell called. She raised her hand towards me; she playfully bit her lip before a transparent force suddenly slammed into my shield, immediately it began to quivering. I groaned, pain burning my arms, splitting my back; my head drummed against my skull.

"I can't," I breathed. "Tell her to stop," I begged Audric. Before, either of them could open their mouths, my hands buckled, and my shield shattered.

Bayona's force slammed into my chest, feeling like a truck had just ran me over. The air was knocked out of me and the next thing I knew – I was flying through the air. Hands wrapped around me and I knew it was Audric; he held me tightly, something hard hit us, and he groaned as we dropped to the floor. Bayona and Mitchell pelted over to us. "Are you two alright?" Mitchell asked as he helped us to our feet.

"We're good," Audric answered with a wince. "I got her." I looked to Audric, who was rubbing the lower part of his back, the tree we'd crashed into groaned as bits of bark flaked to the ground.

"Are you hurt?" I spun him round and lifted his top, thankful that nothing had broken the skin – only a handful of sore looking red marks.

"No, just hitting a tree isn't relaxing. Right, everyone back in position. We go again," he ordered.

Once more, Bayona's power barrelled into my shield, pushing me back; I whimpered as my hands shook violently. I tried to breathe, but only frail gasps left my lips. "Audric," I warned.

"Keep going, stay focused," he coached. "Narrdie, listen to me. You got this." I clenched my jaw and took a few calming breaths. I pushed my hands out, ordering them to keep going; to hold me up, my feet dug into the soil - keeping me steady.

"Good," Mitchell said with a nod, "Very good Narrdie. Bayona, a little more."

Her hand began to glow brighter, I felt myself being forced back, the dirt building up at the back of my feet - like small mountains. My arms cried out - pins and needles consumed my legs.

"Audric," I called as I felt my arms turning numb; my shield began to flicker once more.

"I got you, just tell me when," he said - jumping behind me; his arms stretched out, resting lightly around my waist, ready to catch me if I fell.

"Stop!" I cried out. Mitchell whistled and Bayona immediately dropped her hand, calling her magic back. I slunk back into Audric and breathed out heavily; he slowly brought us down to the floor, his arms still wrapped around me; he stroked his fingers up and down my aching skin.

"Are you alright?" He breathed in my ear, I nestled into him and nodded, an overwhelming tiredness began to pull at my eyes.

"Yeah," I answered with a wince. "Yeah, I'm alright. Can we be done with shield training for today, please?" Audric looked up to Mitchell, who thankfully nodded; he handed me a strange looking biscuit and a bottle of water.

"Astrid made the cookie; it will help with the exhaustion. You did really well today, you should be proud of yourself Narrdie, I know I am." Mitchell gave me a proud smile, Bayona linked his him and playfully made him skip along with her.

"You wanna go inside?" Audric asked as his tilted his head to look at me, his hand came up and brushed back strands of hair.

"Not yet, five more minutes?" He nodded, pulled me in closer and rested his head on top of mine.

*T*he next day's training lasted right up until the daylight had faded, there was no shield training – just plain combat and dodging techniques – I'd been knocked down so much, an imprint was beginning to dent the soil. I wanted to keep going, keep pushing myself – as did some of the others, but Nyda had called Audric and Mitchell away and the way my body screamed with stiffness – it was thankfully.

Bayona breathed out and skipped to her room to take a well-earned nap, advising that I should do the same – tomorrow's lesson would be harder. "I'm going up soon, just want to sit here for a little longer," I assured her with a smile.

I liked the night just as much as I liked the day – perhaps even more; everything seemed to glow, even without the moonlight. Perfectly strung cobwebs glimmering, as they glided from tree to tree, the dark blue of the night's sky, decorated with twinkling stars – covering the forest in a dark blanket. Owls waking up, their wings battering through the air, hooting and calling to each other, echoing for miles – it was all peaceful.

A dark blur began to form within the trees – instantly the forest fell silent, the blur strutted forward and stared into me; its mouth pulled up in a playful and menacing smirk. One that I had seen before. A foul feeling snaked throughout my body, as my eyes locked onto him.

Egregious; he winked, and his smirk turned to a nauseating laugh.

Egregious, the Shade who tried to kill me – twice.

The Shade who Dacre was meant to have killed.

A surge of snarls rippled from my throat as I looked at him, every ounce inside me burned with rage. I closed my eyes for a brief second, imagining his face inches from mine and as I opened them, I found myself standing directly in front of him. "Egregious."

"Narrdie Moon. It is good to see that your abilities are getting stronger, I believe that you just performed a Lacus jump. Well done," he snickered, as he mockingly clapped his hands.

"You're meant to be dead," I hissed, my voice quivered slightly, I could feel my hands beginning to shake; he licked his lips. I cursed myself, after the training I thought I'd be able to face something like him without feeling my body tremble, or the fear fogging around me and choked the breath from my lungs.

"You are still a timid little thing, aren't you? Where are your Watchers? Protectors? Very brave and stupid of you to be without them, isn't it?" I had an urge to scream for help, like I normally would have, I never thought my first encounter would be him. Still, this time I wouldn't run; I could do this – I had to do this.

Something rustled in the trees behind him, bright yellow eyes met mine – wolves, Nyda had informed me that wolves guarded these woods and that they had been gifted unique strength from the mother to help keep the darkness at bay. Every sanctuary had wolves around their land, they weren't tame and wouldn't hesitate to tear me apart if I got too close, however right now – I was the lesser threat, I was friend amongst their enemy. The wolf lowered its head to me, almost bowing – a truce for now and I had to force the smirk that pulled on my lips down.

"I don't need them."

"I will be the judge of that, little girl," he grinned and stepped one foot closer to me.

"No." I hissed, causing him to pause mid stop.

"No?" He repeated.

"No. This time I want to ask a few questions first and you will answer."

He laughed, "I will?"

"Yes, you will and if you make any wrong moves, you'll be hurt...or even killed," I warned.

"By you?" He laughed viciously, I made a point of looking behind him, knowing he wouldn't be able to resist following my stare.

"I've learnt a lot of things here, especially about these grounds. Did you know that this forest is protected by wolves? Not your normal kind, they are bigger, stronger and gifted with a toxin in their bites . . . the kind that is fatal to Shades. Hallucinations start, then a fever kicks in, paranoia, itching, vomiting and then finally a very painful death." I smirked widely, Nyda had introduced us all to the Wolves – so they could get our scent and know we weren't a threat here, we were still warned to keep our distance – it was simply so they wouldn't hunt us.

"You're bluffing," he growled, his voice slightly shaky. I shook my head and gestured for him to turn around. Egregious slowly tilted his head over his shoulder, a grey and white wolf rested its snarling jaws, inches from his face – it heckled a warning. "I'm impressed," he admitted.

"Are you going to try and run?"

"I wouldn't dream of it, my dear." He answered and made a façade of pretending to be offended, I gestured him to take a seat on the ground. "What would you like to know?"

"Your pocket." Egregious's lips pulled into a dark grin, he chuckled and cocked his head to the side.

"Very interesting and what about my pocket?" He teased.

"You know what, the syringe with that . . . liquid in it," I swallowed hard, feeling my hands turn clammy.

"You can feel it can't you?" Its pull was like a magnet, dragging me to it and it was hard to ignore it. It was like it had its own heartbeat and I could feel the pulse thundered in my ears – hear it calling me closer. I had torn through all the books within the mountain and found none about what it was and why it did what it did to me. I'd quizzed Mitchell, Astrid and Nyda and not one of them could give me the answers I wanted. "I was going to use it on you, and then I was going to take you with me." I couldn't help but shudder; I had felt its effects once before – by Melphos. I winced, remember the pain and torment he had asked it to do, that liquid was something I never wanted in my skin ever again – I shook of the memory.

"Unfortunately, your plan hasn't worked," I snapped.

"Don't be too sure," he mocked. A wolf near him snapped its' jaws close to his ear, apparently, they didn't like when Shades were cocky,

"He thinks you're being rude," I warned with a sneer.

"My apologies," he spoke through gritted teeth; he tilted his head and the corner of his mouth twitching up. "Why are you hesitating? Why don't you ask what you really want to?"

"Ask what?"

"You know what!" He snarled angrily, I jumped back, the wolves began to growl and snap their teeth in fury.

"Careful," I warned. "I can't stop them if they decide to attack."

"Ask it!"

"How are you alive?" I finally blurted – I already knew the answer. The Shade spread his mouth into a wide smile, the type that didn't match his face, too big – to monsterish. He glanced past me; a sickening laugh rolled from his tongue. The wolves whined, as their ears went down; they dropped low to the ground – cowering back into the forest.

"Narrdie? What are you doing so far from the sanctuary?" A male voice called, immediately the hairs on the back of my neck stood, shivers crept up my spine and anxiety flashed threw me. I gulped as my hands began to tremble, his footsteps gaining closer.

"Dacre," I managed to breath.

"Egregious," Dacre greeted in an uninterested tone, the Shade smiled smugly as they both fixed their sight upon me. Dacre moving to stand beside Egregious.

"Dacre . . . w-what is going on?" I whimpered; my eyes twitched between them, as though I was watching a sick tennis rally. Dacre's mouth lifted up in an amused yet mocking manner. I fumbled a few steps back and prayed silently that Audric or Astrid – or someone would burst out the mountain and run over to rescue me.

"You seem nervous Narrdie, I can smell it. Wouldn't you agree Dacre?" The Shade spoke playfully, Dacre ignored his teasing comment and kept his gaze locked with mine, I wasn't bothered about Egregious anymore. Right now, I knew that Dacre was the most dangerous person out of the both of them.

"You look puzzled – hurt even," Dacre said calmly.

"Why isn't he dead?" I asked through clenched teeth; my heart pounding so hard under my rib cage, I expected to see bruises. Dacre stepped closer to me and automatically my feet tiptoed back, I didn't want to be anywhere near him – he'd lied to us all. Audric had been right all along.

I'm in danger, I'm in danger, I'm in danger – I said to myself, over and over. Suddenly, my blue orb sprung out around me, stronger and brighter than it had ever been, the electric vines shot out – slashing Dacre to get back. Dacre froze still and raised his hands in an innocent fashion, he lightly tapped my shield and hissed through his teeth as it shocked through his fingers, leaving bleeding cuts up his skin.

"Narrdie. I have to say, I am amazed at how well you're progressing. They haven't let me see you since we first arrived, they didn't want me near you – not until they knew all the venom was out. How long have you been able to do an Arma? Quite a strong one, I might add. Mitchell been teaching you how to strengthen it?"

"Arma?"

Dacre scoffed viciously, "you still have a lot to learn. Arma, it means shield of protection. I'm disappointed that Bayona hasn't taught you the proper names." He took a moment and forced a sickenly fake smile along his wide lips, exposing his razor teeth. "Narrdie, you don't need an Arma around me."

"No Dacre, I think an Arma is exactly what I need around you." I spat.

He kissed his teeth and his eyes flared aggressively, "when did you learn to do this?" His eyes scanned the Arma, looking for any weak points.

"She did a Lacus jump, I think she's been playing with the Witches spell books, don't you?" Egregious snickered, he instantly cringed back as Dacre snapped his head towards him and snarled.

"When Nyda was about to kill you. I did an . . . Arma and protected you, if I didn't, she would have cut you down."

"Oh, I doubt that."

"Why isn't he dead Dacre?"

"Because I never killed him." I was surprised at how unconcerned his voice sounded – my blood boiled.

"I heard-"

"You heard what I wanted you to hear. You all did," he sniped aggressively.

"WHY?" I growled.

"Why would I?" He said nonchalantly. "He was only following orders. Narrdie, I ordered Egregious to collect you from your home that night. Audric got in the way and almost ruined everything, I had to send my associate to step in and end it. So, then I had to plan the attack in the bedroom, I was to distract everyone while Egregious took you. I never thought you'd fight back and when you screamed for help, Astrid heard you." His grimy smile was cynical, I couldn't believe what was happening and what was worse, I could feel the Arma begin to quiver. I was holding it too long; I could already feel the draining begin.

"On the way back to Audric's home, you arranged the attack as well, didn't you?"

"No. Actually, I don't know who organised that one, perhaps Melphos was going rogue. I will have to find out why that happened, it was fun though," he chuckled lightly. "Egregious." Egregious smirked as he pulled out the syringe and placed it in Dacre's hand.

I kept assuring myself that I was safe in the Arma, even though it was quivering it still felt strong, however the moment the black liquid came into my sight – my Arma began to crumble, falling away like burnt paper. Dacre raised his brows and laughed once.

"Seems your Arma is weak against this as well. This won't kill you Narrdie, it'll just send you into a deep sleep for a while. I'm afraid I don't know if it'll be painful or painless – we haven't really experienced it for ourselves. Time is getting on and we have work to do." He walked towards me and came to an abrupt pause in front of my shield, "this needs to come down first of all." With one swift movement, he flicked my Arma with his finger, my heart fell into my stomach, as my Arma dissolved – leaving burning embers, scattering the ground.

I was defenceless.

Wings. Bellowing wings, tearing through the night air – filled my ears, it was deafening, like lightening hitting a tree. Dacre froze, his eyes darting around the sky, Egregious began to cower back into the rubble of the bushes. The flapping gained louder, vibrating off the trees and popping in my ear, a loud thud – big enough to shake the ground, landed behind them.

A giant roar of outrage echoed through the forest, sharp teeth bared down at us in pure fury, big orange eyes glared angrily.

She was more beautiful in person, the thunderstorm grey Dragon. Her eyes rested on me for a split second and my heart fluttered with happiness, she moved to stand beside me; her wing stretching out to cover me from Dacre.

"Indra," I breathed. Relief and happiness swept into me, she turned her head to me; her eyes smiled to me before turning black and facing Dacre. She snarled, her mouth pulled back over her teeth; the spikes all down her back lifted up, as her clubbed tail slammed down on the ground – kicking up the dirt and debris.

"You have betrayed what you sworn to protect Dacre!" She slammed her foot down in front of him, causing the ground to shake, Dacre struggled to contain his balance.

"You stay out of my head!" Dacre warned with a snarl.

"You threatened the life of Narrdie Moon. The others shall hear of your betrayal!" She threw her head back and called out with an ear-piercing screech.

The Shade flung his crossbow of his shoulder and aimed at Indra's throat; a grimly satisfied expression plastered along his face. "I hate Dragons," he hissed as he fired.

"NO!" A voice screeched as a white shadow flew towards the arrow, clashing with it just before it hit Indra.

Aronnia materialized out of thin air, clutching the arrow so tightly – it turned to ash in her hands. Her hair blew wildly, her face masked with anger, eyes fixed on the Shade – who cowered back behind Dacre. Frantic footsteps piled onto the grounds, Astrid and Audric immediately raced to my side, taking positions beside me.

"What's going on here?" Wenona asked in a sharp tone as her eyes looked to her sister's enraged face, Wenona approached her slowly, taking her hand. The sky grew dark and rumbled its protest, lightening hit and stuck all around Egregious and Dacre; forcing them to take a few steps backwards.

"That Shade . . . that Shade, tried to kill my Indra!" Aronnia hissed in a deadly tone; her entire appearance had turned to something that belonged to a nightmare, it caused chills to drip down my spine.

"I am unharmed, thanks you to Aronnia. Calm the skies, my friend. Let the others handle this," Indra gestured in a gently tone as she nudged Aronnia's
shoulder; Aronnia softly stroked down her neck.

"Why have you come out of your realm Indra?" Aronnia asked in a shaky voice, "You know it's dangerous."

"Later my friend."

"The Shade. You never killed him," Mitchell growled as he stepped towards them, it wasn't a question, but Dacre answered anyway.

"Traitorous dog," Audric spat.

"No, I didn't. I am shocked that you never suspected, Mitchell," he mocked. Dacre sneered and raised his hands; he perched his lips together and released a high-pitched whistle. "Now the fun can begin."

Dark eyes and lethal growls crept up on us from the cover of the trees and shrubs, hooded men and horrid looking creatures on all fours, some even on hind legs – emerged from the forest, I had studied many of them, however the books made them look like harmless puppies compared to seeing them in person. "I've always been a man of reason," Dacre began as he pulled up his shirt sleeves, "so I'll give you the choice, Narrdie. Either come with me or watch your friends die and then I'll take you afterwards." Astrid pulled me behind her. Her eyes were a deep red, the whites had turned yellow with dark veins, her face had turned gaunt, and her fangs had extended past her bottom lip – her hand gripped my arm protectively – laced with long daggered claws.

"Over my dead body," she hissed and crouched low – pushing me back towards Bayona. Bayona immediately covered us in her Arma – brightly glowing silver, borrowed from the lingering moon.

"Well then," Dacre cracked. "If it's a fight you want," he paused as he glanced back and nodded to the men in hoods. Their bodies instantly began to vibrate violently, their bones began to crack, and they suddenly shot themselves up into the air. Their hands began to rip and pulled away at their own skin, until the leathery black skin underneath showed – scabby wings, resembling bats sprouted from their backs.

"Half breeds," Nyda cursed.

"It's a fight you'll get."

Chapter Eleven

"Narrdie!" Aronnia shrieked, pulling my attention away from the sudden outburst of war that had erupted onto my peaceful night, the sound of tearing skin, blood splatters staining the ground and bones being snapped echoed in my ears. "Go to Indra!" She ordered in a firm tone.

"Hurry! I need to get you somewhere safe!" Indra called, my eyes darted around to see havoc, everyone was scattered, corned by the winged beasts and hind legged creatures, bodies scattered the floor like leaves from a tree – I couldn't tell if they were ours or Dacres. I couldn't just leave, not when Audric and the others stayed behind, I had trained now; I wasn't useless anymore.

"I can help!" I argued, Indra's eyes frowned, and she slammed her foot down.

"Not now, you are not ready yet." Indra whipped her head around to Aronnia; she was surrounded by vile looking things, dripping with gooey looking skin; their grey teeth were all sharp like a shark, set with different layers – throat tearing layers. Indra effortlessly lifted her tail towards one that was trying to sneak up on Aronnia, she wafted it away like it was nothing but an annoying bug.

Nyda and Bayona rushed forward and spread their hands out, Bayona's silver Arma exploded around us, entwining with Nyda's dark red one, borrowed by the blood that had filled the forest floor – I could feel the strength from both of them.

When someone tried to get past my Arma, they would only get a small shock, but when someone tried to burst through theirs – it was much worse. A pack of rotted dogs snarled and narrowed their red eyes; they scratched their feet on the floor before darting forward, the Arma shook as it blasted out and slashed across them. The dogs yelped and dropped to the ground, cowering and whimpering as their skin began to burn and dissolve away – leaving nothing but a bloodied puddle.

"Still hate shield training?" Bayona called back with an excited laugh.

Wenona, Mitchell, Lenis and Yorg danced around with Egregious; he was strong and seemed more powerful than all of them put together – even Wenona seemed out of breath. Egregious laughed as he flung his foot out and kicked Lenis, the Shade pressed his foot down on his chest and smirked as he aimed his crossbow. I didn't see where Mitchell had come from, but the next thing I knew, he'd dove onto Egregious – pushing him off Lenis, giving Yorg a chance to run over and help him.

Swiftly, Wenona was on the Shade, she danced two moon shaped swords towards him – spinning and twirling them so fast he could barely keep up; she kicked herself up high and slammed her swords down on his own – forcing him back.

"Narrdie!" Indra begged. I needed to see the others, I had to know they were safe . . . alive. My eyes searched and searched for them, but it was carnage, cries of pain and anger burned in my ears, the smell of blood and metal scorched my nose. *"Narrdie!"* Indra's voice was nothing but a mumble in my head.

Not yet, I can't go yet.

Finally, through all the blood and war – I spotted them.

Audric and Astrid flanked each other, keeping Dacre's attention on them, which immediately sent the hairs on the back of my neck to stand. Dacre was sneaky – deadly; he was fast, but Astrid was faster, each time he tried to grab a hold of her, she'd already be behind him. She snarled and dug her daggered claws into his shoulder – he grumbled his pain, she gripped him hard and threw him flying back. Erenna emerged from the tree he'd crashed into, vines covered in thorns shot out all around him, boxing him in. It looked like they all had him under control, but the pit in my stomach didn't ease.

Fyra, Nyda's guards and a Skin-changer called Sharia began to pick off the rest of Dacre's men and creatures, trying to push them back into the forest – away from me and Indra.

Sharia elegantly jumped into the air and shifted into a Panther; she tore at one of the creatures; her claw hooked into its stomach and severed it in half. She swiftly jumped back towards another one and changed into a Bear before brutally ripping it into shreds, for such a tiny girl – she was a brutal fighter. Fyra remained close beside her, flicking her fingers every now and then, burning and boiling them where they stood; she did this in such and effortless way – she almost looked bored. Her eyes caught sight of mine, the air around me turned hot. "Narrdie!" She hissed, anger washed over her face, "leave now! Indra, get her out of here!" Indra moved to position herself in front of me; a stern and demanding look on her face, meaning one thing – no more waiting.

Climbing on her back was simpler than I thought, her spikes lowered when I moved up them, I tucked myself into the nape of her neck and held tightly. Bayona and Nyda's Armas shook as piles of creatures, sacrificing themselves, slammed against it – weakening them.

"Go!"

Indra shot up high and I was surprised I was able to hold on, despite the wind, thrashing against my arms and trying to rip my hands from Indra's spikes. I'd never been afraid of heights; I'd never had any phobias – until now. I kept my head down to my chest and tucked my body in close, at least until Indra calmed to a steady speed, once we were just gliding, it was actually quite nice in the sky – I even felt confident enough to sit up. *"Are you alright?"* She asked softly, her head swaying side to side, searching for oncoming danger.

"I think so."

"Now would be a good chance to try an Animo." She suggested, trying to distract my mind from the ongoing war.

"How?" I shouted towards her, the harsh wind seeped into my mouth, sucking up any moisture and breath I tried to take.

"Think the words you want to tell me, and imagine you are talking." I frowned, the creases in my forehead tightening.

"I don't know how to do this," It was hopeless, I could barely hold my Arma, let alone try and hold a sentence together using Animo. *"It sounds impossible."*

"Narrdie, you just did it," Indra chuckled lightly.

"I did? Am I doing it now?"

"Yes," her laugh grew louder, I felt my body shake – my hands tightened on her spikes.

"That's so cool... how do I stop?"

"You just tell yourself that your thoughts are your own and no one else's and it should stop. Remember Narrdie, you are in charge of everything you do. Try it, think about something that you don't want me to know." I closed my eyes and thought about the only secret I was asked to keep, the time Dacre had given me a ring and told me not to tell anyone. I thought about everything he said, all the lies he'd promised and how deep down, I felt hurt and betrayed by him.

"Did you hear it?" I called down to her, my throat going raw.

"No. Well done, now use Animo, otherwise you are going to lose your voice," she warned playfully.

"Where are we going?"

"To Gatherling. Lazarus mountain is no longer safe, don't worry the others will know to go there. Gatherling is a very strong sanctuary, even if it is found; it is almost impossible to breach. It is Evander's home."

"Who's Evander?" So many people, so many people I'd been introduced to and was expected to trust them – to put my life in their hands.

"A very old friend of us all," there was a longing in her voice, like she was truly excited and pleased that she was about to see him.

"An old friend like Dacre?" A growl rumbled in her throat and I was worried I'd pushed her too far, but Mitchell had said that Dacre was an old friend – look how he turned out.

"No. Dacre was never a friend. He was just... an asset at the time. If Mitchell knew that Dacre was turning against us, he would have never brought him anywhere near you...near his family. Some people are very good at covering the truth, Dacre's been doing it for centuries." I swallowed hard, I barely knew Dacre, but I felt the pain of his double cross, God only knew how it felt for Mitchell. I let out a long breath and ran my hand through my hair, the movement felt harder – like the wind was trying to snatch my arm and sever it from its socket.

This was all so crazy, hidden facilities in mountains, beings more powerful than anything I'd ever seen, men changing into hideous creatures and a Dragon sawing the sky. How did humans not know about all this?

"Indra, how do you hide from humans? How do they not see you when you fly?" She laughed softly and took a gently right turn; the wind licked my cheeks softly.

"This world is not my home Narrdie, so I don't stay here long enough for them to come looking. I come from different realm, one of many, found and created from tears – gaps from a magical imbalance. I pass through if help is needed or if I sense something is wrong. The Watchers keep it all hidden," she explained slowly, which I was thankful for.

"A magical imbalance? What do you mean?"

"Too much power in one place, it can shred through the earth, the sky, the sea and creates a passage to another realm. The Watchers are normally very good at calculating when one is going to form, so they do all they can to fix the balance – remove the power. If they fail, then they seal up the realm, normally a Witch will do it. However, with the increase of power these days, they refuse, afraid it will drain them . . . it might even kill them."

"So, what happens then? They just leave it alone?" Indra slowly began to lower herself, her belly almost skimming on the tip of the trees.

"No, it is too dangerous to just leave it. The Watchers seal off the area, grand level Watchers hold abilities – minor, but still effective. They put a shield around it, like an Arma, but not as strong and not with deadly effects. If a human wanders close to the shield, they suddenly have an urge to return home – forgetting why they ever came that way and if something were to come out of the tear, the Watchers would know instantly." I glanced over the side, I could faintly see the forest floor, people loved to hike in woods like these, they'd spend days doing it.

"Indra, what about now? What if someone sees us?" My voice was panicked; I looked around as if I were expecting to see people staring up at us in marvel, waited for the bright lights of their cameras flashing. Indra's laughed shook me.

"Narrdie, I thought you were a smart one. Do you honestly believe that the Priestesses and the Watchers would allow me to roam freely if there was a chance I'd be seen? No dear, Watchers are not the only race that cover things up, there is a coven of Witches that spend their lives hiding what the Watchers can't from the humans. They spent months maybe even years developing a strong cloaking spell to drape over me, it lasts for ten years and then I return to them so they can put it over me again."

"Cloaking spell? I read that they are one of the hardest spells to perform and to break, their proper name is a . . . Vellera?" I'd remembered sitting in the library at Nyda's sanctuary, it was only small, the size of a living room or master bedroom. It had a long wooden table in the middle of the room, with six uncomfortable chairs dotted around, in total there was probably only about fifty books – but each one was as big as a phonebook. Mitchell had wanted me to learn some of the names of the spells and when I had learnt about the Vellera, I had begged and begged to practice it, but Mitchell thought it too dangerous and unnecessary.

"I'm impressed Narrdie," she glanced back to me and her eyes smiled lightly, I felt a sudden little ego boost; finally, pleased with myself that I was getting better at this.

"Hold on," Indra warned as she speedily swooped down, the wind thrashed against me, my face flushed with pain, branches and leaves whipped at my arms and legs and I had to bite my tongue to keep from crying out. She landed softly and sat up in a magnificent stance, her clubbed tail gently leaned towards me, offering me a hand down, getting off was as difficult as climbing on. The minute my feet touched the ground, relief swam into me, it took everything I had not to get on all fours and kiss the soil; I never wanted to be that high in the air every again.

An array of guards came flooding out around us, each one armed to the teeth with swords, spears and crossbows – all aimed towards us. I jumped back and clung to Indra's leg, I looked up to her, expecting to see the teeth bare and threatening eyes, but she didn't look worried, instead she looked amused.

"Stand down!" A man ordered as he wandered over to us confidently, a gleaming smile across his face, he raised his arms as if he were about to embrace us. "We do not raise arms against friends. Indra, my angel from above and Lady Narrdie Moon, I am so privileged to welcome you into my home! I'm glad you are both safe," he bowed immediately to Indra then turned to me, his eyes caught mine and held my gaze; he bowed slowly; I could feel my cheeks flush red.

"Hello. I'm guessing you're Evander, right?" I cringed at my flirtatious voice and forced my hand to stay down as it tried to creep up and twirl at a strand of my hair. Get it together Moon.

"Lovely to see you again Evander," Indra greeted as she bowed her head, Evander tore his gaze from mine and waved his men away; his face turned serious as he looked back to Indra; his jaw clenched before he spoke.

"The others?" He asked in a concerned voice.

"I've heard nothing from anyone, when we left them, they were already outnumbered. I expected to hear something from Aronnia but nothing," Indra's
voice was shaky, Evander frowned and stroked his hand down the middle of her face – comforting.

"What happened? I wasn't expecting any of you for another few months, we were barely prepared when Bayona sent word that you two had already set off."

"Dacre happened," my voice cracked. Evander stumbled back slightly, his eyes slowly closed, and I could tell that this news had hurt him; he clenched his jaw, as his fists tightened into balls.

"Narrdie, would you come inside and tell me everything? Indra keep an eye out, if anyone or anything springs up, call for me. The rest of you stay aware and be on your guard." Indra nodded.

Evander offered me his arm and I took it without any hesitation.

He smiled and led me inside and walked arm in arm to his infirmary, he sat me on the bed and pulled over a plain wooden chair. "Tell me everything."

I explained everything as fast and as much detail as I could; I was still trying to process it myself, so to him it probably didn't make much sense. I told him everything, from the first day I'd met Egregious, to this day – the day Dacre showed his true colours. He'd stopped me halfway when my voice broke and handed me a glass of water, cupping his hand under my arm and lightly stroking my skin with his thumb – his touch sent tingles around my body.

Evander leaned back in his chair and sighed, the weight of his shoulders almost snapping the wood; he brushed a hand through his hair, "he used to be good, you know. He'd die to protect this world and his friends; he took a knife for me many times. We fought together like brothers – hell, we were brothers. But all this . . . I knew he wasn't right after . . ." He trailed off, his head snapping up as he remembered I was here; he caught my eyes and I could tell he was trying to shake off whatever memory had held him captive. "This is a lot for you." It wasn't a question, but I nodded my head and took a breath. "How are you holding up?"

"Okay I guess," I answered a little unsure.

"You're not okay," he blurted.

"I'm not?"

"No, you're doing what a lot of us have done, you're bottling it all up. You tell yourself that you can handle it, but the truth is, you can't. In my opinion take this time to deal with it now, otherwise it'll all come out at a time you don't want it to, I've seen Witches bottle things up and the next thing . . . a whole forest was set alight." I smiled instantly, Evander was kind, the way he looked at me made me feel like I'd known him all my life and I could feel myself being genuinely relaxed around him, he made me feel...safe.

Evander was striking, the type of guy you'd see all over posters, pinned on a girl's wall, in a heart shape; he had chocolate coloured hair that had been pulled back into a tight ponytail, a slight morning shadow of a beard rested on his prominent chin, his cheekbones perfectly angled and lifted his piercing orange eyes. I could see a faint tattoo or marking on his arms and peeking from his well build chest. He had a scar across his eye, not a thick, discoloured scar, but a thin white mark – from the beginning of his eyebrow to the bottom of his ear. My eyes lingered back to his and he half smiled, I hoped he didn't think I was staring at it.

"Thanks Evander, but honestly I feel okay, I've always been good at dealing with things and even I can tell, that now isn't the time." Evander opened his mouth to speak, but before he could, Indra's roar thundered around us, the vibration tingling as it moved up my legs. "That's Indra," I said as I turned back to find him still watching me, I could feel my cheeks burning red. "We should go," I breathed – my voice shaky.

"Indra what's going on?" Evander asked in a worried tone, his hand clasped onto the hilt of the sword that rested on his belt, ready to draw it at a moment's notice.

"They're back, something is wrong, very wrong." Her eyes had dropped – saddened. My hands turned clammy, as people limped towards us – few, only a few had made it back. I couldn't make anyone out, blood had painted them all – so much blood, they were all hurt; some were even being carried over.

"Get some healers out here!" Evander ordered. I could feel my chest tighten, palpitations drumming over and over, as I searched the small crowd. Relief slammed into me like a wall, when my eyes locked onto Audric, he was hurt and had more blood on him than anyone else.

"Audric?" I wrapped his arm over my shoulder, feeling his weight suddenly lean on me; he winced as I led him to a clear patch and signalled a healer to come over. It was only when I sat him down, that I noticed his injuries, my lips clammed together to keep from crying. His shoulder had been sliced deep, crimson liquid running from it like a fountain, his right arm hanging from its socket, I swallowed down my vomit, as I saw the stained white bone, poking out from his wrist. Three large gashes, had shredded through his t-shirt and torn into his chest – thankfully, they weren't as deep as his others. He winced and groaned as the Healer began to prod and poke around, deciding which one was priority; she pulled out a mossy cream that looked like chewed up kale and thickly slathered it onto his open wounds, before grabbing a bandage and some metal sticks to patch his wrist up. Audric's eyes were empty as they stared into the floor, he opened his mouth to speak, but only air escaped them, I brushed a wet cloth over his face and did my best to clean off as much blood as I could.

Bayona was the first to speak, she slummed against a tree, continuously rubbing at her tattooed palm – it was beginning to turn red. "Things were going good," she began, her eyes distant. "We had the upper hand, had Dacre backed up into a corner, in fact we had them all fading back into the forest – we didn't realise that, that was what he wanted. When we were thick in the trees, more showed up, summoned by Egregious and they just kept coming, springing up like daisies." Evander slowly approached her, his hands placing on each of her shoulders, gently he walked her to a log and sat her down – waving away a Healer.

"What happened then?" He urged softly, he took her red hand into his and moved his hand clockwise around the tattoo – rubbing in a lump of the green cream.

"Egregious came at me, I could feel his power . . . it came for me," Bayona's voice trembled slightly. "So strong . . . but she saved me. She tore out his heart, pulled it straight out his chest," her voice broke.

"Who?" Evander pressed.

"Astrid." Her eyes misted over, she met Evander's eyes and he clenched his jaw, his head lowered. She wasn't here. Astrid wasn't here, she wasn't anywhere. Pain that felt like an electric shock shot into my chest, pulled my stomach into knots and shook my hands.

"Where is Astrid?" I asked, my voice barely a whisper.

"Dead." Sharia announced blankly, "He pierced her through the chest and removed her head from her shoulders." My legs felt like jelly, I slumped to the floor to keep from falling, I looked through my tears, to Audric. He didn't speak, he just nodded – confirming.

"We don't need details like that Sharia," Evander said in a hard tone. "Who did it?"

"He fled straight after," Bayona whimpered.

"Who?" Evander asked gently, his hand stroked a tear from her cheek. She looked to him, her eyes meeting his, his jaw clenched. "You already know who."

"Dacre."

An overwhelming urge to puke grew, a pit burrowed and spread in my stomach, as I looked around – more were missing. "Where is everyone?" I asked, my voice barely a murmur as it fell from my mouth. Erenna took a step forward towards us, she spoke this time as she seemed the calmest out of them all – her eyes were stained with sorrow.

"Mitchell went into shock when he saw what happened to Astrid, shock that then changed into an uncontrollable rage. He went for a herd of Skinners – he didn't make it. Yorg and Lenis were taken also – after they saved Nyda and Sharia. Many of Nyda's other men fell." Dead. So many dead, their lives just...gone. All because I needed to escape, because I had to be protected. My legs gave in and I curled into myself, holding my knees to my chest, I couldn't bring myself to look at Nyda, Bayona . . . Audric. Not when I was the reason they had lost so much. Yes, Dacre and the monstrous things had ended their lives, but I might as well have handed them the tools to do it. The only person I could face was Evander, and he was furious. Evander's hands shook violently, his jaw clenching and unclenching; he was on his feet, standing in front of us all.

"Right. Everyone listen up, it's been a long day and you are all in need of rest. Healers take whoever's closest to you to a room and if needs be, to the infirmary." The Healers nodded, their arms looping around people, slowly walking them inside – even picking people up, if they needed it.

I'd tried to help Audric myself and was met with shock when he shrugged me off and curled his lip up. I stood staring after him, Evander slowly stroked my arm and he offered me a comforting smile.

"Don't take it to heart, he's grieving. Watchers are known to grieve in solitude. They tend to get a resentful towards everything and everyone around them, Mitchell's power will be transferring into him from the moment he died, and it's not a pleasant feeling. Give him time," Evander gently said after Audric had stormed away.

"He blames me."

"No Narrdie, he doesn't – he just needs space; you need rest. Will you be alright on your own? I have a room ready for you, but if you want, I can stay a while?" He offered gently.

"No, I'll be alright, thank you Evander."

"Good, you're a strong one Narrdie. Get some rest." His hand slowly lifted up and brushed my cheek; his fingers were warm and sent hot tingles through me.

I barely slept.

I didn't even know why I kept trying, each time I closed my eyes, bloodied faces of Mitchell and Astrid tainted my sleep. Images of Dacre and Egregious, laughing as they slaughtered Nyda's people echoed in my ears and the worst dream of all, the one that burned every time I saw it – the look on Audric's face. It was a look of anger, disgust...hatred.

I sat up slowly as someone tapped rapidly on my door, I swallowed hard as I felt nerves bubble their way to the surface – I already knew who this was. "Come in." Audric walked in with an emotionless expression, he didn't look well; his skin had paled, his cheeks gaunt – he hadn't eaten at all since coming here. Purple blotches had tattooed the bottom of his eyes and he still had the same blood splattered clothes on. I rose and nervously dared a step towards him, I wanted nothing more than to throw my arms around him and tell him how sorry I was.

"Stop," he growled – causing my feet to turn to stone.

"Audric, I am so, so sorry about Mitchell, Astrid, Yorg, Lenis– everyone," my voice cracked, and I could feel the threat of tears looming to the surface.

"As long as you're safe, it doesn't matter," he said sarcastically.

"Audric, I . . ." I trailed off, not knowing what to say, the truth was, nothing I could say to him would make this better – there was nothing I could say to him, to let him know how bad I felt and how sorry I was.

"Mitchell. Astrid. Yorg. Lenis and all of those other souls that were slaughtered because Narrdie Moon had to be protected. Do you even know the rest of their names?"

"Audric . . . I . . ."

"Do you?" He spat.

"No," I breathed sheepishly. Audric scoffed and rubbed his hand down his face.

"I didn't think so, why should you? They aren't important enough to you, are they? Nothing is, because only YOU matter." I clenched my jaw, feeling tears slowly falling down my cheek.

"I . . .I." He was right, I had never learned any of Nyda's people's names, even though they all protected me – I didn't know who they were.

"Markus, Antonio, Lacey, Alexander, Demetri, Zeke, Imelda, her twin Sister Onia, Kristof, Orion – his son Matais." Each name felt like a knife to my gut – a slash against my skin, but I didn't beg him to stop, didn't tell him how much these names hurt – I needed to hear them, I needed to know who had died for me... because of me. "Lilona, Stephan and Lily – she had just turned eighteen." I had no words, I looked away from him and an angered scoff filled my ears.

"You don't get to look down. You don't get to be upset, no one should feel sorry for you – you are the reason they all died!"

"Audric, please-" With one swift motion, Audric's hand lashed across my cheek, my face tingled with the pins and needles pain. I flinched back and held my hand over my cheek, feeling the hot sting.

"AUDRIC!" A furious voice snarled; Evander stood in the doorway; a cold look upon his face; his hands were clenched into fists.

"This is a private conversation, Evander." Audric snapped.

"I don't care about your conversation. However, I will say this, if you ever lay your hand on anyone in this sanctuary again – you'll be spending your days in the infirmary," Evander warned. Audric opened his mouth and I knew whatever he was going to say, was not going to help the tension in the room. Evander laughed darkly and took a threatening step closer, his eyes darkened; he spoke – his voice laced with venom. "Remember, you are in my house boy. You sleep here, you eat here, and you wash and bath here. You stay here, all because I allow it. Don't make a mistake and take my kindness for weakness, you disobey my rules and I'll throw you out. You want to challenge me, do it – I'll put you down before you're able to raise a hand." Evander's face rested inches from Audric. "Do I make myself clear?" Audric clenched his jaw and submissively stepped back,

"Yes." The aggression had dropped from his voice and his eyes lowered.

"Good. Now, either apologise to Narrdie or leave her be, whatever you decide I suggest you do it soon. I expected so much more from a Watcher, especially one of your bloodline. In fact, apologise to her later, for now, I want you out of my sight." Audric didn't as much as glance at me or Evander as he left the room, he kept his head down and placed his hands in his pockets.

Evander walked towards me and placed his hand gently on my cheek, the burning instantly cooling as his cold fingertips touched my skin, the rest of my body however – prickled.

"Are you alright?" He breathed; his thumb brushing my cheek. "Does it hurt? Should I get some ice?"

"No, it's fine. Thank you for sticking up for me but, you shouldn't have said those things to him, he's going through a lot. Plus, he's right, I don't know the names of the people who died, and they died for me. They died for me, Evander and I didn't even know who they were, I was at Nyda's sanctuary for weeks and I didn't bother to learn anything about them. It is my fault they died, and I deserve more than a slap. You were too harsh."

He fidgeted and his smile slid, "harsh words make people think. I've known his family for many generations. Narrdie, Audric was wrong to say what he said. Those who died, they weren't out there because they had to be – they chose to be. We've trained and prepared for battles like this, since the day we were born and dying in them, is an honour. They didn't die because of you, they didn't die for you, they died fighting those on the side of the darkness. They died protecting this world and believe me when I say this, they were happy to do it." Evander smiled and wouldn't let my eyes leave his. I smiled and for the first time in a while, it was genuine. There had been a pit in my stomach, ever since Audric had returned, a pit that turned food to mould in my mouth, that made water dry up before it graced my tongue and turned dreams into nightmares. Evander dropped his hand from my cheek and laughed lightly, "What I don't get is, he slapped you and you jumped at me for the way I spoke to him. Why?"

"Because he needed to let it out and if him yelling at me helps, then he can shout and slap me as much as he needs."

"You have a good heart, Narrdie Moon. Be careful that you don't give it to people that will use it against you, don't let them turn it into your weakness." His eyes met mine and a certain urge itched at the surface, an urge that I never thought I would feel – especially in these circumstances.

"Thank you for coming to see me, Evander." He bowed his head, before he could leave, I snagged his hand; my fingers lingering on his. "Will you stay for a while? I'm having trouble sleeping, so I could use the company."

"Of course."

Evander stayed with me all night, he didn't yawn, to hint he was tired, he didn't check the time and use it as an excuse to leave. Staying up all night talking and joking on with Evander was everything I needed and as the conversation came to an end, all the tingling and warm feelings I had been getting, finally made sense. "It's getting late, I bet the sun is coming up," I announced, my voice suddenly turning nervous." I sat up and shifted my legs from his lap.

"It is. We should both get some rest," Evander suggested, yet he still lingered on the edge of my bed, his eyes met mine and he leaned closer. "I shouldn't do this," he began, his voice soft. "Stop me if I'm overstepping, but I just . . ." He trailed off and his eyes dropped to my mouth, my heart began to thunder as his gaze lingered. Before I could say another word, his lips embraced mine.

I had never been kissed before, not like this. Butterflies tickled my stomach; goosebumps freckled my skin and my heart was pounding so much – I was scared he'd hear it. His lips were soft as they held mine, his hand cupped my cheek; his fingertips brushing my hair – his other hand snaked around my waist. The touch made shivers shoot up my spine, I leaned closer, daring my hands to take hold of him, but before I could even graze his top – it was over before I knew it. Over before I wanted it to be, I didn't want him to pull away, but he did. I pulled my hair to one side, knowing my face had gone bright red. Evander lightly brushed back a strand I had missed and smiled to me, his eyes still locked with mine. He really did have beautiful eyes. An embarrassed redness took hold of my face, I had never kissed someone after just meeting them, but this felt different.

"Why do I feel like I know you?" I asked my voice softer than a whisper. Evander's jaw hardened and his brows furrowed, he smiled – but I knew it was forced.

"You need to rest, so do I," he chuckled and flashed me a wink as he closed my bedroom door.

Chapter Twelve

It had already been a month since we lost Mitchell, Astrid and all the others that had been killed by Dacre and his monstrous creatures – I'd been reciting all their names over and over in my head. Every night before I went to bed, I'd say them out loud, it didn't make the pit in my stomach any smaller, but it helped me sleep. Evander had given Sharia and Bayona permission to paint one of the walls in the hall, a memorial for all those that had lost their lives. I'd spent many nights awake, just staring and taking it all in, as did others who had lost someone they loved, they'd leave candles and trinkets underneath – pray that they were finally at peace. Sharia had painted most of it, but it was Bayona that had come up with the idea, she had announced it to everyone a few days after – bringing many to tears at the thought.

The memorial itself was beautiful. The purple branches, twirled and wrapped around each other, as they pulled up from the dark purple roots, growing and spreading all across the wall. Leaves of gold, dusted the branches and sprinkled along the floor, the detail was incredible and the different shades of the brush strokes, made it seem so real. If I were to touch it, I was almost convinced that I would feel the rough bark against my fingertips. At the top of the tree, the branches stretched up, twirling around – each other spelling out a name of someone who'd gone. The named branches stretched higher and higher, until they finally reached up and tickled the twinkling stars. "It really is beautiful, you both did a perfect job," I told Bayona, as she linked her arm through mine.

"Do you think she would have liked it?" Bayona asked, her voice shook – the threat of tears crept closer. I knew who she meant; it was the person that I also missed the most – Astrid.

Astrid was a special person in our lives, a friend I could undoubtedly trust, but to Bayona, she was more than a friend. She was a mother. It was Astrid who had found Bayona, the night her eyes were scorched out. Astrid had told me only little about that night, she was out hunting a deer, when she smelt burnt skin and blood – she cradled Bayona in her arms and carried her home, she'd cared for her ever since.

"I think she'd have loved it." She smiled to me and leaned her head on my shoulder, her fingers stretched and gently trailed down the painted branches – brushing Astrid's name.

"I chose purple because it was her favourite colour. I don't know if you ever noticed, but when her eyes are calm, there is a golden shine to them." Bayona's bottom lip quivered as she smiled, she swallowed hard and took a few calming breaths. "She was so beautiful, in and out."

"Do you want to be alone?" She nodded, not daring to speak in case the tears overflowed, I smiled to her and lightly kissed her cheek. Bayona kept her hand pressed against the purple tree, she called back to me before I left, and I could tell from her voice that she was crying.

"They loved you, you know, both of them did. Astrid loved you like a daughter and even though Mitchell didn't show it, he loved you too. You were and always will be family to them and to us." A sharp pain pierced through my heart and a large lump swelled in my throat.

"Thank you," I managed to say, my voice teary.

"Remember that on your bad days."

$$\smile$$

$\mathcal{T}$he Elemental Sisters had announced that they were going away for a while and they wanted to cook the Sanctuary a farewell dinner. I had never seen so much food in all my life and some I had never even imagined to taste.

Evander and Nyda had hunted down a boar, after Erenna had said a small prayer and thanked its spirit; she'd prepared it so perfectly, the skin was crispy, and I knew the inside would be juicy and tender. The smell enticed us all to come and sit, our mouths watering – it even had a caramelized apple in its mouth. A golden sheet made of silk, had been draped over the grand oak table, tall candles neatly spaced out and the boar had been placed in the centre for all to see. The boar wasn't the only thing that had my mouth drooling, the table was full of plates, filled with overflowing food. Golden potatoes with a crispy lining, every kind of vegetable you could think of – all still steaming, homemade Yorkshire puddings, the size of a bowling ball and stuffing, mixed with cranberries and a hint of hazelnut.

The desert looked too pretty to eat, I almost begged Wenona not to cut it. Gateau's had always been my favourite cakes, but I had never had a fifth-tier gateau, the rich chocolate had been shaped into an elegant blend of white and milk chocolate swirls. Around each cake was a thick dark chocolate trimming and teasingly sitting on top of all tiers, were bright, shining, fresh cherries – smothering in a thick berry sauce.

"Narrdie, no," Erenna warned, an amused grin on her lips. "Move away from the cake, you can have some once you've eaten a decent amount. I will not have you skip out on another meal, misses."

"Can't I just have a small piece?"

"No."

"A little finger swipe? No one needs to know," I flashed her my most convincing smile. Erenna gently slapped my hand away and turned me towards the table, she laughed as she pushed me forward.

"You'll lose those fingers if you touch that cake, Wenona made it and she'll destroy you if you ruin it. You'll get some soon enough, there is plenty to go around. Now, take a seat beside Audric." I smiled to her, which instantly faded the moment I turned to the table.

Audric had barely said two words to me since the night in my room, he never looked in my direction when we'd gather for meetings, he never stayed to watch while I trained – he didn't want anything to do with me anymore. Whenever I went near him, it felt like all the warmth in the room, had iced over, when it came to me, Audric was cold.

Evander had done his best to convince me, that Audric was giving everyone the cold shoulder – I knew it was a lie, but I appreciated the gesture. I'd nod and voice my agreement, even my fake smile had become convincing enough, but each time the subject was brought up – it felt like cold blades were being dragged against my skin, cutting deeper and deeper.

Evander and I had spent almost every night together this month, rambling on until the early morning hours. Sometimes he'd teach me defensive moves or show me useful spells from a book he'd store in his library. It was nice, but I couldn't shake the feeling that I knew him from somewhere and every time I brought it up, he seemed to frown and change the subject or decide it was time for bed.

"Narrdie! Pay attention, it's going to get away!" Bayona hissed, snapping me out of another daydream. "Never mind, it's gone. How are we meant to catch Indra a surprise deer if you won't stay focused?" She sighed and tilted her head to me, "what's wrong with you today?"

"Sorry Bayona, my heads all jumbled," I looked down and half smiled; she tugged on my jacket and signalled me back inside.

"It's OK. I'll ask Evander to send someone out to catch one, Indra doesn't have to know that we didn't catch it." She playfully winked and wiggled her eyebrows before beginning to walk off.

"Wait," I called. Bayona turned to me, a comforting smile upon her face, which slowly faded away as she saw the question on my face.

"Narrdie, Audric hasn't said anything to me, was that what you were going to ask me?" I nodded and bit my lip, "just give him some more time." She flashed me a sheepish smile, "come on let's find Evander."

"Actually, I'm just gonna go lie down for a while, I feel a bit sick and tired. I can feel a headache coming." She nodded and gave me a little squeeze of a hug.

I was stretched out across my bed – a wet, cold flannel draped over my forehead – when an extremely happy Evander burst through and dived on me. "Narrdie!" He yelled excitedly.

"Careful! Evander what's happening?" I asked through a laugh.

"I-What are you doing?" He asked as he picked up the wet flannel with a slight crease of his eyebrows. "Never mind, I have a surprise for you," he jumped up and whistled.

A fast-blonde clumsy dog bounded into the room and jumped up at me with a happy whine and an uncontrollable waggling tail. "Freddie! My baby boy! Where have you been?" Freddie instantly whined louder as he licked my face, occasionally stopping to pace around the room then jump back on me; his tail waggling so much his bum couldn't stay still. "I thought I lost you, I was so worried." I hugged him tightly and continued to tell him how much of a good boy he was. Evander sat beside me smiling, his hand outstretched and patting along Freddie's back. "Where did you find him?" I asked as I caught his gaze through my watering eyes.

"Deep in the forest, I was hunting your deer and he came running to me, looks like he was trying to find you, he must have smelt your sent on me because he followed me all the way back. Audric said he was yours when I came up to Gatherling."

"Audric?" He nodded and ruffled Freddie behind the ear, "thank you Evander!" I jumped on him and wrapped my arms around him and held him tight, "I thought he'd been killed . . ." I trailed off as my own words reached my ears and let a long breath out.

"What's wrong? I thought you'd be thrilled?" I leaned back and pulled Freddie onto my lap; my eyes began to water for a different reason.

"I'm so happy to see him, I thought something awful had happened to him but, that's just it. Eventually something awful will happen to him. I have to send him away, he's not safe here and he doesn't belong in this world. Sooner or later, something is gonna get him and either badly hurt him or kill him. I love him too much to watch him die," I breathed out, desperately trying to fight off tears. I ran my hand down Freddie's coat, as he lay across my lap; he looked up to me and licked under my chin; which he always did when I was sad.

"I know," Evander agreed, his voice softened. "I just wanted you to see him first and spend as much time with him as possible. We'll send him to a loving family, where he'll be spoiled rotten. We can go and make the arrangements...when you're ready of course."

"I'm going to stay with him for a while," my voice trembled. Evander nodded, gently kissed the top of my head and patted Freddie, before leaving us.

I hated every moment of saying goodbye to Freddie. The massive pit of guilt reformed in my stomach once again, Freddie had been with me through everything. Every argument my parents had, he'd nudge me and lick my face to cheer me up, and he even threatened to bite my dad once when he was drunk. Freddie was more than a dog to me, more than a protector – he was my family. Would he think I was abandoning him? Would he think that I hated him and didn't care for him anymore?

"I'm so sorry that I'm doing this to you, but it's the only way I can keep you safe. You understand right my beautiful baby boy?" Freddie whined and held his paw out to me, he leaned under my chin and licked me once before pressing his head into my chest. "I love you so much," I whispered in his ear as I held him.

Evander cleared his throat as he slowly approached us, "Narrdie. The arrangements are ready. So, whenever you decide, it doesn't have to be today." Evander said gently; his hand resting on my shoulder.

"Where's he going?" I barely asked, my throat felt like it was going to close up.

"South, far from all of this. He's going to a lovely family; they have a farm and lots of land. He can chase the kids, chickens, horses and everything else he fancies tormenting. He'll be safe, I promise." I smiled, I knew he'd love being around kids and running endlessly all over the place. All I ever wanted, was a home, somewhere in the country where I and Freddie could live in peace – away from everyone.

"Thank you, Evander. It sounds perfect for him."

"Am I interrupting?" My heart immediately dropped, the second I heard his voice.

"Audric. Come in," Evander answered, irritation in his voice. Things had been tense between Evander and Audric since the night in my room.

"I was wondering if I could possibly speak to Narrdie, alone?" Audric was looking down, he fidgeted with the strings of his hoodie. Evander glanced over his shoulder to me, his eyebrow raised in question, I took a breath and nodded.

"Come on Freddie, let's get you some food." The moment Freddie's ears heard the word food, he was out of the room and howling down the corridor, Evander winked to me before closing the door behind him.

"What is it?" I asked Audric nervously.

"I . . . erm . . . well . . . I wanted to apologise for hitting you." His chest extended as he took in a deep breath and eventually looked up to me – his voice sheepish. "I'm really sorry Narrdie, I shouldn't have taken my anger out on you and I shouldn't have put everyone who died on you either. I feel ashamed of myself," he looked down and my heart sank; his eyes seemed cloudy. Seeing Audric standing in front of me, looking so timid and fragile, especially when I hadn't seen him in what felt like forever, made me really realise how much I had actually missed him.

"I forgive you."

"You do?" He asked with a frown, a laugh burst out of me; I grinned widely.

"Yes, you idiot. You think I want to spend the rest of my time without my best friend by my side? Can we just drop this and make up already?"

"That's all I want!" Audric's smile lifted his cheeks, I dived on him and he wrapped his arms around me, lifting me up in a tight squeeze. "So," he began as he backed up from me. "You and Evander?" His raised his eyes teasingly and I jokingly pushed him back.

"This is a discussion we are not and never will be having."

Nyda had asked everyone to gather into the dining hall, which had been completely cleared out so that everyone could fit inside. Evander came up behind me, "everything okay with Audric?" He whispered.

"Yeah, it's great. We've made up and yes he apologised," Evander nodded, and a genuine smile filled his face. "Evander, why are we here?"

"Nyda's about to speak." He warned.

"Greetings friends and family, I would like to start off by thanking you all for coming here." Nyda began as she stood on a plinth in front of everyone; she looked glorious. She wore a sequinned black dress and had her hair pulled back into a long straight ponytail. Smokey grey eyeshadow dusted her eyes and as the candlelight touched her face, her cheeks glittered. "Last month we took a hit, and we lost a lot of good men and women. Each one of them, were some of the bravest warriors our kind could ask for. I am grateful that I've had the privilege of meeting and fighting beside them." I glanced around, most of the group had their heads down, but I could still see the tears that formed in their eyes, the pain that laced the heavy silence. "Tonight, there will be no discussion about our next move, tonight we remember our fallen family and allow those that wish, to say a few words. Audric?" Audric bowed his head and gave Bayona a gentle kiss on the forehead before stepping up and taking over where Nyda stood. He swallowed hard and half smiled to us all, he had a piece of crumpled paper clutched in his hand and a beaded bracelet in the other – a bracelet I remembered Mitchell wearing.

"Thank you, Nyda," he bowed his head to her, a gesture she returned. "I had everything written down that I wanted to say, but now it just seems so . . . rehearsed," he chuckled softly and tucked the paper back into his pocket. "You all knew Mitchell as one of the strongest Watchers in a long time, even The Order relied on him to help with their plans. However, I knew him as only a brother, the brother who raised me to be the man I am today. Watcher or brother, he was strong, brave, smart and tough on us all when he needed to be. After my parents died, Mitchell took it upon himself to become the father I needed, he was my trainer, my guardian and even my enemy when he knew I needed one. I hope that one day, I can be as great as him. Mitchell held so much pride with what he was, but we all saw him turn to that caring and loyal person when it came to his family and friends. Especially his wife and long love Astrid." Evander's fingers slid down and brushed against mine; I couldn't bring myself to meet his eyes.

"Astrid was his partner" Audric continued. "Not just in marriage, but through everything – even in death. I'd never told him how much I appreciated and loved him, and I wish I could have told him how thankful I was and still am for everything he's done." Audric raised his fist into the air and automatically the room copied, his jaw clenched, and I could tell he was holding back the full emotion he was feeling.

Bayona walked forward and embraced him in a hug, she squeezed his shoulder before standing at the front. "Bonjour," she greeted in a sheepish voice. "I'm going to say a few words about someone we all kept close to our hearts, Astrid." My chest tightened, since I first met Astrid, I'd grown very close to her and I just knew that whatever Bayona was going to say, was going to hit me right in my heart. "We all know that Astrid was one of the most wonderful and kind-hearted Elders we all ever met. When I learned about Vampires, I never thought that they could be as loving as her. You get an image in your head about Vampires, they are said to be bloodthirsty monsters, Astrid changed all that, at least she did for me. The moment I met her, I forgot about the stereotypical description for Vampires, I just saw the motherly figure. I used to feel alone and scared, especially when I would get my visions, but when she found me – it felt like home; I never looked back. I asked you all to take a moment and light a candle after this, for Astrid, for Mitchell – for everyone. The mother we all needed. Que les étoiles vous gardent et vous respectent toujours." Bayona kissed her fingers and placed them over her heart, tears falling down her face.

Everyone who wanted to speak took turns taking over the plinth, it wasn't long until everyone's cheeks were stained with track marks from falling teardrops. Apart from me, my tears didn't come anymore; I could feel them, drying up beneath my eyes. I was too angry to cry; instead, I wanted revenge, I wanted the satisfaction of destroying the one person that had done this – the one person, who killed the people who had made me feel at home.

He'd tricked me, made me believe I could put my trust in him. He'd made a fool out of me and I was going to kill him for it.

Dacre.

Chapter Thirteen

"Try again," Fyra commanded with a hiss, I growled under my breath as I jumped to my feet, slapping the dust and mud from my jeans.

"Fyra, go easy," Evander said with a chuckle that didn't quite reach his eyes. His brow creased with worry, each time I fell, I could see him flinch. "Take it easy on her."

Fyra whipped her head in his direction and uncrossed her arms, a cruel smile spread across her maroon lips. "Take it easy?" She repeated in a mocking tone, "Do you think anyone else out there would take it easy on her?" She ran her sharp nails down his cheek, immediately he stepped out of her touch. "Do you think she's ready to face all those things that lurk in the darkness? You praise her, all because she can project her Arma and Lacus jump a few feet?" She scoffed sarcastically; her face dropped into a sneer. "She'd be dead before she even had time to blink." I turned to Evander and offered a gentle smile, shaking my head at him – he wouldn't win an argument with her and the last thing we needed was for her tempter to go up and set everything on fire.

"Evander, she's right. I need to keep going and pushing myself until I can beat you. I'm ready," I assured him. Evander pulled a face but tightened his muscles and crouched ready to attack.

"Good boy," Fyra bit. "Now, begin!"

Evander's boots kicked up bits of mud and stone as he ran for me; he was fast, so fast that it startled me for a second. If I was going to beat him, I either had to be faster, or find a way to get around him – I'd have to outsmart him. I itched forward but Fyra's voice cut into me. "Wait, Narrdie! Focus and stay one step ahead of him." I swallowed and remained still; my blood boiled in my veins. My eyes locked on Evander, taking in every step his feet made on the soil, my head tilted and I had to keep from smirking as I realised a tell-tale sign he had; his eyes quickly darted to my legs – where he was going to attack. I crouched low – ready.

Three, two, one.

He swung at me hard with his fist, I darted to my side and dove onto his back, clinging tight, like a baby monkey holding onto its mama. My arm snaked around his neck, as my other arm locked it in. Of course, I wasn't really trying to hurt him, but I applied just enough pressure – threatening to snap it. I squeezed my legs harder around his waist until his legs buckled and brought us both on the ground, not once did I lighten my hold.

"You give?" I growled viciously – my voice dark.

Evander laughed but it lacked humour; he snarled and grabbed my arms. His strength shocked me as his grip bit down hard; he pried my arms from his neck, almost as easily as if he were snapping a twig from a branch. I winced at the sting of his hold, I already knew that my skin was turning red and sore. He spun me around and threw me forward, my back slammed hard against a tree – the bark scrapping down the back of my arms. It hurt a lot, but I had felt my bones breaking and bruises forming for a while now, I was almost used to it. I slumped down on the bed of the forest and held my hand up in surrender, I couldn't manage to speak through the gasps of air and pain. Evander rubbed his neck as he headed over to me and offered me a hand up, I shook him off and winced as I brought myself to my feet.

"Try again," he teased. I scowled at him and leaned myself against the tree, every inch of my body burned and ached with pain. "You know what you did wrong?" I shook my head, waiting for the breath to return to my lungs. "You got cocky."

"Again," Fyra ordered, looking disinterested as always. Evander rolled his eyes and headed back over to his side. I hissed through my teeth as I took my place – nodding once to him.

Something in me changed. I could feel it – crawling around inside, slithering around my veins – clawing its way to the surface. Whatever it was – it wanted out.

"You ready?" Evander called.

I leaned down, my nails seeming more like talons as they gripped into the tree; my mouth parted, and a smirk pulled at my lips – a low growl rumbled in my throat. My pupils split; I could see everything – every little detail. My hair fell over my shoulder, except it wasn't my hair – it was black and matted. I tried to speak, but my mouth was dry, every move I made, wasn't me – I was no longer in control.

"Narrdie?" Evander's voice was tense as he stood straight; his eyes suddenly widening, he swallowed hard, his eyes catching with Fyra.

"Hello, Evander." The words had come from my mouth, but they weren't mine – they sounded strange, like a cluster of snake- like whispers, forming into one voice. It was like I was watching a movie; I dove onto Evander, my claws began to slash at his chest.

"Narrdie, stop!" He called out as he struggled to keep me back, blood seeped through his shirt from the scratches I'd made. I screamed; I begged, but no matter how hard I tried, I couldn't stop myself. "Narrdie, regain control!" Evander's voice was tense and full of pain.

"Enough Narrdie!" Fyra called, her voice was shaky, she started towards me – her hand raised. "Stop or you'll kill him!" I turned to her, a murderous smile played on my lips, my hand turned into raptor like claws. I snarled as I raised them above my head and slammed them hard into Evander's neck. He roared in agony, his blood pooling around the forest bed – he was going to die.

All of a sudden, I was burning. Fyra stood above me, her eyes wild and hair blowing angrily – fire poured out of her hand. I screamed and cried– writhing around on the floor, the pain was unbearable, the flames tore at my skin, I could feel the heat boiling my insides.

"Enough Fyra!" Evander called breathlessly; his hand gripped her wrist tightly. "I said enough," he repeated sternly. The pain stopped, but I couldn't move – a heavy weight pulled down on my eyes, until everything turned black, and I knew I'd passed out.

*I*t hurt to open my eyes, they felt swollen - like I'd been punched repetitively in the face or stung by a thousand bees. Evander was pacing up and down, rubbing his hands together - the claw marks on his chest already turning into thin white scars. Audric was watching him with a scathing look on his face; he suddenly stood and pushed Evander against the wall. "What the fuck happened to her? What did you do?" He snarled.

"I did nothing," Evander snarled back. "You knew it was bound to happen Audric, it's starting and it's starting a lot earlier than we all thought!" Evander snapped as his eyes darkened. "Now get your hands off me."

"Audric," I called, surprised at how weak my voice sounded. "Let him go." Audric whirled around as I spoke and dropped down beside me, his hand gently gripped mine, as he ran his other over my forehead and down my cheek.

"Hey smiler, how are you feeling?" He asked as he helped me sit up and placed a glass of water at my lips, which I happily gulped down.

"What happened?" I looked to Evander, who was still leaning against the wall. "Evander, I couldn't stop myself . . .I . . .I wasn't in control." Evander shifted slightly and perked his lips together for a moment. He sighed as he crouched beside me and pushed a strand of hair behind my ear. "Evander, what happened to me?"

"I don't know, but I think it's best we stop your physical training for now," Evander suggested. I looked at Audric, expecting him to disagree with Evander but instead he nodded.

"You can't be serious!" I spat. I tried to stand, but Evander gently pushed me back down and shook his head.

"You need to rest, we'll only put off your training for a short while."

"No way! No! I need to learn; I need to learn how to fight if I'm going to kill him!" I blurted then bit my lip to stop myself, unfortunately the look on Evander's face told me, he knew exactly who I meant. Audric however, was too distracted by trying to keep me in bed. Evander raised a disapproving brow towards me, before turning to speak politely to Audric.

"Audric, leave us a moment, Narrdie needs her rest." Audric turned to glare at Evander, I could see the anger beginning to filter through. Evander's face turned hard as he squared up against Audric – a battle of Alphas. "I won't ask again," Evander warned.

"Sure," Audric spoke through gritted teeth. "Get some rest Narrdie, otherwise I'll tell Bayona, and she'll put a charm on you." He teased playfully before he left.

I swallowed hard and waited for the fire storm that was about to erupt from Evander.

"So, you want to kill Dacre?" He asked in a surprisingly calm voice, it was almost comical. I nodded not wanting to look up at him, I knew he would either look incredible mad or look at me like I was a child with her hand in the sweet jar. "I see," he began, as he pulled the forest green armchair closer to the bed. "Well, for one, you have no idea where he is – none of us do. Two, you can barely control yourself and three, he would almost instantly kill you." I scoffed and he gently pulled my chin towards him. "He has so much power Narrdie, you can't even begin to believe what he is capable of. You're not ready to fight him and I'm not ready to lose you," he lightly placed a kiss on my lips. I pulled away from him and let out a long huff.

"You lied Evander. You said you didn't know what happened to me out there." He clenched his jaw and ran a hand through his hair. "You know exactly what that was and for some reason you won't tell me. Why? Why is everyone keeping things from me like I'm some ignorant child that needs protecting?" Evander took my hands into his and half smiled.

"Easy Narrdie. You're right, you aren't a child, but right now you're acting like one. You need to understand, that you are new to this life and the rest of us – we aren't. There are things we can't tell you at the moment, that is not our choice. We have our own laws to abide by and telling you everything straight away, will open up a can of worms. Get some rest and once you're feeling better, I'll come back, and I'll tell you whatever you want to know...within reason."

"Do you promise?" I asked sternly, he half smiled and kissed my knuckles.

"I promise, my Lady."

So far Evander had been truthful, when I woke, he was waiting in the armchair, an old dusty book in his hand. "Enjoying your book?" He smiled as he closed it and set it down beside him.

"I am, you should read this one."

"What's it about?"

"A very stubborn girl," he teased with a smirk. I laughed as I rolled my eyes and threw my pillow at him.

"You're not funny."

"You ready now or do you want something to eat first?" He asked with a worried half smile.

"I wanna know Evander."

Evander linked his arm through mine, as he led me outside; he walked me down the hill and through a deep set of trees. I couldn't see the Gatherling sanctuary anymore and I could feel my hands growing sweaty with nervousness. "Evander where are we going?"

"Just here," he announced as we reached a small clearing in the centre of the trees, I frowned and opened my mouth to speak but was interrupted by the sound of trees straining and groaning as something moved within.

"Evander? Narrdie? What is this?" Indra asked as she stepped into our view; she yawned widely – a puzzled look in her eyes. "Is everything alright?"

Evander bowed his head to her, "my apologies for waking you Indra, I wouldn't have if it wasn't important." Indra nodded and tilted her head.

"What has happened Evander?" Evander ran his hand through his hair and swallowed hard, he signalled for me to take a seat on the forest bed.

"Training with Narrdie has taken a … dark turn," he raised his brows as he looked to her and instantly her eyes widened. She blew out a storm through her nose and lay down – the ground trembling slightly.

"Oh, I see." She was sat in such a picturesque way. *"So, you believe it is time to tell her?"*

"I do, well as much as we can." Evander's voice was cold, and his face was like stone, it grated on me that I couldn't read his face or know what he was thinking.

"But Dacre isn't here, you'll break the pack you made," she cautioned. Evander gave me a sheepish look and bit his lip; he took a deep breath and spoke quickly.

"He's been summoned, that's why we're so far from Gatherling." He let out a long breath and braced himself as he turned to look at me.

"You summoned him here? You said you didn't know where he was!" I snapped, I pushed his chest hard, "you lied!"

"Narrdie," Evander began, but I shoved him again.

"You lied again, Evander." Evander grabbed my wrists and held them tightly in front of me.

"I had to! You were so set on wanting to kill him." Indra breathed loudly through her nose and set her big eyes on me; her eyes smiled, and she nodded reassuringly to me.

"Narrdie, Dacre was there, at the beginning of all of this, as was Evander and myself. There was a pack written in blood that when the day came, we'd all be here to tell you. I know right now you are feeling betrayed and hurt, but it cannot be told without him. If you want to know, now is the time. Will you stay?" She asked me, it was hard to say no to Indra, I don't know what it was about her – but I wanted to please her. I breathed out heavily and sat cross legged beside her, Evander kicked the space beside me – a silent question on his face.

"Just sit," I mumbled.

"Indra, you can start." Indra flashed him a worried look, "Dacre will be here, so the packed is still in tack. You can start."

"Very well."

"One of the most powerful beings this world has ever had the privilege to hold, was the Mage of Light, Lady Ophelia Layvechie Moon. Strong and leader of a large Mage faction, she kept the balance and made sure the tears were controlled. Until Ammon - King of Shades and the Master of Darkness, descended into the world. Both knew how strong the other was and many had died trying to kill them. It quickly became clear that they were the ones capable of killing the other. Both Lady Ophelia and Ammon had a pull to each other, like a magnet, however not in the way that you are probably thinking.

"This pull was created by the Earth itself, nothing and no one was strong enough to kill Ammon, except Lady Ophelia and vice versa. Their magnetic pull to each other wasn't a bond of love, or any other bond you are probably thinking off. It was a bond of death – a fight. One of them had to kill the other. Ophelia wanted to restore the balance and Ammon wanted to break it." I frowned and looked between them; both were intently looking to me.

"But what has this got to do with me?" I asked them, Indra glanced sideways to Evander; he nodded.

"Narrdie, Ophelia was your mother," Evander spoke slowly. My spine locked; my blood turned to ice in my veins – surely this was a cruel joke. It was...impossible. "I know it seems ridiculous, but it's true – your parents were only there to make things seem normal for you," Evander's voice was gentle.

"What year?" I asked, my throat felt dry – like I was swallowing razor blades.

"I don't know exact, Middle Ages maybe," Evander replied as he rubbed his chin. "Well, that's when you came to us."

"Middle Ages?" I was speechless, this couldn't be real. "How old am I?"

"I don't know," Evander said with a sheepish smile.

"So, why . . . why was I with you and not her? Did she not want me?" I asked angrily as I finally managed to get a grip on my voice.

"Of course, she wanted you Narrdie," Indra began, nudging me with her nose. *"You were the daughter of the Mage of Light; Lady Ophelia saw how much power you held the moment you were born; she was so proud to be your mother."*

"Then why did she leave me?"

"When she realised your power, she knew that Ammon and the darkness would see you as a threat. She could easily have protected you, but . . ." She trailed off slightly and looked to Evander with pleading eyes.

"I'll take over," he told her gently, she bowed her head in thanks. "It broke your mother to send you away Narrdie – believe that. However, she had no choice; she saw that you had an almost consuming amount of . . . darkness in you. Darkness which could destroy every bit of light she was sworn to protect." Dizzy, sick, throbbing pains.

"I . . .I have darkness in me?"

"Yes." Evander gently took my hand and gave me a comforting squeeze.

"And it was the darkness that made me, attack you?" It wasn't a question, but he answered anyway.

"Yes."

"How is this possible?"

"Narrdie," Evander's voice was low. "When you were born your soul split, one part filled with the light and the other part – filled with dark. The dark happens to be the part that holds the majority of you power, which is why you change when you lose control. Ophelia knew this the moment she held you; she knew that both sides would want you – claim you or want disposed of you."

"Kill me." He nodded.

"In order to protect you she sent you away, handed you to one of the sacred families, my bloodline. Ammon heard that you were sent away, it took him a few years, but he tracked Ophelia down, tortured her – demanded she tell him where you were. She didn't and . . ." he cut off and looked down.

"And he killed her," I finished for him, he nodded. My heart stung, I'd never known her, never met her – I didn't even know she existed until today. Yet, part of me hoped that maybe she was still alive, hiding somewhere distant and that maybe one day I'd find her, and she'd help me discover who I am.

"After my ancestors heard of Ophelia's fate, they fled and tried their hardest to keep you safe, but the darkness was closing in on them. Ammon's creatures were everywhere, it was getting harder and harder to find people they could trust. After a number of years, they came to me and straight away I sore to protect you. I took you in and my ancestors fled, tried to lead the darkness away."

"I stayed with you?"

"Sadly, not for long. When a high powered being is killed, the Order intervenes and considering you were of importance, they became in charge of who was to protect you. The Order sent you to the strongest and most respected Watchers – Markus and Elizabeth. Naturally, I didn't argue, the Watchers were like royalty back then, in charge of everything – even the darkness kept out of their way. They raised you alongside their daughter and sons, Lilith, Mitchell and Audric." I raised my eyebrows and Evander nodded with a clenched jaw; there was a sadness that glazed over his eyes as he mentioned their names.

"Audric's parents. How old is Audric?" I asked with a nervous chuckle.

"Watchers don't age like humans; they reach an age they feel comfortable at and then they can decide to stay that way, or they can decide to continue ageing." Evander explained with a smile that didn't quite reach his eyes.

"What happened to them?" Evander swallowed; his face shadowed over.

"They died," Indra spoke.

"Protecting me?" I guessed with a sigh; I couldn't handle the thought of being responsible for the death of all of Audric's family.

"No," Indra quickly said, as though she was sensing what I was thinking. *"No, they died protecting Audric. However, Audric does not know that, so I beg you to keep that to yourself, it was Mitchell's wish that he would never know."* I nodded my silent promise and was met with her grateful gaze.

"And Lilith?" Audric had never mentioned his sister, neither had Mitchell or anyone else for that matter.

"Lilith went missing, long before Markus and Elizabeth died. She was tasked by the Order to track down a young Watcher who'd disappeared. Lilith never returned." I looked down, Audric really had lost everyone.

"After Lilith vanished and his parent's death, Mitchell knew neither he nor Audric was ready to protect you. They were still young and training; they had a lot to learn about being a Watcher. Mitchell called upon me to take you somewhere I knew you would be safe, so I brought you to Evander and Dacre – occasionally checking in on you from time to time." Indra explained, she tensed suddenly and the spikes on her back stood erect; she snarled and turned towards the trees.

"You were a lot to handle," a voice called in a wicked tone. Dacre slouched against a tree, tossing an apple up and down in his hands; he smirked as he strutted over towards us, the night light reflecting in his deceiving eyes.

Hate, anger, fury, slammed into me, burning and itching to unleash upon him – an overwhelming urge to pull him apart barrelled against my skin, I growled and rose to my feet. Evander's hand snaked out and gripped my arm tightly – forcing me back.

"Easy Narrdie, he's not really here. He's projecting, his body is elsewhere. We can't hurt him, and he can't hurt us," Evander whispered. "Calm down."

"I've been listening for a while Evander; I hope you aren't going to skip the fairy-tale part. Did you know Narrdie that back then, you and Evander took a real fancy to each other?" He teasingly wiggled his eyebrows and smirked in a mocking way. "Then of course, you tried to kill him...twice. Though, the second time was after you scorched an entire city, destroying and burning men, women and children."

"Dacre!" Evander snarled. I stumbled back and winced, a medley of images began to flicker in my mind – fire and blood, smoke and ash; my ears rang with screams and shrieks. I sank down clutching my head, slamming my fists hard against my temple; my mind felt like a balloon, going up and up – like at any minute it would pop. "Narrdie?" I could feel Evander's hands gripping hold of me, but I couldn't stop the images, I couldn't block out the fear – the pressure in my head continued to pulse against my skull.

"You burned that city and everyone in it," Dacre rambled on. Indra snarled and blocked his vision to me; she hunched low and slammed her foot down in warning – her wing snaked out over me.

I couldn't breathe, the clothes on me felt like they were shrinking, tightening against my frame and making it completely impossible to gain any air. I felt like I was choking, like someone had their hands around my throat and were squeezing the life out of me, the blood in my veins had turned to lava, the moisture to sandpaper – this was going to kill me. Evander crouched over me and took my head in his hands, he held me close to him, saying soothing words into my ear – over and over.

"My head!" I cried.

"Enough Dacre!" Evander barked.

"When we brought you back from the city and into Kibling, which was my sanctuary before it was destroyed," Dacre continued, ignoring Evander; he ducked under Indra's wing and crouched down beside me – his eyes level with mine, holding me in place. "You slaughtered all of Evander's men, like they were nothing . . . nothing but cattle. That feeling you have in your veins, that burning? That's the power, clawing its way out – begging to do it all again. That's who you really are Narrdie – a monster, waiting to be unleashed." He bit into his apple carelessly, and a slimy laugh rolled from his tongue.

"DACRE!"

"I can't remember, I can't remember," I breathed, each word felt like glass shredding against my throat.

"Because I took away your memory and locked you away, it was the only way we could get you to stop killing everyone in your path. I don't remember if you were actually dead or in a very deep sleep. Have you never wondered why your eyes sting when the blood moon comes out, why your body weakens? The blood moon is pure, and it effects the darkness in you – it calls to it and makes it stronger. I removed your memory then I gave you to two people. Aka mummy and daddy, my plan was to get them to beat the good out of you, beat you down to nothing – just a pathetic fragile little girl. Then the dark could consume you and you could become the weapon of destruction, it's what you were born for!" Everything hurt, my head, my stomach and my chest, my whole life had been filled with lies and secrets. I was a monster.

"Enough!" Indra snarled, her voice shaking the trees. *"She needs rest Dacre. What good is she to you like this?"*

"So be it," Dacre snarled, with a cynical smile – he vanished.

"Narrdie?" Evander spoke gently, I couldn't find my voice; all I could feel was the thundering pain in my head. His fingers trying to pry my hands from drumming into my skull, hear his voice echo in my ears – not loud enough to cover the screeches.

I blacked out.

Chapter Fourteen

*E*vander asked me not to tell anyone about Dacre and what had been said, I knew the real reason; he didn't want everyone in the sanctuary to worry; he was scared in case they thought I was going to turn and hurt them. It hurt, but I'd agreed, however one person was allowed to know and his reaction was almost too much for me to take. Audric had gotten in such a rage, that his fist slammed right into Evander's nose and once again I'd had to stand between them, he'd then gone out and given Indra an earful.

"What the fuck did you expect?" He'd snarled at Evander as I struggled to keep him contained on the wall, Evander's eyes had glowed bright as he covered his bleeding nose. "Did you think Dacre was just going to come and help you talk to her? You played right into his hands, look at the state of her! The state you put her in, this is on you Evander!" I wanted to protest, but he was right – since that night I hadn't slept properly and when I did sleep – I'd wake with bedsheets drenched in sweat and screams in my ears, bags the size of ping pong balls camped under my eyes, whenever I tried to eat a meal – I'd throw it up almost instantly.

"Please don't," I begged him. My hands trembling against his weight. He breathed out hard through his nose, but thankfully I felt his weight shift, his tense muscle relax – slightly. Audric had called Bayona to help me sleep, reluctantly he'd made up a cover story, saying that my Arma had gotten the best of me and wiped me out, of course she'd agreed and made me a weird looking pink drink that seemed to ease me.

The nights without her pink drink, were nothing but endless torture. I still couldn't manage to shake the images that continued to carousel in my head, they were like a constant video tape caught on a loop. I was used to sitting in the dark, but now, I was afraid of it, I'd ask Evander or Audric to stay with me most nights – just long enough for me to fall asleep, but even Evander couldn't make the monster go away.

I'd been working hard with them, leaning how to manipulate my abilities and make sure I didn't lose control. Aronnia helped with calming my Spirit and teaching me how to maintain a comfort zone, of course she was more than happy to help – bubbly as always and her methods seemed to work to a certain extent.

When the day would grow dark, Evander, Audric or Bayona would take over and that was when the pain began – each night I'd go to bed with fresh marks – the brown purple of bruised fruit. I got knocked down – a lot, but each time I went down, I felt myself get back up, stronger and more determined.

*A*udric walked beside me with a giant grin and gently batted my arm with his elbow. "So, is your training going well?" He asked, his body jittered with so much excitement – like a little kid waiting to open their presents on Christmas day.

I laughed, "I'm guessing you were watching?" I was still trying to catch my breath, I rubbed the back of my neck and lifted up my damp sweaty hair into a loose bun.

"You bet your little ass I was! I can't believe you out-witted Bayona, she didn't even see you coming!" He bellowed and ruffled my hair. "I don't think I've ever seen her so shocked before, I'm proud of you Moon."

"And I stayed in control," I chimed. He half smiled and plonked down onto the training mat, his hand snaked up and pulled me down beside him – I laughed loudly.

"How has everything been?" He asked and gave me a stern look, I sighed.

"Great," I lied.

"Narrdie."

"Okay not great," I admitted as I rested my head between my knees. "I haven't had a full night's sleep in so long, when I do sleep – I picture the burning city, I hear the screams and they won't go away Audric, it's like I watch myself do it. I beg and beg to stop, but the fire keeps burning and to think I thought badly of Fyra for doing the same thing I did, how's that for hypocritical." Audric sighed and patted my hand.

"Narrdie, you can't blame yourself for that, it wasn't your fault . . . it wasn't you."

"I know, it was the dark in me. The thing that can take over at a moment's notice according to Dacre."

"Narrdie."

"You know sometimes I think I can feel it - sleeking around like a snake, waiting for its moment to strike. I'm scared Audric." He took my hand in his and clenched his jaw. "I'm scared I'll hurt one of you."

"I know you are, but you're not alone. I've got you; I always have, and I always will – it's you and me, always. Besides, every single person in there has your back, not because they have to, but because they all love you. Remember that Narrdie, they love you, not the dark, because that's not who you are. You are Narrdie Moon, strong, brave . . ." He gave me a one-armed hug and pecked me on the top of the head. "And in desperate need of a long sleep and a shower . . . with soap." I scowled and dug him hard in the ribs. "Don't start with me," he warned playfully.

"Or what?" I teased as I dug him in the ribs once more; I jumped to me feet and took my stance. "Let's go Slater, I've got one round left in me."

All of a sudden, Nyda erupted into the room, a frantic look smeared all over her face, she was breathing hard when she spoke; her eyes were wide as they flicked between the two of us. "Audric, Narrdie, come now."

"What's going on Nyda?" Audric asked, his voice held no hint of the playfulness it just had, instead it was serious; he jumped to his feet and pulled me up with him.

"Indra is hurt," she gasped, it was enough to make us both race out of the room and head to the outside grounds.

"Why is there always something?" I cursed.

Indra rested her head along the forest bed; her spikes flopped over on her back and her wings sprawled along the leaves. Aronnia was knelt down beside her, the pale pink gown she wore spread around her like a flowers petals; she hand her hand down Indra's neck, whispering an unknown language in her ear - I assumed it was soothing words. Erenna was knelt on the mud, her olive dress stained and clumped with dirt, her hands were covered in a green paste - that reminded me of guacamole - applying it gently to her right wing, which was smothered in blood. The majority of Gatherling was gathered around her, my heart thudded as I got closer, seeing the full extent of Indra's wound, it was shredded like torn up bedsheets. "What happened?" Audric quizzed.

"Dacre shot me down," Indra answered, her voice slightly shaken, she lifted her lip and growled as pain shot through her.

"The spear has fractured her bone. It has splintered, this will hurt my friend," Erenna warned with remorseful eyes - Indra nodded.

"Shouldn't the healers be here?" I asked Evander.

"The healer's medicine wouldn't work," Erenna answered, her voice tense. "I'm trying my own remedy from the natural gifts of the Earth. Dacre must have poisoned the tip of his spears, I'm afraid you will not be able to fly for a while, not until I am certain I have drawn all the poison out. I will do what I can," Erenna informed Indra, Indra's eyes smiled to her.

"Thank you, dear friend. Your treatment has taken a mass amount of pain from me, I owe you." Erenna bowed her head back to Indra, giving her a warm smile. Aronnia looked to her sister, gratitude in her watery eyes, before they snapped around to the mass crowd that had formed to watch, her hair darkened, and a harsh wind slapped at my skin.

"We do not need an audience," she hissed, her voice a terrifying cluster.

"You have better things to be getting on with, away with you!" Audric ordered, some immediately scurried inside - while others placed their fist over their chest and bowed first. "How did this happen?" Audric asked softly as he turned back to Indra.

"I was flying over the east, he was waiting - I do not know how long he was there. He shot me down and sent a messenger to me when I landed. He said that Gatherling is breached, and the darkness is gathering their army; he is wanting you all to flee. I made sure they didn't follow me here." Everyone began talking at once, their voices ranging from alarmed and angry, to scared

162

and frantic – as they overlapped each other, the tension in the room beginning to thicken like fog.

"But the glamour, how did he see through it?" I asked, projecting my voice over them in order for them to stop, I was grateful that no one looked at me like an uneducated human.

"The glamour only works on humans, but it might be an idea to extend it to the dark dwellers as well," Evander suggested and flashed me a wink that made my insides tingle and cheeks flush red.

"That's if they don't swarm us here first," Nyda sniped.

"How many other sanctuaries are there?"

"I own one more and there are a few others down south, but it's too far to travel by foot and taking cars is risky. Dacre has never been to this sanctuary; I doubt he'll be able to find this place." Dacre had deceived us before – he was the knife in the dark that you never saw coming, Evander may have been convinced – but I wasn't.

"What if he's not bluffing?" I argued. "I know he's a manipulative prick, but what if this is real?"

"What if he is bluffing because he wants to pick us off on the road?" Audric countered; his face had pulled into tense lines.

"What would you rather, being trapped in one place with only one exit and be slaughtered like pigs, or out in the woods. . ."

"And hunted like rabbits instead?" Nyda scoffed.

"We'd have a better chance out their, Nyda," Evander interrupted before myself and Nyda began to bicker.

"So, even you think we should leave?" Everyone suddenly went quiet, waiting edgily for Evander's next words – this was his sanctuary and if he said move, we'd move. Nyda stepped forward and spoke through clenched teeth; her hands clenched beside her.

"We can't keep running Evander," Nyda snapped before he could suck in air to speak.

"We can't stay here if the place is breached either Nyda, we saw how many Dacre has behind him already and I'm not the only one who knows that we aren't ready." Audric barked at her.

"You might not be ready little Watcher, but me and mine are."

"Enough," Evander growled. "You're all giving me a headache. We aren't going anywhere, I strongly believe that Dacre is trying to fool us all, so until we know otherwise, we stay put." The crowd blew up again, half arguing that Evander was right, and we should stay and the other half saying that we were sitting ducks if we did. Nyda and Audric began to square off with each other and I could feel the heat radiating from them both, see the shaking of Nyda's fingers as her power gathered in her palm.

Bayona suddenly dropped down and gasped, her black empty eye sockets bleeding like a waterfall, she cried out pain; her back arching like something out of a horror movie. "Bayona?" Audric darted to her side and quickly gripped hold of her hand – his skin immediately turning pale and gaunt. Aronnia gripped her other hand – feeding her strength to them both.

"D-Dacre," she mumbled with a wince. "I can see him. . . He's leading a handful of his army somewhere. I-It's foggy though, he's got some kind of block on him," she gasped as another strike of pain rippled through her. "I-I can't see where."

"Look harder," Nyda ordered in an aggressive tone, she took a step closer, a small edge of anger vibrated under my skin as I blocked her path.

"Back off Nyda," I warned.

"It hurts to read," Bayona rasped, she shuddered slightly and gripped onto Aronnia tighter – who cooed soothing words into her ear. "Someone is channelling him."

"What does that mean?" I asked as I looked to Evander.

"It means a Witch is blocking us from seeing him. Do your best Bayona," Evander coached her softly. My heart ached for her, the blood from her eyes poured down her face. I wished I knew a way to help her, but even Audric and Aronnia looked strained.

"Take all my strength, dear one," Aronnia lulled.

"Is he coming here?" Audric asked in a soft voice.

"No," I interrupted; I gasped, I couldn't see Nyda or Evander or anyone else for that matter, my vision flickered like tuning an old TV. Then, like a movie playing in my head – I saw Dacre, as smug as always. He was circled by the same kind of creatures that had attacked us, his hands outstretched and mouth moving fast. All my muscles screamed with pain, my head felt like it was being bashed over and over with a hammer, I could taste iron on my tongue and felt a sharp aching in my belly, however my eyes – my eyes felt like someone had stuck a hold poker in them. "He's back tracking," my voice was weak, barely even vocal – something wet slid down my cheek and I knew it was blood.

I felt someone's hand snake in mine, gripping tightly – another rested on my back, keeping me up. The moment my skin touched theirs, I could feel the strength – my body latched onto it, sucking up as much as it could, it was like lemonade on a hot day. "I've got you," Evander whispered in my ear, his breath warming the back of my neck.

"Narrdie, are you seeing this too child?" Wenona asked, her voice full of astonishment. I nodded and winced as I gripped Evander tighter, the block on Dacre burned my skin.

"Lean into me," Evander said as he pulled me against him.

"Astonishing, you are even stronger than we thought. Can you see where or why he's back tracking?"

"He's . . . he's heading to back near our home," Bayona's voice wasn't as pain filled anymore, whatever pain she did have – was now being shared out between us.

"He's leading them past it and towards . . . my college?" I gasped; Dacre was staring at something . . . at me. His face twisted into fury; his lips pulled back over his teeth in a snarl, he lunged.

"No!" Bayona shouted as she appeared in the vision, she gripped my shoulders and pulled me down to the floor. An ear-splitting screeched left my mouth as I felt myself being ripped out of the vision, it felt like a brute forced had just slammed me hard in the chest. I was pushed back, but strong hands wrapped around me and held me tightly, Evander turned me to face him – his eyes scanning me over for any sign of injury.

"Narrdie, look at me. Are you alright?" He quizzed, I nodded and leaned onto him. "How did you do that?"

"I don't know," my voice was hoarse. "I just wanted to take some of her pain away and then I suddenly started to see it, my eyes?" My hand shot up and felt the wetness, I pulled my fingers into view and saw the thick red that lingered.

"A cold flannel will help with the aching," Bayona called to me, her voice as equally strained as my own.

"Don't ever do that again. If you force visions, you could lose your sight or worse, it could take all your strength and kill you," Evander warned sternly. "Still, that was very brave of you," his thumb lightly brushed my cheek – the tip of his thumb smearing the blood on my cheek; her leaned down and kissed the top of my head. "My brave girl," he purred in my ear.

"He's going for the college?" Audric repeated through gritted teeth; his fist balling up, I had almost forgotten about the visions, I was so lost in Evander's touch.

"Why would he do that? What's the college go to do with this?" I asked my voice taking a sudden shake to it.

"It's to get out attention. He wants to see what we've got, and he knows that if he takes a horde to the college, we'll have to stop him, otherwise . . ."

"Otherwise, humans will find out everything," I finished for him, he nodded. Dacre – the definition of a conniving evil monster. I hate him, I hate him, I hate him.

"That coward," Evander hissed.

"Coward or not, he's gotten what he wants. We're gonna have to do something, otherwise a lot of people are going to die." I announced and was relieved when everyone nodded in agreement.

I didn't realise how much preparation had to be done before we could even leave, Evander seemed to have everything under control, he was so quick at answering their questions and barking orders. The rest of us focused on arming ourselves with countless amounts of weapons, Audric was beside me, occasionally he'd turn to me to tighten the buckles that kept my weapons strapped. A row of throwing knives strapped around each forearm, two dual swords rested against my thigh, everything felt so heavy. "We don't want them sliding off before the fight even begins," he teased, I looked at his face expecting to see nerves, but there was nothing – more excitement than worry,

"Shouldn't we have guns?" I asked him, he frowned but it quickly faded and was replaced with a smile.

"I forget that this is still fresh for you," he admitted as he finished tightening the last buckle on my boot – sliding a silver dagger inside. "Bullets don't work on the supernatural, these weapons that Evander and every other sanctuary has, have been around for centuries. Formed for this purpose. Bullets will pierce, maybe even slow them down a little; however, they won't kill. Are you nervous?" He asked me as he took my head in his hands, I swallowed hard; I'd be lying if I told him, I was fine. I'd never been in a fight like this – I'd never been in a fight at all and when it came down to it, could I really take my sword and kill something or someone.

"I'm a little scared," I confessed. "What if I can't . . . you know."

"Kill?" He finished, I nodded sheepishly and bit my lip, to my surprise he laughed and lifted my head up. "Don't look so ashamed about that, it's what makes you, you. When you see those creatures and when you realise that all they want to do is tear you apart, that feeling to fight will push aside the fear. I promise you; we've all had that pre-killing scare. I vomited my first time, so did Mitchell." He smiled confidently to me and I nodded to him and forced my lips to a wide smile. His words were uplifting but it still wasn't enough to stop my heart from falling into my stomach. Audric patted me on the shoulder, before heading over to check on a few other people. I ducked out before anyone had a chance to see me.

The second I reached my room – I vomited.

Everyone had finished getting into armour and locking in their weapons when Nyda spoke up. "I don't think this is a good idea," she began to mumble.

"Nyda, we've discussed this."

"We are all going to die!" She snapped as she threw down her spear. A sudden ominous silence fell around the group, the clattering of swords and steel died away. "This is a trap to kill us all and take Narrdie and you are all so willingly playing into it!" She shouted as she moved around, reaching everyone's eyes. "Fools," she sniped. "We are going to be slaughtered, before this war even begins!"

"Nyda, please," Evander began, his voice a mixture of irritation and tiredness, he rubbed his temples and walked over to stand in front of her. "Enough, we have no time for this."

"She is not ready!" She hissed as she pointed a crooked finger towards me, my blood bubbled. "We are all going to die for some worthless humans!" I snarled and marched over to her, my hand shot out and gripped hold of her hand tightly, forcefully I pushed her back until I had her pinned against the wall.

My voice turned dark. "A large number of human beings are about to be slaughtered by someone, you all," I raised my voice on the last word, so that I could grab everyone's attention and let them know this was meant for everyone to hear. "Failed to notice was no longer fighting on your side! You all should also be aware how dangerous this is for us. The humans aren't weak and pitiful, once threatened they will attack with lethal force and they won't stop until they win or until they are dead. It'll be a blood bath on all sides!" I stepped closer to Nyda, my face inches from hers. "So, get your people ready and keep your mouth shut. Understand?" I glared at her, I could feel her whole body shaking under my hold, it gave me great satisfaction to know that I had won this argument. She swallowed, her breath shuddering and nodded her head frantically, I narrowed my eyes and growled. "I can't hear you; they can't hear you."

"I-I understand," she gulped.

"Good," I whispered and slowly moved back from her. "Go and make sure everyone is gathered outside and await Evander's orders." She bowed and quickly scurried away; clicking her fingers so that her men would swiftly follow her. I turned to face the crowd that still stared at me in marvel, their eyebrows raised – eyes wide and mouths hanging open like they were catching flies. Evander and Audric were stood beside each other, stifling their laughs, they caught my eye and smirked to me, I bit the inside of my cheek to keep myself from laughing.

"Stop standing around," Evander finally announced. "There is still a lot to do, fifteen minutes and I want you all outside. Come on, move!" He bellowed, the elephantine sound of footsteps began almost immediately, whispers quickly turning into load murmurs and the sound of clashing metal bellowed in my ears again.

Audric and Evander swayed over to me, pleased and proud grins on their faces. "Well, well, well Narrdie. You certainly told her, didn't you?" Evander said in a playfully strict voice, "no, honestly Narrdie. I'm amazed, that right there, is the person you really are and the person you always will be. You need to stop shutting it away, use it and wash away the doubts in these people's minds." Evander said cheerfully as he pecked me on the cheek. "Now, outside ten minutes," he ordered lightly before marching off in a gathering of soldiers.

"I knew you had it in you Moon," Audric chimed as he lightly punched my arm. "I'm glad that you're on our side, otherwise we'd never stand a chance. To think I was going to ask you to stay here," he teased.

"Silence!" Evander yelled over the awaiting soldiers. "Narrdie and Audric will be the ones leading us, as they know the college. Narrdie?" I nodded and walked to stand on the rock that Evander had stepped down from, I was quickly aware of all the eyes that were now fixed onto me, I could feel the goosebumps prickle my skin, the hollow pit of nerves in my gut and my hands threatening to shake at my sides. I was never good at speaking to large groups, but this was my life now – I was to be a leader and leaders guided their people. Audric crooked his eyebrows and quickly took a step behind me, I was grateful, him just being there helped confidence swim in my veins.

"The college has two buildings that are separated by the yard, there are two exits, the main gates at the north end and a small gate at the south. The perimeter of the college has an eight-foot fence all around it. However, it will be no trouble at all for Dacre and his followers to tear down, each building is four stories high so I would watch out in case enemies fall from above." No one looked worried or scared like I thought they would be, I suppose they had done this many times over their lives. "I have discussed with Evander, Audric and the other members of the . . ." My cheeks immediately flushed red, I felt so embarrassed that I had forgotten the name Evander had called the meetings between, me, Audric, Nyda, Bayona and the sisters.

"Pura Mensam," Bayona whispered to me, the word curling elegantly off her tongue.

"Thanks," I whispered back to her. I swallowed hard and prayed that I wouldn't sound ridiculous as I tried to repeat the word as easily and gracefully as Bayona. "I have discussed with the members of the Pura Mensam about how we will attack." Audric cleared his throat, I leaned my head back – just enough to give him a subtle nod; he smiled and took a step forward.

"The Order have had people on the inside, a few Tutors and even some students, they have already been contacted and have been tasked with evacuating the college, but in a way that Dacre won't notice. When the attack begins, those members will join us in defending the humans, they will be wearing the Orders crest. Evander?" Audric called moving to stand with me as Evander took his place.

I couldn't help but rack my eyes over him, he looked powerful. Leather plates of armour strapped tightly to his chiselled chest, his hair tied back in a tight plait – even the way he carried himself made my knees weak, my skin flush – I had never wanted him more. "Drool much?" Audric mumbled in my ear, snickering to himself. I stifled my giggle and lightly elbowed him, even Audric looked like a Viking ready to kill.

Evander began in a stern voice. "We'll be splitting into three groups; our main priority is the humans and to get them out. Sharia, Wenona and Indra and the guards that aren't coming with, you will stay here and protect Gatherling, if it is threatened then evacuate as quickly as you can."

"Why can't I come?!" Sharia protested with a snarl, Evander walked off the rock and headed towards her. He caringly stroked her cheek, ever since I had been here, I noticed a strong relationship between them – almost like Evander had taken it upon himself to become a sort of brother to her.

Sharia was a skilled fighter, one I had seen for myself, but I knew why Evander wanted her to stay; he'd said she was young in her race, still coming into her full power and that her changes could become unpredictable – even uncontrollable.

"Because, little lion," Evander softly spoke, his voice cheery. "We need someone brave, strong, fast – someone who knows these grounds like the back of their hand, and you are the only one besides me, who knows the underground escape tunnels. You are responsible for all of these people that are staying behind, as well as the Goddess Wenona herself. I need you to protect and keep everyone safe. Can you do that for me?" Her disappointed and hurt expression completely evaporated, she smiled widely and nodded to him and then to me – she straightened her back and bowed her head.

"I'll have the healers set up for your safe return, as well as everyone prepared in case, we are attacked here." She looked over to Aronnia, Fyra and Erenna, "I will also have someone constantly with Indra and will make sure your sister is safe," she assured them, the sisters all smiled and bowed to her.

"With you here, little one. I know my sister is in good hands," Fyra told her warmly.

"We will be fine," Wenona assured Evander, she turned to her sisters and a flicker of fear crossed her face. "Be safe," she told them, her voice shaky. They all took a moment to place their palms together and rest their heads against each other, it was sweet, but I could see the mist that gathered in their eyes.

"Aronnia," Evander called, regaining the attention of the crowd. "We will need you to give us a bit of cover, the more cover we have, means it'll be harder for the horde to see the humans and harder for the humans to see the horde. Attack from above and keep an eye out, make sure none of them try and ambush us."

"I will watch over you all," Aronnia lowered her head in a slow bow; her hair falling around her face.

"Audric, Fyra, Nyda and troop A are with Narrdie, you will be covering the south of the school, we expect the horde is most likely to attack from there. Bayona, Erenna and troop B, are with me, we will be covering the northern side of the school. Troop C, I want you all to focus on getting the humans out, ignore the horde if you can, you get the humans out and lead them to safety. It is important that you don't lose sight of them, we'll need the Order to contain whatever they have seen. You all know where you are attacking from. Remember your training, don't take any unnecessary risks. Let's move out!" I pulled Audric and Evander to one side and waited until the bulk of the group had shifted away from us.

"The plans are really good, Dacre isn't going to know what hit him," Audric burst gleefully, Evander's eyes narrowed on me, he clenched his jaw.

"What is it?" He asked me in a semi- irritated voice, I had a feeling he already knew what I was going to say.

"I want Dacre," I said bluntly.

Audric snorted, "are you kidding? Narrdie, almost an hour ago you were worried that you wouldn't be able to kill anything and now you've suddenly gotten over that and you want to face Dacre? No way in hell! Mitchell and Astrid, couldn't even face him and they were some of the strongest fighters we had. It's not happening." Audric took a step towards me. "And the minute I see you even attempt to fight him; I will personally drag you back here."

"I agree with Audric. Dacre is far too dangerous. I suggest that everyone try and stay clear of him. It's best to tackle him as a team," Evander suggested, his stare locked me in place – it seemed if I wanted Dacre, I would have to do it when these two weren't around.

"Fine. Let's go."

A white fluffy snow drop lightly landed on my nose; I glanced up and tilted my head as more fluffy flakes drifted from the sky, which was overcast with the threat of a storm. My hand caught a flake, watching as it slowly began to melt in my warm palm.

"Snow," I said entranced – my voice not quite my own. Evander froze, he looked back to me with semi- wide eyes.

Audric lightly pulled on my sleeve; his voice was gently – careful.

"Narrdie, c'mon." I blinked several times before I managed to look back up to them. Evander clenched his jaw and swallowed hard.

Even I felt concerned about what had just happened, I had seen snow loads of times, but this time it had called to something inside me. It was like the snowdrops were hypnotic to me and all I could think about was blood and how blood always looked better on snow.

"I'm alright," my voice trembled.

The college was built around a wide forest, something that thankfully worked to our advantage, it was their way of giving the students a peaceful and private place to study – obviously forgetting that it could also be dangerous when the days grew dark. The snow was gaining heavier, and a cold wet mist began to grow along the grounds, I glanced up, but I could barely see Aronnia anymore.

My eyes locked onto the school, waiting for the horde to strike, my hands were clammy as they gripped the blade – fire burned in my belly and my heartbeat went arrhythmic.

"There," Audric whispered to me as he pointed straight ahead.

Dacre was stood at the south gates, lips sprawled into a cynical grin and a look of hunger shining in his eyes. Prick. I forced a steady breath to fill my too-tight lungs, begged the lightening thrashing through my veins to calm; I knew the horde wouldn't be far behind him. He straightened out his black leather jacket and smoothed out his hair, before he raised his hand – calling the horde forward.

There were hundreds of them, way more than Lazarus Mountain, the vision only showed us a handful, a terrifying chill crawled up my spine – the vision was a trick. This was a trap – *'And like lambs to a slaughter, we shall follow.'*

"Dear god," Audric breathed, his eyes widened – gone was the excitement, gone was the sureness.

The horde raced forwards and surrounded the school; they were practically vibrating with anticipation as they waited for Dacre's approval. Dacre smiled contemptuously before perching his lips together and letting out a high-pitched whistle. The second his whistle reached their ears; they screeched, wailed and hissed as they began to tear apart the buildings and climb over each other to get inside, running like wild beasts on all fours – punching through walls like tissue paper.

Carnage, totally terrifying carnage consumed the school, students and teachers began running for the gates or any other possible way they could escape.

Screams filled the air.

"Evander!" I called over.

"Aronnia, now!" Evander called to her. Aronnia shrieked, the sound as high as a banshee – deafening in my ears. A wave of lightening thrashed to the ground, the sound roaring in my ears; it crashed in a line one after the other, forming a barrier between the darkness and the humans – some dared to cross it and were met with their skin frying or suddenly bursting in nothing but a puddle of flesh and blood.

"KILL HER! KILL HER!" Dacre snarled, his eyes flashing with rage as he pointed to Aronnia. She landed hard on the ground, facing off against them all; hands outstretched – sparks dancing along her arms. They shot towards her in big groups, but each time one reared close, it was sent flying backwards by a blast of skin tearing wind or sharp electric, she opened her mouth and let out another bansheed screech, stopping them in their tracks.

Evander, rushed forward. "Stay close," Audric breathed in my ear, before giving our troops the signal to follow.

Outnumbered. Overwhelmed. Separated.

Everything went wrong fast – too fast and I felt scared for us all. Most of my troop were dead within the first half an hour, Shades had swarmed us, they had been waiting, waiting until they saw me – unleashing such power that I was lucky to evade.

I had lost everyone, and it seemed Dacre was always one step ahead of us. I continued to cut down creatures and shout at the humans to run towards the woman in the white armour – Aronnia, she'd covered them with mist so the darkness couldn't see where they ran. After I had cut down the first creature without vomiting, it had gotten easier and easier. I frantically raced around, diving and weaving in and out, as I desperately tried to find someone. "Evander? Audric?" A bubbled growl echoed in my ear from behind, shuddering across my skin. I turned, only to be face to face with a Skecig – a creature I'd only seen in the books.

It looked like it was made of shadows, bold red eyes were too large amongst the drifting black mist and an array of wide, large teeth spread along the full width of it. Four long arms, each one with several talons on the end. It lunged forward, spinning round, those talons twirling like a blender, I dropped low, spinning on my foot, so that I was almost on the ground. Pulling my twin blades from their hilts and slashed up into what I assumed would be its belly. It shrieked, as black tar spilled out covering over me, the smell made bile burned my throat; I jumped to my feet and swung my sword down its arms, before finally digging my blades into its red eyes.

I had no time to wipe the tar from my face as something hard barrelled into me and knocked me down, a tongue wiped out and lashed across my cheek, the touch scolding into my skin. A Broc, they were the pawns of the dark, expendable, weak and multiplied like rabbits – best thing, they were easy to kill. The reminded me of frogs, hunched on all fours; their back legs slightly to long for their bodies and covered in puss filled boils. I swung my crossbow into my hands and fired two arrows, it cried and gurgled as is shook and erupted into sticky blue liquid.

"Bayona? Nyda?" I called, no one was answering. I fought down that gut feeling that was telling me, they were dead. I wouldn't allow myself to believe it – I refused.

Bodies dotted the grounds like daisies, a mixture of my people, Dacre's and humans – too many humans. How could the Order even think it was possible to hide this from them? In less than an hour so much blood had been spilled, so many innocents had been torn down like they were nothing.

"NARRDIE!" A girls' voice bellowed at me.

I froze and my heart dropped into my stomach. "Alaska." Dacre, curled his lip as he held Alaska in a firm choke grip, his bold yellow eyes locked onto me.

"Hello again, Narrdie," he called in a chirpy voice, his hand stroked Alaska's hair. The other creatures didn't dare approach me; I knew why – I was his to kill and his alone. "I believe you already know Alaska, she said she knows you."

"Dacre, let her go." I promised Audric and Evander that I would stay clear of him no matter what, but now that he was here – I wanted him. Alaska's eyes were wide, shocked that I was here and in full fighting gear and fear that her life could end at any minute.

I spotted Evander a small distance behind where Dacre stood, relief flushed into me, more when I saw he'd found Audric. They pressed back-to-back, surrounded by a small pack of Skinners, Evander ducked under Audric's arm – thrusting his sword forward, until it pierce the chest of the Skinner that lunged at him. He looked around and froze as he spotted me; his eyes widening when they landed on Dacre.

"Narrdie, no!" Evander ordered, both fighting harder and faster so they could get to me.

"Take them out!" Dacre sniped aggressively to two Shades that flanked him. "I don't like interruptions." The Shades shot forward in a cloud of smoke, materializing in front of Audric and Evander – blocking their view from me. I wanted to run to them, help them fight, but leaving Alaska to the mercy of Dacre – was not an option.

"Dacre, let her go, it's not her you want." My heart began to bray against my chest.

"Please, I just wanna go home," Alaska begged before Dacre dug his claws into her shoulder. She shrieked, crimson lines formed along her shoulder; her blood lightly started to overflow and made little indents in the snow – I tingled as I watched them, Dacre's laugh was heinous.

"It grows inside of you; I can smell it. Evander and Audric think they can train it out of you. You know as well as I do, that it bubbles and creeps to the surface, it won't be long until it takes over," he grinned widely.

"If you let her go, you'll have my full attention. I swear it." He snickered but released her. Alaska hobbled over to me and almost dropped into my arms; tears spilled all over her face. "Alaska, run to the main gate, don't stop! Find the woman in white. Go, now!"

"W-What about you?" She asked through little pants and breaths; she gripped onto my hand. "Come with me," she begged.

"Go now! I'll be fine!" She swallowed hard, as much as me and Alaska didn't like each other in the past, I could see in her eyes that she didn't want to leave without me. We shared a look and she finally nodded, she squeezed my hand and quickly ran towards the main gate, where Aronnia would hopefully be waiting.

Dacre and I began to circle each other like animals. Looking at him made my blood burn for revenge, I wanted to make him pay for what he had done; I wanted to cut him open and take his heart out.

"Narrdie!" Bayona called, she raised her hands and began chanting under her breath, Dacre growled with frustration as he set his eyes on her.

"We can't get any privacy with all your protectors hanging around, time for a change of scenery, don't you think?" Before I could react, Dacre lunged at me; he gripped hold of me and I felt my whole body being pulled in all different directions, wind diving down my throat – trying to pull my insides out.

Dacre let me go once we emerged in a dark forest, I jumped back from him and threw my Alma around me – it was glowed grey, dark like my surroundings, "Where are we?" The trees around us were black and rotted from the inside out – nothing had grown here for years, their roots looked infected and a weird pulse beat from the trunk. The floor seemed to be covered in flakes of ash and there was an unpleasant smell, like decaying meat - lingering in the air. I took a step back, my boots crunching underneath me, my skin turned cold, the blood icing over in my veins as I looked down . . . bones. So many bones.

"Somewhere private," he replied casually, as he paraded around with his hands spread out, "you like it?"

"It suits you well," I sneered. "Empty and rotting, like your heart." He scoffed. "Why Dacre? Why betray us? Why betray your friends?" I asked, as much as I wanted to kill him, being alone with him made shivers trickle down me, there would be no one – no one to rescue me, no one to cover my back. Realistically, I knew I was no match for him right now and he knew it, which only made him taunt me more.

"We were friends?" He mocked.

"Not me, Mitchell, Evander!"

"Because good never wins, Narrdie," he answered with a shrug of his shoulders. "Life's not a fairy-tale, no matter how much you try and believe it is." He narrowed his eyes and croaked a laugh, "if only you could see your eyes. There is so much anger, so much hatred for me - I bet you want nothing more than to kill me. Is that it?" He teased, I dug my nails into my palms, I could feel the sharp sting as they cut into my skin, but it was nothing compared to the fury I felt for him.

"Did you even feel anything?" I bit. He paused and raised his brow curiously; his smug smile dropping slightly.

"About what?"

"About Astrid and Mitchell. About all the others, you're the reason they died." His jaw clenched. "The people you once called family and you did nothing." He bared his teeth, his eyes flaming angrily.

"They chose the wrong side; they chose their fate! Just like you! I gave you the option to come with me, you're too caught up in spreading your legs for Evander. I wonder, how long did it take until he had you?" My breath caught in my throat; his laugh was sickening. "I can smell him on you."

"Are you jealous Dacre?" I sneered.

He snarled and dived towards me, but this time I was ready. I dropped down onto the ground and watched as Dacre slammed into the tree behind me – it groaned, the bark splitting down the middle. A low grumble echoed in his throat as he picked himself up and dusted himself off, "this, will be fun," he mocked. "Think you're strong enough to take me Narrdie?"

"I'm strong enough to kill you." He dove at me again. I sprung up, twisting my body over him; I dug my nails into his shoulder until I had a good grip. I forced myself forward, digging my other hand into him, gripping tightly as I lifted him and threw him forward. Dacre slid along the floor, thrusting his claws into the ground to steady himself; he snarled and rose to his feet. My muscles screamed at me, burning – I had already exhausted myself.

The Earth shook and cried out as a tree was ripped from the ground, lifted so effortlessly. My eyes widened as he hauled it forward with impeccable speed. I darted left and winced as the tree scrapped across my arm; I looked, as the blood began trickle down to my hand. Dacre moved on me before I could gather myself; he grabbed me from behind and swiftly plunged his daggers deep into my chest.

I had gone through a lot of pain since I was with Audric and his family, Egregious in the park, Egregious in Astrid's' room. Melphos and the purple liquid and Fyra burning me. However, having two daggers tear into my chest, was one of the worst pains – even worse when he twisted them.

I dropped to the floor, gasping for air – I couldn't even scream. My blood was dark as it poured down my chest and back, covering me like a red blanket.

Dacre walked around me – panting; he crouched down and moved my hair out of my face. "You may be strong little one, but I am stronger." He sighed and wiped the blood from his daggers with his coat. "Your problem is, you get cocky, but I have to admit Narrdie, you're getting much better and faster."

I could feel the blood trickle from my mouth as I tried to speak; I moaned through my teeth – my arms went limp, and my head collided with the ashy ground. Dacre breathed out through his nose and pulled me onto his lap, almost cradling me. "No, Narrdie, stay awake, we aren't done yet." His voice softened, he pulled a cloth from his pocket and gently wiped the blood from my chin. "We were friends once, a long time ago. Me, you and Evander. Travelled all over the world, we were like a pack." I choked and he gently pushed my forward, clumps of clotted blood pooled out my mouth. "There you go," he soothed as he rubbed my back, eventually pulling me back to him.

"Dacre," I whispered then winced in pain.

"Shh, save your strength," he slowly rose, setting me down carefully against the snapped tree. A white raven flew towards him and landed on his arm, it croaked and tilted its head so that its beady eye was looking to Dacre. "Send for her Watcher and be quick." I glanced up at him, my brows creased in puzzlement, why was he letting me go? He turned back to me once the bird had flown away – crouching down beside me. He winked, "it's not your time to die yet. We're not done with you." Just like that, the malicious smirk returned – every ounce of kindness dissolved from his eyes.

"Then . . . why?" I asked, my voice trembled.

"It had to be this way. You had to be an inch from death, so that she can feed from it." He laughed and bowed lowly, like he was excepting a round of applause. "Farewell, my dear, send my love for Crow, I'll send for her soon."

Chapter Fifteen
Evander

*E*vander wretched his sword out of a Shade and sneered in disgust at the stench of the blood, that stained the college grounds – it would wash away but the memories would linger on the bricks. He looked around; squinting his eyes, Aronnia's mist was still looping the air, he wished he could find her so she could clear it and then he could find everyone, especially Narrdie.

"Narrdie," he breathed, where was she? Was she still with Dacre? Was she safe? Finally, the one question that continued to force its way to the tip of his tongue, was she alive?

A cold point of a sword pricked the back of his neck as he stood straight, he froze and tightened the grip he had on the hilt of his sword; he clenched his jaw. "I wouldn't if I was you," a woman's' voice warned him, immediately his heart skipped, and he breathed out in relief.

"Bayona?"

"Evander!" She gasped as she dropped her sword, he spun around and embraced her in a firm hug – thank the Goddess she was alive. "Je remercie la mère de ne pas vous prendre," she cried. "Evander, I couldn't find anyone – I thought the worst,

I thought that maybe you were all dead! The mist is playing havoc on my sight." Evander held her tighter, before pulling her back so he could look at her. His eyes scanned her over, checking for any signs of major injuries.

"You're the first one I've seen in a long while, are you okay? You hurt anywhere?" He questioned. "You've got a cut on your calf, looks deep." He ripped a long strip from the bottom of his top and fastened it around her leg tightly. "Here, put your arm around me and we'll look for everyone else, when your leg gets dangerously numb, we'll have to get you back to Gatherling." Bayona nodded and held onto him tightly.

"My magic is spent," she told him faintly.

"You're alive, that's the main thing."

Evander had fought in wars throughout his life, he thought he'd be used to it – he'd seen so many lifeless bodies, but it always got to him. A dark sadness washed over him when he made his way across the grounds, he tried not to look at the humans, whose lives had been taken – so young, he thought. Some were students and others were teachers, their faces would imprint in his mind.

"Bayona! Evander!" They both froze, their head darted around frantically as they tried to locate the person that the voice belonged to, Bayona pointed across Evander as her eyes spotted Audric.

"There! Oh, thank the mother," she wept. Audric half jogged over to them, his brows creased as he saw the blood on Bayona's leg.

"I thought you were dead," Audric blurted, his voice easing with relief. Bayona practically dove onto him, wrapping her arms around him. Evander gripped his forearm in a warriors greeting.

"You good?" Evander asked, noting the deep gashes across Audric's shoulder.

"Always," Audric chirped.

"We have to keep looking for everyone else," Bayona almost wept, Audric chuckled.

"No need, I've found pretty much everyone," he turned back and whistled. The others emerged from behind the building, swiftly closing the gap between them, quick hugs and hand grasps were quickly exchanged. Evander frowned, there wasn't many of his troops left and by the looks of it there was only a handful of Nyda's men.

"Priestess, did you get most of the humans out?" Bayona asked her.

"Yes, I am afraid we lost so many of them. Dacre's army were faster than they usually are," she sighed. "I have a small group with them now, waiting on the Order."

"They're hungry, they've been dying to crawl back up from their pits and taste blood again, their adrenaline was in full power." Nyda growled as she weakly walked towards them, clinging onto one of her guards for support. "I told you we weren't ready," she snarled.

"Not now, Nyda," Evander snapped. "Where's Narrdie?"

"She's not with you?" Audric asked, his voice dropping into a mixture of anger and worry.

"Dacre took her," Bayona informed them sheepishly, Audric snapped his head in her direction, icy venom laced his voice.

"Why didn't you stop him?"

"I tried!" She snarled, "Don't you dare try and put this on me! I was almost torn apart trying to get to her!" Her hands shook angrily, Audric took a moment and stepped back; he nodded to her, she breathed out heavily through her nose and returned to leaning on Evander.

"I'm sorry," he mumbled.

"I don't mean to interrupt, Sir." A guard croaked as he stepped forwards and bowed his head to Evander.

"Yes Manuel?" Evander asked.

"Sir, it's one of his, it's one of Dacre's," he pointed his finger towards a large white raven, that had perched itself on top of the fence; its head turned so that its beady eye glared down at them. "Shall I kill it?" Manuel asked as he pulled his crossbow from his back and into his hands.

"No," Erenna blurted. "He's come to take us to Narrdie." Her voice suddenly became panicked, "she's hurt! If we don't hurry, she'll die."

Chapter Sixteen
Narrdie

"Nyda, how's Narrdie doing?" Audric asked, his voice sounded bare.

"She let me heal her to a certain point, then pushed me away. She's still very weak, but every time I get close, she snarls at me. I want to help her Audric, I really do but, if I try and force help on her she shocks me with her Arma." Nyda responded in a cold and harsh voice, Audric sighed and rubbed the shadow on his chin.

"Has she spoken?" Evander asked as he knelt beside me, his eyes met mine and I could see dark blotches from stress and tiredness under his eyes. His hand brushed my cheek.

"Not a single word."

"Thank you, Nyda," Evander said dismissing her, Nyda bowed before leaving the infirmary. "Audric." Evander began as he rose, "I'm going to help Bayona, see if anything needs doing. I can't keep sitting here day after day – waiting for her to say something. Inform me if anything changes," Evander's voice was full of guilt – pain.

"Evander," Audric said as he gripped his shoulder. "It's her first battle, shock was bound to happen. Don't give up." Evander didn't respond, he shook Audric's hand off and continued towards the door. I didn't react when I heard the door click shut, I couldn't react.

I felt nothing.

Drained. That's what I was, drained of everything. Every thought, every breath stung, every swallow felt like acid, peoples touch felt like brands on my skin, their voices just ringing in my ear. I was completely empty of every emotion, every feeling I'd ever had, had suddenly evaporated and vanished in the wind.

*T*he moment Evander and Audric found me in the dead forest, I could see on their faces that the battle had not favoured us. I could read how many humans had died, I could see how many people we'd lost, they had tried to hide it – but I knew, it haunted their faces, lingered on their words.

Dacre had killed so many of the humans – just to taunt me. He'd created that entire battle, just so he could lure me out and I'd played right into his hands. Erenna had used some moss to cover the wounds on my chest, as they'd rushed me back to Gatherling and straight in the infirmary. The healers had managed to stop the bleeding but advised that Nyda add her healing powers every few hours, to avoid the poison from spreading and tearing open the stab wounds. The healers wouldn't allow me any visitors for the first two nights, I'd spent most of that time sleeping anyway – not by choice. However, on the third night I had only one visitor and it was to bring me the bad news on the battle.

Audric swallowed hard and tucked his hands into his pockets; he bit his cheek, "Narrdie. Evander thinks I should be the one to tell you, Alaska . . ."

"Dead," I finished for him, my voice was blank.

"Yes," Audric's voice sounded shocked the moment I spoke. "She'd made it to Aronnia, but a Skinner got her while they were fleeing." A Skinner. One of the worse creatures I'd ever come across. I knew what that meant – she'd have been ripped apart, shredded to pieces and then probably died from shock – I winced.

"How many?" I asked

"Narrdie-"

"How many Audric?"

"A hundred and thirty-two, students and ten tutors. Our numbers took a hit, we lost at least half of our people. I'm so sorry, I don't know what went wrong." Audric took my hand, without so much as a grumble, I pulled it away from him and turned towards the window.

"Why?"

"Why, what?" He repeated as his brows crossed.

"Why didn't he just take me and wait for the darkness to take over? Why let me come back here?"

"Dacre? I don't know what game he's playing." Audric mumbled, I could see the resentfulness plastered across his face the moment Dacre's name rolled from his lips.

"Send my love to Crow," I blurted. Audric froze.

"What did you say?" A hint of panic echoed in his voice.

"Before he left, he said, 'send my love to Crow'. Who is Crow?" Audric shifted uncomfortably and reached out for my hand, I jerked it away, but he forcefully gripped it.

"Narrdie, look at me," he ordered, I didn't. He dropped my hand and cursed under his breath, "I can't do this," he told himself. Audric turned from me and began to walk out of the infirmary, I didn't care when he left. I didn't care when he stayed either or when Evander stayed. One word played over and over in my head – one name.

Crow.

Who was Crow and why did Audric look so afraid of the name?

*A*nother week had passed, and I was still stuck in the infirmary. Everyone took turns to sit with me and try and persuade me to eat and speak to them, but I wouldn't. Bayona would brush my hair, while babbling about the latest silly thing someone had done – not once did her cheery voice falter. Audric, would speak slowly, like he was talking to a child who had just experience their first trauma; he'd bring all kinds of foods he knew it loved – cakes, chocolate and my favourite pasta dishes. I still wouldn't eat them.

It was worse when Evander came, he started off begging – begging for me to talk to him, so he could help me cope. Eventually, he gave up with that tactic and just sat, watching – waiting.

When I did speak, it was blank – empty. I couldn't stand to look into their eyes, so I continued to stare at the pale walls and ignore the plate of food that they kept putting beside me. Without Nyda's healing, my wounds stopped mending – some even opened up and bled again, but I didn't want them fixed. I didn't want to do anything anymore, everything inside me had dissolved. The healers and Nyda tried to force aid on me, however when I felt she got too close; I saw myself snarl and snap at her or my Arma would shock her back.

"If she keeps this up, it won't be long until she dies," Nyda informed Audric in a gentle tone.

"Audric, I can't find her future, it's lost," Bayona whimpered.

"What do you mean it's lost?" Audric snarled as he turned on her.

"I mean in my vision; she is neither dead nor alive – it's undecided. Audric, something needs to be done and fast," she warned.

"Apologies for interrupting, but may I speak with Lady Narrdie please?" Erenna asked politely as she gracefully walked into the room, her hands cupped in front of her in an old-fashioned manor.

"Certainly, my Priestess." Bayona bowed, "come on Audric, she'll be okay." Bayona lightly assured him as she tugged on his sleeve.

"Hello, Narrdie," Erenna greeted gently after Audric and Bayona had left the room. She slowly and cautiously took a few steps closer to me; her long crocodile green mermaid styled dress, trailing along the floor.

"The college? What will happen to the college?"

"Do not worry about that, the Order have taken care of it," she assured me. I laughed but it was empty, she raised her brows and fidgeted with her hands slightly. "Narrdie?"

"Yes. Cover it up like nothing has happened, what did they say? That it was a mad man shooting up the place?" I scoffed. "That someone planted a bomb in the hall?" All those parents, family, friends accepting that they lost their loved one – it was a lie.

"Narrdie, everyone is afraid for you; you are not yourself child. If you continue, I am worried something bad may happen to you. Do not shut out your family," she begged.

"Afraid for me? Or afraid of me?" I bit, my eyes shot up to hers and she flinched back.

"Narrdie . . ."

"Go. Away." I growled, pausing after each word, I could feel one emotion beginning to force its way up – anger. Icy cold anger.

"Narrdie, please, let me help you," she said gently, as she placed her hand on my shoulder.

Immediately, I snarled; my pupils split, my hair turned black as it fell down my shoulders and I could feel the strain as my nails extended into razor sharp claws. With a swift movement, I thrusted my hand forward, a vine of black mist shot out of my palm and slammed into her chest. Erenna gasped, her body lifted up and was thrown back, until she slammed into the wall – hard.

The anger that had crawled its way to the surface, had faded as quickly as it had come. I turned back to continue to stare at the wall and drift back into my mind – my hair, nails and eyes slowly turned back to normal. I knew what that power was, I had felt it push the walls of my mind and I had given it full permission to attack.

It didn't take long for the others to burst through the door, with panicked faces and hysterical voices. "What's going on?" Evander growled.

"Erenna? Sister, what happened?" Wenona gasped as she helped her sister back to her feet, Erenna thanked her before gently reassuring the three Priestesses that she was alright and unharmed.

"Narrdie attacked her," Fyra hissed as she took a step towards me, Audric threw out his arm, blocking her.

"Don't," he warned.

"Narrdie, is this true?" Wenona asked in disbelief.

"It's not her fault, as she grows weaker the dark gets stronger." Erenna spoke before anyone could act. "I think it is best that we leave her alone for a while, she has had enough excitement for one day."

"Is that really a good idea?" Evander asked as he stood protectively in front of me, Audric and Bayona flanking him. "If that power is emerging, is it really wise to leave her?"

"Right now, yes." Erenna told him sternly. "Our presence is only causing her more stress. Stress that the darkness inside, will absorb. I am sorry, I should not have pushed her – not now. Let us take our leave."

"*The darkness gets stronger . . .*" Erenna's words echoed in my head. I glanced down at myself. I had been put in a hospital gown and my wounds were still bleeding and weeping threw their bandages. I could see how thin I'd become, my bones so prominent, even threw my clothes, I could see my ribs poking out. "*You know the things she's done!*" Voices began to play like a record, over and over – the echo getting louder. A sharp pain started to pound against my skull. "*You feel it draining you,*" I squeezed my eyes closed.

"Shut up," I whispered to myself as I clamped my hands over my ears.

"*I can smell your fear,*" my blood boiled to hear his voice. Dacre, "*not like other humans.*"

"Shut up!" I begged again and tucked my knees into my chest, I couldn't take how many voices were swirling around in there, shouting over each other.

"*When you were born your soul split, one part filled with the light of your mother and the other part, filled with dark.*" I screamed out; my head felt like it was going to explode. I threw out my hands and the infirmary beds shot across the room, the window shattered into pieces and the walls began to crack. "*The dark happens to be the part that holds a lot of you power, which is why you change when you lost control.*"

"No! Shut up! Leave me alone!" Flames struck the mattresses and the blinds, I held my hands over my ears tightly, trying to block out the voices. I didn't want to hear this anymore.

"*Give my love to Crow.*" I shot my head up and the voices suddenly stopped.

"Crow." I rose to my feet and pulled at the infirmary door. "They locked me in." Locked in – like an animal. Something inside me snarled, I closed my eyes and tried to use my Lacus jump, but it didn't work. Something was cutting it down –

Bayona. She'd put a block on me or the room, they didn't trust me anymore.

Then I felt it.

That dark energy. Slivering its way up, daring me to use it – to allow it to release me from this room. I clenched my jaw; I knew I shouldn't, but I wanted answers and I needed to be freed. Being stuck in this infirmary was one thing but being locked in – I couldn't handle. I needed to know who Crow was and I didn't care about the Order's laws, or whether they all thought I was ready or not. I took a deep breath and closed my eyes, I closed down the block I had built up inside me and allowed the darkness to the surface and taste its only chance of freedom. I knew this could turn bad at any given moment and I didn't care.

"Free me," I called to it and felt its slimy tentacle brush happily against my mind.

"Gladly," it breathed.

I'd blacked out, the second I had given it permission. The dark vine stroked down my mind, as it went back in the depths of my body. I was shocked that it had allowed me to resume control, I made a mental note not to get too familiar in using it, even if its power ignited my bones and made me feel invincible.

I was outside, my eyes were groggy, almost like I was waking from a deep sleep – perhaps I was. It didn't take long for the trees and the leaves to become clear in my vision once again, the sun sung like a fresh cut as it reached my eyes. How long had it been since I'd seen it?

I hadn't smelt the freshness of the air in so long, felt the first nip of the frosty wind as it grazed my cheek and the soft soil under my bare feet – was warm and gentle. The breeze was icy, and it caused my fingers and toes to grow numb, the goosebumps had spread all up my arms and legs. "INDRA!"

I didn't have to wait long until I heard the straining of the trees, as Indra forced her way through them, until she came into my sight – her eyes wide.

"Narrdie, what are you doing out of the infirmary and in the cold?" She asked cautiously, her eyes full of concern. *"Please, let me call for Evander or Audric, you'll freeze out here."*

"No." I hissed.

"Please, you shouldn't be out here," her facial expression softened, but her eyes looked timid, and her ears flicked back and forth.

"You know why I'm here, don't you?" I assumed.

"Yes, I do, and I beg you to leave it be Narrdie, go back inside and rest."

"Leave it be? Why?" I barked.

"Narrdie, you need to focus on getting better, you are not well," she begged. A black vine of smoke shot out from my palm – snapping a cluster of trees around me in half. I was irritated, angry and I wanted answers. No more, would I allow them to gaslight me, to avoid everything I asked them.

"Stop treating me like a silly little child!" I snarled. "I want to know why! Why do both sides want me dead? Who is Crow? I want the truth, Indra!" Indra snuffed out of her nose and wafted her tail around nervously; I could tell she was trying to stall as much as she could.

Before she could speak, Evander marched towards us, guards following him closely and an infuriated look stuck to his face. "Indra leave!" He ordered in a vicious voice.

"Evander, I have not told her anything," she blurted instantly.

"Leave now!" He repeated aggressively as he stared her down, she bowed her head before turning back into the forest. "Narrdie?" Evander's voice turned calm, and he approached me carefully – his hand open.

"She never answered my question," I said, no matter how much I tried, I couldn't shift the empty voice, I couldn't put any feelings back into my soul.

"It's against the rules," his voice was careful. "It's time to come back inside. The guards are going to take you back to the infirmary. I advise you to go with them," he warned.

I tilted my head, they had come armed – each one resting hands on their weapons, weapons they would use on me. So much for family. A hiss rippled from my lips; my hands opened as the black mist began to wrap around me like a snake. Evander's lips tensed into a straight line; he shook his head – eyes pleading with me. "Narrdie." A golden Arma covered over them all, as Bayona emerged behind them, her hand outstretched. "Narrdie, look at me," Evander begged.

"Kill them." A voice whispered in my ears; shadows whispering as they brushed against my mind. *"They don't trust you; they don't care for you . . . but I do."* My head flicked to the side, the mist surrounding me vibrating with anticipation, waiting to be released.

"Narrdie," Bayona called. "Don't make me do this." My eyes snapped to her; she was outside her Arma; her hands twisting her power around. "I know you're hurting; I know you want it to stop and I know that it calls to you, twists your mind. You can't trust it." I hissed, my mist shot out towards her, only to collide and wither away as her own met it.

"Who can I trust," I spat, my voice a collection of whispers.

"Us, your family." I laughed, the sound bitter and cruel.

"My family come with swords and bows to put me down."

"Astrid wouldn't want this." My breath caught, for the first time in these dreaded weeks, my heart stung – Astrid, the mist pulled back into my skin and my arms turned slack at my sides. Bayona took another step forward, her fingers brushed my hand cautiously, testing; she gently entwined her fingers with mine. "Sleep," she breathed, my eyes suddenly feeling heavy. "Sleep, Narrdie."

Chapter Seventeen
Narrdie & Crow

"Narrdie, I can't. If Evander finds out . . ." Sharia protested as she fidgeted uncomfortably with a loose thread on her brown jumper. Things had started to ease, the empty feeling I had clung to was beginning to fill slowly, a few hours a day I had agreed to talk about whatever was spiralling in my head and allowed Nyda and the healers to resume tending to my wounds. Once a week I was even escorted outside to get some fresh air, to feel the sun lick my skin and the grass between my toes. The darkness lowered back into the depths of my soul, but at night I could feel it stirring, Evander refused me books from the library, he banned anyone from answering questions on who Crow was and he hadn't visited since that night.

"He won't." I pleaded. "I have to find something out for myself and then everything will be okay." Sharia stared at me for a small amount of time, she clenched her jaw and swallowed hard – but thankfully she nodded.

"Okay, if it helps. Here." She handed me a long lace dress, which seemed way to revealing for me. I swallowed slightly; the dress was almost see through if it wasn't for the layer of mesh fabric underneath. I shrugged and quickly changed into it and handed her my infirmary gown. Her eyes bulged in her skull as she took in the dress, she raised her brows at me. "It's very . . . baring. So, now I just need to shift into you?"

"Yes. I need you to be convincing, right down to the smallest scar," I warned her.

"Narrdie?" I glanced to her as I walked to the door, "where are you going?"

"To get answers from the only person who will tell me."

There was only one way to get his attention, one thing that I knew he'd come for.

The feeling of being forced out of my own body, was indescribable and more painful than I imagined it would be. It felt like someone had plunged their hand into my chest and was slowly pulling out my heart – twisting while they did it. I watched in the puddle's reflection as my hair, veins and lips slowly turned black. The change filled me with fear, I had never seen myself taken over before – I usually blacked out.

I knew letting the darkness takeover was stupid, reckless and one of the most dangerous things I could ever do. For all I knew, this could have been the last time I was in control. However, this was the only way I could be around him, last time I ended up with two swords sticking out of my chest – I shuddered, remembering the pain of the blades tearing through me.

No, Dacre welcomed the Darkness; he was willing to murder a whole college – just to wake it up.

A ripple of hot pain tore into me, then suddenly, I was gone.

*S*he watched him, her icy blue eyes taking in every step he made. Her tongue snaked out and licked along her cracked lips, she loved nothing more than toying with him – oh how she missed him.

Dacre chuckled to himself as his hand traced the claw marks, she'd purposely left in the tree, a secret way of telling each other that they needed to meet. He smirked and clapped his hands together, "Alright, I'm impressed. Now, come out, pretty bird," he called.

Elegantly, she dove from the branch she was perched on; landing a few feet from him, she ran her long claw like nail, along her lips - smiling widely like a Cheshire cat. "Dacre, my love. It's been a while since we last spoke, I hoped you missed me." Her voice, would have made anyone else shudder - but not him. He'd missed how she sounded, the cluster of whispered voices, all forming into one, the sound of nightmares. The sound used to send shivers spiralling through Evander and the others, but for him - it turned him on.

"Hello, Crow." Dacre's smirk grew wider, he'd forgotten how fierce she looked, beneath those cold eyes, was a deadly creature. "I see you escaped Evander, Audric and Narrdie, bravo." Crow snickered and fluttered her eyes at him, mimicking a bow.

"Thank you, however it was nothing to do with me. Little Narrdie, allowed me to take over - practically begged. It appears she has... figured some things out herself, and dear old Evander, is still trying to protect her from it." She trailed her hand around her neck and down her chest - teasing. "I'm guessing you played a part in helping her along? Sneaky, sneaky Dacre." Crow began to circle him - a lioness playing with her food. He bared his fangs playfully and she purred in excitement.

"I may have," he admitted with a grin.

"You missed me that much?" The wind pushed her black hair, revealing the darken veins - that had now spread around her eyes. Dacre's eyes dropped down, rolling over the tight dress - he practically drooled as he could see the curve of her breasts, her pale skin peeking through.

"Who won last time?" He asked with an excited growl.

"You did, but you cheated," she hissed under her breath.

"Me? Cheat? Never," he mocked daringly.

"Only once, my love. Never again"

"Are you sure you aren't out of practice? It's been a while?" He taunted.

"We shall see," she snarled.

She licked her lips, her whole face darkened as she pounced forward - Dacre grinned and copied her movement.

They slammed into each other, attacking like two vicious dogs - tearing at each other, ripping whatever they could sink their claws into. Dacre gripped her arms, flipping her over him and pinned her to the ground. She giggled and leaned her head up to lick his lips, before bringing her knee up and jamming it hard into his stomach – he groaned. She laughed as she gripped her nails into his shoulder and tossed him over her head, Crow twirled her legs around and sprung up – landing gracefully on her feet. She crouched waiting for his next move.

He rose with a grunt and brushed away the blood from his nose, the corner of his mouth lifted into a smile. "You're stronger than Narrdie, but you're cocky, pretty bird. Something you and Narrdie both share," Crow sneered, straightened up and tilted her head; she licked her lips and a mischievous grin slowly spread upon her face.

"Narrdie. You say her name with such . . . passion," she taunted. "N-a-r-r-d-i-e," she repeated flirtatiously stretching out the word. "I can feel her hatred for you, you really done her wrong. I can feel the sadness, emptiness in her and how she longs to give up and it's all because of you. She feels betrayed by you . . . you broke her," Crow snickered, her smirk suddenly dropped as she looked to Dacre. He frowned; his eyes flicked down as his jaw clenched, a movement she didn't miss – anger bubbled inside her. "This upsets you?" She quizzed in a disgusted voice.

"Absolutely not." He snapped, "Narrdie is weak, of course it doesn't upset me, I have done so much to push her out and it's all been for you!"

"Then why do you look as though you could weep? Do you feel the need to protect her? Care for her?" She closed the distance between them and ran her hand down his face softly. "Do you love her Dacre?"

"No. You're mistaken, I care nothing for her," he laughed, but it wasn't a laugh of humour.

"No?" She scoffed. "Then why didn't you kill her when you had the chance? You forget that whenever you are near her – I can see you through her eyes. You were so caring, holding her, stroking her like a beloved pet. Called for her Watcher to come and rescue her and I know you waited Dacre. I could sense you, watching to make sure she was saved." She growled, "Pathetic. Maybe, it's you, which is the weak one!"

Dacre snarled and flung himself at her; his hand gripped around her throat, like a vice as he pinned her up against the tree. Crow hissed darkly and thrashed against him. "The more you struggle the more it will hurt," he warned and waited for her to calm. He smirked with satisfaction, when he felt her tremble before him. "Remember who you are dealing with Crow. Narrdie Moon, is no good to us dead – not yet. You may share the same body, but if I snap your neck – it'll be you who dies. Do I make myself clear?"

"Snapping my neck won't kill me," she snarled and gasped for air, as he tightened his grip.

"I said, do I make myself clear?" He repeated aggressively, she grunted but nodded and he slowly released her. "Good girl," he praised calmly as he stroked her cheek, she coughed and crumpled to the floor – rubbing her neck. "Melphos!" Dacre called.

"My Lord?" Melphos bowed in respect to Dacre and then stared, wide eyed at Crow - terror struck him and he gulped. "M-Mistress C-Crow," he stuttered, she raised her brows and growled.

"Mistress?" She questioned, "Is that how you address me? Lord Dacre and Mistress Crow? Am I a brothels Madam? Or a King's whore?" Her voice was dark and held a dangerous warning to it, she rose to her feet; her icy eyes glaring down on him.

"No . . . Mistress . . .I mean . . ." He flashed a look to Dacre – begging for help.

Crow snarled, "Don't look at him, snivelling dog! You think he cares if I skin you alive?"

"Crow," Dacre called, his voice bored. "You've had your fun; I actually need this one for a little while longer." Crow smirked wickedly and purred as she ran her hand down Dacre's chest. She nodded; it gave her so much pleasure to watch people squirm under her. Melphos's eyes darted to Crow again, she tilted her head and flashed her sharp teeth. Her hands wrapped around Dacre's chest, she leaned into him and nibbled his ear – smiling when he growled with pleasure.

"Dacre, I would like to warn you, that if this creature does not stop looking at me, I will tear out his eyes, turn it inside out and feed it to a pack of Skinners." Crow warned in a cheery tone, Melphos quickly looked away and swallowed nervously.

Dacre laughed and flashed Crow a playful leer, "Melphos, avert your eyes and escort her to the cave." Crow stepped back with a hiss, "Crow, play nicely."

"Narrdie!" Bayona called as she ran towards them, Audric, Nyda and Evander quickly on her heels, they all immediately slid to a stop as their eyes landed on Crow.

"Holy shit," Audric blurted then turned to Evander.

Evander was the only one out of them that had seen Crow in the flesh, so he wasn't shocked to see the fear that had tattooed itself on all their faces. However, he knew Crow, and this wasn't her full form, her true form – was much worse.

"Crow," Evander breathed.

Crow snapped her head towards him, an animalistic snarl rolled from her tongue; she gasped and clutched her chest. "Narrdie," she spat, before she dropped to the floor screaming in agony.

"NO!" Dacre cursed as he raced for her.

Bayona lurched forward – a chant escaping her lips so fast, no ears could hear it. A bright light shot out and slammed Dacre hard in the chest – forcing him back. She hissed as she raised her hand, forming a golden Arma around them.

"You will not touch her," Bayona warned, her voice venomous.

I gasped and flung my eyes open; bile burned in my throat, I turned over to haul my guts up. After I'd spilled the contents of my stomach onto the ground, Audric pulled me to my feet and held me close to him - a mixture of anger and relief twirled around on his face. I blinked several times, where was I?

Bayona was stood in front of us all, her hands outstretch and powering the purest Arma I'd ever seen. "Audric? What happened?" I asked, his face was cold; he clenched his jaw and pulled me to stand between him and Evander, Evanders hand gripped my other arm tightly – so tight I winced.

"What happened?" He scoffed sarcastically. "You're lucky Astrid isn't here; she would have ripped your head off – I should do the bloody same!" His voice was laced with fiery rage – I flinched back.

"Not here Audric," Evander snapped; his eyes fell on me, there was no love behind them – only fiery anger. "This is the last time I leave you unsupervised," Evander snarled towards me. "You allowed the darkness to take over you – for the second time! You tricked Sharia, she thought you were going to find Indra. This is probably the most idiotic thing you've ever done - seeking out Dacre. He almost killed you last time." His hand tightened around my arm, almost like he thought I was about to run away – I grimaced at his hold, but he didn't release me.

"You're hurting me," I whimpered.

Dacre snarled and took a step forward – testing the strength of the shield, an action I knew he'd instantly regret. Bayona's Arma snaked out like a whip and slashed a deep cut along his cheek; he snarled and heckled – his eyes bold and furious, his fangs bare.

"I'm Crow, aren't I? I knew you were all keeping something from me – I knew this was it!" Audric stiffened, and I knew from then – it was true. I swallowed the urge to scream, to pound my fists into their chests and call them every name under the sun. This whole time, they kept it from me, lied to me. If they had only told me, maybe everything could have been avoided. "I thought I just blacked out, I never thought I changed into . . . into someone else. It's true, isn't it?" I asked more sternly, Evander hissed through his teeth and pulled me towards him.

"Another word out of you and I'll drag you back, kicking and screaming. We will deal with this when we are home." I had never seen Evander so angry, his eyes burned with fury as they looked to me, a tinge of worry swept through me – I had majorly screwed up.

Dacre growled and lunged forward once more, but the Arma struck him again, this time cutting into his neck. "Do not come near us!" Bayona warned as she pushed the barrier towards him, "this is your final warning!"

"Melphos, kill the Witch, she cannot protect herself and keep the Alma up at the same time." A gurgle bubbled in his throat as he lunged at Bayona, her attention was focused on Dacre. Audric drew his blade and ran forward, but the Arma gently pushed him back towards us. Melphos dived, his hands shifted onto claws – aiming for her heart.

"BAYONA!" I screeched in warning.

Melphos gasped he fell to his knees, as a dark shape met him in mid-air – a gaping hole in his chest where his heart should have been. Before a single drop could land on the ground, the shape attacked again – tearing his head from his shoulders.

Fear shadowed Dacre's face; he stumbled back – disbelief rested in his eyes; his face paled. "This can't be," his voice shook. "T-This can't be!"

Tears burned in eyes and a feeling I hadn't felt in several weeks instantly filled me – the feeling of happiness, utter and pure joy as my eyes watched her. She was as extravagant as the first day I'd seen her. The beautiful Vampire Elder, stood with a triumphant smile across her perfectly plumped lips. Her eggplant-coloured hair curled gracefully over her shoulders; her lilac dress clung to her curved body; embroidered silver roses decorated along the bodice and in her hand rested Melphos's heart.

"Astrid," Bayona whispered through a shaky breath, tears overflowing from her scorched eyes and spilling down her cheeks. Astrid looked to her with warmth, her smile stretched wide, before it suddenly dropped; her red lips parting to reveal the sharpened fangs.

"I'm disappointed Dacre," Astrid began, she crushed the heart in her hand until it was nothing but ground dust, each step she took closer to him - he'd take two back. Coward. "Did you really think it would be that easy to kill a Vampire Elder?" She tutted at him. Dacre crouched low and snarled towards her, but Astrid began to laugh. "You do not scare me, little Hybrid," Astrid's laugh was strong, and its melody echoed all around us. "Bayona, lower your Arma," she ordered. Bayona smiled with relief and the golden Arma burned away almost instantly, she fell back into Audric's arms.

Immediately, Dacre lunged for me. Astrid's eyes turned red as she dove into him and struck him hard, the force of her hit, enough to send him back - landing hard on his back. "Stay down, that's a good boy," she warned - her voice lethal. Dacre grumbled under his breath but was smart enough to remain where he was. "He comes back with us. Evander, does your sanctuary have somewhere to hold him?"

"We have cells, enchanted cells - he won't be able to get out of them," Evander assured her.

"Good. Take him there, I'll deal with him later," she ordered. She quickly gave Evander a look and he nodded. Something inside me hit hard against my chest, she was going to kill him once we got back to the sanctuary. A shriek bellowed in my ears, yet no one reacted to it - Crow. She was pleading, begging me to stop them, to save Dacre. As much as I hated it, I couldn't let him die - at least not yet.

"No!" I snarled, I thrust my hand into Evanders chest, hard enough that his hands unwrapped from my arm and lunged myself in front of Dacre - my Arma spreading widely around us. "Don't come near him Evander, I mean it," I warned, my voice surprisingly calm. I circled my Arma around me, just in case Dacre tried to grab me from behind.

"Narrdie, move aside," Evander order, his voice like burning ice.

"I can't let you kill him Astrid, I'm sorry, but I can't. Believe me, I want him dead as much as all of you, but he is better to me alive." Audric's face turned cold, his eyes darkened as he pushed himself forward – inches from my Arma. I could see it beginning to burn his cheeks, but he didn't care – I was betraying him, stealing away his chance at getting revenge for Mitchell.

"You'd even block me?" He asked, his voice not once faltering. "He is the reason Mitchell is dead. My brother, Narrdie."

"I know," I breathed. Audric's eyes met mine and I saw the hurt, the pain I was putting him in – it made my eyes fill with tears. "I'm sorry Audric, but I need him – alive." Audric's jaw clenched, and his hands balled into fists, he sucked in a breath and nodded slowly. I knew it would take him a while to forgive me, but I pleaded with him to understand.

"Narrdie, you need to get away from him and let us handle this. You're still very weak and you need to rest," Bayona begged.

"I've rested enough," I snarled, she flinched back slightly and glanced to Evander. "This war between you and them, lands on me – started because of me. Right? Because I was born?" Evander nodded, his lips tightening into a straight line. "Then we need him alive, we need all the information we can get. What good will killing him do when we can still use him?"

"It's too risky, he's a snake. He deserves to pay for everything he's done. He had blood on his hands, Narrdie. Not just from Lazarus, or the college – it goes back further than that," Evander looked past me, his eyes resting on Dacre – a silent conversation crossing between them.

"I know and he will pay – just not yet." I turned to Astrid and gave her pleading eyes, "Astrid, please. Please, can we just go back home, keep him wherever you want to, but keep him alive. I know you're all mad at the way I've been and I'm sorry, but I couldn't help it. I didn't mean to block you all out or hurt you. Evander, I know you, Audric and Bayona are angry that I let the darkness take over and I'll accept whatever punishment you want to give me. From here on out, I'm good – I swear." I breathed out hard, my muscles screaming. I had been stuck in the infirmary for weeks, I didn't notice how much strength I'd lost – plus, Dacre must have really beaten me when I was taken over. My Arma began to flicker, and I could feel the heavy weight pulling at my eyes. "Astrid," I begged, my voice straining with pain and exhaustion. Astrid nodded but a smile lifted the side of her mouth, she gently laughed – the sound filling me with warmth.

"My sweet Narrdie. How strong you've become in my absence, yet your heart still remains bold and pure. Even in your darkest days, you always find a way to pull yourself back. You have no idea; how much I've missed you." I smiled warmly to her; my eyes almost blurry with tears – my surrogate mother.

"You have no idea, how much I missed you," my voice broke. She closed the space between us, pausing in front of my shield, the look in her eyes was safe – I dropped the Arma. Immediately she wrapped her arms around me, I held her tightly – terrified she was going to suddenly vanish.

"Dacre, will not be harmed – not by any of us," her voice was finally, and I relaxed when I saw everyone nod in agreement. "He shall be under constant supervision, by guards and one of our inner circle. Let's get you back."

I was in trouble.

On the way back, Evander and Audric didn't say one word to me – they didn't even glance in my direction. I could feel anxiety prickling my skin, I didn't know when it was coming, but I knew Evander was going to flip eventually – the bite of his fingers around my arm told me so.

When we got back to Gatherling, Evander offered to walk me to my room – an offer I knew I wasn't allowed to refuse, I gulped. It had been weeks since I was last in my own room, it all seemed so foreign, carpet instead of tiles, my pillows all arranged how I liked them – gathering in a V shape. I longed for a nap, to smother myself under the mountain of duck feathers and wrap the thick quilt around me, but with Evander here – I knew it would be a while before I was allowed to relax. All of a sudden, I was very aware of my appearance, my hair was greasy and tangled, and clumps of dirt lingered under my nails and blotched up and down my arms.

"Oh," I breathed. I was still in the black dress. I could feel my cheeks heating up, I had never worn anything so revealing in all my life. A wave of guilt slammed into me as I caught Evander staring at it; his jaw clenched. I'd purposely worn it for Dacre, to try and distract him into telling me everything I needed to know, I wanted to tell him that I didn't have any feelings for him, but my mouth had gone dry; I wrapped my hands around my body – trying to cover myself as best I could.

"You're filthy," Evander finally spoke – his voice cold.

"I-I'll run a bath."

"No. You can have a bath later, for now have a quick shower."
I swallowed nervously, this was it, once I came out of the
bathroom – Evander was going to rip me to shreds.

"Can I at least put some clothes on?" I asked him timidly
once I came back into the room. "And maybe brush my
hair?" I'd washed it three times, almost using every ounce of
shampoo I'd had – yet the dirt still seemed to linger.

Evander through me an aggravated glare and pointed to
my bed. "Sit," he ordered, his voice sending shivers up my
spine. I glanced down to the towel wrapped around my body
and my long-wet hair dripping onto the floor – he scoffed.
"It's nothing I haven't seen before. Sit." I bit the inside of my
cheek and sat on the edge of my bed without question, my
fingers pulled at a loose thread.

"Would it help if I said I was sorry again?" I suggested, not
able to reach his eyes.

"Do you even mean it?"

"Yes," my voice broke.

"Why? Why are you sorry, Narrdie?"

"For everything." My voice was barely a whisper, each time I
tried to speak – it broke like a mouse.

"For everything?" He ridiculed, "Which part? For lying to
Sharia and getting her into shit with the Order? For letting
yourself be taken over, not once, but twice? Even though, you
know what destruction it can do and has done!" I flinched back;
each word was like a knife in my chest. "And then to top it off
you went to him – Dacre. Do you have any idea what that did
to Audric and Bayona? What it did to me? I had to watch, watch
you break every single day – for weeks, knowing that there was
nothing I could do. You then left." I could no longer hold back
my tears and sobs; I had never heard so much hurt in his voice
before and it was all because of me. "I thought the worse. I
thought...I thought that I had lost you forever."

"I-I know it was stupid," I began, I tried to calm myself, just
enough to get the words out. "I didn't know how else to do it.
Evander, I'm so sorry I never wanted to put you through this.
We got Dacre, isn't that a good thing?" Evander slowly turned
to me, he clenched his fists and sneered.

"Don't try and act like this was your plan all along. I would
rather let Dacre sink back into that pit he was hiding, than have
you open yourself up to the darkness and scare the living shit
out of everyone." Evander laughed and clenched his jaw. "You

made such a song and dance about us all treating you like a child, and then you did this. Snook out like a disobedient teenager, trying to get back at her parents! You demand to be involved in every decision – every discussion we have? You will be – once you've learnt to grown up!"

"Evander, please."

"I could have lost you!" He snarled; he turned and punched the door so hard, it splintered, the wood cutting into his knuckles – I jumped.

"Evander," I began, I stood and forced him to look at me, not caring that my towel had snagged on the bed post and fallen off or how his eyes looked to me with rage, "I didn't mean to scare you, I would never want to hurt you. I'm so sorry, please believe me." His eyes lingered-on mine, then suddenly dropped to look over my naked body. I knew what he was looking at. It was the same thing I'd spent ten minutes staring. Purple and black bruises decorated all over my pale skin, numerous cuts – weeping and red with soreness.

However, that was not what had caught his attention, the wounds from the college – the marks Dacre had made with his daggers. They had never healed properly since that nice, I had never let anyone near me long enough. The wounds still looked fresh, they had split and had started bleeding on the way back – I still winced with most movements. Evander reached his hand out, as though he was going to gently feel them, when I looked to him; he snagged his hand back and turned away from me.

"Sorry, is not enough – not this time Narrdie."

"Evander, I know you're mad, I know I screwed up massively, I know I put this world at risk by letting it take over. I'm sorry, I shouldn't have done it and I wish I could take it back – I really do." My voice turned frantic; I didn't want him to leave me – not like this. "I kept hearing everyone's voices in my head and I . . .I just wanted answers. You wouldn't tell me, none of you would tell me about Crow and why she was connected to me!"

"You need to sleep," his voice had turned cold. "I will have someone come up with food and fresh bandages, you will remain in your room. You will stay here until you have healed up, you will rest when the healers tell you to rest. You will eat whenever food is brought to you, and you will do everything that you are told if it helps your recovery. Do I make myself clear?"

"Evander-"

"Do I make myself clear?" He repeated through gritted teeth.

"Yes," I replied instantly, my voice nothing but a faded whisper.

"I will come back at the end of the week and check on you. If you feel like running off on another one of your amazingly planned adventures – don't. I would hate to have to lock you in the cells. Goodnight, Lady Narrdie." He bowed to me, almost like he was meeting me for the first time, my heart broke.

"Evander, wait, please?" I begged. He clenched his jaw and bent down to fetch my towel, he gently wrapped it around my shoulders.

"If you need anything, just inform one of the guards outside – they will fetch whatever you need."

I stared at the door for a few minutes, hoping, pleading that he'd come back – he didn't. I couldn't find it in me to brush my hair, or even dig in my cupboard to pull on a pair of night sweats. All the energy I had left, was used to crawl into bed and pull up the covers and cry.

It didn't take long for sleep to grab me.

Chapter Eighteen

"*N*arrdie, everyone knows that you meant well – even Evander. You need to remember, Evander lost you once, many years ago; he was overwhelmed when he heard of your return. When you left, you frightened him – he thought you were going to die. Give him time. Still, something good came out of it, Dacre is locked away." Indra's voice was cheery – as always. I half smiled, I was always thankful for Indra – no matter how bad things were, she'd always try to make me feel better. However, I knew she was wrong, everyone was pissed and rightfully so. I wasn't acting on behalf of them, I was being selfish, stupid and reckless.

"Indra, you didn't see him – how angry he was. It's like he . . . hated me," my voice quivered, and I could feel my eyes filling up. Indra breathed out hard, her breath pulling strands of hair from the fishtail plait, Astrid had weaved for me.

"*Narrdie, do you honestly believe that Evander could hate you?*"

"No, but I don't believe he'll forgive me either," I admitted. "I love him Indra and I hurt him."

"*And he loves you. You know what you need to do,*" I stared blankly at her. Indra frowned and gently nudged me with her nose. "*Make it right.*"

"They won't let me see him," I mumbled and picked at a piece of skin that lingered around my thumbnail.

"Who? Dacre?" I nodded and her gentle laugh bellowed in my ears, the ground shaking slightly. *"Of course, they won't. The further you are from him the better. Dacre knows exactly what to say and do to pull the dark out of you, we cannot risk that. We might not get you back this time."* I leaned back against Indra, the sun was slowly beginning to fade – the sky illuminated an orange glow along the horizon, the dark blanket of night following closely behind. Indra released a roar of a yawn and stretched out her wings, which brushed the leaves from the nearby trees. *"Evander let Sharia out of her room on Wednesday,"* Indra announced happily. *"See, he's let go of some of his anger."*

"How is she? I heard the Order wanted her removed from Gatherling and Evander really told her off." I bit the inside of my cheek – guilt eating away at me. I wasn't the only being punished. My punishment was a lot nicer than hers. Evander let me have visitors as much as I wanted, but not Sharia – she wasn't allowed to see anyone, he'd said she should have known better. I could hear her crying from down the hall most nights and each night I heard it, that pit in my stomach burned.

"They did, however Evander refused. Not many can go against the Order, however Evander has earnt their respect. He told them that he would take full responsibility for Sharia and any future mistakes she might make. In return, she's been keeping her head down and spending a lot of time in the library. You and Sharia have one thing in common – Evander. You both cannot stand to upset him."

"I feel awful for what I've done to her," I said in a saddened voice, Indra laughed through her nose.

"You don't get to play the "poor you" card this time, everything you have done, is on your own head." I hated how blunt and brutally honest Indra was at times, but she was right.

"That's true," I admitted reluctantly.

"Indra, Narrdie, sorry we're late," Evander announced as he and Audric strode towards us – sharing a dark look between them.

"Finally. You know I haven't flown in a number of weeks and you two seem to take great pleasure in making me wait – it's taunting," Indra joked as she stood, shaking her whole body.

"Our apologies, you don't need to wait any longer. We've got some business ourselves to see to." Audric teased, "Narrdie, time to restart your training."

"Have fun you three," Indra jumped up into the air and performed a summersault happily, before disappearing out of sight - it seemed her wing had healed better than I had hoped. I turned to Evander and Audric, who were smiling slyly, I cleared my throat and stood.

"I thought we'd try something different today," Evander began, his tone still holding no familiarity towards me.

"Different?" I repeated as I fidgeted with my hands.

"Different," Audric teased.

"There's been reports of a group of Loopins on my grounds and instead of dispatching them myself, I thought I'd let you do it. You know, since you feel you're strong enough to take on Dacre alone - this should be a piece of cake," Evander said sarcastically; his face held no hint of a joke. His stare was angered as he looked at me, I swallowed hard and turned to Audric.

"What are Loopins?" Evander shook his head and Audric kissed his teeth.

"Narrdie, you should already know this, I'm guessing you also haven't been reading up on our world's history either," Evander snapped. "Or maybe you think you already know everything." I clenched my jaw, Evander was still pissed, and I understood why, but his little digs were starting to irritate me.

However, he was right, I should have been reading up on everything, but instead I had gone off into my own little world of plotting and revenge. "Will you tell me or are you just going to shout surprise?" I bit back; Evander's glare cut into me - a warning.

"Loopins belong to the dark world. They are vicious, relentless, emotionless beings. They don't feel pain or fear," Audric began explaining. "They're fast, tear your face and limbs apart, much like Skinners," he explained as he leaned on a tree with his arms folded.

"What do they look like?" I asked, my palms turned sweaty.

"Me, Evander - you. They look like people, it's how they blend in, but you'll see the difference with this horde. The darkness has rotted their insides."

"So, we're going to dispose of them?" I asked, admittedly I was nervous - it had been weeks, maybe even months since I had last trained. Evander chuckled and shook his head; he crossed his arms.

"No, not we. You."

I froze, "me? No way!" My heart began to thunder in my chest, they were going to stick me in the middle of a horde – a horde of creatures I had never even heard of before. Was this a punishment?

Evander's face turned hard; he closed the gap between us in two long strides – his eyes baring down on me; I swallowed the urge to flinch back. "No? So, is this Narrdie Moon, making another decision? Much like when she decided she was big and clever enough to sneak out, while she was insanely ill, weak and find Dacre?" I bit the inside of my cheek, resisting the urge to snap his head off. "If you can do that, then you can do anything, right? Narrdie the big and powerful." I growled under my breath and dug my nails into my palms.

"Evander this isn't fair, and you know it! Audric!" Audric raised his brow and shrugged.

"I agree with him. You brought this on yourself and that feeling you have now, scared, helpless . . . defeated – this is how we felt." Audric clenched his jaw, if this is what it took for them to forgive me, then I was going to have to suck it up.

"Shall we go then?" Evander suggested as he gripped my arm, I raised my brow at him. "You're still under watch and I wouldn't want you running off again."

Audric wasn't lying, the Loopins did in fact, look like normal human beings – with only a few differences.

Their eyes scared me – as grey as a rain cloud and when they opened their mouths, it was a large circle of layers upon layers of shred worthy teeth. They were hairless, some having one or two strands of black hair, their skin was bare, dry and cracked; their feet seemed longer than a human's and their fingers were bony and crooked – I shuddered at their sight. The way they spoke to each other was strange, gargling and clicking their tongue – it made me feel uneasy that I couldn't understand them, how would I know if they already knew I was here? Were they plotting how to attack? They walked around, hunched over – like apes, growling and snapping at each other.

I opened my mouth to speak, but Evander lightly placed his palm over my lips and shook his head. He pointed to the Loopins and then to his ear and raised a brow, I nodded – understanding what he was trying to signal, the Loopins had exceptional hearing. Evander tapped me on the shoulder, counted down from three with his fingers and signalled me forward.

I was mad, what were they thinking? I was surely going to get shredded apart, just looking at these monstrous things – they were created to kill and kill only.

I had no idea how I was going to play this, there were too many of them to try and pick off. I took a deep breath, jumped over the rocks and dove right in the middle of them all. The second my feet landed on the soil; a ripple of angered snarls roared throughout the forest.

Fast feet slammed against the ground as one raced towards me, its lips curled back over its mouth – the layered teeth ready to tear my throat out. Within seconds it was on me – knocking me down, I held it out away from me, it roared and struggled as it tried to reach my face – the spit and saliva pooled on my cheeks. I had to swallow down the urge to vomit at the stench of its breath. Its head sprung left and dug its teeth into my forearm – I screamed. It shook its head side to side, like an animal trying to pull a chunk of meat from a carcass, I could feel my blood spilling around me.

I snarled, my pupils split; I spread out my fingers, willing the nails to grow long and shift into claws. My hand snagged his throat, the claws cutting into its skin, before the Loopin could react – I thrusted my other hand into its chest and squeezed until I could feel my claws pierce his heart. Black blood, oozed between my fingers and down my knuckles, a final gurgle bubbled from its throat – I tossed it to the side and rose to my feet.

The other Loopins began to spit and foam at the mouth - furious high pitched heckles overlapped the air, they slapped their hands against the mud.

One Loopin suddenly stood tall, he was bigger, more muscular and looked more human than the rest. He was cleaner than the others and had a full set of silver hair on his head, his eyes weren't white like the others – they were black and staring right at me. The other Loopins cowered back from him, keeping their heads low in submission – waiting for his approval to attack. "What are you?" I breathed.

"You do not belong here, female." I flinched back – he could speak. His voice was rough, but it still seemed . . . human. He seemed surprisingly calm and sort of amused, considering I had just killed one of his own; he raised his hand to calm the other Loopins.

"You're on the Orders land," I growled. The Loopins around immediately jumped back into their calls of protest when I spoke, his mouth lifted in a smirk.

His forked tongue snaked out and slid along his razor teeth. "Is that so?" His entertained expression suddenly faded and was replaced with rage; he flicked his fingers forward, all of a sudden, the Loopins ran at me, their teeth bare. I gasped, too many – way too many for me to take on at once, the first Loopin was bad enough.

Arrows shot past me – ruffling the hair from behind my ears – each one burying itself deep in the raging Loopins chests.

I spun around and released a breath in relief, Evander and Audric dove over the rocks – their crossbows in hand. Audric whistled me to go to him, as they both continued to rapidly fire at the Loopins.

The Loopin who could speak, hissed and ordered the rest of his creatures forward. He turned as they attacked, slowly backing into the forest – my blood boiled. "Don't let that one leave," Audric snarled towards me. My throat rumbled, I lunged forward, slamming into him hard, digging my claws into the nape of his neck, as I pulled him to the ground. I reached into my boot and pulled out my dagger, aiming it straight for the creature's heart.

"Narrdie! No!" Evander ordered, grabbing my wrist, Audric aimed his crossbow between the Loopins eyes. "Keep this one alive – he's a half breed," Evander said the words with such disgust, it surprised me. "Audric, you got it?"

"Yeah," Audric grumbled as he wrapped a black chain around the Loopins neck. "It's not going anywhere unless I want it to."

"Good, get it back and put it in the cells, if it tries anything – take a limb," he suggested with a dark smile. Audric wiggled his brows and laughed as he began to pull the chain, forcing the Loopin to follow him.

"As for you," Evander began as he turned to me. "Well done, you were amazing," he smiled widely and winked at me, it filled me with butterflies to see him finally look at me like that – I almost thought he never would smile to me ever again. His hand graced my waist and he leaned into me, his head fell against mine and I closed my eyes – breathing him in, I had missed being close to him.

"You forgive me?" His placed his hand under my chin and lifted my face up.

"I should have forgiven you ages ago, instead of ridiculing you and for that I ask - will you forgive me?" I leaned on my tiptoes and lightly placed my lips to his. "I'll take that as a yes," he chuckled and leaned in closer - I winced. "Shit," he blurted as he gently examined my arm. "One bit you? We should get you back. It's deep, it's gonna need healing - luckily, the venom doesn't look like it's kicked in yet."

Nyda wasn't gentle as she bandaged my arm, she'd protested and complained about being woken up in the middle of the night - just to heal a wound that wouldn't kill me. I winced with every pull she made, throwing a look to Evander - who just covered his laugh with a cough. "Loopins," Nyda grumbled. "They are horrid creatures, they have such nasty claws - each claw holds a different kind and amount of venom, and their teeth," she spat. "Some can make you believe you are on fire, while others can make you hallucinate terrifying things. Loopins - abominations."

"I was scratched by one once," Evander announced, he was sat crossed legged on the floor - twirling one of his throwing knives around his fingers. "It felt like someone was scooping out my eyeballs...slowly. Hurt like hell, how did yours feel?"

"Like death by a thousand bee stings," I admitted and shrugged. "I've had worse pain," Evander nodded in agreement and smiled to me sympathetically.

"And you survived," he reminded me with a smile.

"That I did . . . just," I teased.

Nyda scoffed and rolled her eyes, "after all of this, you brought one back. Why?"

"It's different, it's more human than the others. What did you call it again?" I asked Evander, he frowned and dug his knife into the floor.

"Half breed."

"Like Dacre? Astrid said he was a Hybrid."

"Yes and no. Half breeds are created in the dark realm, abominations that shouldn't exist. Created for one purpose and one purpose alone – to kill," Evander explained, something dark lingered in his eyes.

"Sounds like Dacre," I mocked.

"A Hybrid is someone who is a mixture of two powerful races. They are normally created by Necromancers – not many survive when the bloods are mixed however, too much power to be contained in one person."

"But Dacre . . ."

"Dacre is rare. He was born a Hybrid; his mother was a wolf, and no one knows what his father was. Believe me if he were a half breed – I would have killed him already," Evander spat – his words lined with anger.

"Why do you hate half breeds so much?" Evander stilled, he through a look to Nyda; she clenched her jaw and stormed out of the infirmary – a hateful sneer on her face.

"I had a sister once, Graya," he began; his eyes turned cloudy the moment he said her name. "Little Graya, she was younger than me and smaller, however that never stopped her – she was a warrior. You would have loved her Narrdie, she was so strong, would never back off from an argument if she knew she was right – a lot like you. She would have made a glorious leader – legendary even and I'm not just saying that because I'm her brother. Gatherling, is the biggest sanctuary in the Order and they thought no one but Graya, was worthy enough to run it." He smiled to himself, and I gently took his hand in mine.

"Were you going to run it with her?" I asked gently, he laughed lightly.

"No, as much as me and Graya loved each other and trained well together – you couldn't have two Alpha wolves in the same sanctuary – instincts." I smirked as I looked down and he raised his brow. "Something funny?"

"No, it's just...do you know that's the first time you've ever talked about being a wolf to me?"

"It is?"

"Yeah, Indra told me what you were months ago, but I always wondered why you never spoke of it."

Evander shrugged, "it's not a secret. I guess I just forgot that you didn't remember the old days," he half smiled, and I knew it was meant as an apology – I leaned up and kissed him on the cheek.

"So, if Graya was going to be in charge of Gatherling – where would you have gone?"

"Nathina, the sanctuary to the west – the second largest. Everything was quiet for a few years; you had been placed into the deep sleep – practically comatose. The dark realm, were like fish out of water with no one to lead them. Then . . . then," Evander's voice faded, and he clenched his jaw. Tears threatened to spill in his eyes, I squeezed his hand – bringing his eyes back to me.

"You don't have to, Evander."

"No, it's alright. I had just finished having a meeting with some members of the Order, when we had gotten word that Lazarus Mountain was under attack – a lot of attack."

"Nyda?"

"No, Nyda was in Gatherling with Graya – they were good friends those two. Narcissa, a Vampire Elder was the reigning leader of Lazarus back then. When her sanctuary fell under attack, she called to the closest sanctuary for help - Graya. A horde of half breeds, had descended on Lazarus by the hundreds – it was overrun. By the time I arrived with reinforcements, Narcissa and . . . and my Graya were dead. Their bodies hanging upside down outside of the sanctuary. We found Nyda inside all cut up – but alive. After time, the Order believed that we'd gotten all those responsible. I was never satisfied and now I know why. The half breeds were led by a Hybrid."

"Dacre," I finished, my voice nothing but a whisper – he nodded. I didn't know what to say to him, what could I say? I stood and wrapped my arms around him. "I'm so sorry Evander."

Before any of us could say another word, a light knock padded on the infirmary door. "Come in," Evander called, after her wiped his eyes and cleared his throat.

"Bonjour, forgive me for interrupting." We both jumped up as Bayona poked her head through the door, she had a half worried and half curious look on her face. "I hope you're feeling better, Narrdie." I smiled and lightly tapped my bandage.

"A lot better than I was an hour ago, is everything alright?" I asked her, her breathing was rapid, and she kept looking between me and Evander – worried.

"Well, we . . . we have company. You two should probably come outside."

Guards stood in a line around the Gatherling entrance, each one armed with crossbows and swords – aimed toward a small group of people. The strangers exchanged a nervous glance and closed in the space between them; their eyes flickered around us; my heart skipped a beat when several of their eyes landed on me. One of the guards raised his crossbow higher and glanced to Audric – waiting for the order.

"You're frightening them," I whispered to him as I carefully stepped closer. "Tell the men to stand down, they could be here to help."

"Or they could be here to hurt," Audric growled. "We can't take that chance."

I was worried that this torturous staring between our groups would never end, it seemed no one wanted to be the first to speak. I rolled my eyes and took a step forward before I could even breathe – Evander snagged my arm and pulled me back.

"No," he warned. "They came to us if they need help – they talk. Not us and especially not you." I glared at him; I didn't know if this was the way things were in this world, or whether it was just his wolf, alpha ego – poking its way through.

Finally, one of the men unlinked his arm from the girl beside him and took two steps forward, he swallowed hard and rubbed his hands together nervously. His eyes darted along the line of our people, until they paused at me – he dropped his head low in a bow.

I bowed my head back and bumped my shoulder with Evander; he nodded and offered me his hand. I knew what this meant and with a smile I happily took it, he led me a few steps forward – Audric dropped back to flank us. "I-It is an honour to meet you Sir Evander, Sir Audric and an even greater honour to meet you, Lady Narrdie Moon. We have heard a lot about you and your people, it took us a long while to find you." They all bowed, and we returned the gesture.

"Forgive the high security, we've had a rough couple of weeks and the sanctuary is on high alert." Evander explained respectfully.

"Before we talk any further, I ask you and your companions to surrender all weapons that you and your people may have." Audric ordered in a polite manor, the man hesitated for a moment – exchanging a look with his people, before calmly pulling out his sword and handing it carefully to a nearby guard.   "Thank you," Audric said with a smile. "We will keep them safe for you," he assured them.

"How may we help you all?" Evander asked a little too hostile, I nudged him and he quickly through me a tight smile.

"What are you?" I blurted, before either of them could say another word. They both looked to me with surprised expressions, a smile tugged at Evander's lips. "You're not human," my eyes moved from the man to the rest of his people. "Only one of you is."

"How do you know that?" Evander asked warmly. "I can't smell anything," he whispered - leaning in closely.

"I just do," With a nod of permission from Evander, I took a step forward and offered him a friendly smile. "There's no need to feel scared, we can help you if you need it. I swear none of our men will lay a hand on you, as long as you and your own don't plan on harming mine." I met his eyes and he smiled warmly.

"I assure you, we are no threat to you," he spoke as he placed his hand over his chest and bowed. "My name is Demir, and Lady Moon, you are correct. I am not human," he blinked hard several times and his eyes changed from brown to the same lavender, that I had seen in Sharia.

"You're a Skin-Changer," I said with wide smile.

Evander chuckled. "As a sign of good faith - I will introduce my people. Of course, you already know the Lady Narrdie, as well as myself and Narrdie's Watcher - Audric, one of the high-ranking Watchers in the Order." Audric flicked the top of his head in greeting. "Welcome to Gatherling, my sanctuary - which I am Alpha of." Evander smirked as his orange eyes glowed bright. I bit my lip, heat flushed to my cheeks, and I could feel butterflies spinning around in my stomach.

My Alpha wolf.

"Our Witches," Evander continued. "Nyda and Bayona," they both stepped forward and did their elegant bows, both with friendly and beautiful smiles on their faces. I could tell they had all done this many times over, I had to admit it made me self-conscious.

Demir's eyes rested on Bayona's blackened sockets, and his smile faded. A low growl rippled from Astrid - a frightening sound. She'd moved so fast; it had taken me a moment to register where she had gone; she'd placed herself only inches from Demir's face.

"Stare any longer and I will make your eyes, exactly like hers and then you can glare at yourself instead," she warned darkly. I bit my cheek to keep from smiling.

Immediately, Demir looked to Astrid and lowered his head. "Forgive me, I didn't mean any offense. It's just...I have heard stories of you," he clarified quickly to Bayona.

"Astrid," Bayona called softly. She walked forward and gently took hold of her elbow. "He meant no insult," she assured her. "Leave him be." Bayona flashed Demir an apologetic smile and he nodded nervously to her.

"I apologise if I offended anyone," he repeated, his voice held a shaky note. "We have heard of the Lady Bayona, the grand Psychic Witch – your story is glorious." Bayona's laugh fluttered around us, and I made a mental note to ask her to tell me some of these stories.

"Thank you," she chimed. "However, over the years I think some of the stories have been exaggerated." Everyone chuckled, everyone except Nyda – jealously tainted her eyes.

"The Lady that almost tore out your spine, is the Elder Astrid – our Vampire," Evander explained with a chuckle. Three people behind Demir suddenly gasped and exchanged quiet mumbles between themselves, Demir through his hand back to silence them. "I see some of yours know her also," he chortled.

"Hello, my dears," Astrid spoke gently to the three behind Demir, they looked at her with wide eyes and dropped to the ground in a bow. "That is not needed, stand please – we will talk more later."

"We too, have our own Skin-changer," Evander raised his hand and smiled as he gestured Sharia forward – she didn't move or even glance Demir's direction. Sharia bit the inside of her cheek, she seemed stiff and uncomfortable; her eyes kept glancing towards Gatherling entrance, as though she wanted to run back inside. "This is Sharia," Evander continued with worry in his eyes. "And these," he began with a gesture to the guards – all still with their crossbows raised. "Are the Guardians of the Keepers, each man and woman you see bearing the purple colours of the Order – are the protectors of the sanctuaries. You will also find that hidden amongst the ins and outs of the grounds – sanctuary Monks." This wasn't an introduction, but a polite caution, if they were here to harm us – we were more than capable of defending ourselves. Demir nodded in understanding, gulping slightly at the mention of the Monks.

The moment they had crossed Gatherling's borders, Evander had ordered Indra and the Elemental Priestesses to leave – just until it was safe. A build of trust, Audric had called it. If they prove to be allies, then in time they would be introduced to them.

"It is truly a pleasure to meet you all," Demir began in a happy tone, I was thankful that he didn't seem to notice Sharia's inhospitality, no doubt Evander would speak to her later. "These are my people, there may not be many of us – but we are good people. Illythia, Adelina, Talon," the ones who'd bowed to Astrid. "Our

Vampire siblings."

"Ciao a tutti voi," one of the sisters said politely as they both bowed – Talon just nodded.

"When we heard of your return, we came from Italy – to help," the other sister said to me, her smile was sweet, her voice lined with a light Italian accent.

"Rosie-Anika-Yoland, a hunter from one of the human factions." Demir announced as he continued, he looked disapprovingly towards Talon – it seemed we weren't the only ones who didn't like unknown company.

"Ray for short," Rosie-Anika-Yoland jumped in with a smile.

"Human factions? Forgive me, but I thought humans weren't involved – isn't that what Watchers and the Order make sure off?"

"That is true, however the Order can't erase every human's mind that had seen something or someone belonging to this world. They helped organised different human factions to help keep things contained. It's why you don't ever see this stuff on the tele or the internet – it's always monitored and taken down," she explained happily. Demir and the others from his group frowned and once more all eyes were on me – perhaps they didn't realise that I had no memory of certain things.

"There's something else about you, isn't there?" I asked as I looked into her eyes, I could sense it – like a bug crawling around her veins. "What is it?" Ray laughed; pleasant shock filled her eyes.

"A syrim. It took me a while to perfect, but it works a lot in her favour – she's not much of an easy target anymore." A tall man explained as he stepped forward – not daring to reach any of our eyes.

"Mazruriuk, is very skilled in many ways," Ray chimed as she linked her hand with his.

Once more Astrid launched herself forwards in front of me and snarled, instantly the cheery mood – turned dark and tense. Ray flinched back, however Mazruriuk didn't move and inch, his jawed clenched.

"Astrid!" Audric barked, he raised his hands – like she was a ferocious animal turned rabid.

"Introduce yourself Mazruriuk," Astrid ordered in an aggressive voice. Demir swallowed timidly and stepped in front of Mazruriuk, blocking his view from Astrid; his hands raised in a calming manor.

"Mazruriuk . . . is a Shade." The moment the word reached everyone's ears, an array of snarls and hisses spread all around – our guards stepped forward, all their crossbows turned on Mazruriuk. "Wait, please!" Demir begged.

"Evander," I called, he turned to me – his face dark. I breathed out heavily and nodded once to him – he frowned, distaste smudging his face, but released a high-pitched whistle. Hesitantly, the area silenced, and our guards stood back – there crossbows dropping only slightly. "Speak quickly," I urged.

"Mazruriuk, is a white Shade – he is on the side of the light!" Demir's eyes were wide; his breathing was fast, and he looked around us all frantically. I shared a long look with Mazruriuk, before looking over my shoulder to Evander – who glared so hard at the Shade, I thought he was going to burn holes through his skull.

"Evander, is that true? Are their white Shades?" I asked.

"It's rare – very rare, but true. He doesn't look like a Shade of dark, and once tainted by the darkness – they can't change what it does to them." Evander replied, not taking his eyes from him.

"So, what now?" Ray uttered, "Are we just going to stand around deciding whether or not to trust each other?"

"Rose," Illythia snapped.

"Perché non chiedere a quello psichico? Bayona," Adelina spoke, her voice like a melody.

"Forgive me, but what did she say?" Audric asked as he turned to Talon and Illythia.

"She wonders if Bayona would use her abilities to look into Mazruriuk," Talon replied, his voice sounded bored and uninterested. "Forgive my sister, she doesn't speak English."

"Bayona?" Evander asked softly. "Would you?"

Bayona tilted her head with a smile, she nodded and stepped forward – offering her hand to Mazruriuk. "I won't hurt you," she ensured him warmly. Astrid growled in protest, but Evander shot his hand out to silence her. Mazruriuk didn't hesitate when he took her hand, nor did he look nervous, his hand touched hers and she gasped instantly.

The seconds it took felt like minutes, the minutes felt like hours, and everyone had fallen silent and still while we waited for Bayona. She breathed out hard as she let his hand go, she smiled her appreciation to him before turned to Evander. "I saw no darkness," she announced, Evander nodded once.

"You'll have to forgive our hostility," I said with a lightly chuckle, trying to defuse the tension that clogged the area and filled my lungs. "We have had a bad history with Shades."

"Come all of you, let us continue this in the grand hall. Gatherling opens its doors to you," Evander said with a cheery voice, he signalled them all inside with his hand.

Astrid didn't once take her eyes from Mazruriuk, if looks could kill – he'd be a pile of blood and bones by now. All the members of the Pura Mensam, a handful of guards and the new group – were all spread around the grand hall. Evander had ordered food to be brought out, an assortment of cheeses – marinated in a creamy sauce, meats on skewers with picked onions and peppers. Stuffed peppers with caramelized garlic mushrooms and spicy rice, steamed into my nose – my mouth instantly watered. Audric laughed and gently pushed me towards the food.

"Go on," he urged.

"I will later."

"You may as well go and stuff your face, you're hardly paying attention anyway. When did you last get something to eat?" He picked up a skewer and waved it around in my face playfully, I snagged it from him and pulled a chunk of beef into my mouth.

"Right now," I teased with my mouth full, sticking my food filled tongue out at him – Audric rolled his eyes.

"You're disgusting." I wiggled my eyebrows at him, and we held in our laughter. I pretended to silence him and pointed to Demir – who began to happily tell us his story.

"I came amongst Illythia, Adelina and Talon in Tuscany – they almost killed me, well Illythia almost did. I had no passport, no papers – so getting around was difficult as a human. I had shifted into a deer and was running through the groves; little did I know I was being hunted by three very hungry Vampires." He laughed along with the siblings, even Talon - who was slouched away from us on a wall, chuckled.

"You should have heard his squeals," Illythia snorted.

"Pensavo che stavi per piangere," Adelina said through a laugh.

"I was not going to cry," Demir protested. "Anyway! Illythia dove on me, and I immediately changed back and thankful she eventually let me go. I waited at their camp until they had finished hunting and they'd told me that Narrdie Moon had rose up again and were heading over here to find her. We were heading to Gretenval," Evander's head snapped to him, and he frowned as he set his cup down.

"Gretenval?" Evander repeated, Demir nodded and shared a curious look with the siblings. "Gretenval was breached and burned down centuries ago, who told you to go there?"

"When we arrived here, a man called Dacre was waiting for us and warned us that Lazarus was breached. He said we should head to Gretenval, and he'd have someone come and meet us," Demir's face creased with puzzlement. Evander slammed his fist on the table, causing bits of food and cups to fall all around, anger washed over his face, and he laughed sarcastically.

"I should have known!" He hissed; Evander's eyes met mine. Demir exchanged a puzzled look with his people.

"Dacre, is the reason Lazarus was breached, he betrayed us all and is the reason a lot of ours have died. He was probably going to kill you or force you to turn over to the dark realm when you got to Gretenval," I explained and took hold of Evander's hand under the table.

"I see," Demir said; he swallowed hard and bowed his head to us all. "I'm sorry for your losses."

"What brought you here instead of Gretenval?"

"We were on our way when Adelina caught Ray's scent - it was full of fear and blood. Then we all heard her screams and the worst sound any of us hear . . . Skinners."

"We couldn't just leave her," Illythia chimed in, she shook her head and shuddered slightly. "When we got to her, she was up in a tree, her leg was torn up and the Skinners were chewing through the bark. Before we could even take another step, Mazruriuk had ripped their heads from their bodies and crushed their hearts. While Mazruriuk was taking care of the

Skinners, Talon got Ray down and healed her up. We told them where we were going and that they were welcome to join, but Ray told us that Gatherling was closer, and they were arming up."

"We agreed that no matter what we found, we'd stay together," Ray jumped in. "You may be wary of us Sir Evander and even kill us if you choose not to trust us. If that is your choice, then I will do anything to protect them – not matter what the outcome is," she said with a glance in my direction, before turning back to Evander. "You have your family and I have mine." I couldn't contain the smile that spread widely on my face, and I could see that same smile mimicked in everyone's faces – even Nyda's stone face seemed to crack.

"I like her," Astrid announced cheerfully.

"Wait, so you were already with Mazruriuk?" Bayona asked Ray in surprise, Ray nodded and slipped her hand into his. "How peculiar, a Shade and a human . . . companions," Bayona teased with a raised brow.

Evander and Demir continued to talk about their travels, not leaving out any detail in case it was useful to us. I spent my time in the hall looking over our new friends, seeing if I could find anything that might trigger some warning bells – they seemed safe enough.

Demir was older than us, his stubble was a mixture of dark and grey hair – the grey more prominent against his black skin. He was toned, with wide shoulders and buried in animal tattoos, each one covered in so much detail – they looked like the real thing. Perhaps each tattoo represented an animal he had shifted into, I made a mental note to ask him about them later.

The three Vampire siblings were almost identical. Adelina and Illythia both had incredibly long silver hair – it reminded me of the Moon. Adelina's hair was straight, while Illythia's was wild and wavy, the silver began to blend into black towards the end. They had perfect angled cheekbones that seemed to shimmer in the light, their plump lips were deep purple. Illythia was fuller and curvier than Adelina, she had a strange symbol that seemed to have been burnt above her collarbone; she spotted me looking and pulled up the collar of her V-neck grey jumper.

Talon's hair stayed silver, it was long – at least down past his shoulders, he was broad, and his face was as hard as stone. His eyes were bold and...red – bright red. I looked to Illythia and Adelina, their eyes were also blood red, I knew exactly what that meant – hunger.

"Astrid?" I called over lightly as everyone spoke amongst themselves. Astrid was still glaring at Mazruriuk, every movement he made, every time he spoke – Astrid was there. She tilted her head to the side, and she slid into a chair beside me.

"Yes, dear?" She whispered.

"Adelina, Illythia and Talon, look at them," reluctantly she moved her eyes to the siblings and nodded.

"Oh, I see. That's not what you want."

"Apart from Ray, does Gatherling have any humans?" I asked, I had never really stopped to ask what everyone was – there was too many people in and out.

"Yes, a few. I'll handle this," Astrid turned to the others and cleared her throat. "Forgive me for interrupting but, you all had a long journey and have been given food and water. However, some of us don't eat this food, would you mind if I took Sir Talon, Lady Adelina and Lady Illythia out hunting with me?" Their eyes shot up instantly and they all grinned, wide fanged smiles to her.

"That does not sound such a bad idea, Lady Astrid, I would be honoured to join you. Sisters?" Talon said with an excited tone, it was the happiest I'd seen him since he'd gotten here.

"Sono affamato," Adelina said happily.

"I agree with Adelina, I'm starving," Illythia cheered.

"Then follow me, I know the best area." The four Vampires hastily skipped out of the hall, I smiled, and the tension seemed to filter out with them.

Ray, was standing very close to Mazruriuk, his hand linked protectively with hers – she nestled her head on his shoulder. She was a plain girl, naturally pretty with light pink lips and freckles decorating her cheeks. Her orange hair was bright – like a fire on a dark night, she had half of it waving down to her shoulders – two little ponytails rested in green bobbles on her head. She was cute in all aspects, even the clothes she wore – blue washed tight fitting, dungarees with a white long sleeved top underneath. Her dark olive-green eyes, stayed fixated on Mazruriuk– who side glanced to her with a grin.

Mazruriuk's appearance scared me slightly, his skin grey and pale but, his eyes were two different colours, one black and the other – the palest pink I'd ever seen. His hair was braided, white with a single black streak, trailing all the way down his back. His veins were spread around his face and arms like Egregious – but not as dark. His fingertips were navy, like he had stained ink all over them; Mazruriuk was taller than Egregious, bigger and no doubt stronger – but the fear he made me feel was the same.

"I can smell your fear," I heard Mazruriuk's voice in my head – my eyes shot towards him, but he wasn't looking towards me. *"I know who you are and what lies inside you."* I could feel my heart pounding against my chest from his words. He knew – he knew about Crow.

"What do you want? Why are you here?" I through towards him.

"I am not here to harm you or anyone else, we've all be truthful, and we've meant every word. We are here to help you; help you fight against the darkness – all the darkness." I clenched my jaw, feeling a subtle warning in his words. I felt his eyes on me and looked back towards him; he bowed his head once to me and I copied his movement – not being able to respond back to him. This seemed enough response he needed.

"Evander, I'm going to get some air, I feel a bit sick," I turned to walk but Evander grabbed my arm and gave me a stern look.

"Narrdie?"

"It's okay, I just need air and then I'm going to lie down," I smiled and planted a light kiss on his lips, I lightly lifted his hand from my arm. "I'm not running off, I promise." This had all been enough excitement for one day.

Chapter Nineteen
Everyone

*R*ay opened her eyes and let out a long huff, another night being wide awake, as much as she enjoyed the syrim – the side effects were still an issue, she had gotten used to the occasional headaches, sickness and dizziness – it was the sleepless nights she hated. She looked to her side, Mazruriuk was sound asleep – she frowned and leaned her ear against his mouth and waited a few seconds. He always seemed so...dead when he slept, even though she had been with him for almost a year – she still had to check he was breathing.

She pulled on her mossy green jumper, the warmth from it instantly prickling her skin, wiggled into her grey jeans and crammed her foot into her black combat boot – which had seen better days. She frowned, where was its twin? She began searching for the other boot, tiptoeing around and cursing quietly to herself.

"Under the bed – my side," he grumbled in a sleepy voice. She crinkled her nose and swore at herself for waking him, before reaching under the bed and snatching it.

"I was trying not to wake you," she whispered, as though he was still asleep.

"I'm awake whenever you're awake," he rolled over onto his back and watched her. "Where are you sneaking of too anyway?" He asked as his hand lazily reached out to caress her cheek, she forced her foot into her boot and dived onto the bed beside him.

"We've been here for a week now and I haven't been hunting or exploring, I feel like a caged animal." Mazruriuk stroked her arm with his fingers and yawned.

"Fine, I'll get dressed and come with you," he offered and leaned up, Ray frowned and pushed him back down gently – dropping a kiss on his lips.

"No, I'll be fine on my own. It's still early and we were up late last night – you should sleep, come find me later or better yet, don't leave the bed and I'll come and find you," she purred with a wiggle of her eyebrows. He frowned, he hated leaving her – it always set him on edge, still he nodded.

"Be safe," he ordered softly.

Ray walked happily down the hallways, there weren't many people awake at this hour and the ones that were awake, stayed in their rooms until everyone else woke. This made her happier, she wasn't one for crowds – never had been. "Excuse me?" She called to a guard standing outside the grand hall. He turned almost in an aggravated way, still he bowed and forced a smile.

"Lady Yoland, what can I do for you?" He asked respectfully, purple bags lingered under his eyes – he must have been on watch all night.

"I want to go hunting, but since we came, they've removed all our weapons. Who do I speak to, to get my bow and arrow back?" She asked with a smile, the guard couldn't help but smile back to her. A lot of people found it hard not to enjoy her company, she was one of the sweetest people, kind-hearted – everyone instantly loved her.

"Please, forgive us Lady Yoland, the removal of your weapons is the protocol for the sanctuary. If you wish to get your weapon back, you must get permission from one of the members, most are still asleep, I believe Sir Evander is in the hall."

"Ray! Good morning," Evander greeted instantly, he was hunched over at the table reading a thick book – a bundle of smaller books scattered around him; he smiled widely. "Early riser as well I assume."

"Good morning, Evander, enjoying your read?" She asked with a distasteful tone, she perched her lips as she read the title of the page he was reading, 'White Shades and their power.' Evander let out a long breath and smiled apologetically; he closed the book and kicked out a seat beside him – offering it to her. She remained standing.

"I know it looks as though I am checking up on Mazruriuk, but I can assure you – I fully believe he is on our side."

"It looks it," she bit.

"It is, otherwise, none of you would be in my home. I have never met a white Shade, never really heard much about them either – I'm curious to know their heritage. Curiosity, that's all." Ray nodded and the warm smile she always wore returned to her lips once more.

"I get it. I'm sorry, I'm very protective of him – everyone we've come across has either turned us away because of what he is . . . or tried to kill him. So, I get very defensive," she smiled sheepishly.

"Then he is very lucky to have you. Maybe now you can relax a little, no one here will harm him, you have my word," Evander promised her. He tilted his head; his eyebrows creased slightly. "Mazruriuk isn't why you're here, is it?"

"No, I have actually come to ask if I can have my bow and arrow back, please. A guard said only a member of the . . . P- Pura Mensam, can give permission for weapons." Evander's mouth twitched up, he nodded towards the opened chair beside him.

"Sit with me?" She hesitated, but only for a second. "Hunting? Very well, I will let the watchmen know to release your weapons."

"I'll bring it back once I'm done," she offered.

"No, keep them. Once the rest are awake, I will return theirs as well. I'm going to wait for everyone, but I think I'll just tell you and then the others later. I've spoken with the Pura Mensam members, and we've all agreed that we'd like you and your people to join us." He said with a wide smile.

Ray blinked several times, the side of her mouth twitched up in a smile. "But it's only been a week."

"I know, but I have had people keep tabs on you all and as you all know, Bayona has been using her abilities to look into you and I believe that we really can trust you. We need more people on our side, Dacre beats us in numbers and if we start turning people away, who offer help - we'll lose. So, what do you say, Ray?" Ray squealed and practically jumped out of her seat; it had been so long since she'd been accepted somewhere - since Mazruriuk had been accepted.

"I can't speak for the others, but I'd be happy to accept."

Evander met her wide smile with his own and chuckled lightly. "Well, I am pleased to have you. However, do me a favour, until I have everyone's answers, I'd like to keep it hush for now. So please don't say anything?" She nodded. "Thank you, now off you go - go hunt and have fun."

Ray hummed a lullaby as she stalked around the forest; she ran her fingers along the rough bark and the melody of her lullaby turned eerie - the bark had been tainted. She froze, allowing her senses to consume over her, feeling the rush of the syrim sawing through her veins. Her eyes flew open as it hit her - the smell. It was the smell of decay, the overwhelming smell of damp and mould, it smelt like rotten mushrooms and spoiled meat. It belonged to something that shouldn't be there; something that was in no way good or kind - no, this smell belonged to something that she should fear.

Run. Run. Run.

The thought screamed at her, slammed against her head, stabbed between her chest and begged her legs to move, to turn around and run back to Gatherling, back to Mazruriuk- back to safety.

Run. Run. Run.

No. Ray wouldn't run. Mazruriuk had given her that syrim because he saw something in her, she wasn't a week little girl - she was soldier and soldiers didn't run, they'd fight.

She crouched to the floor, her hand hovering over the disturbed soil - warm, something was here, and it wasn't that long ago. She tracked her way past the trees, allowing the syrim to ignite her senses, fuel her blood and awaken her muscles, the more she tracked the more the forest had been infected. The more trees she pasted, the stronger that dangerous scent became, until finally - she reached the core of the foul smell. She expected to find a dead animal, a decomposing body or even a creature from the dark world -

they were known for their horrific smells. What she didn't expect to find, was the unusual pool of gloopy blood – pulsating on the ground.

If there was something you didn't understand, don't go near it and never under any circumstances – touch it. Those words had been grilled into her on a daily basis, Mazruriuk used to be so afraid that her human curiosity would get her killed – he'd even get her to recite it before she went to sleep and the minute she'd wake up.

She knelt down beside it, only to try and examine it more. Her brows pulled together in a tight knot, as she willed calm into her shaking bones, this blood in no way was from and animal or a human, not only was the stench and consistency a big giveaway, but this blood was...alive. "Darkness," she whispered – her breath jittery. She knew she should have headed back to Gatherling and inform the others; this was still within the Gatherling grounds and that meant that the darkness was getting close – dangerously close. However, the hunter inside her wanted to find the creature it belonged to, she had nothing to prove to anyone, she showed how strong she was a long while ago, this was pure human stubbornness. Her fingers stretched out in front of her, edging closer towards it – perhaps if she could feel it; her senses would get a better reading.

Suddenly, a hand snaked out and gripped her – pulling her back roughly. Instinct shot through her, the syrim came alive in her veins and she felt the fire of battle swim around her blood. She swung her fist around, knocking whoever it was holding her; she kicked up – flipping back and landing with a painful thud on her heels, the vibrating pain shooting up her calves. She pulled the engraved dagger – that Mazruriuk gave her for her birthday – from her boot and gripped it hard in her hand.

"Nika!" The voice called – shocked.

"Riuk!" Dropping the dagger back into its sheath, she closed the distance between them and held his face in her hands – wiping the black blood from his lip and kissing his head over and over. "I'm sorry, you scared the shit out of me!" She cursed him, he laughed and brushed her hands with his own.

"You have some punch on you Nika, still your landing is wrong. You hurt your feet, didn't you? I saw you wince," he said sternly; he turned her around to gently massage her calves, using his powers to heal the stinging.

"I'm alright, I just got spooked." She lightly kicked him off and stun around to kiss his lips, "I'm sorry I punched you. Why are you skulking around here for anyway?"

"I go where you go, but I never thought you'd be foolish enough try something like this." He said softly, his expression darkened, and he gently took hold of her arm – pulling her away from the gloopy blood. "You said you were hunting, not tracking a creature. Has nothing I've taught you sank in?"

She groaned in frustration and wriggled out of his hold, looking back towards the blood pool. "Riuk, something's not right, this blood it's . . . it's like it's alive," she began as she took a step towards it again.

"Not to close," he warned her. "If I left you for another second, you would have touched that and right now I'd probably be watching you die. This blood is alive, and it is very toxic – non treatable. Do you understand what I'm saying, it would have killed you, Nika." She heard the pain in his voice, Mazruriuk had been her protector since day one.

She'd come across him one night, while she was hunting a gathering of Brocs, he'd had a run in with a large horde of Sivvs; she'd aimed her crossbow right for his head, but he'd seen her and when their eyes met – sparks electrocuted her veins. Instantly, he'd felt bewitched by her, this frail tiny human, who had his life in her hands - was now leaning over him, wiping the blood and muck from his wounds, damping the sweat on his brow, she'd even sang to him on nights where the night terrors tried to consume his mind. He'd stayed with her ever since.

Her eyebrows raised and she gulped, "I get it, again I'm sorry. What creature has blood like that?" Mazruriuk frowned; he took a step closer to her - not liking the way she kept pulling towards it, like she was stuck in a trance, hypnotized by its very presence. He knew exactly what that could mean - the blood called to her, the second her foot had set down on the ground beside it, it had clung to her like a tick on a dog. Gently, he hooked his hand around her arm and pulled her back towards Gatherling, his eyes not once leaving her face.

"Come on Nika, it's time to go back. It's not safe here," Ray grunted and ripped her arm from his hold. Mazruriuk's temper rose, something uneasy was lingering in the air and he didn't want to endure it any longer than he had to.

"You know, don't you?" She hissed to him.

"Rosie," his voice was stern.

"I'm not moving until you tell me." Stubborn little thing.

He growled and stormed over to her, "then I'll drag you!" He snapped as he gripped her arm, his fingers were like vices around her wrists, simmering into her skin – she winced.

"Riuk!" She protested, he'd never acted like this – at least never with her; she dug her feet into the soil and slammed a hand into his chest. "You're hurting me!" The words snagged him, he stopped – his fingers lightened their hold; his jaw clenching as he saw the red marks on her wrist.

"I'm sorry," he breathed as he lightly kissed the finger marks.

"Just tell me." She demanded, but stroked her thumb along his to let him know she held no ill thoughts about his actions.

"It's a Shade," he finally blurted with a growl. Ray scoffed; she knew Shades, it was the first thing she was taught to kill in the faction – she'd had one warming her bed for the past year.

"Bullshit. That blood is alive, you really expect me to believe it's a Shades?" She was aware that her voice sounded panicked, but she couldn't help it, if he were willing to lie to her – then this must be bad. Mazruriuk exhaled – calming himself, before taking her hands once more and pulling her to him.

"Nika, look at me. I have never lied to you, nor have I ever questioned your ability to sense or kill before," he began, reading the anger that caused her face to harden. "You need to listen to me carefully, this is a Shade's blood. This Shade is nothing like me or the one we killed in Boreal Forest, he is the stronger, older and deadlier than we could ever know." Ray had seen all kinds of Shades – light and dark, each one would either cower in fear or bow in respect as Mazruriuk approached, as far as she knew; he was the older and strongest.

"Even older than you?" Her voice cracked.

"Yes." Her mouth went dry, shivers danced around her skin, she knew exactly what this meant – they were all in severe danger.

"We need to get back to Gatherling."

⌈

"You are sure Ray?" Illythia asked, wanting to make sure she hadn't been daydreaming – humans were notorious at that. "Mazruriuk?" He nodded, confirmation.

"I was with her, I smelt what she smelt – saw what she saw," Mazruriuk answered. Illythia glanced to Astrid who then glanced to Evander. Evander was normally the one who remained calm – unreadable, it was his way of keeping everyone from falling apart. Today was different, after hearing this news – they all saw the fear in his eyes, and it was beginning to taint the rest of his composure. Evander's eyes swept across the looking group, until finally they set on Narrdie. His jaw clenched – shame washed over him, he didn't have a plan, or any kind of encouraging words for them all, like they hoped.

Pain pulled at Narrdie's heartstrings, she couldn't bear to see him looking so defeated; she wanted to run over to him, to wrap her arms around him and tell him that she didn't care if he was scared. Why would she care, why would any of them care? In fact, seeing him so vulnerable, made her love him even more. Yes, every girl loved the brave warrior fantasy, liked their men tough – able to take on a whole army alone and be able to throw them across the room when it counted. She loved the fact Evander was powerful, respected and a hell of a good fighter, but seeing his carved face, crumble and turn away from them all with fright – made him more human, it made him real.

She closed her eyes and took in a deep breath. *"Evander,"* she called to him; her Animo ability was rusty, it was the one ability she had practiced the least – had it even worked? She peeked one eye open, holding all her fingers and toes crossed, thankfully Evander glanced over – his face was like granite, but his eyes were gently.

"Look who's playing with her Animo," his voice sang to her. *"Is everything alright?"*

"I was going to ask you the same thing, you can act tough around everyone else – but not me. I know you, Evander." Evander looked down, hiding his smirk from everyone; he looked up to her, in the way that sent the butterflies skittering around in her stomach and made goosebumps freckle her skin.

"Can't hide from the great Narrdie Moon," he teased.

"Evander. I'm serious. Stop acting around me, I can see it in your eyes. Tell me, what's going on in your head." She dared a push, sneaking her Animo further into his mind – only to be met by snaking vines, whipping her back.

"It's rude to neb," he taunted, she could hear his laugh echo in her head.

"Evander, please."

"If this is as bad as Mazruriuk is saying then...then we are more fucked than we thought. If this Shade is as strong as he is saying, then we need to round up more people and get everyone ready sooner than we wanted. I am scared Narrdie, not because of the fight or being outnumbered – I'm scared for you, for Sharia – for everyone. I'm scared that I won't be able to help you, that my time with you keeps getting cut shorter and shorter. I'm scared I will lose you – for good this time." Her heart stung at his words, tears burned in her eyes, and she had to cough to cover the whimper that escaped her lips. She couldn't reassure him, she couldn't tell him that everything was going to be alright, because they both knew it wasn't.

"Promise me something," she said, hating how her voice sounded so fragile, even in her Animo.

"Anything."

"Whatever happens – we face it together." Evander's eyes met hers and a warm smile stretched across her lips.

"Always."

⌣

"*N*yda, take some troops and go and get a sample, be careful not to touch it thought," Evander began barking orders, he turned towards Astrid. "Send word to the Monks, tell them to check the grounds thoroughly, let nothing slip by. Once everyone is back, I am putting Gatherling in lockdown."

"Lockdown? Is that really necessary Evander?" Sharia whinged.

"Until we know the grounds aren't breached then yes, it is necessary, and I will hear no word about it. Do you understand?" Sharia nodded and flinched back. "Mazruriuk go with Nyda, be on your guard." Mazruriuk and Nyda bowed, Nyda clicked her flingers, and a small group of men quickly grabbed their weapons and rushed after her.

"Dove è Narrdie?" Adelina asked. Evander raised his brow as he looked to Illythia for help.

"She said where is Narrdie," Illythia translated; she looked around and frowned. "She was here earlier; shouldn't she be here?" Evander's jaw clenched, he plastered on a smile and shrugged nonchalantly.

"She's with Audric, she . . . she wasn't feeling the best." Illythia nodded sympathetically. During their hunts with Astrid, they had all been filled in with the events that had happened at Gatherling. Including Narrdie's memory being wiped, Dacre's betrayal – the attack on the college and how it had affected Narrdie. Illythia understood more than most, what grief and betrayal could do to someone, it made her heart ache.

Adelina swallowed slightly and took a few moments to gather her words; she spoke slowly, glancing to her brother for reassurance. "So . . . what do?" She began, everyone had been helping her with her English and every time she tried – everyone smiled. Evander turned to her and offered her a smile, encouraging her to continue. "If bad Shade here, we . . . we . . ." She frowned and breathed out with annoyance; she turned towards Talon. "Se è una brutta Ombra, corriamo e lasciamo Gatherling?"

"She wants to know if we are going to leave Gatherling because of the Shade," Talon murmured.

"No. We are not leaving again," Evander growled. "Moving to a new sanctuary can take days – months even. Months we can't afford to waste."

"So, we just stay here and wait for this grand Shade to find us?" Talon scoffed. "Or worse bring the darkness to us? We're not ready for that – you've made that very clear!"

"I will not waste time running," Evander snarled. Talon pushed of the wall and closed the distance between them in three big strides – standing inches from Evander.

"Talon!" Illythia hissed as her hand snaked out in an attempt to stop her brother.

"Then you stay. You think I'm going to allow you to risk my family? I will not watch them die just to water your ego flower!" Talon's eyes turned black as his fangs extended, Evander met his stare with his own – the orange glowing bright as his claws pushed through his own skin.

"Back down Talon," Evander warned, Audric moved to his flank as Adelina moved to Talons.

Meanwhile, Ray remained standing in the corner of the room – silent. Something didn't feel right with her, her eyes stung; her hands trembled by her sides – her mouth was dry and every time she tried to swallowed, it felt like razor blades. Between her skin and bones, something thrummed and pounded. A loud thumping began to repeat over and over in her head, causing the room to turn dizzy.

"Rosie." A voice. She didn't know this voice, it didn't belong to anyone in this room, and the only one who could reach her from a distance was Mazruriuk. *"Rosie,"* it called to her again. The voice ached her bones, made her head twang – her blood turn to ice in her veins, she could feel her breath tingle as she sucked in the air around her, but it was stuffy and even the temperature in the room seemed too hot to bear. Her feet took a mind of their own as they headed for the door, summoned by the voice. *"Come to me. Come and find me, Rosie."*

☾

"**N**o one is to touch this," Nyda ordered sternly. "It certainly smells . . . different," she spoke as she knelt down beside Mazruriuk – who nodded in agreement. "In all my years I have never come across anything like it," Nyda's voice wobbled.

Mazruriuk frowned, the blood had changed since he'd last seen it, a dark Shade's blood was a deep red, but this - this was thick and had turned to a dark purple – it still pulsed and seemed to have developed a bubbling. "I though it to belong to a Shade," he announced. "I have seen only one blood like this."

"But?" She urged, sensing the hesitation in his voice.

"But this has changed, see for yourself," he inclined.

Nyda clenched her jaw and hovered her hand over the blood, instantly her whole body went ridged, shivers decorated her skin and a dull ache vibrated around her bones. A pain filled gasp captured her throat. Pain - desecrating her body, ripping her from the inside out, she couldn't make it stop, couldn't move – she was frozen, caught like a fish on a hook. She could feel the call of the blood, the grip it had – like it had a hold of her hand and was pulling her down, she was only inches away from it.

"Nyda?"

Nyda's eyes widened, her breathing became rapid and unsteady, whimpers of pain were the only noise she was able to mumble from her lips. Mazruriuk swore under his breath and wrapped his hands around her waist; he could feel them both being pulled down towards it, its strength too strong for even him to face. "Here!" He called to the troops around them, "here! Help me with her!" Two men found him first and exchanged a puzzled look. "Pull her away from it!" Mazruriuk snarled, "Now! Pull!"

Whatever this was, it was tough – almost overpowering, when they managed to pull her away, they were all sweating. They fell backwards and immediately Mazruriuk jumped up and gripped Nyda's face in his hands, shaking her until her frightened eyes met his. "Nyda?" He said carefully, his eyes searched hers.

"It . . . I . . ."

"Nyda, hey!" He raised his voice, snapping her out of whatever spell the blood burned into her. "Hey, hey, Nyda, focus on me! Are you alright?"

"Y-yes," she answered as she rubbed her chest, her hands trembled as they gripped his shoulder. "It had a hold of me, I couldn't do anything – I was trapped, I couldn't see you. I was caged in my own head, shadows and darkness clouding around me." Her voice quivered as she spoke, Mazruriuk gently helped her stand, her skin had turned to ice, her face like a frightened child. Mazruriuk jumped as she suddenly gripped onto him, holding him so tightly – her knuckles turned white. "Rosie. Did she touch this blood? Mazruriuk, did Rosie touch it?"

"No," he assured her, tenderly pulling her hands free and lingering them on her arms, attempting to comfort her fear filled jitters. "I stopped her."

"Are you absolutely sure you stopped her?"

"Yes. Nyda, what is it?" He dared ask, feeling the prick of worry pull down his brows.

"Everyone back to Gatherling. Immediately!"

"*R*osie."

The voice.

It kept calling to her, gaining louder and louder the further in the forest she went; she knew where her feet were taking her. The sound of crunching twigs and leaves under her foot, the hooting of the night owls and the breeze of the forest air rustling the trees – wasn't enough to drown out to call.

Yes, she knew exactly where it was leading her, she could already smell the familiar foul stench – burning her nose and the branches seemed to bend away – showing her the path to follow. Before she could convince herself to turn and head back, her eyes landed on the blood. A thick fog began to swarm around, filling in through the trees until finally – she couldn't see.

Hot breath licked the back of her neck, instantly her whole body went still, shivers crawled down her spine and her heart began to pound hard against her ribcage. Twigs snapped behind her, something was moving around, her hands shook by her sides – she'd left all her weapons at Gatherling; she cursed under her breath.

"Who's there?" She growled in as much as a threatening tone she could manage, each word was shaky on her tongue. She had no weapons, but that didn't mean she was going to go down without a fight, she had been trained in combat and that human stubbornness she kept close, refused to let her fall.

"Hello Rosie," it wasn't a whisper this time, or a voice in her head. It was rough, hoarse, but strong and the worst part, the part that consumed her with terror, made her teeth shatter, her skin cold and her heart race – it came from behind her.

He was standing close – very close, too close for comfort, if he were to lift his hand; he'd be able to touch her, the strand of hair that drifted out of her ponytail. She knew what he was the second she laid her eyes on him, his pebble grey skin – the white veins that formed into thick tribal like markings; his eyes were a bold mixture of yellow and blood orange; his teeth were stained as he trailed his black tongue along them and there was a strange tattoo covering his bold head. His hand snaked out towards her; his thick long black nails barely touching her cheek before she batted his hand away and took a few timid steps back. "Dear little, Rosie," he sang, curling the R in her name.

"Stay away from me," she warned. She jumped back, snatching up the first heavy looking rock she could find; she knew it wouldn't hurt him – wouldn't even leave a graze on his skin, still it would give her a chance to run if she threw it.

"Well, aren't you a fierce little one." His eyes narrowed and he tilted his head, "you smell different...for a human."

"I'm stronger than most as well – so don't try me."

He smirked, his tongue tracing the roof of his mouth; he raised his hands in a mocking gesture of surrender. "I come in peace, little Rosie."

"Then why are you here?"

"I need your help, sweet girl."

"Why would I help you?" She laughed but it lacked humour; her eyes explored him, watching for any signs of danger; he was injured – gloopy blood pooled from a deep cut in his stomach. "You're hurt."

"That I am, that is why I need your help." His mocking tone dropped; his voice almost desperate as it took a pleading whimper to it.

"Why me?"

"Because your heart is pure. If I wanted to kill you – I would have already done it." Ray was taught from day one, that dark Shades were nothing but cruel, lethal and were predators. They were the darkness that festered the Earth, they fed from it; they were consumed by it – they welcomed it. Dark Shades felt no compassion for anything, the only thing they loved – was to torment and torture anything they could get their hands on.

"Can't Shades heal themselves?"

He scoffed, the movement causing him to wince, "usually yes. However, that all depends on the creature that inflicted the damage."

"What did this?" She was almost afraid to ask.

"The darkest creature of them all – Crow."

Chapter Twenty
Everyone

*A*udric swung his blade, the metal clanging as it collided with mine; I brought my knee up, slamming it hard into his groin. He grimaced, stifling a groan as he reared back, I dropped low, aiming to swipe his foot from under him, halting as I felt the cold tip of his sword lightly digging into my throat.

"Dead," Audric growled. I knew he was pissed, and I knew a lecture was about to come my way, I kept going for the easy way out and Audric knew that. "Fuck sake Narrdie."

"I know," I whined, as I threw down my blade in sheer frustration. "I'm sorry."

"Where are you right now?" He snapped, "Because you're not here. You're not focusing, you should be one step ahead of me at all times!"

"I know."

"Your swings are sloppy, your movements lazy and that knee – was a cheap shot." He sighed as he leaned forward and gripped my forearm, helping me back onto my feet; he kicked up my blade into his hands and held it out. Since fighting the

Loopins, Evander and Audric had been training me even harder; they'd wake me at the crack of dawn to train and then again straight after dinner. Even Mazruriuk would volunteer and show me how to take out a Shade properly, help me learn their powers. "Narrdie," Audric began, pulling back my attention. "You need to remember that some creatures are faster than others, you can't turn your back on them or let them get too close. I could have killed you three times over there."

"Jesus, Audric I know," I bit. He breathed out and raised a playful brow at me.

"You normally bring your game when we train. What's on your mind Moon?"

"What do you know about white Shades?" I asked as I brushed the dirt off my jeans and gulped down my water, Audric stretched out his arms, cracking his bones and shrugged slightly.

"Mitchell mentioned them to me once," Audric's eyes turned foggy at the mention of his brother – they always did. "They're meant to be stronger than dark Shades, however there are more dark Shades than there are white. Mitchell was adamant that white Shades are on the side of the light; he said it would be a bonus to have one on our side." Audric frowned towards me, "you don't trust Mazruriuk?"

"That's not it, I do trust him – he's helped me a lot with training. I'm just curious, can they turn towards the darkness?" Audric laughed lightly, but it was bitter.

"Narrdie, everything can turn to darkness, sometimes they don't even know it – you of all people should know that." I bit my lip and Audric playfully tapped me on the shoulder with his sword. "Mazruriuk's been here for a three weeks now and so far, the only change he makes is when he sees Rosie-Anika-Yoland."

"Ray," I corrected him with a smile. He wasn't wrong, Mazruriuk's face was carved from stone, never moved – his eyes cold, yet whenever Ray walked in; he was like a love-struck puppy.

"Think fast," Audric warned as he suddenly lunged at me – frantically swinging his sword. I leaned back, the sword skipping past me, I dropped down – diving myself through his legs. I flung my leg out and kicked him forward, diving on his back before he had a chance to react. I raised my sword to his throat and smirked.

"Dead," I sang. Audric smiled widely and cheered; he pulled me down and granted me his usual wink.

"Better – much better. It needs to be like that all the time, no matter what you're thinking. Keep your mind focused. That's enough for today, the sun's coming up and we need to get some sleep at least." He took my sword and began to pack it up with the rest of the weapons, an assortment of throwing knives, stars, bows and arrows and different varieties of swords.

"I know, I'm just having an off day today. I'll be more relaxed later," I assured him with a confident smile.

"How've you been sleeping?"

"Meh," I mumbled, making him laugh loudly. "What?"

"What's meh?"

"Meh is meh. It means not great," I explained with a kick to his side.

"Still sleeping crappy?" he turned to me with a sly smile. He picked up the weapons bag and chucked it in the doorway. "I have an idea; it might help you relax, but it comes with rules," he warned humorously.

"Yes, because rules equal relaxation," I teased sarcastically.

"Shut up and listen. So, the rules are, no training, no talking about training, no talking about the upcoming battle and the most important rule – no talking about the darkness . . . or Crow. Just me and you, going for a walk, like old times." I raised my brow at him, and he sighed. "Narrdie, it's a chance to be normal . . . even if it's only for a second." He stretched out his hand to me, I could feel my heart skipping a beat, butterflies pirouetting in my stomach at the chance of being normal. "What do you say, Moon?"

"I'd love to," I replied as I took his hand.

It felt like a lifetime since I had done this with Audric. I missed it, the false sense of security that nothing could touch us here – we were safe in our bubble. I'd almost forgotten what it was like to lie in the sun, forgot how it felt when the light rays would gently caress my skin and tickle me with warmth. Audric had taken us to the hilltop and the moment my eyes set on the view, they filled with tears. At that point, I would have traded anything – anything just to stay there and let this brutal world I'd been thrown into, pass by.

The grass glittered with the morning mist; I ran my hands through the blades feeling the water drift along my hand. The grass was soft – welcoming, I didn't care that it was wet; I laid my head on Audric's lap and let out a happy breath.

I promised myself that I would never forget this image – I'd take a photograph in my head and save it, keep it safe and only bring it out on my darkest days. I'd always remember it, the glowing sun lighting up the cloudless sky – beaming down and making parts of the forest glow with a golden shine. The sky, a beautiful mixture of pastel blues, purples, pinks and oranges, illuminating everything it hung over – everything the rays touched, sparkled and twinkled. "I miss this," I breathed.

"I thought you'd like it here, it's peaceful," he replied gently as he lightly played with a strand of my hair.

"Why didn't you show me it earlier?"

"Because you needed it now – not then."

"I wonder how many times I get to see this before the darkness-" I trailed off and picked at a blade of grass.

"Hey, nothing is going to happen to you Narrdie. I promise that after all this comes to an end, we'll come back here. We'll march up this hill and we'll sit here – me and you, in our spot," he playfully nudged me.

I looked to him and smiled, "out of all the crap that's happened, you've stayed by me and always treated me as normal, I owe you so much Audric."

"I'm your Watcher . . . I have no choice," he teased; I turned to scowl at him and we both laughed.

I wished we could stay here forever.

*T*he sunrise had turned to a misty sunset by the time Audric woke, he groaned as he slowly opened his eyes, shocked to see he was still on top of the hill . . . when had he fallen asleep? He clutched his head and hissed through his teeth – a pounding pain beat against his skull; his head was damp and not just from the moist grass, no this was something else – blood. He winced as he sat up, the sky was dark – thick clouds smothered the stars. He was alone. A dreaded feeling slammed into his gut; he wasn't alone before – where was Narrdie?

"Narrdie?" No answer, the forest was dead, no owls, no night bugs - even the wind didn't want to make a sound. "NARRDIE!"

He bellowed, his voice carrying along the forest, echoing from tree to tree. The sickening feeling of panic because to curdle in his stomach, he looked around – searching for any sign that would tell him what had happened. The moon light caught his eye as if reflected onto a long black hair that rested on his shirt, he caught it between his fingers and brought it to his eyes – the clotting feeling icing over. "Crow."

$$\smile$$

*C*row stood outside Gatherling; her icy eyes slowly turned black as a feral smirk stretched across her lips. "Play time," she hummed.

Mazruriuk perched on a rock, drinking a cup of spicy coffee, he frowned as an unrecognisable scent seeped into his nose; he paused and set down his drink and slowly turned towards the smell – her voice reached his ears first. He knew exactly who she was, he'd met her once – a long time ago, but that was a story for another time. He moved into her line of sight and clenched his jaw, a laugh rolled off her tongue. "I haven't seen one of your kind in some time," she purred. "I've come for Dacre, where is he?" Crow asked in an unconcerned tone as she examined her razor-sharp nails; she didn't care for this creature; however, she didn't like the way it was looking at her either. She didn't like the lesser beings looking at her. She released a low hiss, Mazruriuk suddenly stiffened as a warning streak shot into him.

"He isn't here . . . Crow," he said in a hard tone. She tilted her head and took a taunting step towards him, a playful laugh echoed around. She lived for these moments, watching these creatures try to pretend they didn't fear her – everyone feared her.

"I'd say it was a pleasure to make your acquaintance but . . . I'd be lying. Now, where is Dacre?" She repeated as she began to play with a ball of what looked to be black lightening, in her hands. "I asked twice, something I don't normally do. Don't make me ask a third time."

"You're not welcome here," he snarled. She raised her brow. A long-carved sword formed in Mazruriuk's hand, his eyes darkened, and his skin shifted to hard reptilian scales.

"Impressive, normally I would jump at the chance to play some sword games. However, I'm afraid, I'm in quite a rush." She snarled and hurtled the ball towards him; he swung his blade in front of him, the steel cutting across her power. "Disappointing," she mumbled, before unleashing another, this one was faster, larger than he'd anticipated; it slammed into his arm, fizzing into his skin. Another followed close behind, it crashed into his chest, the lethal energy of it lifting his body and threw him back. "White Shades, such a waste." She spat.

Crow retracted her blades after the last guards body slumped to the floor, she'd warned them not to get in her way; she snickered then glanced up as she heard a door close - her body shivered with excitement. She hadn't had this much fun in years. "Who could be behind lucky door number one?" She sang as she booted down the door, with one swift kick. She smirked and laughed through her nose at the young human hunter; her teeth grew sharp, and she mockingly clapped her hands. "Aren't you a pretty little thing?" Crow teased; her voice was poisonous. "My, my, Evander is getting desperate if he's relying on the strength of . . . humans," the word tasted bitted on her tongue.

Ray's skin tighten, her hands felt clammy as they gripped the axes, the very appearance of Crow - sent shivers up her spine and consumed her with fear. She could feel the darkness's energy radiating from her. "I know who you are," Ray's voice shook. "And I know why you're here," Ray tried to make her voice sound strong, regardless of her whole body vibrating with nerves - she had never faced something like Crow before.

"Do you? So, right now, the best thing for you, would be to tell me where I can find him, wouldn't it? Because then I won't have to kill you - I'll just hurt you a little bit." Crow grinned widely; her black hair roared around her like tentacles. Ray glanced behind Crow and towards the door, hoping that someone would burst through and save her, she was no match for the kind of creature Crow was. While traveling to Gatherling, she'd heard stories of Crow, stories that Mazruriuk and Demir told, but even they seemed to shudder at the thought of her. Crow followed her gaze before letting out a sarcastic cackle, "there's no one out there dear, unless you can see the spirits of the dead. They tried to stand against me and lasted...five maybe ten seconds? You'll last only two I think, or you could just tell me where Dacre is."

"I don't know where he is," Ray blurted aggressively, Crow raised her brow and tutted as she circled her.

"I do not believe you, Rosie." Crow snapped, she could feel herself growing bored and impatient – a combination that always ended deadly. Ray gulped, hearing her name on Crow's lips, was more terrifying than fighting a pack of Skinners, a cold shiver shot up her spine.

"I wouldn't lie to you, they never told us. They don't trust us yet, not with this sort of information."

Crow nodded then sighed, "I guess you're no help to me, just as useless as the white Shade." Ray's head snapped up and her grip tightened on her axe.

"Mazruriuk?" Her voice quivered, the sound of a broken heart – it was like music in Crow's ears.

"Yes, Mazruriuk, the white Shade. A waste if you ask me, so much power and they do nothing with it, all they do is fall in love with human hunters," she growled and spat on the floor. "Disgusting."

"What have you done to him you Witch?!" Ray snarled.

Crow hissed, icy glittering rage filled her eyes; she sprung towards Ray, pinning her against the wall; resting her hand around Ray's throat. Ray thrust her axe forward but was met with Crow's hand – gripping the blade. Crow smirked as the blade cut into her palm, her blood dripping onto Ray's cheek.

"You want to play with me, little human," she purred as she pulled Ray close. "You'll have to do a lot better than that."

"You know even if I did know where Dacre was," Ray wheezed – shaking with each word. "I would never tell you, not for all the torture in the world. You'd have to kill me." Panic filled her the moment she spoke the words; she didn't want to die – it would break Mazruriuk.

Crow laughed joylessly; her fingernail extended and traced along Ray's cheek. "Like I said sweet girl, you're no help to me." Crow twisted Ray's hand, the snapping of her wrist pleasing, Ray shrieked. "Is that all? Is that all the fight you have in you?" She bared her teeth as she lifted her high – the movement barely any effort. "You're not even worth a kill," she rumbled, before tossing Ray, crashing hard into a set of draws – the impact of the crash sent the shelves above to shatter and collapse on top.

Crows claws screeched against the walls, thick lines tearing up the brickwork as she fluttered down the hallway – curious as to who her next playmate would be. She didn't have to wait long until three Vampires stood at the end – their eyes red and fangs extended.

Talon stood at the end of the corridor, Illythia and Adelina stood at his flank; they exchanged a glance with each other – a conversation that only they understood. Crow spun around and chuckled, looking them up and down, "three? Three to play with, I'm being spoilt today," her laughter increased bouncing along the walls. "This is my favourite game yet, there's so much sport here – you all just keep popping up like daisies."

"You shouldn't be here! Abomination!" Illythia hissed and took a step forward, Talon flung his arm out, stopping her with a warning growl.

"Un'attenta Illythia, lei è pericoloso," Talon warned her, Crow moaned in pleasure.

"I don't know what you said, but it sounded heavenly. Say my name," she purred, Talon didn't deign to respond, instead he lifted his lip in a distasteful sneer. "No? That's too bad. However, I hope you told her to get out of my way... maybe you should tell her, to go check on your red headed human pet." Their eyes widened.

"If you've hurt her-"

"If you hurry, you might be able to save her." Crow teased. Adelina snarled and took a step forward – instantly freezing when Talon shot her a look, when it came down to danger – he was in charge.

"What have you done to Rosie?" Illythia asked, her voice full of rage and worry. Crow didn't answer, she smirked widely – all her teeth changing into sharp fangs.

A deep anger consumed Adelina, she was no longer a rational thinking Vampire – she was a feral beast, devoured by animalistic rage. She shrieked and pushed her way past her siblings, snarling as she lunged towards Crow – who growled with excitement and through herself towards her. "Adelina no!" Illythia called. Adelina and Crow slammed into each other hard, attacking with a violent display of slashes and bites, tearing into each other – attacking any way they could. Crow didn't bother to use her powers; she hadn't had a good scrap in years – this was more fun.

Illythia and Talon could only watch, fear coiling around them; they wanted to help, but each time one of them got close enough – they were pushed back.

"Illythia, andare a trovare Ray," Talon ordered, she glared at him in protest; she opened her mouth to argue, but he shook his head. "Vai ora!" Illythia clenched her jaw but nodded, she through a worried glance to her sister, before racing back to find Ray.

Crow spun and dropped Adelina to the floor – pinning her with her claws, her poisonous tongue snaked out and glided along Adelina's cheek – burning her flesh. "I will tear you apart from the inside out," Crow sang.

Talon crashed his body against Crow, knocking her to the side; he sprung to his feet and dragged Adelina towards him – holding his arm out protectively in front of her. Crow cackled as she lay on her back, she rolled over and perched her chin on her hands – wiggling her feet in the air.

"Se hai fatto del male a Rosie, ti ucciderò," Adelina hissed.

"You," Crow said as she pointed to Talon. "What did she just call me?"

"She said, if you've hurt Rosie – she'll kill you. Same goes for me," Talon growled.

"You'd harm Narrdie like that? I thought Vampires were meant to drain humans...not protect them. What is this world coming to, first white Shades, then this – disappointing."

"I reckon if I kill you, Narrdie would survive – I'm willing to find out," Talon spat.

Crow's face turned hard, all the liveliness vanished as quick as water down a drain; she stood slowly and cocked her head to the side – her eyes held a murderous glare, "and if you're wrong?"

Crow sprang up, Talon scowled then mimicked her action without a second thought. Crow couldn't help but smirk with victory, he was doing exactly what she hoped he'd do; her nails slowly grew into sharp points – like daggers.

Adelina gasped, Crow was baiting him, and he didn't know; he had fallen straight into her trap. She didn't hesitate. She didn't hesitate as she pushed her feet flat on the wall, using it as a spring to glide her through the air; she didn't hesitate as she pushed Talon out the way and felt the full force of Crow crash into her.

Crow's nails dug up deep into Adelina's chest, she smirked as she heard Adelina's flesh tear open and a gasp escape her lips – she wouldn't scream, not unless Crow wanted her to. Crow landed on the balls of her feet; her hand drenched in blood; her eyes watched with pride as Adelina dropped to the floor – gasping for breath, whimpering with pain.

Talon dropped to his knees beside her and pulled her onto his lap and safely away from Crow – his hand shook as he wiped the hair from her face. "Adelina? Adelina, svegliati!" He begged, she was bleeding heavily from four slits that had buried deep in her chest, he pressed his hand over them in a desperate attempt to keep her blood inside. Vampires didn't burst into dust, they didn't dissolve in embers or erupt in a bloody way, just like the myths said they did. When pierced in the heart, Vampires instantly became paralyzed, unable to cry or scream out, their heart slowly and painfully shrivelling and disintegrating, until eventually – death.

Talon's head sprang up as he heard the dark poisonous laughter bellow out of Crow, he wanted to tear her tongue out, press his fingers into her eyes – torture her until she begged him to stop. However, right now – his sister needed him.

"Oh no," Crow mocked sadly. "Is she dead?" She looked down on the two Vampires, the hate filled smirk plastered on her face. Talon snarled as his eyes locked onto her. "Should I get a healer? Oh, that's right most of them lie in ribbons."

"Get away from her!"

"It's too late," Crow spoke with no emotion in her voice, which only added to Talon's anger.

"She is not dead!" He hissed, Crow rolled her eyes and picked at her fingernails.

"No, but she will be very soon. So, will you." She hovered her hand over him, instantly his body seized, bending to her will; she pulled him in close and lightly kissed his lips; her tongue slithering out along his cheek. "You are a lovely one to look at, maybe I'll return for you," she hummed in his ear. Without another word, she thrust her hand to the side flinging his body away, like a crumbled-up ball of paper. She glanced once at Adelina, a pain hit Crow's chest and she whimpered and dug her hand hard into her skin. She sneered and forced herself to stand straight, hissing lowly, "no you don't Narrdie, I am not finished yet." She snapped.

Dacre rose and began straightening out his jacket; he could hear the gunfire outside the door, the thunder of swords banging together and the crackling of power striking any who dared stand in its way. He grinned, the cruel smile widening each time he heard a limp body drop down, how many times had him and Evander told them all – guns don't work, he never did understand why they kept them. A light chuckle rolled out his mouth when all the shootings rapidly came to a stop. "What an amazing woman," he chimed. He began clapping his hands as the metal door groaned, the sound deafening as the hinges popped and snapped, with a

loud thud it dropped to the floor. Crow elegantly stepped over it, she was drenched in blood, but that predatory smile spread wide as her icy eyes landed on him. "Crow, what touching surprise, you come all this way for me?" She quickly stepped towards him and pressed herself up against the bars seductively.

"Dacre, my love. Seeing you in a cage, does something to me – it's a good look for you," she purred as she stroked her hand down his chest and hooked her finger on his trouser belt; she flashed him a flirtatious smile.

"Now is not the time," he replied, matching her smile with his, "I take it you weren't quiet about this?"

She licked her razor teeth, "am I ever?"

"That's my girl," she bit her lip, before taking several steps backwards.

"Stand back, my love," she warned, he nodded. Crow raised her hand; the cell door shrieked as it crumbled to tiny pieces on the floor. A vicious growl, mixed with pain and excitement, grumbled in her throat, she leaned against the wall for support. Dacre quickly crossed over to her and wrapped his hand around her waist, his face crumpled with concern, she swayed in his arm; her head lolled to the side.

"Easy, pretty bird."

"I'm growing weaker, I can feel it. Why?" Her voice was fragile.

"It's a blood Moon tonight, that's all. You are not as strong as you used to be," he explained as he helped her walk.

"That's because you forced me to sleep for too many years, which is why Narrdie has more strength over me," she snapped.

"I did what needed to be done, you knew that."

She huffed and rolled her eyes, "I didn't think it would be that long."

"We never agreed on time."

"I don't think I can fight anymore off," her voice was gravelly, she leaned into him; her feet almost dragging behind her. Dacre soothed in her ear, he picked up one of the dead guard's swords, before leading her out - keeping his hand tight on her waist.

$$\smile$$

A line of men and women were scattered outside the entrance of Gatherling, led by Nyda, Audric and Astrid; all were armed as best as they could be - they had to be when faced with Dacre and Crow.

A deadly combination.

Audric paced, over and over - eager to get inside, to find Narrdie and pull her back to surface, he jerked forward but Astrid pushed him back. He turned on her, a dark temper flaring in his eyes. "Let me go in," he growled.

"No."

"Astrid-"

"I said no," she growled, her voice deadly. "You don't know what you could be walking into, we all wait." Astrid shot her eyes around, making sure everyone understood, Evander had left her in charge, the moment she's arrived she'd smelt the blood. So much had been spilled inside and she was not going risk anymore lives.

Crow and Dacre slowly walked into their view, wide teasing smirks across their faces as they met a number of furious eyes. "Look Dacre, our leaving party," Crow sang, her voice drained.

"Audric." Dacre called, "a pleasure as always, we'd love to stay and chat but, we must be off, and you really should tend to the wounded inside." He flashed a grin to Crow, "she doesn't really play nicely with others, I have told her to be gentle - she prefers it rough." Crow smirked sadistically and ran her hand down Dacre's arm, Audric tensed, and a low growl bubbled in Astrid's throat; her eyes slowly burned red.

"You are not leaving with her," Audric snarled as he drew his sword, Nyda and Astrid close behind him.

"Dacre," Crow warned as she felt her knees buckle under her, she gripped onto him tightly for support; her nails digging into his arm. Her skin had paled, her eyes lolled, stained with exhaustion.

"As much as I like a good fight, we are struck for time. So, I'm going to have to cheat and do this the old-fashioned way."

248

Before anyone could run to them, Dacre grasped hold of Crow tightly and vanished.

"NO!" Audric roared and desperately raced over, his fist swung out into a tree – which snapped and toppled over. "Narrdie! He has Narrdie!"

Chapter Twenty-One
Audric & Bayona

"Audric, we will get Narrdie back, but right now, we must help the wounded," Nyda snapped. Audric lifted up his lip in a sneer, choosing to ignore her. "Or we could just let our people die," Nyda sniped sarcastically. "I'm sure Narrdie would love more blood on her hands." Audric paused, anger flashed across his face.

"On her hands?" White hot rage consumed him, he darted forward; his hands gripping her throat. "You dare put the blame on her? Where were you, Nyda? It was you turn to be on watch, how convenient you weren't here."

"Audric!" Astrid snarled. "Let her go!" Audric nostrils flared, but he released her with a push.

"I'm sorry, I didn't mean that," Nyda rasped as she rubbed her neck. She gently placed her hand on his shoulder and smiled sheepishly, "I didn't mean it."

"Me too," he responded, and stroked her hand with his.

"Astrid, I've ordered the Monks to search around the outskirts of Gatherling, to make sure no more nasty surprises come out way. I also have asked Lindon to do a head count, find out who's missing, who's here and who's . . ." Nyda trailed off and swallowed down the lump that formed in her throat, Astrid stroked her cheek.

"Thank you," she said softly. "Take yourself a minute if you need to.

"Find someone to fetch Bayona," Audric announced to no one in particular, "we'll need her to help heal the wounded," his voice was rough.

"I'll go," Astrid offered. He nodded and faked a smile as she kissed his cheek and vanished with inhuman speed. "No one goes inside or near the sanctuary until Bayona arrives, Crow might have put a dark enchantment on it." Audric announced, his voice wavering.

"But there could be more wounded inside," a young Watcher called to him.

"I'm aware of that Ameer, but until we know it's safe, we can't take that chance. Not right now."

It didn't take long for Astrid to find Bayona, she was right where she said she would be. Sitting cross legged, at the highest point of the forest, where the stars burned bright, and she could tap into her abilities without the pain and the bloody eyes. Astrid didn't have to say anything when she found her, one look at her and Bayona knew, something was wrong – very wrong.

"Audric!" Bayona almost cried. She threw her arms around him and squeezed him tightly, he clung to her – relieved that she was safe. "Astrid told me what happened, we'll find her and bring her home." Audric smiled to her and pecked the top of her head with a kiss. "Nyda," she greeted with a clasp of arms.

"I am glad you're safe, sister."

"As am I. Nyda, may I loan some of your power to see if Gatherling is safe? You know these grounds better." Bayona asked. Nyda nodded and reluctantly rested her tattooed palm against Bayona's; their other hands outstretched towards the forest. Power sharing was never pleasant. Audric tapped his foot impatiently, scrapping his fingers along his stubble, he opened his mouth to complain but Astrid shook her head. It felt like a lifetime to him, yet it had only been a few minutes before Bayona let out a tiring and saddened sigh. "It's clear," she announced, bringing everyone's attention to her. "I can feel how bad it is inside," her voice wobbled.

"Everyone listen up," Audric began. "Everyone who is capable help with the wounded, take them to the infirmary and watch out for any others along the way. Crow and Dacre are sneaky – remember that. Nyda, head into the forest and round up the Monks, we are going to need them close."

Astrid froze at the doors; she breathed in and shuddered, a sad whimper escaped her lips, she sighed, "there is so much blood in there." Her voice quivered as she spoke. "It's a massacre, I don't think Crow left anyone alive." Audric's jaw clenched; he nodded and gently squeezed her hand.

"We'll do this together," his voice matched hers.

Rustling in the trees made everyone pause, Audric signed with his hand for everyone to remain still, he drew his sword and slowly began walking – two other Watchers dropped to his flank.

"Audric!" Mazruriuk called from under a cluster of collapsed trees and stone.

"Mazruriuk?" Audric called out, he raced towards him – the others quick on his heels. "What happened?" He asked as they all carefully pulled the trees from his body, Audric threw Mazruriuk's arm over his shoulder and helped him stand.

"Crow, she attacked Gatherling. I tried to stop her, I underestimated how powerful she is!" He winced and hissed through his teeth painfully.

"Put him down here," Bayona cooed. "Where are you hurt?"

"My ribs, shoulder and my arm," he groaned as she pulled off his shirt carefully. She gasped, seeing the burnt skin where Crow's ball of energy hit him, it stretched from his ribs – like spider webs, crawling up his chest and down his arm.

"Hold still," Bayona advised as she placed one hand over his ribs and the other over his shoulder. "She left with Dacre," her voice was bland.

"What?" He jerked up but was met with hands pushing him down gently.

"Later. Audric, Ameer, Wesley hold him down. This is going to hurt, ma belle," she warned – he closed his eyes and nodded.

"Bite down on this," Astrid suggested as she placed a thick piece or bark in his mouth.

A bright light began to glow from her hands, instantly he groaned and clenched his teeth together. She closed her eyes, speaking under her breath so quietly, no one could make out what she was saying. Mazruriuk shrieked through the bark, agony tearing through him as his broken bones began to twist and snap back together, the shredded skin pulled towards each other; his body tensed – his back arching. "Almost done," Astrid assured him; she weaved her hand with his, making soothing sounds in his ear. Audric and the other Watchers strained as they held him down, trees began to splinter and the forest bed around them seared black.

"There," Bayona blurted out of breath. She raised a shaking hand and wiped the blood from her eyes. "I've done the best I could, you'll need to rest it," she told him with a weak smile.

"Thank you," his voice was strained – tired.

"We should go," Astrid suggested. "Others inside could need help."

"If anything has happened to Nika . . ." Mazruriuk began, he trailed off, not being able to find the rest of the words; his head began to flop down.

"Ameer, Wesley, help him to his feet."

"Monstrous," Astrid breathed, "this is simply awful." Astrid's voice quaked, her eyes misted over as the threat of tears crept closer, and her hand fell over her mouth. Bodies. Scattered on the floor like litter, Crow hadn't just killed them – she'd mutilated them, savoured every rip, basked in every cry. The forgotten limbs send shivers up everyone's spines, the blood painted the walls, creating puddles and pools along the grey tiles. Astrid gripped Audric's hand, she was used to blood – they all were, but not like this.

"Wait!" Mazruriuk called, Ameer and Wesley froze – holding him still. Mazruriuk breathed in, picking up two very familiar scents, Ray. He pushed Ameer and Wesley off him and burst through the grand hall doors. His heart dropped, seeing the red headed girl cradled in the arms of Illythia; she looked so small, so fragile, so – human. "Nika!" He dropped beside them, afraid to touch her in case she crumbled under his touch.

"You're alive," Ray chimed weakly.

"Nika," he took her hand, noticing how small and shaky it was in his hand. He gently kissed it, "what happened?"

"I found her in here, underneath a load of shelves and rubble," Illythia informed him.

"Crow," it wasn't a question, but Illythia nodded to him. "Anything broken?"

"She broke my wrist, my arm's slit and it feels like I've cracked a few ribs, but apart from those, I'm fine," he nodded and breathed out in relief. "Probably have a few more bruises by tomorrow morning."

"You're fine," he repeated over and over, kissing every part of her face and hand. "You're fine." What a fool he felt, thinking that if he trained her enough, she'd stand a chance against something like Crow, Ray was a human – humans were fragile, compared to his world. "For a moment, I thought I'd lost you." Mazruriuk carefully lifted her into his arms; he smiled appreciatively to Illythia and stroked his hand down her arm. "I'm glad you're safe too," he told her. Illythia couldn't find her words, a lump had clogged her throat even since she'd left her siblings, she was worried that if she kept speaking – she'd crumble right there and then.

"Here," Bayona called as her healing hands began to glow.

"No," Ray said softly. "Will I die from any of my wounds?"

"Well, no, not unless you get an infection, but I doubt that will happen. You'll have pain thought," Bayona replied, turning to look at Mazruriuk.

"She doesn't like to be healed by magic, Illythia dress the wound, so it won't get infected, then we'll sort it out later." Mazruriuk said, Illythia ripped a strand from the bottom of her top and tied it tightly.

"Thank you Illythia, for this and coming to find me." Illythia swallowed and gave Ray a weak smile, Ray had become an extra sister, (human or not), she loved her.

"Have you seen any of my family?" She dared to ask Astrid.

"Not yet."

Silence.

Nothing but silence, it was sorrowful – like the sanctuary itself was mourning.

Healers had dropped off one by one, as they dove deeper and deeper into Gatherling, finding more and more injured. . . some beyond help. They knew Crow could be vicious, brutal, but they never expected this.

Their footsteps came to a sudden stop, the voices faded into quiet, shaking raspy breaths, "Illythia," Astrid called softly; her voice nothing but a shaking breath. Illythia pushed her way forward and for a few moments Illythia felt like everything was moving in slow motion, the voices that called her name were stretched out mumbles. Then, everything hit her at once, she dropped to her knees beside her brother; his hands were shaking as they pressed his shirt over Adelina's chest.

"T-Talon?" Illythia stuttered, the burning of tears stinging her eyes, her heart dropped into her stomach, she felt like she was going to throw up everything inside her, all over the blood-stained floor.

"She was going to kill me," Talon sobbed, his voice trembling. "Crow had the drop on me and I missed it . . . I missed it. Adelina jumped in the way . . . her claws, they were like daggers. S-She's not healing, she's drank but she's not healing." Talon looked up to Illythia, his cheeks were stained with tears. "It should have been me."

"Adelina?" Illythia's voice wobbled, she lightly took hold of Adelina's hand and held it against her own cheek.

"Don't speak, la mia dolce sorella. Bayona!" Bayona's hands were already glowing with her healing light, she dropped down beside them. "Help her," Illythia begged.

 Bayona rested her palm over the gaping wounds, but there was nothing – no sharp twinge as she took the injuries, not bleeding eyes . . . nothing. "Bayona," Astrid called tenderly, Bayona met her eyes and whimpered, the healing light dwindling.

"Bayona! Heal her!" Illythia repeated, her voice becoming panicked.

"I'm so sorry, I can't," she replied in a hushed tone.

Illythia snarled, "why?!"

"Illythia," Astrid began, moving Bayona out of view protectively. "It's too late," her voice cracked, and she bit the inside of her cheek to keep the tears down. "She's already fading, there's nothing that can be done. I'm so sorry."

"Oh god, Adelina," Ray cried, burying her face into Mazruriuk's chest, his face turned hard – unreadable like stone, but his eyes had misted over.

"No!" Talon growled as he held his hand down over her wound, Adelina placed her hand on top of his and smiled weakly to him, her eyes droopy.

"Illythia, Talon, fermata, è troppo tardi," she said weakly as more blood dripped from her mouth, which Illythia wiped away with the back of her sleeve.

"It's not too late, we'll get you back on your feet in no time."

Two birds flew around Mazruriuk before crashing into the ground, Sharia and Demir rose and stretched out. Audric immediately pulled off his over shirt, wrapping it around Sharia, to cover her naked body, Wesley did the same to Demir. They both nodded their thanks. "We shifted when we sensed something was wrong," Sharia informed them quietly, her throat bobbed.

"Adelina?" Demir gasped as he followed everyone's eyes, his head snapped to Mazruriuk with a questionable look, Mazruriuk clenched his jaw and held Ray tightly. "Oh, please no," he slumped down to his knees, Sharia placed her hand on his shoulder in comfort; he reached up and clung to her fingers.

"Talon, Illythia, lasciami andare," Adelina told her siblings gently; she knew it was her time. Illythia snivelled and rested her head on her sister's shoulder.

"Talon, stop," Illythia whimpered.

"No, I can help you; I can save you," he insisted, refusing to meet her eyes. Adelina pulled his hand down, clenching it tightly.

"Talon," she breathed. "You already save me," she told him her words coming in faint fragile whispers. His jaw tightened but he nodded and carefully lifted her head onto his lap. "You all save me, I feel . . . no . . . no pain," she announced with a peaceful smile; her eyes drifting past them.

Illythia took her hand into her own and kissed it, her other hand reached out for Talon's – he took it while lightly stroking Adelina's hair. "Do you remember . . . being human?" Adelina asked them, Illythia's tear struck face lifted up into a fragile smile.

"I do," Illythia admitted.

"Me to," Talon's voice broke.

"Ray, voglio che sentano questo, puoi tradurre per me?"

"Sarei onorato," Ray wiped her tears, she swallowed – trying to gain control over her voice. "She . . . she wants me to translate," she told the others.

"Adelina," Illythia whimpered.

"I remember the sun," Ray began to translate. "I remember the warmth of it on my skin, I liked it best when we'd go to the beach, playing in the sea, the waves crashing over us, the sand between my toes." Ray's voice broke and Mazruriuk pulled her into him and lightly stroked her hair.

"It's okay Nika, I'll take over," he whispered to her. "Talon would pretend he was coming to help us build up the sandcastle," Mazruriuk began. "Then he'd chase us and throw us in – you hated how it made your hair feel." Adelina laughed softly, they all smiled as their minds filled with the old memories of their human life. "I can feel it, I can feel the sun!" Talon glanced to Bayona; her hand was hovering above Adelina, a light warm beam falling over her, he nodded gratefully to her.

"Sono pronto ora," Adelina announced in a weak voice, though she wasn't saying to her siblings or any of the others, but someone they all couldn't see.

"She's ready," Mazruriuk told the others, his voice quivered; he clenched his jaw and held Ray tighter as she buried her crying face into his chest, sobbing lightly.

Adelina turned to her siblings and gave them a loving, yet stern look. "You both better take care of each other," Mazruriuk translated. "Protect and comfort each other and always remember to help each other no matter what the cause."

"Ti amo," Adelina's voice was barely a whisper; her eyes fluttered before finally closing, her chest stopped moving and her whole body went stiff.

Talon placed his head down, tears falling down his cheeks, while Illythia burst out; she buried her face in her sisters' shoulder and shrieked out. "Adelina!" She sobbed.

Astrid lightly tapped Audric and Bayona. "Come, let us leave their family to grieve," her voice was hushed, not wanting to disturb the siblings.

The leaves and twigs crunched under Audric's boots as he once again, paced up and down; he was beginning to make an imprint in the mud. Illythia lay across Talon's lap, still quietly sobbing; his hands lightly stroked her long hair. "What now?" Talon asked Audric.

"We wait here for the others to turn up," Astrid announced, as she checked Ray's bandage. "I'm going to change it, so it might sting," she warned her – Ray nodded.

"What if they don't come back? What if they're dead?" Illythia grunted through clenched teeth. Everyone suddenly went quiet and looked over to her, she was right, what if they were dead, and what if the head of all sanctuaries - Evander, was indeed dead?

Evander was the only one who had all the connections to the other sanctuaries, he was the one who knew the locations of other covens and potential races that could help them, without him – they were as good as sheep in a field of wolves. The guards shifted amongst themselves, each one becoming more and more concerned with every minute that passed, until finally Audric spoke.

"We'd know if they were dead."

"Would we?" She said in a bitter tone, "how would we know? Crow could have easily killed them like she did with . . ." She trailed off and began sobbing again, Talon held her tighter while quietly consoling her.

"She has a point, we could be sitting ducks here Audric, Dacre has Narrdie, he knows where Gatherling is, and Evander is nowhere to be seen. The next move is ours," Mazruriuk uttered as he glanced into the distance, as if he were waiting for a sudden horde to run at them, he was perched high up in a tree, posing as a look out.

"I don't care if we are sitting ducks," Sharia snapped towards him. "We are not leaving until Evander comes back! Indra and the Priestesses will come for us if something is wrong!" Sharia protested, she suddenly widened her eyes and slammed her hand over her mouth.

Audric glared at her in anger and annoyance, the day Demir and his people had arrived, Evander had ordered that Indra and the Priestesses stay away from Gatherling and that no one was to mention them until he gave the order. "Sharia!" Audric hissed.

"Indra? The Priestesses?" Talon asked in a puzzled tone, Illythia lifted her head, her brows creased into a frown.

"Audric," Astrid called, grabbing his attention. "Evander has made Ray and Mazruriuk members of the Pura Mensam; he was going to do the same to Demir, Talon and Illythia. I think we can tell them now; they have proved that we can trust them." Audric met her eyes and nodded, he cleared his throat and ruffled his hair.

"I suppose," he finally said.

"Good answer, considering our sister has just died trying to protect this place," Illythia sniped, Audric swallowed hard and gave her an apologetic look.

"When we say Priestesses, we mean the Elemental sisters," Bayona told them, Illythia and Talon jumped to their feet, their eyes wide with shock.

"The Elemental Sisters?" She gasped, "As in Earth, Fire, Water and Air?"

"Yes," Bayona chimed.

"They've offered to help? They never step in – never." Mazruriuk said as he jumped down from the tree, his face had paled.

"That is true, but this isn't any kind of war, this effects all of us, if this doesn't end the way we want it to - everything ends in blood." Talon and Illythia nodded agreeing with Astrid as she spoke, no one liked to say what could happen out loud and to hear it, frightened them.

"And Indra?" Talon asked, his voice tense.

"Indra is one of the Elder Dragons, she's here in favour to Ophelia Layvechie Moon – the grand Mage and . . ." Audric trailed off and glanced to Astrid.

"Tell them." She urged.

"And Ophelia Layvechie Moon is . . . was Narrdie's mother." Anger twitched at their faces; Talon's hands balled into fists as they shook at his sides; his eyes glimmered red.

"Is there anything else you have kept from us?" Talon asked bitterly.

"That's everything, you know what we do." Audric told him, in a stern voice.

"Why have you kept this from us," Illythia growled.

"It was protocol, we needed to know that we could trust you," Astrid said regretfully, she offered them a sheepish smile.

"Sharia!" A voice shrieked out, the voice was strained, exhausted and full of pain. Sharia jumped up and snapped her head towards the trees, relief slammed into her like a brick wall at the sight of him.

Evander dragged himself out of the trees before collapsing onto the ground, cold sweat coating him like blood, Sharia was the first to reach him. "Evander!" She almost wept; shaking his vigorously, when his eyes closed. "Evander? Evander? Is he dead?"

"Move out of the way," Mazruriuk ordered; he carefully lifted Evander up in his arms and brought him down on a bundle of blankets. "He's out cold," Mazruriuk said in a worried voice.

"Lady Nyda," a guard called as he bowed to her.

"Cole?"

"It's clear inside, it will take a while to clean the rubble, but the . . . the dead have been moved," he announced, she nodded to him and turned to address everyone.

"Listen up, all wounded are to be taken to the infirmary, if that is full then move people into rooms. Cole, take Evander to his quarters and bring a healer with you. Samuel, send for the Elementals, we are going to need their help. As for everyone else, no one is to leave Gatherling, we are on a strict lock down." She turned to a small group; her voice low so only they could hear. "Spread out around Gatherling, if someone approaches and they are not with us – kill them."

$\left(\right.$

*E*vander winced and groaned, slowly regaining consciousness; he licked his lips, they were tight, and his bottom lip had split in several places. He opened his mouth to speak, but words had escaped him, his mouth and throat felt as dry as a desert; he coughed but it sounded wheezy. "Here," Bayona spoke tenderly, "drink this." She lifted his head and placed a glass of water against his lips, slowly lifting it up until the water graced his skin. He closed his eyes as he drank, wanting to take it from her and gulp it down, but before he could – she pulled it away.

"Thanks," his voice croaked. "Where am I?"

"You're home, safe in Gatherling. Nyda thought it better to bring you to your room, here, have another drink." After a few more sips, he pulled away and looked to her; she set down the glass and pulled down the blanket that was draped over him, revealing the bandage tightly bound around his chest. "This needs changing, try not to move."

"What happened?" He asked then hissed through his teeth as she ripped off the blood-stained dressing, in one swift movement.

"I don't know what happened to you, only that you came to us with a wound in your chest and silver in your body."

"What aren't you telling me?" He asked as he scrutinized her – she wouldn't meet his eyes. He lightly grabbed her hand and shook it until she looked to him. "Bayona."

"Dacre escaped . . . Crow let him out." His eyes flared, before he could jump up, Bayona flung her golden Arma around them and gently pushed him back down. "If you go after him now, you'll be dead before you get to the exit," she warned him. He breathed out hard through his nose and reluctantly nodded to her. "Promise you won't try and leave if I lower this?"

"I promise," he grumbled. "Now, will you tell me what happened?"

"Crow attacked the headquarters, Evander eighty died trying to stop her - including Adelina. By the end of the night, the healers think we'll lose ten more, she butchered them like cattle." Bayona's eyes filled up, her voice whimpered. Evander roared in anger and drove his fist into the wall, Bayona snatched his hands into her own. "Stop," she begged. "That won't help anything."

"The siblings are to have as much space as needed and we will have a burial day for all those that we lost, Adelina will have a traditional Vampiral send off," Evander ordered.

Bayona nodded, "I'll inform everyone, after I've sorted you out. Nyda has put the sanctuary in lockdown, we've lost a big number Evander - from just one person. We have to focus on reaching out to other sanctuaries and covens, we need numbers." Evander squeezed her hand and gave her a small smile.

"I know, we'll get the numbers." He sighed again and scratched his stubble. "This is going to kill Narrdie when she snaps out of it. I should go to her." Bayona froze before shifting uncomfortable, she sat back and perched her lips, dreading what she was going to have to tell him; his eyes met hers and a sudden coldness filled the air. "There's more?"

"It's Narrdie." Her voice had turned timid.

"What about Narrdie?" He snapped, making her flinch back.

"She's . . . she's with Dacre," she replied nervously.

Evander jerked up. "What?" He growled, then groaned loudly in agony.

"Stop moving! You're going to rip open your wound!" Bayona hissed.

"I don't care about my wound; how did he manage to take her?"

"When Crow attacked, she broke Dacre out and then left with him." Evander swore; his hands trembled as anger and worry poured into him; he'd failed Narrdie - again. Bayona rested her soft hand over his, using her power to calm him, she'd noticed the purple blotches forming under his eyes - he needed to rest. "We will get her back Evander, but you are no good to her like this."

"We need to get her back now," he said calmly. He glared at her, he wanted to be angry – he needed to be angry. "I know what you're doing."

"Good. I've told you; you need to rest and if you refuse to, then I'll make you," she smiled sweetly. "I do this because I care."

"I know, but we need to get her back. Bayona, we can't delay this."

"We don't have the numbers, more than half of our people are wounded, badly. Plus, our leader is lying in a bed with silver very close to his heart, may I remind you that silver can be fatal to your kind!" Evander rolled his eyes. "The Priestesses are on their way and are bringing some extra healers and Monks with them, to help secure the sanctuary. Once they've arrived and everyone is healed, we'll discuss what to do then. Until that time, please, just rest," Bayona said in a firm tone, she gave him a look that meant, this was not a conversation up for negotiation. "We need you Evander – now more than ever."

Chapter Twenty-Two
Narrdie

*S*omething was wrong. Very wrong.

I wasn't in my room, and I had a deep fear that I wasn't in Gatherling either. I opened my eyes, but I couldn't tell if they were blurry or whether the room was just dark and gloomy. I couldn't feel the warmth of my blanket or the fluffiness of my pillows. No, they had been replaced with a wet and damp floor and the smell of mould and smoke – a constant dripping echoed in my ears.

The blurriness in my eyes cleared – my heart began to beat so fast, I thought it was going to burst out my chest and leave me – when I set my eyes on the cold, thick, cell bars.

The sound of a crunch pulled my attention, saving me from having a panic attack, the crunching reached my ears again and I knew who it was straight away. I clenched my jaw as I turned to face the dark figure, which was slouched on a rusty chair, in the corner of the room – biting into a bright green apple. Dacre.

"Good morning, Narrdie," Dacre sang, as he tossed his apple to the side – rats immediately swarmed it. My hands instantly turned sticky, as they always did when I was faced with him; I raised my hands, summoning my Arma to surround me. Dacre rolled his eyes and stood. "Come now Narrdie, if I wanted to hurt you, I would have already done it, who do you think brought you here?" He raised his brow, that cocky, insufferable grin stretching across his lips.

"How did you get out?" A horrid thought slammed into me and I could feel my breath begin to quicken. "What did you do?" My voice shook slightly, his playfully grin turned sinister.

"I did nothing. You on the other hand . . . did lots of things, including walking in here yourself." His voice was gentle, as though he was talking to a hospital patient that was receiving bad news.

"Crow."

"The Queen herself," Dacre chimed. "Don't fret, Audric was left unharmed at Gatherling, Evander on the other hand; he may or may not be dead, it depends on how quickly he reacts to silver. I did warn you all that Crow doesn't play fairly."

Crow.

Crow did this.

I couldn't remember anything yet, I felt a dark weight hanging over me – guilt circling inside, eating away. I squeezed my eyes together, trying to force myself to remember, recall everything that had happened over the past twenty-four hours. All I could remember was the hill, sitting and laughing with Audric; I was happy because it made me feel . . . normal. I could still see the view, the glittering forest, the feeling of the grass on my fingers and then . . . nothing. It was black.

"Narrdie, stop trying to remember – you'll hurt yourself." He snickered and flashed his fangs at me. I stood and winced as a thumping pain blasted into my head – there was a tender spot when I reached to touch it and it seemed to be forming a lump. "Sorry about that, you began to change so I had to knock you out."

"Let me out of here!" I demanded.

"Get some rest, your day is about to get much harder than a sore head." He slammed the steel room door with a bang that made the cell bars vibrate, I could still here him laughing as he grew further and further away.

My fingers strummed along the cell bars, back and forth, back and forth – over and over again. I had no idea how many hours had passed . . . or had it been days? I leaned against the wall and slumped to the floor, tucking my knees into me; I needed to get out of here and the urge to scream was overwhelming, I bit the inside of my cheek. Screaming would do nothing, it never worked for the kidnapped girls in horror movies, and it wouldn't work for me now.

"I have to get out of here . . . think Narrdie, think!" I told myself, the sound of my own voice was comforting, made me feel less alone.

"Poor, pathetic Narrdie," a voice sang in my head . . . no, not any voice – *her* voice. Her laughter was like frost, snaking around me, biting into my skin. Shut her out, I told myself. *"You can't,"* she snickered, I could feel her dark tendrils brushing against my mind, caressing down my skin – I recoiled.

"What have you done?"

"What have we done." This wasn't the first time I had her skulking around; I had never mentioned it to anyone – not my greatest idea to keep secret. I feared that Evander would get scared, that Audric would never let me leave Gatherling . . . that Nyda would demand that I stayed locked up.

"I am not, you."

"You are part of me, the blame also lies with you."

"Get out of my head," I snarled, braying my fists against my temples.

"Make me," she taunted, her sickening laugh was bitter on my tongue.

I screamed, I screamed out everything. I screamed Crow to leave, I screamed about Dacre and his annoying love for apples, I screamed for Gatherling and everyone that Crow had cut down and I screamed for me. My Arma shot out, it was dark – oily, formed by the very cell I was trapped in, trapped – locked in a cage like an unpredictable beast. The Arma thrashed against the bars, slamming harder and harder with each hit, until I fell to my knees, gasping, the dampness of the ground sticking to my hands. Trapped, trapped, trapped. My Lacus jump ricocheted on the bars, hauling my back against the wall – adding to the ever-growing bump on my head. Useless, pathetic, disappointment.

The doors burst open, the smug laughter filling and tainting my ears, Dacre slandered towards my cell; his eyes scanning over the crumpled bits of debris, until eventually his eyes landed on me. "Anything work?" He teased.

"Bite me." The corner of his lip twitched in amusement.

"Pleasure later Narrdie, business first." His head tilted to the side, I knew what they were the moment they walked in, by now I had seen enough of them; their pale, dark veined skin, how the darkness had tattooed their very soul. Shades, three of them. "I'm afraid you aren't going to like this part," Dacre warned.

I spat on the ground, the clumps of blood forming a small pool; my arms shook, my knees clattered, I looked up – as best I could through my swollen eyes. The three Shades loomed over me, red staining their knuckles from each hit they'd given me, their boots imprinting on my ribs, Dacre was perched lazily in a wooden chair behind them, watching with a sparkle in his eyes. "Again," he mumbled blandly, like he had better things to do than watch them beat the shit out of me over and over. I braced myself for the next wave of pain, the pins and needles to shoot through me – I didn't have to wait long.

One of the Shades gripped a fistful of my hair, hauling me to my feet; his hand snaked around my arms, pinning them to my back. The other two descended on me fast, taking turns to drive an array of punches into my ribs, my stomach – each one getting worse, I'd stopped screaming after the fourth round, the saliva in my mouth had dried until my throat felt like sandpaper. Faint grunts and whimpers of pain were the only things that managed to escape my lips, blood spouting from my mouth like a fountain, they snickered louder with each hit and I swore to remember them – memorizing each scar, each symbol they had carved into their skin. "Enough," Dacre called, rising to his feet. The Shade holding me dropped me down, not bothering to be gentle about it either. "Put her back in her cell," he ordered without so much as a glance my way.

I had never been more thankful for sleep that night.

*Eight days.

Eight days, I was forced to endure this. My bruises never faded, the cuts never closing, blood dried on top of old crusted blood, my hair was coated with it, matting together to form one sticky ponytail. I didn't have the energy to climb into the dusty, rotting bed, the cold floor was more soothing – stinging into my wounds and making the burning less painful.

"Good morning," Dacre announced as he strutted over to the cell, the bars had been left open, I couldn't leave even if I tried, the broken ribs and shattered knees made moving more of a task – even breathing came with riling agony. "How are we feeling today?" He asked in a sarcastic voice, he crouched beside me, flicking away the gravel from my face.

"Screw you," I mumbled into the floor, wincing as my split lip tore and began to bleed, the iron taste lingering in my mouth.

"Still as pleasant as ever," he mocked. His hands gently wrapped around me, lifting me up with ease and laying me on the bed - every spot of contact was abhorrent, unbearable. "There we go, that's better, isn't it?" My eyes finally looked up, searching for the Shades that took delight in my pain. "Not today," he said softly, following my eyes. "I thought I'd give you a little break, a little bit of kindness." I scoffed; his expression turned dark; his hands snagged out around my throat. "You might even want to say thank you." I didn't, my thanks was a spit of blood to his face; he grumbled, the boiling rage bubbling to the surface. "That, was not very nice." His hand clamped over my mouth, sensing my determination to spit at him again. "I dare you," he snarled; his eyes were ablaze as they burned down into mine. "I was going to offer you a bath, but you backhand my kindness."

"Your kindness comes with claws," I managed to say, each word felt like swallowing glass. He laughed through his nose and tossed me back onto the bed.

"Please yourself. I suggest you try and get as much rest as you can, tomorrow will be much, much worse for you." Without another word he rose and shut the door, leaving me once again in darkness.

My head thrummed, I could feel it pulsating with pain, the ringing in my ears almost deafening. *"Narrdie?"* A faint whisper, easily missed if it wasn't for the silence. *"Narrdie, please, if you can hear me, call out to me."* I knew that voice, I had felt its wisps swimming in my mind before, heard its dark voice reach out . . . no not dark, white – a white Shade, Mazruriuk.

"Mazruriuk?" I didn't bother to hope my Animo would be strong enough to reach him, and for a few minutes my only response was the tapping of the leaking roof.

"Narrdie! I've tried to reach you days!" He replied with surprise, his voice echo-y, distant. *"Narrdie, are you alright? Are you hurt?"*

"I'm alive," was the only response I could think to say. I was more than hurt. *"I can't hold it,"* I could already feel the Animo wavering, a blanket of tiredness began to curl around me. *"I don't know where I am."*

"Sit tight, we're coming." I felt like I was being thrown backwards the second the Animo cut off, I lurched over and vomited bile and blood all over the floor, the pounding in my head thumped louder against my temples. They were coming, they were coming to get me, I prayed they'd hurry and that soon I'd be back safe in Gatherling.

Dacre ripped open the door, his hand clenched around the handle so hard it crumbled into pieces, I could feel the rage radiating from him – the hairs on the back of my neck stood up and I gulped down the urge to shriek for help.

Two large Skinners – both with chunks of flesh and meat hanging from their jaws – flanked him; their red eyes fixed on me. By the look on Dacre's face, he knew exactly what I had just done, he waggled his finger at me. "I don't take kindly to people disrespecting my home." He snarled, the Skinners heckled and snapped their jaws. I begged my Arma to spring around me, to shock the three of them into the wall – but I hadn't mustered up the energy for it in days. I gripped the sides of the bed, my hands shrieking at the sudden movement, my body threatening to snap as I hauled myself upright.

The Skinners crouched low – ready to pounce – spit and foam falling from their mouth as they snarled, my eyes snapped down to them and a snake like hiss, wrapped in shadows rolled from my tongue. The lowered to the ground, whimpering as they took a few paces backwards, not daring to raise their blood red eyes to me again. Dacre raised his brows as he watched them and tutted towards me. "Borrowing power from Crow? She won't thank you for that," he warned.

"Mazruriuk says hello," I spluttered, my voice weak, brittle. Dacre tilted his head, a question raising his brow. "You haven't had much experience with Shades of light, have you?" Dacre's clenched jaw was all the answer I needed, and I swore fear flickered in his eyes, as quickly as the beads of sweat that began to gather on his forehead.

"So that's who you called."

"He said, he'd be here soon. I don't know if he'll bring the others – not that he needs them. You and I both know that you're no match for a white Shade, Dacre." He stiffened and I couldn't help but grin, ignoring the sting it caused my lips and bruised face. For once I had him; I'd managed to wipe that mug smirk he wore – like a badge of honour – right from his face.

"I guess it's time to leave then," he snarled as his hand gripped my arms tightly; he froze, tilting his head towards the door, where shouts and the sounds of a fight had begun.

"Times up. So, now what Dacre?" The fighting grew louder, closer and calls of my name reached our ears - Audric. "You don't have time to gather your followers and me and get out of here. I promise you, if you try, I won't come quietly." His eyes burned red, he raised his fist and struck me down with one hard blow – looming over me, his voice icy venom.

"You may think you're smart, little girl, but your power isn't yours! There will come a time again when the darkness consumes you and you'll come crawling back here for help and I'm going to stand there and watch as it chokes you from the inside." I had never seen such wrath in his eyes, such hunger to kill. "Your power belongs to Crow, and you know it does, you're not as strong as Evander and Audric think you are! You are just a shell!" My hands were shaking, in that moment, I felt trapped – frozen by fear . . . he terrified me and he knew it.

"You should be running, Dacre," my voice was shaky.

"I didn't want to hurt you Narrdie, I didn't want it to turn this way, and this was not my way of doing things." I scoffed, I didn't believe him one-bit, I knew he took massive amounts of pleasure in watching everyone around him suffer.

"You think saying that makes you a better person Dacre? It doesn't and if you think I believe you, then you're more delusional than I thought," I growled.

"Until we meet again Narrdie, I suspect it won't be long."

I didn't know how long I was waiting – lying on the holey, soggy mattress – until Mazruriuk kicked the door off its hinges, his power flared all around him, the deadly shadows snaking out around the room, ready to devour anything that dared get close. "Mazruriuk," I called weakly. Immediately, his power pulled back into him, he dropped his blood-stained sword and ran to my side, relief softening his features. His jaw tensed as he looked over me, the crumbled broken and bleeding mess I must have looked.

"You're safe now," he breathed softly. "We'll go slowly, OK? Nice and easy, put your arms around me while I lift you," he coached. My whole body exploded with pain the second I was off the ground and in his arms. "Here!" He called to no one in particular, "I've got her." I couldn't stop myself from sobbing the moment I saw Audric, he fought hard against his own tears as he took my appearance in, my bones protruding from my skin – I hadn't eaten in days, only scraps that Dacre deigned to give me. "Careful," Mazruriuk warned as Audric reached for me. He handed me over and I felt the warmth of Audrics body wrap around me, licking at my aching limbs. "Stay close to me," Mazruriuk ordered, that power once again being brought to the surface.

"You frightened the hell out of me, Moon," Audric's voice was croaky. "I've got you now, we'll get you home."

"Dacre . . . he said I'd attacked the sanctuary...I hurt people." His eyes landed on mine, a stern look.

"You listen and you listen good Narrdie Moon, you didn't hurt anyone, Crow did. You and her are not the same person." Before I could protest Bayona came into our sight, she raised her tattooed hand in the air and spoke a thankful chant to the mother, before quick stepping over to me.

"Narrdie. You two, get her back – we'll follow close and make sure we aren't trailed. I'll see to her once we are all back at Gatherling." Bayona smiled warmly to me, she placed a gently kiss on my head, before opening her palm – a long staff, carved with runes and wrapped in golden leaves emerged in her hands. "Go," she ordered as she raced back towards another Witch, a Witch wrapped in lilac fabric, a similar looking staff in her hands – Nyda. They were alive, unharmed, relief hit me like a tidal wave.

They were alive, they were alive, they were alive.

Chapter Twenty-Three

*A*nger and hatred.

That was what waited for me at Gatherling, that was how every person looked at me when I was carried in there; their tear-stained faces, their cries and their low chattering, fell silent the moment Audric carried me across the threshold.

Regardless of what Audric and Bayona thought, regardless of what they told me – this was my fault and everyone else, believed it also. I buried my face in Audric's chest, I couldn't look at them, I couldn't face what I had done – what I had put them all through.

"There you go, easy does it," Audric breathed as he carefully tucked me into my bed, my bed – it welcomed me instantly, the pillow sinking and surrounding my thrumming head with feathers, the soft quilt wrapping around me and warming up my clattering bones. The coloured sheets, instantly stained, as my blood leaked onto them – but I didn't care, I was so fatigued, drained of every bit of energy I had. "Bayona will be here soon," Audric's mumbled voice echoed in my ears.

"Mm-hmm," I couldn't find words to say, I could barely muster a sigh.

"Until then you just rest," his warm fingers brushed my cheek, sweeping my hair to the side. He walked to the green armchair opposite my bed and breathed out hard as he sank back into it, allowing his own eyes to close.

"Wait here," Audric said, as we entered the grand hall. He gave me an encouraging smile before walking to a small group of guards. The grand hall was the last place I wanted to be, it was full – crowded with mourners, echoing with cries and saddened voices, each sound, hurt. I didn't belong here, didn't deserve to be here – didn't deserve to grieve with them.

Then I saw her, Illythia.

She knelt beside Adelina's body – whispering to her in their mother tongue – as she stroked her sister's lifeless hand. Adelina's body had been placed on a red silk bed, candles spread all around her, spreading around the wall and tables. She was dressed in a white satin dress, embroidered with silver tulips, her hair had been curled and entwined around a white tiara; her hands clasped across her stomach. She looked beautiful, like a sleeping goddess – worshipped by her family.

I lingered in the doorway, not being able to take my eyes from her; my heart broke for Illythia and Talon and what I had taken from them, my heart broke for everyone – everyone in this room, everyone who was cradled beside their fallen loved one, lying on similar laid out beds. Talon appeared next to me; his face as hard as stone, there was no warmth, no kindness as he looked to me – only icy cold detest. "Talon, I . . ." I trailed off. What do you say to the person whose sister was killed by the dark creature inside you?

"I think you should go," his voice was like fire – whipping me with every word, I swallowed the lump that had clogged my throat and nodded, the moment I was out the room – I bolted.

I couldn't stay in Gatherling, not with everyone mourning from what Crow or I had done, every room I went into, someone was either wounded, dead or grieving. The way people looked at me, the fury in their eyes – it was too much for me to bare. If it would make things better, I would stand in a room and let them stare with as much distain as they wished, I would let them shout, scream at me – call me every name under the sun.

I sat on a small patch, my arms wrapped around my knees; I wasn't far from Gatherling, but it was enough distance so that I couldn't hear the grieving. The forest was silent, not a peaceful sort of silence, it was like even the forest wanted me to feel the burning emptiness of my victims. It wanted the silence to consume me, crush me into nothing but dust. "What have you done Crow? What have we done?" I was surprised at how weepy my voice was, I thought I'd be used to the devastation that came with the darkness, but no matter how many died – it didn't feel any easier.

The sun was setting, the clouds were a blend of pink and orange, as they travelled towards the horizon; they turned into a buttercup yellow, but even something as beautiful as this was tainted. "I can't take this anymore. No matter how hard I train, no matter how stronger I get, Crow will always beat me."

"That's simply not true," Audric said lightly, as he came up behind me. "Budge over," he playfully kicked me, before dropping down beside me and smiled.

"I have to use every bit of energy I have to keep her down – she's too powerful Audric." Audric sighed and caught a piece of hair that had escaped its clasp; he tucked it gently behind my ear and breath out hard.

"Adelina, Molly, Santos, Bo and all the others died because of Crow. They all jumped into a fight they knew, they couldn't win. It sounds harsh to say out loud but, it's the truth. No one – apart from you – is strong enough to fight Crow."

"Evander-"

"Evander, knows everything about Crow, he's dealt with her for years, he's fought her countless times and each time he's almost been killed," Audric argued.

"Evander knew what she was going to do and somehow; he managed to manipulate the situation and survive. Always remember, Crow isn't you, you may share a body, but she is not you. You are strong Narrdie, caring and more powerful than you realise; you're everything Crow pretends to be. You think you can't beat her, but you already are, you are here right now – she's not. If she was more powerful, she'd be in control – not you." His fingers lightly gripped my chin – forcing me to look at him, "Right?" He held our stare – unfaltering, until finally I smiled and nodded.

"Yes," I said with a chuckle.

"And, as for you getting stronger, look at how much you intimidated Egregious, or at the college, you fought like you'd been doing it all your life. Things will take time, it's annoying having to wait but it's worth it."

"But, how much time do we have left?" I asked, causing the grin to slide from his face, he looked down and shuffled. "That's what I thought," I mumbled disappointedly.

"Others will come and join us Narrdie, they've realised this war is happening, at the end of it, we'll be ready. Nyda has already sent her people out to the covens and the sanctuaries and called them in for help – we'll have our army." I frowned and bit my lip; I tilted my head towards him; he raised his brows at me with a puzzled expression. "What?"

"A lot of our army hasn't had any experience fighting the dark, they don't know how strong they are. Even if we warn them and train them, they still will get a shock when faced with them and I know the sanctuaries and covens are amazing fighters, but I've seen what the darkness can do, and I've felt it first-hand. I think as well as having the light fight for us, we need the dark," Audric studied me for a few heartbeats; his brows raised.

"You want us to reach out to . . . the dark realm?" A chilling thought strummed its fingers along my mind,

"I have an idea . . . but you aren't going to like it."

*E*vander woke with a jerk, his eyes still blood shot – watered with pain. "There's a face worth waking up for," he teased. I half smiled and helped him to sit up – biting the inside of my cheek each time he moaned or winced.

"Maybe I should have just let you rest."

"No, no. It's about time you came to see me, what kept you for so long?" I looked down guiltily. "Narrdie? What's on your mind?" His hand slipped into mine – he squeezed it lightly and I looked to him; his bold orange eyes holding nothing but kindness as they locked with mine.

"I almost killed you," my voice turned weepy.

"That's why you haven't come." It wasn't a question, but I nodded.

"I feel like there's a hole in my chest and after each time – it gets bigger." He frowned.

"Each time?"

"Each time I kill someone, this hole is getting so big – I'm scared I'll never fill it again and then I'll just be something different." He sighed and rubbed the back of his neck, huffing a laugh.

"Narrdie, I don't know how many times we have to tell you; you haven't killed. Crow did. You didn't do this to me either. Crow did. You and Crow both have control over one body, but you are both different people, with different thoughts and different actions. Do you remember hurting me?" I shook my head and he chuckled softly. "That's because it's not your memory to keep, it's Crows." He gripped the sides of my face, not tight enough to hurt, but strong enough that I couldn't pull away. "I hate to say it, but you need to toughen up and tattoo it into your brain, that you and her – are different people. Different people, who do different things," he tightly tapped my head, pretending his finger was a drill. "Am I getting through to you?" I laughed and swotted his hand away. "Besides, it'll take a lot more than a silver knife to kill me," he said playfully as he gently tugged my hair. I lightly hit him on the shoulder, "Ow! Don't abuse me I'm injured!" He whined sarcastically.

"Don't be a smart ass." His gaze turned hard as it raked over me, to the split in my lip, the lingering purple bruises and markings that were still fading from Dacre. A muscle feathered in his jaw; his eyes flickered with distaste, I could see the icy unyielding rage of the beast beneath his skin, inkling to the surface. "It's fine," my voice was hollow.

"Bayona told me the state they found you in, what Dacre had done to you. I swear when I see him-"

"Stop," I breathed, my hands leaning to rest on his cheek. He leaned his forehead against mine, his jaw clenching. "I'm fine." He slid incredulous eyes to me, as if he could see the shredded soul underneath my eyes – my throat bobbed. "Dacre once told me that Crow tried to kill you many times over, why didn't she ever do it?"

Evander breathed out hard and leaned his head back against the headboard.

"I think deep down, way down in that black heart of hers, she cares," he admitted. "If she wanted me dead – I'd be dead."

"And Dacre?"

"Dacre would never kill me." His name was like fire on his tongue.

"Is that because you're his Alpha?" Evander burst out in a laugh, coughing as the laugh turned to sharp pain.

"Me? Dacre's Alpha?"

"Well, Dacre is part wolf and you're a wolf and you lived together. Who was the Alpha?"

"There was no Alpha, Dacre is half Wolf – the Alpha instinct isn't in him, only pure-blooded wolves like me and my sister have the Alpha gene." I frowned, watching him, every time he mentioned Dacre – his eyes darkened.

"Were you ever friends?" I dared to ask him; his smile dropped – his mouth cutting a cruel line.

"No, not really. We fought like brothers, but that didn't mean we always saw eye to eye."

"Why?" He looked away from me and stared at the wall – lost in a memory, finally he yawned widely and winced as he turned on his side; his hand stroked down a strand of my hair.

"Shouldn't you be doing your research?" He asked casually, I pulled away from him; my brows creasing into a line.

"You're avoiding the question, Evander." His jaw clenched and he gave me a look – a look which I had seen more than once and knew exactly what it meant. "It has something to do with me, doesn't it?" He smiled, but it quickly faded.

"Back then we'd contained Crow, she wasn't full of hate . . . well not as much hate, she'd even help us," he began, his eyes became distance. "We were naïve, got too comfortable – too familiar with her. Especially Dacre." He gave me a look and my mouth gaped open like a fish.

"Dacre loved Crow?"

He nodded, "Yes."

"And you loved me?"

"Yes," his jaw tightened. "Crow quickly became a problem; she'd engorged herself, welcomed too much darkness . . . too much blood. Dacre and I argued about her, as much as it hurt Dacre; he agreed to stop her. It hurt me too – although he didn't believe it did – when we put you to sleep, he lost Crow and I lost you." My lip quivered and I began to pick at the loose skin around my thumb.

"You miss the girl I was back then." I tried hard not to let him see how much I was hurting. He'd loved the old Narrdie, the one who knew her power, the strong warrior they all expect me to become. The one that didn't shudder, cower or fear the nightmares that consumed her at night.

"No. I used to, but now I have her back." His hand rested on my cheek, and I leaned into his touch, breathed in its warmth. I smiled and leaned up to kiss him gently, I tried to pull away as he winced, but he kept me there with his hand resting on the back of my head. "I love you."

"Is my real name Narrdie Moon?" Evander snorted a laugh.

"Yes, your real name is Narrdie Moon. Changing your name wasn't necessary," he chucked as I breathed out in relief. "Dacre, I don't suppose he fed you anything we could use when he held you captive?" He flashed me apologetic eyes, "Nyda wanted to pull you in for questioning the moment you returned."

"There wasn't much talking, he'd come in and order the Shades to break my body." I shuddered, feeling the sudden heaviness of the dark damp cell cramming down on me, the pain of each kick into my already broken ribs, the smell of dried blood staining my hair.

"I'm sorry, I shouldn't have brought it up." Shame washed across his eyes.

"Towards the end, he said one thing, but I'm not sure whether he was trying to make me believe he was the good guy." Evander sat up, his eyes carefully surveying me; he nodded for me to continue. "He said, that this wasn't how he wanted to do things, that it wasn't his plan. If it wasn't his plan, then who's calling the shots? I thought Dacre was in charge."

"So did I," Evander admitted; his forehead creasing into a tight frown. "It seems whoever is in charge, is staying far from sight." I laughed a humourless laugh, as something clicked into place.

"So that a certain Witch doesn't see him."

"Bayona. Dacre is purposely keeping in her sights. The Witch they have isn't blocking him, it's blocking whoever is leading them." Evander sneered; his face uncharacteristically solemn.

"We're more in the dark than we thought, aren't we?" I breathed; Evander's silence was answer enough. "What is Crow to the dark Realm?"

"Sorceress of Darkness, some refer to her as their Queen – who knows what she really is to them. Whoever this mysterious shadow is, we need to draw him out. It'd be too dangerous for Bayona to start skulking around in Dacre's head – he'd likely trap her there." I could see the clogs turning in Evander's mind, his eyes suddenly looking stained, thick purple bags began to pull his eyes down.

"You need rest," I told him softly. "I'll leave you be," I offered. His hand lightly grabbed mine and he pulled me onto the bed, lightly pressing my head down onto his chest and running his fingers through my hair.

"So do you. You look just as weary as I do. Stay with me tonight – you owe me, I stayed with you the first night we met, remember? I had to put up with your snoring," he teased in a tired voice.

"I don't snore," I protested.

"You do, as loud as a bore," he snickered.

"Do you know when you're a wolf," I began, he responded with a tired mumble.

"Do you chase your tail?" I giggled, as I felt his fingers dig into my ribs.

Chapter Twenty-Four

"Remember, we're right outside this door," Audric reassured me for the fourth time – as we stood outside the Gatherling cells, which were located in the darkest depths of the sanctuary.

A cell, dark, trapped, left to die.

I dug my nails into the palms of my hands, reminding myself that I could walk out of here whenever I wanted, that I wasn't locked away or left on the cold damp ground; I was in Gatherling, and I was safe. I plastered a confident smile across myself, ignoring the panicked beating my heart had begun to orchestrate.

Both Audric and Mazruriuk had come armed to the teeth; Mazruriuk gripped onto a large sharp knife, embossed with black onyx and a strange language along the blade, another sword on his belt and the dark shadows of his power swimming around him. A black crossbow lingered on Audric's back, an assortment of daggers on both sides of his legs, (two on each side) and a double-edged sword, gripped hard in his hand.

"I'll be fine," I assured them, my voice not as convincing as I hoped. "If I need help, I'll call." They both exchanged an unconvinced look, before signalling the watchman to open the cells door – keeping my shaking hands behind my back.

The Loopin man snarled as I walked towards the bars that contained him, noting the runes that had been carved in and enchanted by Nyda and Bayona so no amount of strength could break them – a measurement they'd taken after Crow had turned them to rubble. "I already know you speak," I snapped, after the second wave of heckles and snarls. He cocked his head to the side and smirked widely, a wicked laugh rolled off his tongue.

"Very well then." I was still shocked at how polite and articulate the Loopin sounded. I gave him a warning look, before twisting the key in the lock and throwing open the door – he raised his thin brow. "Brave girl," he mocked.

"You're well spoken . . . for a Loopin. You'll have to tell me how you learnt our language."

He grumbled a snort, "who said it was your language."

"I thought it would be more civil if we talked without a bar between us. Like equals," I offered.

"You think we are equals?" He sang, that grin going razor sharp.

"I could close it and let you rot in here instead?" The side of his mouth lifted in a sneer, he slowly sat opposite me and gestured me to have a seat – I did.

"Are we going to negotiate? Either that or you're about to kill me?"

"We'll see how this conversation goes. I want to make a deal." His forked tongue snaked out, licking along his sharp teeth.

"Go ahead, try your best," he urged.

"I'll keep it simple. I want you and your kind to join and fight with us," I kept my voice blank, empty – careful.

"That's it?" He asked.

"Yes." The Loopin erupted in a roar of laughter, the sound bouncing off the walls – ringing in my ears. Ringing in my ears, like the ringing after the Shades had beaten me down, after Dacre had tossed me onto the cold pavement.

Cell, cell, cell. Trapped, trapped, trapped.

My lips pulled back over my teeth, I could feel the sharpness they had shifted to, along my tongue, a dark rumble swelled in my throat, rippling into a feral snarl – he flinched. "Why would we fight with you instead of them? They have Skinners, Jackals, Crawlers . . . Sivvs." I shuddered, trying to hide how much those creatures made the hairs on my skin stick up. "Creatures you've never even heard off. Why choose you?"

"Because, I'm going to win." I kept my eyes locked with his, allowing my power to consume them, allowing it to clog the air – just enough to make his body jerk.

He forced a smile – but it quivered, "If I fight with you, how do I know that I won't be double crossed? How do I know you won't kill me and mine after the war is over?"

"I give you, my word."

"Your word means nothing," he spat; his claws protruding under his grimy nails.

"And my oath?"

He laughed humourlessly; his face turned dark. "An oath means nothing to you. You have no idea what it really is! You think I haven't heard the whispers amongst the wind? You, girl, have not an ounce of power you may have once possessed – the sleeping defender." His cackle was sharp, cutting into me like a knife.

"You want reassurance? Fine." I rose, noting his sudden recoil, almost tearing the hinges from the cell doors as I retched it open – where Mazruriuk and Audric stood like guards outside a palace.

"Mazruriuk, can I borrow your knife please?" They both swivelled around on their heels and gave me suspicious brows, I could see Audric's eyes swimming over me, taking in the anger that poured from my skin like sweat.

"My knife? W-h-y?" He asked as he stretched out the word.

"What you up to Moon?" Audric asked as Mazruriuk rested the hilt in my palm, the onyx stones scratching my calloused fingers.

"Be careful with that, it's older than Illythia and that's saying something – don't tell her I said that either." He whispered, we all shared a quiet chuckle, before Audric spoke, asking the one question I hoped he wouldn't.

"What do you need it for?"

"A blood oath." I turned to head back to the Loopin – when Audric and Mazruriuk lifted me up by my arms and headed back upstairs, mumbling and swearing under their breaths.

"Lock that thing back up," Mazruriuk ordered a guard.

They carried me all the way to the dining hall, my feet waggling around underneath me, I felt like a child – being flung over the shoulder by her father. Finally, they set me down on a chair, in front of a rather confused looking Nyda; her eyes shot up and her face twisted into the familiar annoyed look she always wore. "Good evening Audric, Mazruriuk, Narrdie. What is with this unexpected visit? I'm assuming it isn't a social one?" Audric kept his hand on my shoulder – holding me down. Mazruriuk pulled a chair beside Nyda, leaning his body close to me – like he thought I would bolt for the door; he cleared his throat.

"Narrdie, was about to make a blood oath . . . with the Loopin." Nyda's eyes widened; she glared at me in disbelief as she closed her book and set it down beside her; she let out a long breath and I just knew that a lecture was about to come my way.

"Tell me this isn't true, Narrdie." I sighed and shrugged Audric's hand off.

"Audric, I'm not a child, you don't need to keep me restrained," I snapped. "Yes. I was going to make, a blood oath; I've done my research; I know what to do." Audric snorted sarcastically – I really hated his arrogant side.

"How much do you know about blood oaths?" Nyda quizzed.

"Just what I've read, Evander has a section on oaths," I admitted, beginning to feel like an idiot once again.

"Just what you've read?" Nyda repeated – her tone bitter, she scoffed and shook her head.

"Nyda. That's enough, don't mock her – you should know better," Evander said with a stern voice. Ray had her arm linked with his; she slowly helped him to the seat Mazruriuk had offered, a crutch resting under his right arm. He was shirtless, the fresh white bandages wrapped tightly around his chest, were already beginning to turn yellow from his weeping wound. "Thank you, Mazruriuk and thank you Rosie – my little helper." Ray smiled warmly and stood beside Mazruriuk – who I caught winking at her; his fingers brushed hers and I couldn't help but smile. "I thought I'd stretch my legs, you can imagine my surprise when I saw Narrdie – dangling between two warriors," he winced as he placed his crutched on the ground; he turned to me. "Now, what's this I hear about blood oaths in my house?" Evander's tone was soft, and his eyes were gentle as they looked towards me. I smiled sheepishly to him.

"I was going to make a blood oath with the Loopin we have in holding." I said it all in a rush, before giving him a nervous look and put my head down. I expected him to bite my head off, to tell me I was being reckless and stupid and that I was going to be under watch once again – but he didn't, instead he breathed out and offered me a gentle smile; his hand reaching for mine.

"Ah, I see," he began, as his thumb brushed the space between my fingers. "Well, you may have read one of my books, but Narrdie those books are loosely based. A mix between fact and fiction, blood oaths haven't been done in centuries – they are tricky and can be fatal." He winced slightly as he leaned closer to me, he lifted my hand and pressed his lips to it, my skin tingled. "To make a blood oath, you need the basics. You need to know what you are making the oath for – every little detail, don't leave anything out. Then you need a Witch to seal the oath." I nodded, it didn't sound too difficult; I shrugged and rose.

"Fine, that's easy enough. I know exactly what I want, down to every detail. I'll ask Bayona unless you'd do it for me Nyda?" Nyda went speechless; her skin drained of colour, she glared with wide eyes to Evander – signalling for help.

"Narrdie, do you know what happens if you break a blood oath?" Evander asked gently.

Unfortunately, I hadn't gotten up to that part yet; I slumped down and huffed which made Audric nod with satisfaction. I had a feeling I wasn't going to like the answer. "If you break a blood oath, you, the creature and the Witch . . . die." I gulped. I wasn't scared for me but putting Nyda or Bayona's life at risk . . . I couldn't do it; I didn't want more blood on my hands.

"It is not a pleasant death either," Mazruriuk added.

"And if I did it without all the right people?" I asked nervously, my palms turned sticky.

"You'd die," Audric answered blankly.

"And you can guarantee that that Loopin would have let you do it – to watch you die, slowly, painfully," Mazruriuk added.

"She gets it Riuk," Ray told him, her lips perched playfully.

"It's a good thing we stopped you, isn't it?" Mazruriuk boasted – Ray dug her elbow into his ribs.

"I still want to do this," I decided.

"You've got to be fucking kidding me," Audric snarled – Evander shot him a warning look.

"Having the Loopins on our side gives us more numbers – a lot of numbers and more of an advantage. They're vicious, fast and don't think before they attack!" I argued, flaring my eyes at Audric. Audric rose and began to curse and mumble to himself – I chose to ignore him. Evander's reaction surprised me and for a split second I thought I had been zapped into a parallel universe.

He laughed, not sarcastically, not aggressively – but happily. "Once an idea is in your head, you don't back down, do you?"

"Nope."

"That's my girl." My insides fluttered at his words, my blood burned, my body tingled, and my heart felt like it was dancing around in my chest; I had a sudden urge to dive on him – I had to grip the chair to stop myself. "Well," he began – pulling me out of my animalistic desires. "I suppose having Loopins on our side does give us the numbers and the brutality. If you find a Witch that's willing to do this, then I guess none of us can stop you."

"Evander-" Audric began, Evander raised his hand – cutting him off.

"Narrdie is not a child to be coddled, she is a leader and good leaders make tough decisions for the good of their people, I think it is about time that we all start allowing her to choose things for herself," his voice was stern, final. "However, I ask for one favour first." I frowned; I knew how sneaky he could be.

"Which is?"

"Give it some time, just to think this over – a week, maybe two. Do it for me, for Audric, because I think his head is about to pop like a balloon. Come to one of us before, not after. Narrdie, promise me this." I released a breath, I didn't want to waste time; I wanted to do this now, I supposed I still had one idea I could do in the meantime.

Reluctantly, I nodded, and Evander smiled – yet I could see the concern reflect in his eyes. "I promise."

Chapter Twenty-Five

I was convinced that Evander and Talon were gonna bail on me, neither one of them liked this idea and had spent numerous hours and days trying to talk me out of it, I'd wake up and Evander would either be sitting awake next to me or pacing up and down my room - listing everything that could go wrong. Saying I wasn't nervous, wouldn't have been an outright lie; I couldn't tell if I was going to pass out or puke my guts up all over the forest floor. My eyes stung, I had been going over every scenario that could possibly happen all night, my hands lightly shook, and a bead of sweat dotted my forehead.

Talon and Evander strutted towards me, everything inside me turned tense, my heart began to pirouette against my chest as my eyes dropped to Evander - he was topless. Topless, muscular, tattoo covered Evander - my mouth watered, it had been a while since we had been intimate. "You've cut your hair," I cringed at my voice, the voice I always ended having whenever I felt the tingles from him. His ponytail was gone, his hair was cropped short on the top, gradually fraying into neat shaven sides; his beard was trimmed, but still holding the messiness to it that I loved.

"You like?" He asked as his eyes looked me up and down – lingering at my slightly exposed cleavage, it seemed I wasn't the only one who thought it had been a while. He winked, and I bit my lip playfully, my eyes dropping to his chest . . . his muscular . . . chiselled chest. Talon coughed awkwardly and raised his brows to us, bringing us back to the current task at hand. Evander stifled a laugh, but the look in his eyes meant that tonight – it would be just us.

"Remind me why we are doing this again?" Talon asked me, as he glanced down to my sweaty restless hands and raised his brow. I wiped my hands on my jeans and painted on the best smile I could muster.

"Because every sanctuary has them as guard, they are evolved, strong and having them stand with us, makes our numbers larger than Dacres," I had recited this over and over, in an attempt to convince myself.

"And you're sure you want to do this?"

"Yep." Lie. "One hundred percent." Such a lie. "I'm ready." Complete utter lie.

"I can smell your fear," he pointed out with a harsh brow.

"Me too," Evander added.

"Fine, maybe I'm more sixty – forty," I admitted. "I'm not sure I want to go through with this, but if I don't do it now – I never will, and I'll just kick myself for chickening out." Talon gave me a gentle pat on the shoulder – the most human gesture I'd seen him make.

We'd only just made up a few hours ago. He'd come to my room, with a cup of hot chocolate – which tasted like gravel – it was the first one he'd ever made. He'd wanted to talk and tell me how awful he felt for blaming Adelina's death on me, he'd apologised over and over – no matter how many times I told him I forgave him. He'd asked to come with me, in place of Mazruriuk, to prove that he would always be on my side. I was grateful – extremely grateful.

"Talon." Evander nodded towards him, Talon lightly gripped my arm and moved me to stand behind him. Evander groaned as he began to bend and twist in all kinds of uncomfortable looking positions. "I haven't done this in a while, years even. I might be a little . . ."

"Wild?" I teased, the look he gave me was playful, animalistic, I almost purred.

"You might want to look away," he warned, I could see in his eyes that he really wished I would.

Crunching, the chilling snapping of bones, the squelching of blood hitting the floor and the tearing of flesh, stained my ears. Evander screeched, the sound echoed and bounced around the trees, with each break, each splinter; his cries turned more blood curling.

I clasped my hand over my mouth, to keep in my whimpers, my eyes aching as they filled with tears; I wanted to turn and run to comfort him, but every time I gestured that I was going to look - Talon gripped my arm and shook his head. "This is normal for him," he assured me, he held my hand - not flinching when I'd dig my nails into his skin.

"He's in pain," my voice was nothing but a rasping wobble.

"He's a werewolf who hasn't changed in a while. He's pushed down his instincts, it's as bad as a Vampire not having blood, or a human refusing to sleep. It messes with the system, after this he'll be able to change quicker and without pain." Talon smiled at me, and there was truthiness behind his eyes.

Darkness was falling around us - the sky engulfed in a black blanket and a sea of stars began to light up the forest. An hour passed, an antagonising hour - full of Evander's ricocheting shrieks and screams. Eventually, Talon squeezed my hand and offered me a comforting smile, his finger gently wiped my tears. "He's done, you can look now." My blood turned to ice in my veins, I didn't know what to expect when I turned around - would he still be my Evander? The one who held me at night when the nightmares would swarm, the one who made me laugh on my dark days, would he even know me? "Go on," Talon urged.

I expected to feel the kernel of fear when I looked to him, but there was nothing - nothing but a crack of a smile as my eyes met him. He was a giant. The biggest wolf I had ever seen in my entire life. His tongue hung out his open mouth, his hot breath ruffled my hair, his bright orange eyes connected with mine - freezing me in place. I waited for the savage growl and heckles to spout, the uncontrollable animal instinct to launch at me and tear my throat out, but instead; he sat down - his tail waggling. Evander's fur was a beautiful blend of whites and greys, he had one black ear, making him more unique that I thought. The scar across his eye still remained in his wolf from but didn't take away how stunningly majestic he looked. My hand lightly fell forward, wanting to touch him, to feel his coat,

I pulled back nervously. Evander whimpered and didn't hesitate, as he lowered his head, his ears gently folding as he stepped to me. He licked my fingers, before pressing his head into my hand, my fingers sank into him, his fur thick, silky and softer than any blanket. "Hey Evander," my voice seemed shaky, and I hoped he didn't think I was afraid of him.

"Everything good here?" Talon asked.

"Lead the way," I whispered as I scratched his black ear and dropped a light kiss on his forehead.

This part of the forest was different, it was untouched – unsullied in all its glory, no human or being had tarnished it's bed. The trees groaned, but there was no breeze to shake them, the air was tight and stale – this part of the forest was alive, and it didn't take kindly to us being here. My eyes had lost Evander, he'd ran so far ahead that the forest mist had swallowed him up. Anxiety gripped hold of me, and my hand shot out to grab Talon; he chuckled lightly. "It's OK to be scared," he said, keeping his voice low.

"The forest..."

"This forest is changed," his voice was tense; he didn't take his eyes from the trees as he spoke. "It's probably best you stay close, it will consume you faster than death," he warned.

"What about Evander?" I could see my breath clouding in front of me as it left my mouth.

"He'll be checking to make sure our path is safe, don't worry – he knows these woods." My blood went cold as the woods around me as a brand snapped beside us, Talon paused, pulling me to a stop with him. His eyes turned red, and his fangs and nails extended into sharp points. Evander padded out of the trees – panting so loudly, I could feel it vibrate in my chest.

"Here, we wait," Talon announced; his voice sounded like something from a nightmare.

The pack was big, bigger than any of us anticipated, within a breath we were surrounded, each one had fury in their eyes – fury like I had never seen. My heart sang into a thunderous beat; this was a mistake – a mistake that could cost us our lives. They parted, cowering back as he came through, I knew he was the leader, the Alpha – his size alone gave that away. He towered over the rest, his paws making thick dints in the ground; his fur was thick and as black as the shadows. His lips pulled back, revealing the array of large teeth, teeth that could snap off our bones in one bite; he snarled as he took a step closer – Evander blocked his path; his teeth also bare. This was going to turn into a battle of Alpha's if I didn't act quickly. Evander and the black wolf snarled and snapped their jaws at each other, neither one of them balking from the heated look in their eyes.

"Talon?" His hand shot out to silence me, his voice a hushed whisper as he spoke.

"Evander's talking to him, the wolf is furious we are here. Especially Evander, it's an insult."

"Because he's a potential Alpha," I guessed – Talon nodded.

"He's agreed to let you speak. Use your Animo, be respectful, don't lie and watch your tempter – this is his house we're in, don't let him trick you." I nodded and swallowed hard; the wolf's gaze was like a brand as it set on me.

"We are not here to cause any harm to you or your pack." The second I used my Animo I could taste the tremor of power, the darkness laced within it. The wolf spoke, his words were like a hiss of a breath.

"You're trespassing," he snarled.

"I know, and I am sorry for that, we wouldn't have come if we weren't desperate."

"Why have you come?"

"Dacre." The moment his name slipped through my lips; the wolves suddenly erupted furiously – their jaws snapping as the saliva splashed on the floor. Evander dropped low beside me, ready to pounce.

"Narrdie," Talon warned.

"He is nothing to us, once maybe – but now, we'd see him die." I bit the inside of my cheek to keep myself from grinning.

"You and your kind have always guarded these woods, guarded all the sanctuary woods – yet no one asked you too. You want Dacre dead? Then fight against him, fight with me." The uproar of the wolves around them began again, but the Alpha tilted his head.

"Why would you fight against him? You fought with him in the old world... you are as untrustworthy as he is, Crow," he spat.

The name – *her* name. Whenever I heard it, it ignited icy hot rage within my blood, a rage I couldn't control. The nails on my hand shifted to claws, I leapt forward and slashed once across his eye – my nails barked as they tore his hard skin. The forest came alive with howls, snarls – every corner of the wood echoed with the anger of their Alpha being hurt

– anger directed towards me. They crouched low, ready to dive and rip my throat out in one swift bite.

"Narrdie! What are you doing?" Talon demanded, through clenched fangs, Evander paced around, eyeing up the wolves that had taken a step closer.

"I will tell you this once and once only. I am not Crow," I began, pushing my Animo out to reach them all. *"I fight against her. You call me Crow again and I will tear out your heart, regardless of your pack,"* I warned.

The wolf stopped, eased up from his stance slightly; his eyes sizing me up, his teeth bared towards his pack – silencing them. His eye met mine and I could see some feral part of him beamed with savage delight. *"If you are not Crow, then who are you?"*

"I am Narrdie Moon, and I am asking you to side with me, protect your pack and future. Fight on our side, before it's too late for us all." The forest fell silent, and I knew he was talking amongst his pack.

After a moment's breath, his eyes fixed back onto me.

"We request time. You will come back alone when we send for you." He tossed his head back and let out a deafening howl, it echoed throughout the forest – carried by the wind. Slowly, cautiously they backed up – their eyes still fixed onto us before the only thing I could see was the brightness of their eyes.

"Well?" Talon urged, once they were all gone. "You want to explain that little outburst that nearly turned us to chum?" Talon asked as he snagged my arm.

"He called me Crow." Talon nodded, as if that was answer enough.

"What did he say?"

"We should go back, then we can talk." I warned, signalling to my ears.

"I can't believe it, all three of them are back, alive and unharmed – did you even do it? Or just hang around for a few hours to make us thing you did?" Bayona harassed playfully, the second we came through the door. "Not one of you are harmed – not even a scratch."

"I have to say, even I thought you would have been wolf chow, brother," Illythia admitted as she placed a relief filled kiss on Talon's cheek – she didn't once look in my direction.

"Did it work?" Nyda asked; he voice sounded uninterested. I dropped into the seat beside Audric and let out an exhausted huff. Audric handed me a cup of mint hot chocolate-swarmed with whipped cream and marshmallows – and tucked a fluffy blanket around me, I didn't realise how stiff my frozen limbs had become.

"I don't know yet; they want time to discuss it," I mumbled as I pulled my hot chocolate towards me. The warmth of the stream seeping into my nose, the alluring smell of mint following close by; the marshmallows turned gloopy – melting into the milky chocolate river, the whipped cream slowly losing its peak. I place it to my lips, savouring the taste as the heat flowed down my throat, warming my cold core.

"If they don't fight with us, do you think they'll go to Dacre?" Bayona asked.

"No, I don't think so, they hate Dacre – almost as much as we do."

"The air has changed," Astrid announced as she stared at the wall, causing everyone to fall silent and turn to her, a worried mist tainted her eyes. "You can all sense it as much as I can. Those that don't want to fight have evacuated and the ones that haven't, they will be forced to pick a side."

"And Crow would kill them if they refused her side," Illythia added with a sneer towards me, her words were cold – hard, as they sank into me. Astrid frowned in her direction – a subtle warning – before she glanced over to me; she smiled her motherly smile at me and patted me on the knee.

"Bed for you Miss Moon," she decided as she signalled me to stand up. "You two as well," she ordered as she pointed her finger playfully to Evander and Talon. None of us bothered to argue, the events with the wolves had shattered us completely. Sleep would do us good. "Your own beds," she added as she glared to me and Evander.

"Tomorrow, you're mine," Evander whispered in my ear.

It was noon by the time I woke, I stretched my legs and arms out – thankful that everyone had left me to my lie in. I wanted to stay in my bed, bask in the peace and quiet I rarely got, perhaps even light some candles and have an extralong bath. The reality of why I couldn't lounge around hit me hard. I leaned over and screamed into my pillow – kicking my legs out in a tantrum.

The Loopin.

It had been well over a week since I wanted to do the blood oath, in respect to Evander, I'd agreed to think it over and to their displeasure – my answer was the same. No one dared to bring up the oath or the Loopin, in the hope that I'd forget about it. Reluctant to leave my room I pulled on my leggings and my favourite baggy jumper – a dark grey turtleneck, which was way too big for me – and slipped into my furry black boots.

I slumped into the corridor, my nose instantly guiding me. The smell of crispy bacon, fried eggs with a sprinkle of cheese and sausages scattered with black pepper and herbs – drifted into my nostrils. My mouth watered and my stomach rumbled, begging my feet to move faster, the closer I got to the dining hall the more the smells swayed around me. Homemade golden hash browns, caramelized fried mushrooms, black pudding and giant grilled tomatoes – I wanted them all.

Almost everyone was in the dining hall, sat around the table; their faces happy and plates full – I loved seeing them like this. I lingered in the doorway, just for a moment – just watching and listening.

"How do you find these people Evander?" Demir began as he stuffed a handful of bacon into his mouth, Ray slapped his hand and spiritedly scowled to him.

"Use your fork – pig."

"What do you mean?" Evander quizzed through a laugh, his plate bare and hands cradling a mug filled with coffee. He looked shattered, his skin was grey and gaunt – his body stiff and tense, Talon had warned me that it would take a few days for the aching and exhaustion of shifting to his wolf form, to die down.

"Your kitchen staff, how do you manage to find ones who can cook up such amazing food and are still terrifying warriors in a fight?" Demir asked with his mouth full.

"Swallow your food!" Ray cursed, mumbling under her breath.

Evander laughed, "I'll have you know that I cooked all this. There are no kitchen staff, we all take turns cooking here. Everyone's first priorities are as warriors and to protect Gatherling. Instead of standing in the doorway admiring the food, why not sit down and eat it, Narrdie." Evander called back – making me jump. He turned to flash me a warm smile and pulled out a chair beside him, patting the cushion. I grinned widely; my stomach singing with hunger, I kissed him on the cheek and started piling my plate with anything and everything I could get my hands on - topping it all with a mountain of tomato sauce. "Don't make yourself sick," Evander warned, slapping my hand away as I tried to grab my fourth slice of toast.

"You're not eating." Evander raised his coffee cup towards me, as if that would be enough. Astrid's voice cut into him, her stern mothering tone, causing a smirk to pull at my lips.

"Coffee is not breakfast and if I see you reach for another one, I will throw it into the river," she warned as her blue eyes landed on him. "Try me."

"How many have you had?" I leaned to whisper.

"Six." I battered my eyes at him, disbelief. I guessed werewolves had a better tolerance for it, I would have been bouncing along the walls.

"Vile liquid," Astrid sniped - scowling at his cup. "I swear Evander, you better get some food down you." Evander wiggled his eyebrows, before leaning over me and snagging the sausage - that was waiting to be devoured on my fork - with his teeth; he glanced over to her as he chewed.

"Happy?" He teased.

"Very," Astrid shook her head, but a bubbling laugh fell from her mouth.

"I'm not!" I grumbled, staring at the now bare pricks of the fork.

"I guess, you'll just have to eat one of the other five sausages then," Evander told me with a light chuckle.

"I don't mean to spoil this lovely brunch, but ... I've made my choice on the Loopin?" I announced, fighting my cringe as the cluster of chatter, rapidly faded.

Audric set down his cup and began rubbing his temples. "I'm not going to like this, am I?" He grumbled through the food lingering in his mouth.

"I know, you were all hoping that I'd forget but I didn't; I know the risks and I've thought about them. We've talked it over and we've decided to do it." Audric's head snapped up and he glared at me with flared pupils - I flinched back.

"Whose we?" His voice wiped like a snake. Bayona shifted in her seat and pressed her lips together; her palms spread on the table - bracing herself. His enraged eyes slid to her; they were hard - unflinching. "Are you serious Bayona? Haven't you learnt enough about dealing with creatures of the darkness? I thought you wised up when they took your eyes!"

"Audric!" Astrid hissed – rising from her chair. Bayona snarled as she kicked her own chair back, she slammed her hands down on the table – the dishes rattling, sparks jittering from her palm. Evander leaned back and let out a long breath which meant one thing – here we go.

"How dare you say that to me! My eyes may have been taken, but my power grew stronger because of it! You never seem to have a problem asking me to use them for your own need Audric!" Bayona's voice was feral, burning like ice as she snapped back, the air around us became thick with her magic – it radiated from her, choking down my lungs and filling my nose like a cold. Immediately, Audric flinched back, his jaw clenched and I could see the balled-up fists loosening at his sides. I couldn't help but smirk, I loved when Audric got told off – especially when he was being a giant ass. "I know the dark magic better than you, boy."

"That Loopin could break it the minute it's bound together!" Audric argued, his voice releasing hold of the scolding anger. Bayona scoffed and I knew that if she had eyes – she'd be rolling them.

"How little you think of me, do you honestly believe that I would risk Narrdie and myself like that? Maybe you're the one that needs to spend more time in the library, go read up on blood magic and you'll see it can be manipulated. Do you think I was just going to waltz in there and give everything up? I'll be adding my own extension to this oath, a loophole if you will. I may be blind Audric, but I can still see, I can see the evil inside that thing down there and how it wouldn't hesitate to tear us apart. This oath is happening, so get on board or move aside."

Chapter Twenty-Six

"Narrdie, please rethink this," Audric pleaded as we stood outside the cell room door; his hands were clenched by his sides – his eyes unreadable. I rubbed my eyes and gave him a lazed look, he'd spent most of the morning trying to talk me out of this, practically ambushed me the moment I woke up and even shouted through the bathroom door while I showered.

"Audric, please don't make me go through this again – it's getting annoying, you're starting to sound like a broken record." I took his hand into mine and smiled lightly to him. "Look, none of us are happy about this, heck I don't even want to do this. It's no secret that we're extremely outnumbered, the Loopin and his kind could really help us, but he doesn't trust us and I don't blame him for that – we did kill most of his pack. If you don't trust him then at least trust me." My eyes met with his, mercifully he nodded, blew out a breath of air and laughed through his nose.

"You don't need a Watcher anymore, you're too strong for that now." I wrapped my arms around him, not letting got until I felt his own drape around me and squeeze.

"I may not need a Watcher, but I need an Audric – always."

The Loopin cackled; the menacing slimy smile – that made shivers skip around my skin – grew wide on his lips, those pointed teeth glistening in the light. "Come to a decision? I was beginning to believe you'd abandoned your plea," he mocked. I called the power to me, letting it coat around me like mist, before tearing open the cell door once more.

"You would have let me make that blood oath with you, knowing that the second I tried to do it – I would have died." The Loopin snickered, a predatory gleam flickered in his eyes.

"Yes, I would have, and I would have lapped up your blood afterwards," he sang.

"And I would have torn you limb from limb," Evander snarled.

"I would have helped," Audric chimed in.

"You could have been fooling me," the Loopin spoke, ignoring Audric and Evander. "Killed me straight after I helped you fight your war."

"It's your war as well!" Evander growled, the Loopins' eyes snapped in his direction, he sneered; his rage rippling around him.

"Would you fight if I gave you, my oath?" I asked him, pulling his attention back to me.

"I said before, oaths are useless," he turned away from me, resting his hands behind his head as he lay back down.

"You didn't let me finish." He looked to me lazily and arched his brow. "Would you fight if I gave you, my oath – my blood oath?" He stilled and I knew I had his attention. "Do we have a deal?"

"Terms?" He growled. I signalled Bayona forward; she was hesitant, and I could tell she was afraid of him – he was chilling after all. The Loopin tilted his head in her direction; his eyes examining the burnt sockets; his eyes were shining – lit with amusement. I could see Audric trying to contain the anger, I felt it too – we all did when it came to Bayona and her eyes, I wanted to press my thumbs into the Loopin until his eyes were nothing but mush.

"If you swear your oath to fight with us and cause no harm to Narrdie, our people and future companions that may join our ranks, then Narrdie swears that you and your own will not be harmed by her. Once the war is finished, you will be released from the oath and free to go – without any follow ups." Bayona finished in a rush.

The Loopin glared at me, as though he was waiting for something. "That simple?"

"That simple," I repeated, hiding my shaking hands behind my back.

A wolfish grin stretched along his face; his yellow teeth glistening. "I accept."

Bayona gripped our arms tightly, instantly a tremor shuddered through me as I felt her magic engulf me. She side glanced to Evander; her voice eerie. "Evander, this is your home, you are the one who needs to make the cut – grant the permission." Evander nodded; a faint smile ghosted on his face; he placed a light kiss on my cheek.

"Sorry my lovely," he breathed in my ear, he quickly slit his knife across my wrist – I winced. His face turned hard as he looked to the Loopin – cold rage seeping into his eyes, he wasn't gently as he cut the Loopin, a satisfied smile beaming as the Loopin hissed through his teeth. The moment our bloods broke the surface, Bayona gasped, I tried not to look as her blackened sockets began to violently bleed, her skin paled to a washed out grey and her back arched.

"A matre Dea et sorores coram me. I, Bayona Alarie – sister of the Pleiades, servant of the Elemental Goddesses and all those before me. I call for these two bloods to come together and bind, bind into an unbreakable bond – join together as one." I held my breath, shocked in amazement and pure disgust, as the blood from my arm began to float in a snake like line towards the Loopin's blood, until they began to entwine themselves with each other – looping around like a plait. They turned, bound together and headed towards Bayona's heart. "I bind these two creatures in an unbreakable oath, an oath of words, an oath of trust – an oath of blood. An oath to never be broken on pain of death!" Her voice was no longer hers; it was dark, unworldly – evil. She turned to me, and shivers rippled over my skin. "Narrdie Moon, do you sacrifice your life and blood to the oath?" I swallowed down the urge to scream and run.

Thankfully Nyda had told me what I was expected to say.

"I, Narrdie Moon; do sacrifice my life and blood, so that I may keep the oath and I accept that if I break my vow – my heart should stop, and I should die. May the Goddess bear witness to my plea." I felt a pain in my chest, a burning, skin tearing pain – like someone was pushing a red-hot needle into my heart. I wanted to pull away, but I couldn't move, I couldn't scream – I couldn't do anything. I was just stuck. Bayona clenched her jaw and turned her head towards the Loopin.

"Do you sacrifice your life and blood to the oath?" The Loopin glanced to me, that half smile danced on his mouth.

"I, Nakoma, do sacrifice my own life and blood so that I may keep the oath and I accept that if I break my vow . . . my heart should stop, and I should die." Hearing his name shocked me, it made him seem more . . . human. I could see in his eyes that he was feeling the same pain I was – yet he couldn't react either.

"From here on out, Narrdie Moon and Nakoma are bound in life and in blood. You are bound to each other and bound to your own or smite you down. Ut Dea tueri te et dirige." Our entwined bloods shot forward, slamming hard into Bayona's chest; she gasped – flinching back slightly. She dropped our hands; she swayed; every bit of colour had drained from her skin. Evander swooped in and steadied her, wrapping one strong arm around her waist. "It's done," she managed to breathe – her voice a weakened whisper.

"It's that quick?" Evander asked.

"Were you expecting thunder, lightning, for the ground to open up and the sky to tear?" Bayona teased.

"No . . . at least not the ground opening or the sky, it just seemed rushed." Bayona scoffed, a wince whispering through her teeth as another spike of pain pierced her.

"It is best to get straight to the point with an oath, especially a blood one – you play with it too long, the dark magic will change. May even consume you."

Nakoma collapsed to the ground – clutching his chest; his body began to twitch and jerk on the floor like a fish out of water. Audric grabbed me just in time as I felt my legs turn to jelly under me and lifted me into his arms – I still couldn't speak, I couldn't move and I could feel my breath tight on my chest, a silence torture. "Bayona, what's happening to them?" Audric asked in panic, he brushed his hand along my forehead; his eyes scanning me over, like he was hoping to find the danger and grab hold of it.

"They're alright, just in shock. The bond can be . . . overwhelming," her voice shook. Audric waved his hand in front of my face and gave Bayona and unconvinced look. "She's perfectly fine Audric."

"She's not moving . . . or even blinking!"

"Neither is Noko there," Evander announced.

"It's Nakoma," Bayona corrected. "They won't for another few hours, best to put Narrdie in her room and put Nakoma in one of the empty rooms," she suggested.

Audric scoffed, "You're joking, right? You expect this thing to get its own room now?" Bayona groaned out her irritation.

"Audric, he made a blood oath; he's with us now. We're going to have to trust him sooner or later."

"I pick later," he spat.

"Until Narrdie is back to normal, Noko stays here," Evander decided. Audric snickered and Bayona let out a huffed breath. "He is the least of my concern at the moment. I think you need to rest as well, come on – put your weight on me."

Chapter Twenty- Seven

Six hours.

Six hours, I was left to endure my silent torment, left with the horrors that began to dance and taint my mind. One thing Bayona never mentioned, was the dreamlike nightmares that would attack, they were brutal, terrifying and unescapable. It was like the oath wanted to remind me – in every little detail – what would happen if it was broken, a slideshow of images projected across my head, my bones being snapped, misted into nothing but dust; blood seeping from every part of me. Shadows wrapped around my arms and legs, shadows made of adamant, unable to break, unable to escape; they held me in place as the skin was carved from my bones, the muscles burned to ash. I wanted to scream, scream until my lungs gave out and my voice box shattered.

When everything started to come back to me, I had intense and painful pins and needles, every time I moved – it felt like my body was burning, like the fire was dancing along my skin.

As if he could sense it, Evander waltzed through the door with a monstrous sized bunch of fresh sunflowers, instantly brightening up my room. "You're favourites right?" I laughed – which felt like razorblades scrapping against my chest.

"Is it even time for sunflowers?" My voice was hoarse, begging for water. He hopped onto the bed and pressed the sunflowers into my face until I took them from him, wincing as the movement of lifting my arm ached.

"No, but I know someone who can manipulate the Earth, they've been growing all around for weeks," he winked. I made a mental not to thank Erenna.

"Thank you, I love them." He tapped his cheek and my grin widened as I kissed him. "I love you."

"I know, it's hard not to." He raised his brows at my groan. "How are you feeling?"

"Stiff, just six hours of no movement really makes my body ache," I said with a light chuckle, I'd decided to keep the tantalising hallucinations to myself. He nodded and lifted my legs onto his laps, I smiled appreciatively, as he began to massage up and down – his hands making my skin tingle.

"Once we get the feeling back into your legs, I can help put the feeling back into your body," he teased with a flirtatious wink – my cheeks flushed pink. "Astrid and Ray are making a beef dinner – smells great. We should be done in time. I promise I'll be gentle . . . for round one at least." I giggled and bit my lip.

The smell was enthralling, the food that had been laid out on the table was even more inviting. My mouth watered at the sight; my nostrils flared – trying to savour as much of the smell it could breathe in. I was surprised at how many people were sat around the table – to the point where a couple of extra tables and chairs had to be brought in, even those who didn't eat normal food were huddled – laughing happily. I glanced to Evander – his hair and clothes still ruffled – he huffed a laughed. "Ray thought it would be nice if everyone in the sanctuary has a family night, at least once a month."

My blood chilled as I spotted Nakoma, awkwardly wedged between Talon and Mazruriuk, Nakoma's eye surveyed the room – examining every move anyone near him made. Finally, his eyes landed on me, and he nodded to me once.

"Family night," I repeated, looking from Evander to the Loopin.

"Bayona said he should be included, especially if we're trying to gain his trust," he half grumbled. "Come on, let's eat."

Evander pulled me into the chair beside him, as Astrid put a large plate with a few generous slabs on beef in front of me. "What took you two so long?" Astrid asked with a raised brow. Evander choked on his water, suppressing a laugh; his eyebrows rose, and he grinned to her as he tore into a giant Yorkshire pudding. "Animals, the pair of you," Astrid smirked. "How are you feeling?" She asked as she gave me a one-armed hug, being careful not to squeeze too tightly.

"Stiff," I admitted with a wince as I reached for some mashed potato.

"Let me, dear," Astrid offered with her mothering smile. "I want you to have a full plate, Narrdie and I want you to have all the vegetables on your plate Evander – not just the meat and mash." She gave him a stern look and he rolled his eyes.

"Yes, mother," he mocked, and groaned as she slapped him across the head.

"He means, thank you Astrid," I corrected.

"Kiss ass."

The room had erupted in laughter and chatter, almost like we were just one big, happy, normal family – without the weight of a war about to erupt, hanging over our heads. Evander leaned over to me – keeping his voice low; he spoke through a mouthful of meat. "So, what do we do with the Loopin?"

"His name is Nakoma, and I think he should have his own room," I suggested. Evander and Audric both snorted and shared a look of distaste.

"A room with a lock!" Audric spat, I rolled my eyes and pointed my knife at him in a threatening way.

"Don't test me today Audric," I warned in good humour, Audric smirked playfully, wiggling his own knife against mine.

"Audric has a point. I'm just saying that I don't trust him Narrdie, I don't feel comfortable with it running freely around my home," Evander added. He glanced over to Nakoma – who had went so still, he looked like a statue. It made me question how good his hearing was.

"Well, you need to. He's made a blood oath; we all need to trust each other. If we keep him under constant supervision, he'll never trust us - we don't need that kind of issue within our walls." Evander opened his mouth to argue, but before he could get a word out – I shoved a piece of broccoli into his mouth – bursting into laughter when he grimaced.

The next few weeks were as normal as they could be, lockdown restrictions had been lifted and training was in full swing once again. The sanctuary was getting crowded, with more and more covens and groups coming to join us – we were all anticipating an attack with each arrival. I had hardly seen Evander and Nyda, they had gotten word about several sanctuaries that had been breached and burned, with that news they had doubled our watch – making sure at least three different groups patrolled the grounds, even the Monks had doubled in numbers.

Astrid had taken charge of the Vampires, keeping them at bay and away from the humans. Some not understanding why they had to hunt only animals – a shiver went down my spine every time I was faced with one of them – faced with the skin crawling bloodlust that curdled in their eyes.

Most days I kept to myself, racking through Evander's books and combat training with Audric, wandering around had become almost impossible. Most of the races kept to their own groups, some I knew and some I had never seen before, yet they were as terrifying as being lost in a misty wood at midnight. No matter how busy we all were with training and teaching – making sure our army didn't eat each other became a priority – Astrid made sure that everyone was around the table when it was time to eat. As the head of the sanctuary Evander made sure the members of the Pura Mensam ate first. "It's important to make sure everyone remembers the ranks," he'd say whenever I'd question him. However, Astrid and Ray would always make sure that every single person in the sanctuary went to bed will full stomachs and smiling faces.

Audric and Mazruriuk persisted on dragging me outside to train my body up, they were convinced that instead of reading I should be fighting. Bayona disagreed and it would turn into their usual debate about brains over brawn. Most nights I'd go to bed black and blue – my muscles screaming with agony, but I was always happy for Evander to rub them better.

"So, I ripped his heart right out and crushed it to dust in my hands," Mazruriuk said with a giant grin on his face. Bayona had gathered the Pura Mensam members in the lounge, where we all sprawled out on bed of pillows and soft blankets – swapping different stories.

Ray threw a pillow at Mazruriuk's head and scowled playfully to him, bunny ears on her dressing gown, bobbing with the movement. "Don't be smug and don't exaggerate! His heart didn't turn into dust, and you didn't rip it out. You stabbed him in the chest, and he bled out," Ray altered.

"Nika! Why do you have to ruin my story? I had these lot eating out of my hand!" She snickered and shook her head; her eyes gleamed at him, like the fresh green of spring.

Amongst the playful bickering, something twanged in my chest – like a hot needle piercing my heart, I leaned over, pulling in as much air into my lungs – even that didn't stop the mound of vomit that spilled from my mouth onto the pale pink blanket. Evander jumped towards me, rubbing idle little circles on my back, Bayona's healing light twinkled in my eye. "Easy girl," Evander soothed in my ear.

"She's alright," he said to Bayona, a grateful smile on his lips.

"Narrdie? Are you unwell?" Demir asked, running over with a glass of water. "Food not sitting right?"

"I think that was the wolves," I said through gasps, Evander's hand rested on my back – the only think keeping me steady; he rubbed idle circles along the curve of my back.

"How do you know?"

"I can feel it," I said as I rubbed my temples, a ripple seemed to pass through me – goosebumps dotting along my skin. It was a feeling I knew all too well, because a big part of it resided within me.

"Looks like we've arrived at the right time," Erenna announced as she glided into the room with her sisters – I had almost forgotten how magnificent they were.

Today, they looked exceptionally Goddess- like, dressed to impress our new members. They all matched each other, their gowns representing their Elements and looking like mist falling along their bodies. On the top of their heads rested subtle but stunning headpieces, fashioned beautifully into their hair.

Erenna's was like ivy, the golden vines twirling and knotting around the circular emerald that rested in the middle; her olive-green dreadlocks had been decorated with leaves and flowers as it rested high in a strong ponytail.

Wenona's crown was silver, woven amongst her crimped bob, silver shells circled the small cluster of sapphire and sea-coloured stones.

Fyra's looked like a weapon, a three-pointed stone of ruby stood bold in the middle, there was no decoration – no engraving or playful patterns. Instead, the golden crown rose up into sharp golden points – sharp enough to kill. Her crimson hair was straight, and I could see the full-length hovering over her breasts, not a single strand out of place.

Aronnia's crown was my favourite out of the four, it looked like wind and clouds, carved into silver – the three moonstone gems that were lightly spread across the band, looked like they were surrounded by mist and as the light shone over it, I could see it shimmer and glow like a morning sun.

Seeing the sisters again after weeks of no contact – felt like coming up for air after a long dive, like seeing the sunlight after a dark cave. It was refreshing – almost healing every little fear that had buried itself inside me. They smiled over us all – even Fyra's mouth seemed to curve up, the harshness of her eyes diminished slightly.

Demir, Illythia, Talon and Ray stared at them with shocked opened mouths, however Mazruriuk seemed to stiffen, his face becoming like stone - unreadable. I had almost forgotten that they had never met them yet, Demir rammed his fist into Talon's ribs and signalled them all to bow. I wanted to run to them and engulf them in a never-ending hug, I hadn't realised how much I'd missed them, I wanted to shower them with questions about where they'd been. Bayona and Nyda immediately bowed with their tattooed hands in the air, a motion the sisters were quick to accept with warm smiles on their faces.

"We are glad to be back with you all," Aronnia sang, her voice joyful.

"Yes, we cannot wait to talk with you all. However, it seems Narrdie has something more important to deal with. Child, you said you felt the wolves call to you?" Erenna asked, her voice sounded on the verge of excitement; she walked over – her gown whispering along the floor and took my hands in hers. She closed her eyes; her smile widening, "Yes, I can feel them.

Very eager indeed." She looked to me, with nothing but warmth and love in her eyes and playfully winked; her hand brushing my cheek. "I have missed you," she whispered for only my ears. The coldness in my veins burst with warmth, my heart fluttering with happiness and a broad smile pulled across my lip – a smile I thought I would never fully feel again.

"Forgive me, my Lady," Illythia began, taking a nervous step forward. "What kind of Wolves are these? To be able to send her a signal like that?" Erenna turned to her, that loving smile not once wavering from her face and spoke.

"Special wolves – rare and powerful, old and ancient. Narrdie go to the wolves, see what they have to say," she suggested with a comforting smile.

"Right, best get ready then, Talon?" Evander said as he downed his coffee.

"No, they wanted me to come alone." Silence filled the room.

"It's risky" Evander snapped – a mixture of anger and worry in his voice.

"If I don't go alone, they'll think I don't trust them. If it's a trap, I'm strong enough to fend them off. I'm sure that Bayona or Erenna will sense if I'm in danger." He exchanged a look with Bayona – needing reassurance, she nodded.

"I don't like this," Evander growled.

"What happened to not coddling her?" Audric cut in, he winked towards me, and I looked down to hide the smirk. Evander's eyes snapped to him, shocked at the sudden change; Audric was normally the one that agreed in making choices for me. "Narrdie's not a child to be coddled, remember?" Audric said, repeating the same words Evander had said a few weeks ago.

"Very well. Seems we don't really have a choice," he gripped the arms of his chair, his knuckles turning as white as chalk. "That Alpha is head of numerous packs, that could add hundreds to our side," Evander announced. He sighed and reluctantly nodded to me – he knew there was no choice.

☾

*M*y blood chilled as I perched on a rock; scratching my arm, until they were red raw – the air was tight and stale, the cold bit at my cheeks; I hated this part of the forest. It made my mouth taste bitter, like ash and decay, my skin felt like ice, like it would never feel warmth again and I expected the shadows to pounce and swallow me up the longer I sat.

Finally, the wolves emerged out of the bushes – the Alpha was first, closely followed by a white female, her fur as pale as untouched snow; she nuzzling at his fur. I had almost forgotten how big he was, forgot how the power that radiated from him swarmed around me, waiting to crush into me – even the forest turned silence, fearful of the energy that floated around him. He studied me for a few heartbeats and a spike of dread shot through me, I almost braced myself – expecting him to dive on me and tear my head from my shoulder. Thankfully, he bowed and set his eyes on me.

"You made your decision?" I asked him, being careful to keep the voice in my Animo respectful. The white female eyed me suspiciously, her buttercup yellow eyes calm – terrifyingly calm.

"We have," his voice bellowed in my head. *"We accept your offer."* This time I didn't bother trying to cover the smile that spread along my lips; my heart almost leaping from my chest. *"The world is changing and whether we like it or not – it affects us all. For the sake of our pack – for the sake of our family."* He turned to

lightly nuzzle the white wolf's face, gently nibbling on her ear – so she was his mate, the Alpha female. *"My packs are with you."* He lifted his muzzle into the air and released a howl that echoed around the forest, a wave of howls from all directions began to sing across the woodland, so many wolves – hundreds even.

As his howl reached into the air, the forest awoken, the eerie night air turning solemn, the bone crushing shadows that threatened to swallow me whole, licked my skin with warmth and as the howls travelled further, my urge to scream with glee grew more. I'd done it. I had gotten us the numbers we needed, I had shown everyone that I wasn't just the darkness's vessel, the bomb waiting to go off – I was here, and I was ready to fight. For the first time since being pulled into this world, I had felt the one thing I feared I would never feel . . . Hope.

"Thank you, thank you all," I bowed to him and laughed as they all continued to howl.

The sound of wings, fluttered to my ears – catching my attention. There it was, perched on a tree branch, it's head cocked to the side; it's beady red eye watching me – a white raven.

"I know you," I whispered, it twitched it's head like it had heard me, and I could have sworn I heard its voice in my head.

"I know you too."

*T*alon had gathered the members of the Pura Mensam outside, as requested by me and my Animo – Nakoma was also present, stood in the middle of Audric and Bayona, an unreadable expression marbled on his face. I'd done my best to bring everyone up to speed, Evander helped me in warning everyone to be respectful, helped explain that these were no normal wolves.

The Alpha wolf – whose name was Karro – was the first to approach, not allowing his pack to emerge from the trees until he knew they would not be harmed. He turned his head to the side, watching cautiously as his Alpha female – Oyku – lead a few members of his pack out of the trees and onto the clearing outside of Gatherling. Karro had agreed that only a handful of them would preside at Gatherling, the rest would wait amongst the trees, but I'd shared with Evander and Audric how many belonged to the pack.

Oyku was nervous; she pressed herself against Karro, liking under his chin; her buttery eyes slowly met with each one of my people – a silent threat hidden in her stare, a warning that she'd sooner kill than see her Alpha and pack come to harm. Karro let out a low grumble, ordering the pack to stop, they stayed close – flanking their Alphas. Karro may have chosen to trust me, but that didn't mean he trusted my people and by the way his eyes scrutinized certain members – I knew it would take a long while, he let out a low snarl towards Nakoma and Mazruriuk.

"Ana't net alon," I told Karro and the pack with an encouraging smile. Evander arched a brow at me, taking a careful step forward; he glanced sideways, his eyes meeting with Astrid.

"Narrdie, what did you just say?"

"I said don't be afraid. Why?" I asked with a frown.

"It was not English," Astrid answered after clearing her throat, "nor is it a language I have ever heard before." Wenona suddenly laughed, making everyone jump and turn in her direction, she turned to her sisters, each one smiling warmly – even Fyra. Erenna walked forward, approaching the wolves without an ounce of restraint or fear; her hand outstretched to Oyku – who to my surprise – pressed her snout into her palm, licking at her fingers; her tail high and waggling, some of the other wolves approached – each one as happy to see the Earth Goddess.

"A bond with the wolves already? You were right Erenna," Wenona beamed.

"I told you so, sister," Erenna chimed, politely greeting each wolf.

"A bond?" Nakoma spat, earning himself a snarl of warning from Karro.

"Yes. Narrdie, I don't think you understand these type of wolves, the power they have had recognised the power you old. Think of it, as formed from the same weave, they call to each other, joining like long lost family. The moment you agreed to become allies, that power ignited and entwined together – forming a bond. A bond that will only gain stronger with time, you were with them only a few hours and their language has already imprinted on you and might I say, you speak it beautifully," Erenna praised.

I froze, taking a moment to comprehend what had just happened, I hadn't even noticed that the words coming off my tongue were different – foreign to me. Evander approached me slowly, his hand lightly holding onto my arm – expected me to turn dizzy with fright or shock, he jumped as a bubbling laugh burst out of me. "That is...AMAZING! I've just learnt a new language; I've always wanted to do that." Evander's mouth flicked up in an amused expression and I noticed the others stifling their own chuckles.

"A language of the ancients," Wenona added, her eyes beaming proudly.

"You're just full of surprises aren't you, Moon," Audric bellowed with a wide grin.

"That's all great and all," Nakoma grumbled, cutting the pleasant atmosphere instantly. "But, does that mean Narrdie is going to have to translate everything we say to them and everything they say to us?" He snorted, "I don't see that ending well in battle." Evander's eyes cut into Nakoma; his face a mask stone as he cautioned him - a warning to watch his mouth.

"Maybe I can help with that," Nyda offered. "I can put a translation cloak over them, they'll be able to understand us and communicate with us whenever they wish. With their permission, of course." Nyda looked to me, waiting.

"Karro, Oyku, Nyda omeci se enchantago, te henlo bon undina tigo. Son bay ruta?" I asked as I looked to Karro, containing the excitement I felt. Karro hesitated, exchanging a look with Oyku, Oyku yelped lightly and licked under his chin, her ears back and eyes soft. He bowed his head to me, then again to Nyda. "Go ahead," I encouraged with a smile.

I thought she would need to chant, gather energy or even ask Bayona to assist her, instead she just waved her hand once - like she was dismissing a servant. "There," she said blankly.

"That's it?" Audric asked with an unconvinced frown. "No twirling or dancing around? Singing or calling to the Goddess," he mocked teasingly.

"It isn't that hard to do," she bit. Perhaps Nyda had more power than she was letting on and by the way Bayona stared in her direction - she must have thought it too. "Are we done out here?" Nyda snapped.

I locked eyes with her, staring down her sudden hostility. "Yes. I only ask you all to introduce yourselves to the wolves and help make them feel part of our home." The moment I had finished speaking Nyda turned from us and vanished inside, Bayona bowed her head to the wolves and was quick to follow - no doubt to question her. For now, I'd push it from my mind, understanding that the Sanctuary leaders were under a lot of pressure with the mass numbers and war preparations.

Evander happily told the wolves that they were free to roam as they pleased, offering them a friendly smile, Karro bowed his head in gratitude, Oyku nudged his hand - a respectful gesture. "You may stay anywhere inside or if you'd prefer to stay outside here, our home in now yours and from us all at Gatherling, we are pleased to have you here and fighting by our side." He approached me, after everyone began to disperse; his hands wrapping around my waist from behind and pulling me to him; his breath was hot on my neck as he whispered in my ear. "I want you. Now." I leaned my head back onto his shoulder, my hands wrapping around him - teasing him; his hand brushed up my thigh, a predatory growl rumbled in his throat as he bit my earlobe. I had to dig my teeth into my bottom lip to keep from moaning.

I leaned my head on Evander's chest – still panting. "Give me a few seconds and I'll be ready for round three," he teased as his hand trailed down my side, a bubbly giggle rolled from my tongue, my leg was spawled over him – the blanket barely covering us; our bodies laced with sweat.

I leaned up and kissed the crook of his neck, running my fingers lazily along his chest, tracing the tattoos. "We may have to wait until the morning for round three," I managed to mumble. Truthfully, I was tired; it seemed that these days I was always tired – the undesirable perks of being the defender of light. At least that's what Bayona called me.

I thought Evander had just stopped talking, I didn't realise that I had fallen asleep – at least not until I was jerked awake by the sound of the white raven– cawing at me; its beady eye locking me in place. It's talons shot out, slashing and digging into my arms, pinning them at my sides; it spread its wings wide, blocking the moonlight – casting me in shadow. His sharp beak reared up and before I knew it, I was screaming. Hands gripped me, shaking and pulling at me, a voice – filled with panic, called to me, begged me.

"Narrdie?" My eyes flung open, but it was dark, my hands shot out – batting and clawing at whatever – whoever held me. "Narrdie, stop!" Evander's voice filled my ears; his hands grabbed my wrists and pinned them above my head; he was on top of me, naked and panting as his eyes filled with concern. "Easy, my girl," he spoke softly and slowly released his hold and pulled me into his arms. I didn't realise I was crying until he crooked his finger and gently brushed the tears from my cheeks. "You're safe," he soothed.

"I'm sorry," I wept.

"It's OK, nothing but a dream." It was anything but a dream, dreams were nice little stories that your mind would play for you, to help keep you sane, dreams were memories, hopes and fun. This was no dream; it was a nightmare – built to torment and sow fear into your insides. "Want to tell me what it was about?"

"After Karro agreed to join us, I saw something – something that I didn't expect to see."

"What was it?" He asked in a tired voice, he pulled me down back onto the bed and ran his hands through my hair.

"A white raven." His fingers stopped and I felt his body go ridged.

"As in Dacre's white raven?" His voice turned cold, I nodded. "It came to you?" I was almost too afraid to answer.

"Yes." He cursed as he dove out of bed and scrambled to put his clothes on, a dark feeling began to build in my stomach, knotting tightly around my chest.

"Evander?"

"Narrdie, why didn't you mention this earlier?" I grudgingly began putting on my own clothes.

"I don't know." A muscle in his jaw twitched and disappointment washed over his eyes – I knew what he was thinking, I had just jeopardized the entire household and I still couldn't understand how. "What have I done?"

"Get everyone outside and I mean everyone. Let's hope it's not too late – I thought you were smarter than this Narrdie. Let's hope I can sort this out before someone gets killed," he growled. I flinched back and I felt everything inside me fall into an empty pit – bile rose in my throat.

"Because of the raven?" I asked sheepishly. Evander paused and breathed out hard as he turned to me.

"The white raven is Dacre's spy; he sees through its eyes. It's seen what we've been doing, and it will go and report everything back to him. When he finds out we have Loopins and the wolves, he'll send a horde over to attack – to keep our numbers down." My insides burned, once again I had put everyone I loved in serious danger and all for what? So, I could get my leg over with Evander for a night.

"How? How did it know where we were?" My voice was nothing but a trembling echo. Evander's eyes – as chilling as they were, looked to me, surveying every inch of me, until they landed on my hand.

"Where did you get that?" He asked as he pointed to the ring on my finger, the grave look on his face meant he already knew.

"Dacre," my voice shuddered.

"And you never thought to take it off?" He voice cut into me, hard. "Even after he betrayed and tried to kill you?"

"I-I forgot I had it on," I admitted. It was true, this small silver band had become weightless to me, like it was part of my skin – not once did I think it was used to track me.

"Get rid of it," he hissed. He turned towards the door, nearly ripping it from the wall, I shot forward, grabbing his wrist and holding it until he looked to me.

"I'm sorry," I almost sobbed.

His eyes softened, "this isn't just on you, it's on me as well," he admitted. "I should have done this when Dacre escaped."

"Done what?" I asked, worry crashing into me like a wave.

"Please gather everyone outside," he ordered, before darting down the hall, shouting for everyone to wake up.

"Evander, done what?" I called after him.

I couldn't figure out what to say to anyone as we all stood waiting for Evander, couldn't even bear to meet their eyes, no, I'd kept my gaze firmly on the ground. Even when they had bombarded me with so many questions – questions that I couldn't answer; I couldn't find the right words to tell them that I had put the entire sanctuary in danger, I couldn't even muster up a single word to say to them. I took myself to stand behind them all, slumping down onto the fallen leaves and bundles of mud, I ran my hands through my hair, resting them at the back of my neck. My breath caught on the harsh wind, my bare skin prickling from the cold. I wiped my numb fingers across my eyes, hating how much they shook, I hadn't even noticed Audric approach, didn't hear the crunching of his boots; he slung his jacket over my shoulders and breathed out hard.

"You messed up again, didn't you?" He asked with a light chuckle; he plonked down beside me.

"Yep," I admitted, my voice a strained croak.

"How bad? Scale of one to ten?"

"Eleven." Audric laughed and tapped my knee with his own, he flung his arm around my shoulders – giving me a gentle squeeze.

"I'm sure it will work itself out, it always does." I shrugged and he playfully squeezed me tighter. "What do we do, we move forwards . . ." He raised his brow, waiting for me to finish.

313

"Never looking back."

"If you have messed up as bad as you say, I know you'll find a way to fix it." I eventually tore my gaze from the ruffling mud and met his eyes, eyes that greeted me with kindness and love, eyes I didn't deserve at that time. I surveyed his face, he looked like he'd aged; his eyes were weary, tired, his skin was paler than usual, and he looked like he hadn't had a full night's sleep in a long while.

"You look tired, like there's something going on behind the mask you wear." His jaw tightened and he swallowed hard, like a thick lump had been gathered in his throat.

"You know me," he joked, the humour not quite meeting his eyes.

"You're right, I do know you and I've been hard on you, but not as much as you've been on yourself." Audric's stare dropped from mine, he reached down to grab a thin looking twig and snapped it several times over before he spoke.

"In this kind of life, there's no time to dwell on things lost." I knew what he meant, Mitchell, the serge of power that had been transferred into him, the Watchers and friends he'd lost. "What's lost is lost."

"You need time, Audric. Time to heal."

He scoffed, "time is a luxury none of us can afford anymore. When Mitchell died, I knew I'd never be able to give him a Watcher's final goodbye, because not only did we not have his . . ." He grimaced, the word choking in his voice. "His . . . body, I felt his power slam into me, the power transferring to the next Watcher in line – me. I didn't even have time to process that power, because before I knew it, I had thirty young Watchers under my belt, maybe when this is over . . . I'll light the fire for Mitchell and all the other Watchers that have ended their journey." I took his hand into my own and leaned my head on his shoulder; he gentle squeezed my hand and rested his head on mine.

"Maybe we can find time sooner," I offered, the kiss on the top of my head was gratitude enough.

A high-pitched whistle rang in our ears, the ring lingering even when he'd stopped blowing. Evander walked in front of us all – his jaw clenched as his eyes met mine. "Listen up!" He bellowed, forcing the crowd into silence; his face was blank – empty, like it had been carved out of stone. "I know you are all wondering why I summoned you all out here. Some news has come to my attention – news that has endangered this sanctuary beyond repair." I looked down. In these past few months, I had faced a pack of wolves, Loopins and even survived a Skinner – but I was too spineless to look anyone in the eyes, the moment I did – they'd know.

Audric lightly brushed his fingers against mine, offering me a comforting smile. "Head up, don't let them see you sweat," he whispered.

"I've talked some things over with the Priestesses, and the safest thing for us to do right now is to relocate . . . all of us." Everyone burst into gasps and mumbles – demanding to know what had caused this sudden decision – I slumped down, praying that the ground would open up and swallow me whole. "Staying here is no longer safe!" Evander shouted, hushing the crowd once more. I knew that tone he was using, it was stern, deciding and final.

"Evander, what is the meaning of this? Are we under attack?" Nyda asked as she settled her guards – this was the most emotion I've seen from Nyda in one burst.

"No, we aren't under attack – at least not yet. Dacre knows where we are and it's my fault, after the attack with Crow; I should have moved us straight away." My head snapped up to him, bewildered as to why he was putting the blame on himself – the simmering pit of guilt in my stomach, began to curdle.

"Where will we go?" Sharia asked – her voice close to tears. "Evander, everywhere else either is either breached or burned, we can't just leave!" Evander's eyes softened as he looked at her, the girl he had adopted as a sister; he walked over to her and stroked her cheek. "This is our home," her voice broke.

"Home is wherever we make it – together. The Priestesses have offered us haven. It's up north and will take us a few days walking, I promise you all that it's safe there." He stood straight and his voice turned to serious once more. "I want everyone out here in one hour, pack light – essentials only. Sir Asta, fill a cart with supplies, water, food and whatever the healers believe we may need. Madam Keeper, fill another cart with the ancient books and scrolls – only the ones that could benefit us, we can return for the others." The two people he called upon bowed swiftly and snapped their fingers at the people around them, ordering them to help.

"Walking? Evander, we have cars," Audric protested.

"It's not safe for cars," Evander snapped. "From now on everywhere we go – we walk, no vehicles and no Lacus jumps, they might be tracked." He signalled everyone to go and get sorted – tapping his watch to remind them to be quick.

"You coming?" Audric asked as he brushed dirt from his jeans.

"In a minute, just need some air." He watched me for a moment, eyes scanning over me; he nodded and headed inside. I stayed slumped on the ground, Evander was still outside; his eyes taking in Gatherling, I tried not to meet his gaze.

I heard his breath push out from his nose as he crouched down and placed his hands on my knees.

"I'm so sorry Evander," my voice broke.

"I know," he kissed me lightly on the top of my head, cupped my chin in his fingers and lifted it up, so my eyes met his. I wasn't sure if that meant he had forgiven me, or he just needed a second of normality. "I know," he repeated softly; his lips found mine and he remained there for a few seconds, I didn't know I was sobbing, until his finger lightly smudged away the tears that escaped. "I don't blame you," he breathed into me.

"You really think it'll take a couple of days? It's a long time to be walking."

He nodded, "I know the route we have to take, but I won't know when we are actually there. The Priestesses have a glamour on their house, when we arrive at the right spot – wherever that is – they'll lift the veil." Evander's voice quivered, it seemed even he, couldn't alter the worry in his voice. This didn't help with the rave of sickness in my stomach. I breathed out heavily; I could feel my hands shaking as they wrapped around my knees. Evander frowned, "What's going on?" He asked; his eyes searching mine. "C'mon, talk to me."

"A couple of days, a couple of days can quickly turn into a week, which then can turn into two weeks and then . . ." Evander's hand gently clasped around my mouth.

"You're spiralling." He teased, his hand moved from my mouth and lay against my cheek, "tell me what's really on your mind."

"Crow. Do you think she will stay down for this? If she appears, this could end really badly, especially when people are drained and aching. Are we prepared for that?" Evander took my vibrating hands in his and gave me an uplifting smile – I knew him enough to see the doubt tweak at him.

"Crow is one of the most powerful beings to walk this earth," Evander began – not soothing my worries at all. "She's weakened right now and there is a lot of people here that could put her down – including you. I believe that we'll all be fine." Lie. A generous lie. He glanced to the side, where Karro patiently waited to approach, Evander kissed me once more and bowed his head to the Alpha wolf. "Don't forget to pack some stuff."

I breathed out a huff, my breath feeling like ice on my skin, as it fogged out in front of me; my ears tingled with the sound of padding paws as Karro skipped towards me – hitting my arm with his snout. He studied me and flicked his ears – waiting for me to speak. The words lingered on my tongue, too hesitant to say, because I knew an argument would form.

"Karro, me ben bon so te promes me semago, fi me trun – Kilba me." A growl rumbled the moment I'd spoken the words, he pulled his paw back and slammed it on the ground. I forced myself to meet his eyes – burning with rage, hurt, and thankfully understanding. He knew as well as I did, that this would be the only way to stop Crow and I knew, he would be the only one who would do it.

I didn't have anything important to pack, I grabbed Freddie's collar – the most valuable thing I possessed – I lightly traced the soft teal fabric, embroidered with silver paws and a bone tag with elegant font. I wrapped it in the handkerchief that Evander had given me the first day I'd met him and zipped it in the inside pouch of my backpack. I searched through my draws for anything that would call out to me, I was never one for things, even my bedroom at my old home was bare.

I'd packed a thick jumper, the current book I was reading, a fidgety wooden puzzle, that I had swiped from Audric's room and a couple of throwing daggers that I had been practicing with. As for weapons in general, I had my twin blades tucked into the straps on either thigh and a dagger with a golden handle tucked into my hiking boots – always be dressed for a fight, even when you don't expect one – Audric had drilled into me.

I paused at door, feeling something dark thrum in my ears, calling – whispering in my ears, my hand tightened on the frame, my nails shifting into claws as they pierced the wood, I turned to it. Dacre's ring, sitting abandoned on the dresser, begging me to slide it back onto my finger, the ring he had tricked me into wearing – the one that he'd used to track us. "No," I hissed, that pulse almost deafening in my ears. "NO!"

Darkness exploded from me, scattering across the room, the dresser split, the blanket and pillows erupting until they were nothing but shredded bits of cloth. The mirrors shattered and burst onto the ground like glitter. I gasped willing myself to calm, calling the cold of the air to consume me and sooth over my burning rage, the birdsong to fill my ears, to overpower the ring's calling. I slammed the split door closed and prayed that no one would enter it, prayed that no one would see it, figure out what had happened and report it to Evander.

I was one of the first ones outside, I wasn't surprised. For a lot of them, Gatherling was a home, a safe haven when they had nowhere else to go; they had lived here for years – centuries even and here I'd come and shattered that. The pit in my stomach churned, devouring me from the inside and I could have sworn that I heard her – laughing, cackling like a witch at how much I had screwed up. I clenched my fists, feeling the icy hot rage tingle at my fingertips, that darkness licking the surface – waiting to erupt once more. I wanted to scream, tell her to get out and leave us alone, but just as I felt like I was about to burst, a wet nose prickled my skin.

Oyku lightly licked my fingers until my fist uncurled, her tongue was cold, damp and exactly what I needed to stop the fire that almost erupted at my hands. She pressed her nuzzled into my cheek, pushing until my hands reached up and stroked the soft fur down her neck, I closed my eyes and pressed my forehead against hers. "Thank you." She didn't say anything in return, she just gently licked my nose and trotted back over to her pack.

When the time hit the hour, a horn bellowed throughout the grounds – it was time. The contents of Gatherling was now spread around outside, all with two or three bags max – it made my little backpack look pathetic. The wolves shifted uneasily and moved closer to the side I was sitting on, the tuff of fur on their backs standing up. Karro and another wolf of similar size and dark brown fur – dropped to his flank, taking protective stances in front of their pack. I'd almost forgotten it had only be a day since I'd brought them here, that they'd still not had a chance to trust or talk to anyone yet. However, when it came to me, I could feel a bond the bond, just like Wenona and Erenna had discussed, I could feel their power and they could feel mine, latching onto each other like two long lost lovers.

Oyku nuzzled Karro and licked under his chin, looking for comfort. *"Easy, no one means you harm, you can trust them – all of them,"* I reassured her; my palm outstretched, but still a distance away so that she had the choice. She pressed her nose into my hand.

"Do you trust them, Narrdie Moon?" She asked as she sat opposite me – I nodded and gave her a warm smile. *"Then so do we."* Her golden stare, lifted happily and her tongue rolled out her mouth as she panted and wagged her tail, she playfully battered herself against Karro and the other wolf, snapping at them to relax. "I'll even trust the false wolf, Evander." She teased, causing a loud laugh to burst from my lips.

"Heads up Moon," Audric cautioned, as he threw me a sleeping bag and a second backpack – I arched my brow at him. "Just the essentials. Clothing, water, deodorant . . . a toothbrush." I smiled; Audric always made sure to take care of me. "And also, I have a pillow and blanket for you, it's on one of the carts." I rolled my eyes and gave his hand a little squeeze.

"Thanks, Audric."

"It's what I'm here for, I can't handle it if you end up . . . smelling the whole way there. I mean c'mon Narrdie – personal hygiene is a thing!" He chuckled, as he quickly dodged out of the way of a rock I threw in his direction. "Missed me . . . and again . . . seriously Narrdie, I expected more." He sang as he swayed side to side, evading more projectile rocks.

Once again Evander stood at the front of the group – a giant backpack over his shoulder, he waited until everyone fell silent. "North, that is where we are heading, there will be no splitting up – we go together, and we arrive together. I'll lead from the front – Narrdie from the back, that way the pack can follow at their own pace." I flashed him a grateful smile and he fought hard to resist giving me one back. "Remember, if I give the signal everyone stops and goes down on the floor. Sivv's roam the northern woods and they don't hesitate. Some of you have dealt with them, others have only read about them, either way – they'll kill you all the same." Audric shuddered and rubbed the side of his torso, I knew the memory that haunted him, had heard about the Sivv that had left the huge purple scar that tattooed his skin and how it had almost completely gutted him.

It was his first training exercise, Mitchell had sent him to track a Skecig – a lone one that had wandered to close to a human village – Audric had found it, already torn into shreds. Before he could send a signal to Mitchell, the Sivv had come from

319

behind, its claw digging into his back and slicing right around to his belly button. Astrid had smelled the Sivv, the blood and had distracted it, lead it away – giving Mitchell a chance to drag Audric to safety. If it wasn't for Mitchell and Astrid and their constant healing and monitoring his fever, he would had died.

"Is everyone out?" Evander asked a nearby guard – who immediately nodded.

"Yes Sir, all valuables, scrolls and books, are locked away and shielded in the vault."

"Nyda, Bayona, light it up." Silver tears reflected in their eyes as they walked to stand in front of the Gatherling building, raising their palms out in front of them. Tears fogged over my own eyes; this couldn't be happening – it wasn't right. *No, No, No!* This is all wrong! I went to take a step forward and protest – Evander threw his hand out to stop me, his face like adamant.

"Evander, no," I begged – my voice holding the threat of breaking into tears. His jaw was clenched, and his expression was unreadable, but I knew this was hurting him.

"This has to be done, they can track it otherwise. It's protocol when a sanctuary is breached." I opened my mouth to speak but a stern look in his eyes, had me cowering back. "Burn it."

Fire burst from both of the Witches hands, a blaze so hot, I could feel it singeing my skin and turning it pink, the fire attacked like snakes – hissing and lashing anything in its path. Within seconds, Gatherling was swallowed by flames and the sound of walls clashing, ceilings collapsing echoed around us, no one spoke – no one could speak as they watched their home turn to ash.

For a few moments, we all just stood in silence – eerie silence. Evander was allowing everyone to say goodbye I realised, his fingers brushed against mine and I couldn't bring myself to look at him as I lightly hooked my finger with his.

Evander didn't speak, he didn't need to; he was a leader, the very essence of his power seeped through his pours, the power we all sensed and automatically followed as he turned and began to head into the woods. I waited until the vast of the herd were already amongst the trees, finally I began to move with my group, which consisted of Audric, Mazruriuk and the unfortunate company of Nakoma. Nakoma's eyes flicked around nervously, occasionally giving Audric and Mazruriuk a vulgar gesture, he had the right idea to flinch, whenever he strayed too close to the wolves, their teeth snapping at him to keep in step.

Chapter
Twenty-Eight

$\mathcal{E}$vander's promise of a few days had vanished as quickly as it had come, barely sleeping, barely eating – nothing but exhaustion and aching limbs. A lot of the group that began in the front of the movement, had now fallen back with me, leaving me with the most to keep an eye one, I had asked the wolves to spread out around them, to gather everyone's scent so that no one would be left behind. Our people had become weak, I could see it in their eyes, the pain, tiredness – the amount of force they'd pull from their body, just to make one foot move in front of the other. The worst thing I saw, was the suspicion – no one admitted it, but I knew they were all thinking it, that Evander had gotten us all lost and I was ashamed to say, I was beginning to believe it to.

A small black bird with a blue shine on its chest and strained violet eyes, landed on Audric's shoulder and tweeted in his ear; it nuzzled its beak against his cheek, a gentle request. He smiled.

"Sure Sharia, you can rest on me." Audric, stretched the pocket on his t-shirt and brushed her little bird cheek. Sharia spun several times, before changing into a small rodent and climbed inside – no doubt setting herself down for a long-needed sleep. Jealous, so incredibly jealous.

"Any room for me?" I kidded, my voice croaked – my throat felt itchy, the type of itch you'd feel before a sore chest infection took hold. Audric froze and raised a questioning brow towards me; he sighed and waiting for me to catch up.

"Your waters empty, isn't it?" I nodded sheepishly, waving the hollow bottle for him to see – my stiff limbs protesting at the movement. He rolled his eyes and laughed through his nose; he reached into his pocket and pulled out his bottle – which was wrapped in soft brown leather – and tossed it to me. "You need to ration better. Drink as much as you need, I'm gonna take the mouse and run up front – see if Evander will be setting up camp soon." Audric's gaze dragged past me, he frowned, his throat bobbing. "You've got stragglers behind you." I nodded my thanks – I could barely even whisper my throat hurt that much.

Luckily, that feeling was washed away the moment the water hit my mouth, I had never really enjoyed just water before, but after the refreshing liquid licked my insides awake – I would never judge it again. I could feel my muscles, bones, limbs, shooting out, all fighting to get a piece – to hydrate once more.

"Narrdie," Nakoma called back, gaining a distasteful grumble from Karro. "Camp." I nodded my thanks to him, smiling at the outbursts and gasps of relief. I slung my backpack off and flung it towards a tree stump, before making my way through my group – offering and helping them with their own luggage. Weak, fatigued, every single one of them; they barely even made it here, a shudder skidded down my spine, and I knew that if this journey lasted another few days without proper rest, food and water – we'd be burying our people along the way.

Karro yawned widely before letting out three deafening howls, the first to signal that camp was to be made, the second calling the ones far out to return and the last, letting the pack know that they were free to do what they wanted.

Wolves began pouring into our campsite, like the tide engulfing the sand, one of the younger wolves hobbled over to us – limping and panting more than the others; his weak legs shaking where he stood. He was still fresh, Karro had told me, still trying to find his rank among the other wolves, I felt my heart strings pull as I looked at him; I was sure Audric wouldn't mind if I shared his water . . . even just a gulp. "Bakka," I called to him and waved him forward, his eyes strained as they looked to me. Using my hand as a cup I poured a small puddle into the depth of my palm. With his tail high and waggling, he lapped it up so fast, I thought he might have been sick.

"Thank you," Oyku called over to me, her eyes smiling with warmth, I winked my response to her.

"Lady Narrdie?" I turned – being careful not to spill any of the water in my hand – and nodded, appreciating the fact she kept a comfortable distance back from the pack.

"Is everything alright, Madam Keeper?" She smiled sweetly, her gentle eyes nervously flicking around the wolves; she pulled out her decanter.

"I have some extra water, would any of the other wolves like a handful?"

"I have some as well, my Lady," A healer chimed.

"Me to."

"I've still a whole two bottles." I couldn't fight the tears that burned in my eyes, as more people slowly approached – each with water bottles in their hands and food in their bowls.

"Thank you," I managed to say after a hard swallow. *"Karro, Oyku. They have water for you all."* Karro exchanged a look with Oyku, a conversation I was not to intrude on. The wolves were slowly becoming more comfortable with the group over the past few days – at least enough to sleep around them, but was this too much? Oyku whined and licked under his chin; he licked her back and her eyes lit up – permission granted. She moved first, the others staying back with impatient anticipation, she crouched low, her movements slow. She approached Ray cautiously, her ears back and tail straight.

Ray sat cross legged, glaring at everyone else until they followed her movement; she smiled in her sweet way, keeping her hands outstretched, Oyku's tail immediately began to wag as she lapped up the water. It didn't take long until the other wolves were forming little lines – waiting patiently for their turn. I could feel the lump in my throat as I looked around, it was like I could see the trust forming – it looked like gold flakes twinkling around them, surrounding them in a blanket of sparkles. My eyes landed on Evander, crouched down, hand cupped out and letting Karro take as much water as he needed, I caught his eye and he winked before turning to pour Karro another.

"You did this," Audric breathed in my ear, a wide proud smile on his face. Words had escaped me and each time I tried to speak, it felt like glass shards poked in my throat, Audric laughed and slung his arm around me – gently squeezing me to him. "Narrdie Moon, the great softy."

☾

I rested my head on Karro and Oyku lay her front paws across my stomach, her eyes fluttering around lazily, the rest of the pack had spread around the camp, pushing past their comfort zone and taking to sleeping beside the others. I laughed as two pups chewing on my boots, high pitched yelps and playful growls rumbling from them. *"How are these two not sleeping?"* I asked Oyku with a chuckle, I wiggled my feet playfully, laughing as the pups yelped and dove over each other. Oyku yawned as she forced herself to stand, allowing a few moments for a long stretch; she whined as she nudged and nipped the two, pushing them towards the rest of the pups – clustered together, sound asleep.

Unfortunately for me, sleep was not a luxury given to me quickly on our final night at this camp, I felt tired, the heaviness of my eyelids told me so, but I felt uneasy. Each time I tried to close my eyes, the uneasiness would creep in like a thief in the night and clasp its hands around my throat.

I always imagined camping in the woods to be fun, the burning fire crackling as you roasted marshmallows, the sleeping bags spread in a circle and the swapping of stories, but it wasn't fun at all. The forest was quiet – scarily quiet, like it had terrifying secrets about to unfold, it set my teeth on edge. Normally I would here the owls, hooting the forest alive, signalling that the stars were out and that it was time for the nocturnal creatures to have their play, fireflies would dance, spinning and twirling – looking like fairies in a child's movie.

Finally, after what felt like hours, I slept – it just didn't last as long as I hoped it would.

☾

$\mathcal{A}$ footstep on crinkling leaves and a snap of a branch, shocked me awake; my eyes shot open, a gasp caught in my throat; my heart began to pound as fear dug it's claws into me – pinning me to the ground. Nakoma leaned over me – a dagger in hand and a treacherous look in his eye, was this the knife in the dark I had been anticipating?

Just as Wenona had expected, the wolves sensed the change in me, the panic in the pounding of my heart, the vibration of my shaking hands and the sudden trembling fright that swam through my veins. Within seconds Nakoma was completely surrounded, angered heckles and snarls echoed through the trees – waking everyone. Karro circled Nakoma – Oyku and a patchy brown wolf called Dakiva – at his flank; he didn't move closer, or give the order for the wolves to attack, but his voice rang in my head – waiting for my permission.

"Evander! Audric!" Sharia yelled in a frantic voice.

Karro snapped towards the on looking crowd, warning them all to keep their distance, making them all aware of the knife, now resting at my throat. Even surrounded, Nakoma didn't let up, didn't lift the blade from my skin, but the look in his eye told me it was for his own protection now – the only thing keeping the others from tearing him apart, was that knife.

"Nakoma, what are you doing?" I asked, my voice trembling. "You kill me, you kill yourself."

"Evander, I could take him," Bayona offered, her hand beginning to glow as she crouched low. Evander didn't speak, his eyes didn't once leave me, almost like he was worried his very breath would startle Nakoma and that blade would jitter in his hands and slide along my skin.

Talon hissed. "Bayona don't. He'll slice her before you hit, we can't risk it." Nakoma didn't speak; his eyes were fixated on Karro – his grip on the knife tightened, as Karro stepped a paw forward.

"Karro, na! Ami iv bon saya bekk," the words came out quick, like a panicked mumble, but thankfully he heard; his paw taking a cautious step back – the other wolves following.

"Were you going to break the oath?" Bayona asked, her eyes panicked, after all this included her life as well. Audric gripped her arm – steadying her; his other hand gripping tightly to his double ended blade, he too didn't speak – only watched and waited.

Nakoma finally spoke, his voice a vicious growl, "No."

"Then what were you doing?" Talon demanded. Again, he didn't answer, he looked from his knife to Karro and shifted uneasily.

It hit me and all fear I held, had dissolved away – replaced with a burning hot rage. Rage that caused my fingertips to burn, singeing the leaves underneath them. Rage that summoned the power inside, to mist out and cover the forest bed around us in black fog. My pupils split as they narrowed in and locked in on Nakoma, the sweat on his brow, the shudder of his Adam's apple and finally fixed on the wideness of his eyes. He flinched back at the snarl that rumbled from my throat, the nails that had now stretched into razor sharp claws, I no longer cared for the knife near my throat – in fact I leaned into it. Nakoma immediately cast it aside; he dove away from me, his eyes flaying around frantically; he raised his hands in a surrender pose. "Narrdie," his voice shook slightly. "I wasn't going to hurt you." Karro and Oyku dropped to my flank as I rose to my feet.

"Narrdie, stop!" Evander warned – his voice drifted to my ears, but it was a muffled blur. I was going to shred Nakoma to pieces.

"Narrdie! Don't please," Bayona begged. I froze, my hands stretched out to stop Karro and Oyku.

"You wanted to hurt Karro," I accused, the wolves turned frantic, each one snapping and heckling. "You were going to attack the pack?"

"Why would you want to hurt the pack?" Mazruriuk quizzed; he'd taken a protective stance in front of Ray, his voice was bland; his face solemn and bored, but I could sense his power on the edge of his skin. However, I couldn't tell if it was for Nakoma . . . or me.

"You may choose not to believe me," Nakoma began, keeping his voice calm, careful. "I did not want to kill any of the pack, I wanted to test the blood." Oyku heckled and crouched low.

"You dare take an Alpha's blood!" She snarled; her teeth bare and ready to take out his throat, I rested a hand on her back – ready to grab her if she lunged.

"Risky move, in normal circumstances, you would be the pack's property to deal with if you harmed the Alpha," Evander informed, taking a step closer to Oyku, reading himself to jump and stop her. "However," he continued, turning his gaze to Oyku in warning. "If you get hurt or die, so does Bayona and Narrdie."

Oyku growled lowly as she lowered her head to Evander, she didn't move back but her stance eased – only slightly.

"Why did you want his blood?" Audric asked, his voice tense.

"To see if the pack have become part of the oath," Bayona cut in, Nakoma clenched his jaw and nodded rapidly.

"Can that happen?" Evander asked her, she swallowed hard and rested her hand on her chest.

"Yes. In some cases, it can – mainly if you've shared blood."

"There is another way," Mazruriuk interrupted – his finger tapping his chin. My heart began to thud so much – it was like listening to a marching band playing in my eardrum. "It can happen through a bond or an imprint, it's rare however, and oaths are stronger – made so nothing can intrude on it." I gulped, Audric's face had flushed of colour and Evander looked like his bowels had watered.

"How?" Evander managed to say; his teeth clenched.

"Oaths and bonds are some of the most powerful links in all the realms, formed by the very thing that makes the world run, unfortunately I cannot say how it exactly works."

"Has it happened?" I asked, swallowing down my urge to vomit. Mazruriuk scrutinized me for what felt like a lifetime, none of us breathed while his eyes racked over me – finally, he shook his head and I breathed out hard in relief.

"No, but it might someday and before you waste countless hours searching," he said as he glanced to Bayona. "It cannot be stopped, can't be changed and can't be undone." Everyone fell silent – looking from one person to the next, as if waiting for a miraculous miracle. Astrid shook her head and rolled her eyes, she tapped Sharia on the shoulder and began making her way through the gathered crowd – steering people to bed.

"Right, this is enough for one day," she said in her stern mother tone. "I've had enough of this constant dreariness. Come on, everyone back to bed, save your strength for tomorrows drama. I'm sure it will be just as fun." She looked to the wolves and playfully scowled at them. "That includes you lot, march your tails."

"Nakoma," Evander growled as he snagged his arm, his eyes burning into Nakoma, they were furious, deadly and held a dark warning. "From now on, you will stay under the watchful eye of Mazruriuk," Evander decided with an arrogant smirk. Mazruriuk stepped forward – twirling a black fire ball in his hand; he smirked and signalled for Nakoma to start walking.

"Don't worry if you get cold on a night, I like to sleep close," Mazruriuk warned.

Nakoma hissed lowly and Mazruriuk took a hostile step forward. "Try me Nakoma." Mazruriuk's veins turned a bold red and even I could see his powers fizzling to the surface.

"I said, that's enough!" Astrid snarled over them – her eyes ablaze.

"I'll pay you any amount to try and fight Astrid," Bayona dared them both with a giggle.

It was still dawn when Audric woke me, I winced as I felt the burn of the mornings frost hit my chest – I'd give anything for a hot chocolate with huge marshmallows. "Come on, we need to get going," Audric spoke softly – I couldn't manage to speak, I was never too good at interaction in the early hours. I nodded and pulled all my hair to the side, scrapped it up in a bobble and stretched my arms out; I leaned over and bumped Karro lightly on the back.

"Wena un," I said lazily, my words slurring with the overwhelming tiredness that still lingered in my voice and limbs. Karro grumbled, grudgingly he rose and began handing out nuzzles of encouragement to wake the pack – some whined, begging for a few more minutes, while others sprang up and began skipping around. Audric's hand clamped around mine as he hauled me to my feet, the wariness still staining under his own eyes. "You look like shit." I teased with a smirk, Audric made a point to look me up and down, circling around me.

"Speak for yourself, have you even bothered to us the deodorant I gave you; I mean can you even get a comb through that bird's nest you call hair?" His lips pulled up in a teasing grin and he laughed as I slammed my body into his, almost knocking him to the floor. "Our mighty leader Evander, has bestowed a few more rules onto the camp," Audric announced as he came back over to me with some water, I could hear the eye roll in his voice. I dreaded to think.

"What now?"

"We're all taking shifts on a night, thanks to Nakoma's little midnight show." Audric through a distasteful look in Nakoma's direction and lifted his lip in a sneer. "So, when you're up all night and day because you were on night patrol – blame that thing."

$\mathcal{J}$ust as I thought hiking to the Priestesses home couldn't get any more draining – the weather shifted. This whole journey I had been thankful for the cold breeze, the morning frost on the tip of my nose, the subtle rain, licking at our burning limbs – it had kept us all cool and refreshed. However, today – it was hot, and I didn't mean a nice summer day or a relaxing bath hot – no. I meant a volcanic eruption, melt your skin, and boil you for eating – type of hot. The unexpected change, messed with my insides. I paused to take a sip of the water Astrid had given me, my stomach cried out as one drop dared to grace my tongue, I wanted to down the lot – but Audric had warned me that the camp was running on empty, dangerously empty.

A breathy groan tickled my ears and I paused; I could feel the hairs on the back of my neck begin to stick up, wrong, wrong, wrong – something's wrong. The leaves rustled – almost like a footstep had disturbed their slumber, I breathed in – grimacing at the sudden thickness of the air. My ears rang, but not with the usual birdsong and skittering of forest rabbits, no – it rang with silence, unnerving silence.

"Narrdie Moon?" Oyku questioned as she followed my eyes, the tuff on her back stuck up – ready for whatever was troubling me. *"You see something."* It wasn't a question, but I nodded, tearing my eyes through the trees, flicking from one bush to the other.

"I think there's something out there." Her ears flicked, and three wolves approached her, two nuzzled her respectfully, listening to whatever command she was ordering; with a quick nibble under her chin two raced each other towards the shadows of the bushes – the other ran up towards the front of the group. The last thing we needed was for one of Dacre's people to follow us.

It only took seconds before Evander jogged down the hill towards us, his face crumpled in a permanent frown, his hand brushed down my arm and he laced his fingers with mine – his other hand moving to cup my cheek. "Are you alright?" He asked, his eyes searching mine – I knew what he looked for, the fear that had been following us since we left Gatherling ... Crow.

"Listen," I whispered to him, using my finger to turn his head towards the trees. "Listen and look, I mean really look." Evander studied the trees, which began to darken in their silence, the air

329

turning thicker, foggier – like at any moment it would seep down our throats and choke us. An echo of a hiss traveling on wind, blew in our ears, a warning that something was coming. Evander crouched low and pressed his hand against the forest floor, his fingers curling until he'd scooped bits of mud and stones in his hand – rubbing it between his fingers.

"Audric," Evander spoke, his voice low – barely even a whisper, but Audric approached. "Get them to stop, keep them quiet – no one is to make a sound. Be on your guard, we're not alone here." Audric nodded once and pulled his sword from its sheath – the blade ringing and hissing in his hands.

"Oyku has already sent some wolves to go and see if they can catch a scent," I informed him, keeping my voice as low as his.

"Better safe than sorry, now you're thinking like a leader," Evander smirked to me.

Oyku whined, Karro began to pace up and down nervously and I had to grip hard onto the twin blades in my hands, as the clamminess had made their hilts slippery. *They've been in there ages,"* Oyku whimpered. The silence was heavy, no one dared make a sound or even breath hard, Audric had spread his Watchers around us all, each one armed to the teeth.

Finally, for what felt like forever, the bushes rustled, and Kadin emerged, his ears back and eyes wide – he was panting, hard. Oyku and Karro raced to him and nestled him with their snouts, he whimpered and pushed into them. *"Are you harmed?"* Oyku asked him as she licked his snout, sniffing around for any sign of injury.

"Where is Mako?" Karro demanded, pulling back the silence. He stood strong as he looked into the trees – expecting Mako to run out at any moment, but there was no noise, no howl, no padding of paws – on the other side of the foliage, there was nothing but that frightening silence – gaining thicker and thicker. My heart dropped and I felt Evander's grip squeeze my arm, comforting. *"Kadin, where is Mako?"* Kadin didn't answer, instead he pushed through his two Alpha's and stepped to Evander. He spoke to Evander and only him, and whatever transpired between them, made Evander's skin turn ghost white, made his jaw lock and knuckles turn white as they gripped the hilt of his swords.

With seconds, the wave of fear plastered all over him had dissolved and his face had turned to granite, unreadable. He clenched his fist tightly and with a hard gulp he raised it high in the air for everyone to see – everyone dropped to the floor, including me after a stern look from Audric.

"Evander?" I kept my voice low, his eyes cut into me – silencing me.

"Try not to breathe," he whispered.

I don't know how long we were all on the ground before they came, the forest had gone as still as a corpse, no animal dared make a sound, not leaves rustled and even the wind refused to whistle. The air thinned, like all the oxygen had been sucked out and an icy cold smog swept along the floor, engulfing and clogging around us. Spider shivers ran down my spine, biting into my skin and I knew – even before I heard the rippling grumbles, the echoing shrieks – what had just walked into our herd.

Sivvs.

Chapter Twenty-Nine

Sivvs.

One was deadly enough; one could kill our entire group without even breaking a sweat – this wasn't just one Sivv . . . this was three.

Three, full grown adult Sivvs.

The most terrifying creatures I had ever encountered – were now walking around our camp – listening for one of us to make a noise. I focused hard on trying to keep my body still, scared they'd hear the vibrating of my shaking bones, the scream bubbling in my throat.

Most people had curled into a foetus positions; keeping their eyes closed and breathing quiet. I noticed Ray, she was curled into Mazruriuk; eyes squeezed shut and her shaking body was pressed into him. Mazruriuk kept his hand tightly over her mouth and leaned his head on hers – pulling her closer to him. His eyes had gone clear, and I realized he was using his magic to put a glamour over her. I dared a glanced around, desperate to make sure my family where all down and safe, but Nakoma caught my eye.

He was standing.

Nakoma was still standing, he wasn't scared or shortening his breaths, in fact he looked bored. I glanced to Evander – his hand clenching tightly around my own – he gave me an expression which meant, he didn't know what Nakoma was doing either. Did he have a death wish? Was being in an oath with me so bad, that he'd rather be torn apart by Sivvs?

A Sivv's foot slammed down beside my head, and I had to clamp my lips together to contain the scream that wanted to burst out – the smell of its skin stained the insides of my nose, it was like rotten eggs and sewage all mixed together, it burned my eyes. I bit down on cheeks instantly feeling the blood fill my mouth as my teeth ripped into my flesh, Evander squeezed my hand – reminding me that he was here, that I wasn't on my own. I looked up and caught Nakoma watching me; he lifted his finger to his mouth, shaking his head.

"Not a sound," he mimed. The Sivv leaned down towards me, I shuddered as I felt its warm stench breath hover over me, I was surprised I didn't pass out from the fumes. My heart was thrashing so much – I thought the Sivv was going to hear, I tried to stop my nails from digging into Evander's palm, but I felt the bite as my nails sunk in deep.

Evander caught my gaze, nodding at me; he kept hold of my eyes with his own, as the Sivv's poisonous forked tongue wriggled out towards me, one lick and I would be paralysed; I tried to shuffle out of the way, but the leaves crunched under me. Evander sucked in a breath, and I looked to him with panicked eyes. I'm going to die; I'm going to die.

The Sivv snarled, the sound a gurgling click, it lifted its talons – the talons that had almost torn Audric in two bits – towards me, the other two Sivvs turned; their own hisses bouncing along the tree bark as they slumped closer, closing in around me. Audric's hand drifted to his knife, but Nakoma shot out is hand – ordering him to stop. Close, they were so close – too close – their sickeningly pale leathery skin almost grazing against my own. They froze as a hiss reached the hole in sides of their heads, where their ears were, yet it didn't come from them – it came from one of ours.

Nakoma let out another low hissed and the Sivvs snapped their heads towards him, within seconds they'd surrounded him; their lipless mouths stretched across their face – jaws dislocating as a display of teeth, upon teeth, grew sharp. Nakoma stiffened as the Sivv's tongues began to creep around him; he opened his mouth, a chattering of gurgles rippling from him so fast, none of us could understand. The Sivv's cocked their heads to the side, as if they were listening – understanding whatever he was saying. My eyes dropped to Evander, a bewildered wide-eyed stare plastered on his face, he looked from me to Mazruriuk.

Mazruriuk was old and had seen many things in his life, but the look he gave use read one thing – he was stumped. Nakoma's hiss deepened into a gurgle, he opened his jaw wide; his teeth suddenly growing sharper and longer; his eyes clouded over – looking like a sky before a hurricane was about to strike. The Sivv's snarled once more to each other and sucked in their wicked venomous tongues and without so much as another sniff around; they slunked back into the trees.

No one moved, no one dared even breathe until we felt the forest shift underneath us, the winds once again graced the trees – ruffling the leaves, making the branches hiss as they scrapped across each other. The songbirds, found their voices once again and bellowed out their tune – a sign that it was safe once more.

"You can move," Nakoma mumbled. Just like the Sivvs had – we surround around Nakoma, bombarding him at once with the same question – what had just happened?

"What the fuck was that?" Audric spat, jabbing him hard with his finger.

"How are you, not shreds on the floor?" Demir quizzed – shuddered at the thought.

"My blood is toxic," He explained nonchalantly, as if it were answer enough.

"How toxic can your blood be? I've seen Sivv's devour Skinners by the dozen," Audric interrogated.

"Toxic enough to kill them if they tried a taste, I called them over to me and their tongues sensed it. Narrdie is lucky that I did, otherwise she'd be dead. You were too loud," he spattered, I raised my eyes, at my unexpected knight in shining armour.

"Perhaps, you should say thank you. Instead of just staring at him," Illythia snapped. "Perhaps you all should."

"Thank you, Nakoma." I never thought I'd be giving him gratitude for saving my life – almost as much as I didn't think Illythia would jump to his defence. The world was certainly turning upside down today.

"You sounded like them," Demir pointed, Nakoma froze and his jaw clenched – a movement Audric didn't miss.

"We should keep moving," Nakoma suggested.

$$\smile$$

*T*he encounter with the Sivv's had terrified us to the point where no one wanting to risk talking, footsteps became as light as feathers along the debris of mud and twigs, even the sun had taken shelter behind the thick clouds, but even with the hidden sun – the heat stayed blistering. I could feel the skin on my arms burning and perhaps even smelt it too, my pale skin had gone from an icy white to tomato red. "You alright Narrdie?" Ray asked as she paused to take a sip of her water – her freckles seeming more vibrant in the sun.

"Yeah, fine – just a bit shaken from the Sivvs," I admitted – instantly feeling like a coward. "So much for the strong defender of light," I joked, yet we both knew it held some truth.

"I thought you looked . . . well like you said, shaken. You know, the first time I saw a Sivv was with Mazruriuk – he held me so tightly that he almost crushed my bones, in fact I think I had little finger bruises. I was sick when it left, threw up all over Mazruriuk's shoes, couldn't keep food down for two days." We both shared a laugh, a reaction not too common when it came to Sivvs. "The way the Sivv's suck the life out of everything – it's unnatural, enough to make someone go insane. It took days until I felt normal again." I nodded, I'd known that feeling all too well, I wanted to run and lock myself away forever the first time I felt like that. "Everyone has similar stories of their first time with Sivvs, they can make even the strongest of warriors, wet their trousers."

"Their smell doesn't help either," I swallowed down my urge to retch. "I got a face full of it earlier." Ray grimaced and finished off the rest of her water; she shook the bottle – begging for another drop to fall on her tongue.

"Shit," she cursed.

"I'm out too."

"Everyone is, one of the healers collapsed before and is now resting on the cart. Bayona says that there's a river along the way where we can refill, hopefully we'll reach there before dark." I nodded in agreement, another night without water and we'd surely be picked off – like pawns on a twisted chest board.

Ray caught my arm, her eyes kind as she looked to me. "You may be the defender of light, but you're also a being with a heart, soul and emotion. Don't be ashamed or embarrassed about them, don't get disheartened when you feel the wave of fear when faced with danger, don't get angry when you cry over something sad. The day you stop feeling those things, that's when you should worry. Narrdie, all those things you hate about yourself, is all the things we love about you, because it makes you, you." Before I could open my mouth to thank her, or before the fogging in my eyes turned to tears, she skipped off and linked arms with Astrid – who smiled and brushed her cheek, no doubt hearing every word we'd said.

Hopes of reaching the river before nightfall were gaining slim and with each passing moment, my throat was getting as dry and scratchy as sandpaper. However, one good thing that the night had brought, it meant the boiling heat, was beginning to be eaten away by the murky night clouds. A wave of yawns and tired stretches rippled through our herd and I found myself stifling a yawn; my legs felt like jelly and my stomach pained like never before – hunger.

I craved one of our Gatherling family meals, craved the roasted potatoes cooked in goose fat, the pink beef, juicy and tender and all the steamed vegetables with a lump of butter. All we'd managed to eat so far were squirrels and rabbits, and that was only if we were quick enough to catch them before the wolves did.

A chilling thought echoed throughout my mind and a menacing laugh in the back of my head only confirmed it. Soon I wouldn't be strong enough to keep control over my body and once I couldn't take it any longer – Crow would be the one in the driver's seat. I had focused so much on building a wall in my head, adding layers and layers to keep her from breaking through – now those walls were starting to crack and crumble. I wouldn't be able to last another night, it would be a mental suicide. "Evander!" I shouted as I swayed myself through the crowd, smiling and brushing my hand on people's shoulders so they wouldn't panic.

"What's wrong? Everything OK?" He raised his hand slightly – ready to halt the marching parade. I lowered his hand and smiled as to not worry him, entwining my fingers with his and kissing the back of his hand – gaining me a warm smile.

"Most of the people haven't eaten in days and they are all almost out of water. I know you want us to camp but, most are weak – I'm scared if they fall asleep, they might not wake up." Evander sighed and rubbed the back of his neck; he looked drained of colour and a gloomy yellow had tainted the whites of his eyes. "You look bushed Evander, more than anyone else." I pulled him to a stop, "there's something you're not telling me."

"It's nothing." His eyes darkened and he tore his fingers from mine. "What would you have me do? We won't reach the river for another few hours," his snapped coldly.

"Then we'll keep going. Our people need water, if they sit another night without it, we may very well lose some!" I protested; his nails shifted into claws as he pushed me back – I gasped. "What is going on with you?"

"We're stopping to make camp. End of discussion. Go back to your post Narrdie," he snarled.

"NO!" I bellowed, the group paused and fell silent – watching us as if we were a show on TV or a dramatic theatre play. I pulled him to face me, his eyes flaring like wildfire.

"I said we're making camp. Do as I say for once in your messed-up life! Why do you always have to make things difficult? It's always an argument with Narrdie Moon, isn't it? It's your fault we're out here in the first place." I wanted to strike him where he stood, and I could feel Crow's claws – scratching their way to the surface, daring me to do it, almost heard her voice hissing in my ears.

"People need water!" I spoke through clenched teeth – grinding them together to stop from ripping out his tongue. "If we stop now, people will die."

"What do I have to do, to get it into your skull? We are making camp." He grasped my forearm roughly – tightening his fingers until they were like a steel grip. "Now, go back to your post. Before you piss me off." I snarled as I pushed him back and swung my fist into his face. He stumbled back; his hand lifting to wipe the blood from his lip – he slowly turned to me. "Are you out of your senses?" I'd forgotten how fast he could be. Suddenly, he was behind me; he locked my hands behind my back, pushing them up until they seared; his other hand shooting up to grip my throat. I leaned my body forward before thrusting it backwords – my head smashed into his nose. I swirled to the floor – flinging out my leg and kicking his from under him. Before any of us could launch and tear chunks from one another, Bayona and Astrid rapidly stood in-between us; their face consumed by surprise and anger.

"Stop this now!" Astrid ordered with a frightful snarl. I could see Bayona's hand begin to glow, ready to strike us back if we lunged for each other again.

"What the hell is wrong with you? I don't care if you're tired, hungry, or dehydrated! You ever grab me like that again and I'll do worse!" I shrieked, feeling Astrid's hand digging into my chest as she held me back. "These people need water, if you want to stay here all night, then fine. However, I'm taking these to the river, so they can get some water!" I turned away from him and signalled everyone to keep walking – not once turning to look back at him.

$$\smile$$

It was a little after one in the morning when we'd finally made it to the river, the big hill seemed more like a steep mountain by the time we'd all got over it, some of the weaker ones, having to be carried – but we'd made it. The moonlight shone down on the stream, like a beacon calling us closer, I almost didn't want to touch it, didn't want to disturb the reflection of the moon, highlighting it like little diamonds – I wanted it to stay pure and untouched.

The wolves were the first to break the seal, tails high and waggling as their tongues lapped up as much water as they wanted; rolling around until they looked like drenched rats.

"Fill up, get cleaned up; do whatever you have to do – half an hour then we find somewhere to make camp," Evander announced. His eyes met mine, I swallowed hard and turned to a part of the river no one gathered.

The water felt satisfying as it hit my skin; I cupped my hands before repeatedly splashing the water over my face, enjoying how much it made me feel clean and refreshed – it was like the feeling of putting cream on a scorching burn, instant relief. After the twentieth time of splashing, I submerged my water bottle and watched as the bubbles floated to the surface, popping once they reached the air.

As the water filled up, I felt my heartstrings twinge, pulling my eyes to look at Evander once more. He was leaning on a log – his hand holding his side, wincing as he pressed his fingers in – wincing like he was in pain . . . serious pain. This time, he was not going to evade the question, one way or another he would have to tell me or show me what was going on. I screwed the cap on my water and stuffed it into my bag, before calmly walking over to him – not wanting to worry anyone else into thinking another fight was about to happen.

"Evander?"

"Hey," he greeted sheepishly.

"What's wrong?" I demanded as I pointed at his side.

"Just a cramp." I scowled; in the amount of time, I'd known Evander – he'd never once gotten a cramp. He smiled innocently, I perched my lips and arched my brow – he was lying.

"Lift up your shirt."

"Narrdie-" He began, but I interrupted him.

"Lift up your shift, or I'll knock you down and do it myself," I warned. I kept my face as hard as stone, he swallowed hard – clenched his jaw and lifted his black shirt, hissing through his teeth at the pain.

Just as I had suspected, the place where Crow has stabbed him, where I had stabbed him – hadn't fully healed. The wound wept with puss and clotted blood; patches of purple bruises had blotched around his skin. I pressed my hand against my mouth to keep from crying out. I did this. "Evander, you said you were healed," I meant it to sound stern, but my voice was barely a whisper.

"We didn't have time to be concerned about me. If you all knew, we wouldn't have left Gatherling." He pulled me closer to him – to cover the wound from spying eyes.

"It's swelling up. Evander this is serious, why hasn't it healed up?" His eyes met mine and for the first time since I'd known him – he looked scared for his life.

"Crow broke part of the dagger off and stuck it inside, Nyda thought she got it all – turns out Crow buried it deep." His hands found mine and he cupped them softly.

"How long have you known?" I tried to keep my voice calm – tried to hide the tears that painted over my eyes. How could I have fought with him.

"A while. I could feel it, polluting my blood, my head – it's everywhere. Making its way to my heart, let's hope I can hold out until we reach the Priestesses, because it's going to have to wait until then." He huffed a laugh to hide his fear.

I scoffed, "Like hell it will! I'll get Bayona or Nyda, they can fix it." Evander snared my arm as I turned from him – the look on his face made my heart sink.

"They've already tried, it's too deep. I'll need surgery and if they try it here, infection will kill me. The Priestesses will know what to do," he assured me with his familiar smile.

"Not doing it will kill you," my voice had turned teary. I shook my head; I couldn't believe what I was hearing and to make things worse, I could hear Crow laughing. Evander's face softened as he saw the tears stream down my cheeks; he pulled me onto his lap - with a pained groan and kissed the top of my head.

"I'm sorry about earlier, I would never want to hurt you Narrdie. Silver changes me, it's poison in my veins - consuming everything that makes me . . . me." I lifted his chin and kissed him hard, brushing my hand down his cheek.

"I know."

"Go, make sure everyone has refilled. Here." Evander handed me another empty bottle and I frowned, "Audric said you ran out a while ago, said he gave you his."

"This is yours." He gave me, a gentle smile and lightly pushed me forwards.

"Go and fill up. Trust me, I don't need it, it tastes like ash to my anyway."

"Karro, have the pack drank to their hearts content?" I asked with as much cheeriness as I could fake. Karro was lapping up water faster that Astrid could run - it was like he'd gone years without it.

"Yes, but they are hungry," he spoke through gulps. "It has been a while since we hunted, me and Oyku can last, but not our pack." I sighed and surveyed the pack - they looked like they were thinning by the hour, their ribs almost poking through their fur.

"We're making camp once everyone has got water, you can all hunt then."

Karro's tail immediately started swaying from side to side. He yelped happily and rubbed his forehead against mine - an act of affection and respect that I had come to learn.

"Time's up! Let's head out and find a place to camp!" Evander called; he stood on the very top of the hill - his finger outstretched as he performed a head count. I mimicked him, doing my own count - just in case the silver that was poisoning him, compromised his vision.

Thump, thump, thump - my heart was deafening in my ears and for a good reason - we were missing eight. Demir, Illythia, three wolves and three of Nyda's troops. "EVANDER!" I screeched. Eventually, his eyes picked me out; his eyebrows creased into a harsh line – his mouth twisted. "We're missing people – two members of the Pura Mensam, three of the pack, and three of Nyda's people, Cody, Shel and Una." Talon and Karro darted to their feet – their eyes desperately trying to seek out their family members.

Mazruriuk raised his hand – his eyes vibrated in their sockets. "There not nearby either," he announced. "I can't pick up their heartbeats."

"You can feel our heartbeats?" I blurted. He shrugged; his face almost shocked that I didn't know this – it gave me an old feeling of just being human.

"All Shades can . . . it is how I found Nika after I smelt her sent." Ray's cheeks flushed with red as she beamed happily behind him. Shades could feel heartbeats . . . a chilling fact.

"I'll go look," I offered. Audric and Evander's faces matched each other, as they both pulled and unconvinced face – my face flared with annoyance. "I'll go look," I repeated more forcefully.

"Fine. Take some of the wolves with you," Audric ordered. I nodded and glanced over my shoulder – already a handful of wolves including Karro and Oyku stepped forward as volunteers.

"I'll go to," Nakoma decided.

"Seriously?" Talon grumbled, "I'm meant to trust you to bring back my sister?"

"I don't see you volunteering," Nakoma snarled. "What if they've been taken or are trapped by a Sivv? Are you going to let it kill you instead? Tear your flesh off, rip out your insides? Suck it up like spaghetti" Talon stiffened – thinking about the long bone claws of the Sivvs was enough to give you nightmares for a year. "If there are Sivvs around, I stand a better chance than any of you."

"You know what spaghetti is?" Audric asked with a tilt of his head.

"Nakoma is right," I cut in, Talon shot me a look of disgust. "What? He is! We all saw how the Sivvs acted around him and Evander said these parts of the woods are where they roam. Also, it'll be interesting to see if he can keep the word of the oath." Plus, I'd rather he gets hurt than anyone else – but I wasn't going to say that out loud. I glanced at Astrid for help, she winked to me and placed a calming hand on Talon's shoulder.

"Talon, Narrdie is right, Nakoma cannot do anything to harm your sister or anyone else for that matter – it'll break the oath. Come, you and I will check the east side, we have a better chance of picking up one of their scents," she smiled her familiar mothering smile. Since Talon and his sisters arrived, the never disagreed with Astrid – neither did any of the other Vampires on our side.

I paced up and down as the wolves and Nakoma inspected the missing people's things – handing it around like a game of pass the parcel, picking up any scent they could muster. Karro had asked the wolves for volunteers instead of just picking who would come with us – the other wolves which padded around all looked strong. I could easily tell them apart, as each of them had an aspect that was different from the other.

Loka, was a decent size, he almost matched Karro . . . almost. His coat was dark brown – like the murky puddles after heavy rain fall and one of his eyes seemed more crooked than the other.

Tallani, I had seen her fight before; she was small, but what she lacked in height; she made up for in speed and sneaking. She resembled more of a timber wolf than the others; her underbelly was pale, while the top of her coat was a mixture of ashy brown.

I remembered Nook from the forest, the first time I had met Karro and the pack. Nook was one of Karro's youngest pups, almost twinning with Bakka – he looked the spitting double of Karro, only a few sizes smaller.

The last of the wolves, was Rev. The next in command after the two Alphas, Rev wasn't the biggest out of the pack – he was the strongest. Most vicious. His coat was the colour of soot and his claws gleamed as they protruded from his paws, I was thankful that he was loyal to Karro, because if it came down to it . . . Karro would lose against him.

"We ready?" I asked somewhat impatient. "Nakoma, stay where Tallani and Rev can see you," I advised. Rev growled lowly, projecting his hatred for the Loopin; he snapped his jaws – threatening to bite the back of Nakoma's leg. "Esay, Rev," I warned, worried he'd rip him apart then and there. "Esay."

Chapter Thirty

Illythia and Demir weren't at the riverbank and the wolves couldn't pick up their lost packs scent either, Oyku began to whine with worry, Karro nudged her softly. "They didn't pass here, and if they did – the river's washed away their scent," Nakoma reported; his expression almost looking concerned.

"You look worried Nakoma," I mocked. He glared at me – unimpressed. *"Tallani, Oyku, could you run along the river, just the parts where we all refilled. See if you can pick anything up,"* Oyku bowed her head to me; before she raced towards the top of the river – Tallani at her side.

"You seem to have grown close to those wolves, like you'll be their new Alpha soon." Karro and Rev let out a cluster of snarls and heckles, I took a step back as they rounded on Nakoma.

"I'd take that back if I was you. You disrespect the Alpha and it's out of my hands, I'm not a wolf – I have no say in pack laws and what action the Alpha takes if you disrespect them. So, you better quickly realise – Karro is Alpha. The wolves trust me, and I trust them, they know I am not interested in being their Alpha. I'll say this again, I'm not a wolf." He laughed unpleasantly, I was about to argue more and threaten that he keeps his mouth shut – when a howl bellowed to us. "Karro?"

Karro's ears perked up; his head whipped behind me. *"Oyku, she needs us."*

Oyku was leaning over Illythia's collapsed body, she was slumped against a tree, whatever had attacked her had thrown her so hard – bark had splintered away. Beside Illythia lay one of the wolves, Aneha, blood oozed from her neck. Karro whimpered as he nudged her, waiting and hoping that she's react to his touch, deep down he knew. *"I'm so sorry Karro,"* I rested my hand on his back, offering him comfort.

"I don't know if this one is alive," Oyku spoke, her voice saddened; she moved back and hid her face in the crook of Karro's neck.

"Illythia?" I shook her gently; I couldn't tell if she was alive either – Vampires didn't need to breathe, and I had never seen on die.

"Move," Nakoma barked as he pushed me to the side; he leaned over her and placed his hand over her eyes. Tallani lowered herself – ready to dive on him if he tried anything.

"What are you doing?" I demanded; he didn't answer – which only pissed me off more. He was such an arrogant ass. "Nakoma!"

"She's not dead," he announced blandly – my chest heaved in relief, Talon had already lost one sister. "She's very weak, been poisoned by something – it's hard to tell." His fingers traced her cheek softly and a muscle feathered in his jaw. "She needs a Vampires blood . . . the Elder one – Astrid." He gently swooped her up into his arms; a hint of a smile was pulling at the corner of his mouth – not a normal twisted Nakoma smile, but a warm, almost loving smile. He held her into his chest, his arms wrapped round her protectively, it was strange to see him . . . care. The smile faded as quickly as it had come, as he remembered that I was watching him, and the usual uncaring look returned. "We need to get her back."

"You go, we still have people missing." Nakoma froze and flashed me an unconvinced frown.

"I don't think that's a good idea. I think we should all go back and get more people. We don't know what or how she got infested by a deadly poison, it could be air born for all we know."

"We might not have time, if we all go back now, Demir, the wolves, Nyda's men, could all be dead by the time we find them. Take her back, I can handle myself – I took out your kind without issue." Nakoma met my eyes, the corners of his mouth lifted up in a smirk; he nodded and shuffled Illythia, so her head rested on his shoulder.

"Fine," he mumbled. "I'll take her and then I'll come back, try and find Demir but if you aren't sure about something. Wait for me."

"Bring someone back to get Aneha, I won't leave her here." Nakoma nodded to me and offered Karro a respectful nod.

Noses pressed to the floor – desperately trying to pick up anything, the wolves padded over and over the spot Illythia lay. I felt uneasy, almost like something or someone was watching me – perhaps they were, perhaps this was a test to see what I could do. Either way, this had to be down to Dacre; he was as bad as a dog – pissing on everything, marking the territory he wants.

Nook heckled all of a sudden, crouching low; he glared into the trees across the river and signalled for us to follow as he pelted forward. I felt the temperature drop the moment we started to run, the icy wind slammed into me, and it felt like I'd just been thrown from a moving car.

Demir was alive . . . barely. He was crumpled on the floor breathless and screeching out with pain, blood stained the ground around him . . . so much blood. "Demir! Hey, hey, look at me – focus on me." His eyes drifted up and he blinked several times, almost like he couldn't believe we were real. Horror ghosted over his face; he shook his head from side to side and forced himself to sit up.

"No, Narrdie, you can't be here – go now!" He demanded. "W-where's Illythia."

"It's alright Demir, just calm down. What happened? Illythia's safe, where are the others?" He continued to shake his head and attempt to push me away; his skin had paled and the whites of his eyes where bold – panicked.

"Dead, they're all dead or being eaten. Narrdie, you have to get out of here – run." He tried to stand, but the only movement he made, was opening his mouth to let out another pained scream. His hands clasped around his leg and my eyes trailed down his body.

My blood chilled.

I wasn't sure how I hadn't noticed; I knew there was blood everywhere, but I didn't think to find the source of the wound. Demir's right leg had been completely stripped of skin – all the way up to his mid-thigh, the exposed muscles, wept and pulsed out blood and even some parts revealed bone. I tried to mask the horror that had no doubt reached my face, I had never seen a wound like this before and it was one I wouldn't easily forget, the mangled mess of his leg, would no doubt cause me more nightmares. A tangy smell intruded in my nose, and I had to swallow hard to keep from gagging – it was already becoming infected, parts of it had even turned yellow, my throat pilled with sick. "What did this?" I asked – though the words barely manage to reach his ears. I took a second to gather myself, before I rushed out of my jacket and did the best DIY bandaging, I could do.

"I-It's not that bad. Just . . . just a scratch," he repeated over and over. All colour had washed from his face and the cold had clasped its hands around him; his body practically dancing as he shook.

"Demir, you're in shock. I need you to focus on me, what did this?" He opened his mouth to speak, but suddenly he froze, a mask of horror pulling at his face. His eyes were the widest I'd ever seen – he stared past me; a scream caught in his throat; his bottom lip quivering. I looked to the wolves, but they were also looking past me – the fur on their backs sticking up, their lips pulled back over their teeth. I followed their gaze slowly and found myself wishing that I had an army by my side, I thought back to the first time I had seen one.

The way it's flesh looked like it was melting, the way its claws where perfectly sharp – belly slicing sharp, the way my ears bled when it shrieked.

Skinners.

Skinners were soulless – they were violent. They earned their names from the way they killed – so it wasn't hard to guess, yet it was still terrifying to think of. Slowly peeling off every part of the flesh before tearing their food to shreds – while alive, they were the piranhas of the darkness. Evander had said that Dacre had recruited them and even used them at the school attack – I shuddered as the chorus of screams and cries of terror from the students rang in my ears, the PTSD of that day caused the goosebumps to pepper over my skin. I shook the thought from my head and forced it to the darkest depths of my mind, locked it in a chest and melted the key – now was not the time to reopen those wounds.

The Skinners jumped from side to side – unsure of why we had suddenly arrived there, angered that we now stood in the way of their meal. I remembered Evander's words when I asked him about Skinners; he'd said they were lethal, fast, and very rarely were people able to kill them – my palms grew damp and sweat slid down my temple. Dacre had killed the one in the woods, but that was only possible for two reasons, he was faster than it and it was too focused on me.

Karro and Rev moved to my flank as I slowly stood in front of Demir, my breath was raspy – Loopins were nothing compared to these. Oyku and Loka dropped back to protect Demir and Tallani and Nook dropped around the sides – ready to circle in the Skinners. *"You're going to die,"* Crow sang in my ear.

The Skinners outnumbered us – badly. There were at least a horde of twelve in front of us and I had no doubt that there'd probably be more on their way; they opened their mouths widely, the sound of snapping as their jaws dislocated – revealing the layers of shark like teeth.

Teeth that could very easily cut threw bone – my bone.

"We're going to die," Demir began chanting, over and over. His voice caused the Skinners heads to whirl in our directions; their acidic saliva burning wherever it fell.

"Shut up!" I hissed back at him – not once taking my eyes from the aggravated Skinners, neither side wanted to attack first, but if Demir kept talking, the choice would be made.

"We're going to die!"

"Demir!" The Skinners screeched their ear bleeding sound, I clamped my hands over my ears, feeling the blood slowly dripping through my fingers; my legs went weak and my mind was slowly beginning to feel like a mushy puddle. I moaned, the ringing pain pulsating, my eardrums ready to rupture. "Karro!"

A flicker of rage shone in Karro's eyes; he lunged forward, a predatory snarl rippling from his jaws – the other wolves following instantly.

Chapter Thirty-One

$\mathcal{W}$hen feral and ready to strike, Skinners seem to grow in size - not just double, but triple. One of the Skinners, one of the biggest, barricaded through the others, it's blood thirsty eyes met mine - foam dripping from its mouth. "Demir, try and shift, shift into something small - something they won't notice. You need to find the others and get us help, we'll try and hold them off as much as we can. I need you to do this, otherwise we are all going to die."

"It's too late. We're going to die." If I had a chance, I would have slapped him hard in the face.

The monstrous Skinner hurled towards me; I dug my feet into the soil - bracing myself for the impact. Loka lunged up and crossed over me, his jaws open and aiming towards the creatures throat; the Skinner curled it's paw, it's razor claw shifting and digging deep into Loka's shoulder. Loka yelped, whimpering as the Skinner heaved him up and tossed him to the side, leaving him to bleed - it didn't want Loka, it wanted me. Oyku snarled in fury and raced forward, Karro and Rev as her sides, the three of them moved like one, the strongest defenders of the pack - watching them was like watching a dance. Rev slid to the left, dodging as the Skinner's jaws snapped together, he crashed into its legs - knocking it down, hard. Immediately, Oyku sank her teeth into its leg; severing those razor talons from its body, Karro wasted no time, as he clamped his jaws around its jugular and in one swift motion – tore it wide. Its thick, black, gloopy blood spilled all over the ground – the leaves sizzling and curling up under its touch.

Panicked, I turned to Demir – hoping he'd come to his senses, "Shift! Please, Demir!" He shook his head and lifted a trembling hand to his mouth; he mumbled.

"I . . . I can't." Suddenly, a Skinner jumped onto me and pinned me against the muddy soil, I winced as the sharp rocks pricked into my back.

I struggled to keep it at arm's length; it's jaws merely inches from my face, it cocked its head to the side and a gurgle bubbling in its throat; it turned and bit down hard on my arm. I screeched out as I felt a surge of antagonizing pain ripple throughout my body – my insides lit on fire and a sudden hazy of dizziness sank its swaying grip on me. I heard a snarl from behind me, a fast-white blur collided with the Skinner, they rolled into the trees – out of my sight. I rolled onto my side, clutching my arm; I heard a mixture of snarls and yelps within the trees, horror struck me as the trees ran silent.

The bushes rustled, and I knew Karro wasn't breathing, couldn't breathe – not until he knew if she was safe, that she was alive. Oyku padded through the leaves – black blood covered her snout, instantly Karro was beside he, rubbing his head against hers, scolding her for taking one on alone.

"Narrdie Moon, you are hurt!" She announced and took a step to me, she paused and arched her head to her left. Another Skinner began booming towards us – Oyku snarled; she reared up as it came to her and dropped down hard on it, she wasted no time before her mouth forcefully gripped its chest, seeking out its heart. For such a gentle and small wolf – she was frightening in a fight, it didn't shock me, one of her pack lay wounded and the others were dead. *"Go! Make that Shifter get help, I can smell more coming!"* She ordered as she ran to Tallani's aid. *"Nook, protect Loka!"*

I forced myself to stand, the pain in my arm boiling beneath my skin; the delusion beginning to grip hold of my blood; I dropped beside Demir and forced him to look at me, "Shift now – or we all die here!" I pleaded with him; his eyes met mine and I could have screamed with relief when he nodded – his body beginning to vibrate.

A yelp had pulled my attention back, two Skinners had Tallani backing up into a corner; she snapped and snarled, desperately trying to drive them from her. A wave of pain shot up my arm, warning me that I was in no position to help her, fighting Skinners one handed was a death sentence. "Karro!" I called drastically, Karro skidded to a stop; his head snapping around to face me. I pointed to Tallani, instantly he growled and dashed to her – diving on top of the first one. I'd never seen a wolf move so quickly, his mouth was like a machine as he began tearing chunks from it, he was filled with anger, and it unleashed the Alpha inside him. A familiar feeling crept around me, a familiar dark thrum – Karro's power, the same type of power that flowed in my own veins and the power that had clung hard to mine and formed our bond. Karro's jaws sank it, a sudden crunch of bone, as he shredded the Skinner's head from its body. The other Skinner turned and screeched ferociously, Tallani seized the opportunity and made a dive for its throat, holding it in place for Karro, who made a quick meal in ending its life.

"They will die," Crow purred in my head. *"You can't save them, let me help you."* I gritted my teeth and created a wall in my head, closing her in – pushing her down.

A pained yelp caught my attention, a Skinner plunged its teeth into Karro's back, picking him up, as easily as a dog would pick up a bone. It bit down and the crunch of Karro's ribs went right through me, even as the agony rippled throughout him; Karro turned and buckled. The Skinner dug his teeth down harder, before tossing him aside and turning to face the remaining four wolves – who began to circle him. I dropped beside Karro, my heart performing pirouettes, pounding with the fear of losing him.

It didn't take long for the others to remove the last Skinner, their fury was enough to guide them into tearing it apart, until it was nothing but ribbons on the floor. The wolves, crowded around him, they lay on the floor beside him – softly whimpering. Oyku crouched low and crawled to his side; she nuzzled, licking softly at his snout. My eyes teared over – he was going to die.

"What can I do?" I chocked; they didn't answer me. *"Oyku, please!"* She didn't respond to me, instead she let out a broken howl and then licked her mate.

"I wanted his blood to see if he has become part of the oath . . ." Nakoma's voice ran in my ears, I'd asked Mazruriuk if that was possible, it they could become part of it . . . what had he said? My mind was fuzzy and sieving through it stung, I pressed

my fingers into my temples – forcing the thoughts to push their way through. *"Yes, in some cases it's happened. However, only if you've shared blood."*

Blood – my blood.

I could save him, I could save Karro – all he needed was my blood, our bond was strong; our power was like a magnet to one another. I didn't bother weighing up my options, I didn't stop to think through the consequences, I wouldn't let him die like this – I couldn't.

"Oyku, tell the others to step back," I asked as I edged closer to him – Oyku growled deeply towards me, a warning. *"Oyku, I know I am overstepping, but please, trust that I wouldn't if it wasn't important. I swear to you. I can save him. Oyku, I can save him."* She paused and studied me for a heartbeat; she met my eyes and shifted away from Karro – the others followed.

"Please," she begged.

Karro whined as he looked to me weakly, my hand gently stroked down his neck, *"I'm going to help you."* He gently lay his head back down – his breathing calmed, I had to do this now. The nails on my right hand grew, until they resembled sharp slender claws, I winced as I raised my arm and cut a deep line across my wrist. Crimson liquid began to immediately overflow, I slowly lifted Karro's head up and nodded at him. *"Trust me Karro, this will help you."* Without another thought, his tongue reached out and traced along the ruby droplets.

I could feel it, feel the bond flowing through me like electricity, watched as a white tethered jumped out of my chest – another tether jumping from Karro. It was like I was watching a ballet dance – the tethered spun together, swirling and swaying, until finally, they entwined together. A bright light flashed, and the tethered erupted into tiny dust particles that sprinkled over us – like glitter on a page. I could feel it as it seeped up my nose, flowed down my throat and pierce into my heart and before I could gather my thoughts, Karro was on his feet. Oyku whined as she buried her face against his– no doubt she was giving him a good telling off for scaring her. Karro's eyes met mine and he nodded his head slowly, a shade of uneasiness darkened his eyes, I could feel it on myself – we were going to be in serious trouble.

"A bond only broken by Death," Crow snickered.

"*N*arrdie?" Audric's voice was faint as it drifted over to me, through the thickness of the trees.

"Here! We're here!" I called to him and winced. I looked to my arm and grimaced, my wound was quickly becoming a mutilated mess, my skin hung in shreds where it's teeth had torn and the venom from its bite, journeyed up my veins.

"Narrdie?" Audric slashed a branch with his sword; his face softened as he saw me, in three big strides he was beside me; his hand resting at the back of my head as he kissed my forehead multiple times. "Thank the mother you're alive."

"It's about time, you missed all the fun," I said back to him, yet he knew too well that I'd hated every second of the fight. Nakoma and a couple dozen guards burst from the footpath Audric had made, each one more armed than the other – Nakoma nodded to me, relaxing slightly. Audric's eyes ran over me, trying to decipher what blood belonged to the Skinners and what blood belonged to me.

"Are you hurt?" His eyes travelled down to my arm – which I kept hidden with my hand.

"It's nothing – a scratch." I don't know why I lied or tried to hide the severity of it. Perhaps I didn't want him thinking I was some breakable doll. "Did Demir reach you?"

"He did. Rambling like an idiot, it was hard for us to even figure out what in the hell he was saying. Luckily, Nakoma sniffed you out." Audric turned to bark orders at the others, telling them to lift and help the wolves with extreme care.

"Don't blame Demir, he's in shock." Audric counted down from five before he lifted me from the ground, apologising as I moaned with the burning pain that had been set off by the movement. He held me tight against him; his heartbeat comforting as it eased my own, his breathing lowering to match with mine and if I didn't force my eyes open – I would have fallen asleep there and then.

"Hey, stay awake," Audric breathed as he shook my carefully, I groaned my protest. "I know you're tired, you can sleep once a healer has checked you. Nakoma, you got him?" Audric called back, his eyes narrowing as he watched the Loopin lift Loka in his arms - taking extra care not to harm him.

"I have him, we'll follow your lead."

Chapter Thirty-Two

"They're back!" I heard Madam Keeper announce, her voice full of concern. Audric outstretched his arm – signalling people to give us some space, I was grateful for that. Evander was beside us in an instant, Nyda close on his heels.

"What happened? What attacked you? Where are the others?" Nyda began, firing questions before I even had a chance to sit down. Evander gave her an unimpressed look and snapped towards her.

"Back off a bit Nyda, give her some room and go and tend to Demir," he ordered; his eyes staring her down until she looked to the floor and bowed. His eyes checked over me, looking for any kind of injury, until eventually they rested on my arm; he grimaced through his teeth at the state of it. "Looks nasty, but I feared you'd be worse – considering it was a horde of Skinners that you faced." He brushed a hand along my cheek, frowning as he felt my temperature radiating from my skin, almost burning his fingers.

"I would have been nothing but a pile of blood and bones if it wasn't for the wolves," I mumbled, the exhaustion pulling me down. I jerked up, my eyes searching around desperately, "Loka?" Audric's hand stopped me in my tracks, he shook his head, a warning to stay still.

"He's with Lotus, she's doing her best to heal him. You stay here and I'll go check on him, stay here Narrdie," Audric's voice was stern.

"Your fever is spiking," Evander locked eyes with Bayona and with a tilt of his head, summoned her to me. "Skinner bite," he informed her as he carefully pulled my arm free from my jacket, kissing my hand as I cried out with pain. "Easy, girl."

"I'll try and make this as painless as possible," Bayona assured me. Her hands hovered over my wound - the bright light glowing bright, before instantly fading, she frowned and shook her hands in the air - placing them over my wound once more. The same thing happened, and I watched as she pulled away and bit her lip. "I'm afraid I can't heal this; the poison is too thick for healing magic; it needs to be drained and washed out. Still, there is no need for panic - your blood is strong, and it'll hold back the spreading for now. However, what I can do is keep it contained in one area." She moved her hands down until they grasped my own hand.

She froze; her eyes snapping up to me; she clenched her jaw - tapping the cut on my wrist, the cut I had made for Karro and I knew I'd been caught. I prayed and squeezed her hand - pleading with her, begging that she wouldn't say anything, at least not yet. I didn't realise I was holding my breath until she subtly nodded and continued to block the poisons path, the look in her eye reading one promise - we'll discuss this later.

"Evander, how's Illythia and Demir?" I asked, he sighed and glanced behind him, Talon sat beside Illythia and held her hand in his; his other hand lighting brushing a damp cloth along her forehead.

"She hasn't woken up yet, Astrid fed her blood, and nothing happened." He leaned closer, so that his words would only reach my ears. "Skinners didn't do this to her - it's not how they attack."

"You think someone set this up?"

"I do and I think you know who I suspect." I clenched my jaw; I knew exactly who he meant. "Demir calmed down after Nyda put a glamour over him, however it's not looking good for his leg, I'm afraid when we get to the Priestesses - it'll have to be removed." I shuddered and Bayona tapped my shoulder - letting me know she was finished with my arm.

"Thank you Bayona, could you please check on Loka? He got hurt pretty badly," I asked her sheepishly.

"Of course. I take it the others aren't harmed? Karro?" A threat carried in her voice, I swallowed nervously – hoping that the others didn't pick up on anything.

"N-No. Just Loka."

"Very well. I will speak to you later, Narrdie," her voice was tight, angered. That would be a conversation I wouldn't be looking forward too.

"You should rest," Evander advised and for once – I didn't argue.

I'd slept through the full day and was thankful for the undisturbed slumber. The night had swallowed up the sky when I opened my eyes. The camp was still, everyone captured in a deep wave of exhaustion – everyone except Evander. He caught my eye – it was his turn to keep watch over us, though with his wound, I wasn't sure what use he'd be. He tilted his head and gave me a smile, that immediately made my insides burn for him; he winked and made his way to me, tiptoeing around the sleeping bodies. "You should be sleeping," he whispered in my ear before kissing my neck.

"Behave," I purred. He chuckled lightly and sprawled out beside me, his hand drawing lazy patterns along my collarbone. "How long have I slept?"

"Day and a half, we wrapped you up and put you on one of the carts, I'm more anxious than ever to get to that house. I never expected we'd lose any along the way, I should have been more prepared." I caught his hand in mine and kissed his knuckles over and over.

"You're too hard on yourself, none of us expected this to happen." He smiled his appreciation, the gesture not quite reaching his eyes.

"How is it?" He asked as he unbound the bandage on my arm.

"Hurts, but I can live with it for now. How's the silver?"

"Hurts, but I can live with it," he mimicked, we both shared a quiet laugh, he carefully wrapped his hand around the back of my neck and pulled me closer to him.

"How are the others?" I was almost afraid to ask.

"Loka's awake, he's resting in the cart, his mama Oyku warned him not to move around unless Lotus gave him, the all clear. Bayona has had to place Demir in sleep, every time he

355

came around, he was hysterical, a rot is beginning to take hold of his leg." I winced at the thought. "Illythia still hasn't woken either."

"Evander what if we don't make it to the house soon? What if another horde is waiting for us?" I looked to him, waiting for those burning orange eyes to swallow me up. He swallowed hard, his jaw tightening; his fists clenching slightly. "You're scared." It wasn't a question, but his scoff was answer enough.

"I am, not from the Skinners or whoever is setting them on us. I'm scared for you, for me, for our people. If we are attacked again, I'm scared a lot of us won't make it." I knew it took a lot for him to admit it, since I'd know Evander; he preferred to play the strong, confident role.

"Evander, Narrdie," Mazruriuk greeted with a lazed tone. "It is time for you two to get some rest," he paused and narrowed his eyes as he looked at me – his eyes glancing at wound on my arm; he raised his brow. "You shouldn't even be awake." I rolled my eyes playfully, Evander snickered.

"Thank you, Mazruriuk," Evander said with a tired smile; he pulled the blanket from behind me and flung it over us both.

"Rest well," Mazruriuk wished with a bow of his head, before turning and beginning his checks.

I curled up into Evander, being careful not to knock his side; his arms wrapped around tickling down my back and through my hair, a little trick he used to help me fall asleep.

$$\smile$$

I was beginning to hate the sight, the smell and the feeling of this forest; it was all seeming to merge into one big green and brown blob and with each hour that passed – my arm seared with pain. The venom had begun to spread around my body, coursing through my veins and no matter how many blankets Astrid lay over me, the cold still iced my skin. Every bump the cart made, sent my body screaming, burning with agony. Bayona's barrier that she had used to contain the venom, was broken, she'd tried to restore it but found the poison had hardened, strengthened beyond magical repair and with each tormenting breath I took, I could hear the bitter cackling of Crow in the back on my head. It wouldn't be long until I was too weak to hold her off.

As if he could read the thoughts across my head, Evander spoke; his hand feeling the heat across my head. "Bayona can sense a shift in the air, it won't be much further. Just hold on a little longer."

"I hope you're right." Illythia still hadn't woken up, for a Vampire it seemed she'd gone even colder; she'd been laid out on a stretcher – carried by Talon and Astrid, as well Demir who was lifted by Mazruriuk and Basso – a warrior for Nyda. Demir quietly spoke to himself, words that no one could quite make out, the Skinner's toxin already infecting his mind.

Bayona quick stepped and rested her hand on the side of the cart. "How are you feeling?" She asked in a cheery sing-song voice, for someone who hadn't eaten or slept properly in a number of days – she seemed awfully happy.

"Drained," I admitted.

"It seems my barrier wasn't as strong as I thought it would be." Evander clenched his jaw and gave me a forced comforting smile, Bayona's smile widened. "Do not be worried, today is a glorious day! Today is the day we reach the Priestesses home, I'm overjoyed! Witches rarely ever get to meet the Priestesses, let alone go to one of their homes and we'll be living in it! This is a true dream come true!" Bayona burst, she looked as if she was going to jump up and take off into the sky. I was curious, I wondered if Nyda held the same feelings.

To my surprise, Nyda was practically dancing around her men – it was the happiest I'd ever seen her.

"Here!" Bayona called – halting the march. I forced myself into a seating position – using the back of the cart as a back rest. My brows pulled together, there was nothing – no door, no house, not even a clearing where something could be hiding underground. All there was, was the never-ending forest, nothing but dirt, stones, bushes and trees.

"Where? I don't see any-" My words were cut in half as the ground beneath me began to shake, the wind picked up my hair and made it dance around my face, I felt the spit of water, rain down on me and felt a sudden heat lick my cheeks.

"Easy," Evander said, calming the panicked voices, people had suddenly drawn their weapons and ignited their powers. A haze of leaves began to spin around in a circle – lifting higher and higher until my neck hurt from watching.

Erenna appeared in the centre of the pirouetting leaves, standing with her hands cupped in front of her; she looked breath-taking – an image no painting or camera would ever be able to capture. She'd chosen a more comfortable style of clothing, a deep green turtle-necked jumper, brushing above her knees and the same-coloured leggings – barefoot as always. Erenna offered us all a comforting smile, it didn't once fall as she saw the weapons aimed towards her – her brows rose.

"My dear children," she began softly. "I pray you, please lower your guard, you are safe here." She turned towards Nyda, "What brings on this cloud of hostility?" Nyda bowed and raised her tattooed hand, only rising to speak once Erenna recognised her.

"My Priestess, it has not been an easy journey. We have faced many of the darkness's children along the way, our own are injured and we have lost some along the way. The wounded are beyond Bayona and I, we have healed as much as we can." Erenna's eyes widened, she took herself a moment, swallowing down a lump, before moving towards us; her eyes scanning each and every person for injury. She reached Demir, who had now taken to rocking back and forth; his eyes frantically darting around.

"How has this happened?"

"Sivvs and Skinners, my Lady," one of Evander's men announced – his voice wavering.

"How many?" Erenna pressed.

"Three Sivvs, they seemed to pass on thanks to Nakoma. I think there were around twelve Skinners, they attacked some of our people who went missing," I stated. "They're dead now, but I wouldn't be surprised if there's more, frolicking about." Erenna tilted her head as I spoke; her eyes surveying the group for me.

"My dear child," she breathed as she walked beside me. She carefully took my arm in her hands, before pulling the blanket down to reveal my bare skin. The venom had created a spider webbed effect along my skin, the wound itself oozing black and yellow puss. "You fought them." She stated, I looked away.

"No. The pack did, they lost two and Loka was hurt." I could feel Evander's eyes surveying me; his hand brushed mine.

"You went to find the ones that were separated. You made that choice; you should be proud at your bravery – I know I am." Her fingers gripped my chin and lifted my face up until my gaze met hers. "You should be proud," she repeated. She held our gaze a few moments longer, before releasing my chin and turning towards Karro and Oyku. She bent down to them, I knew she was speaking to them, acknowledging their grief for their fallen, Oyku leaned forward to lick Erenna's cheek once. "Who is wounded?" Erenna asked to no one in particular as she straightened up.

"Illythia has been unconscious for a number of days now, the Shifter's leg is missing it's . . . skin," Nyda began. She paused to swallow, and I assumed she was holding down the urge to vomit. "He is also dealing with Skinner venom, as well as Narrdie, many are fading from hunger, dehydration and exhaustion. It is just as well you turned up when you did, otherwise I fear the worse for our numbers." Nyda's voice had been completely evaporated of emotion and I wondered if she really would care if our people . . . her people, died. Erenna rubbed her hand along her neck, she swallowed hard and after a few breaths she nodded.

"Come. We will see to your wounds, there is food, water, hot springs to bath yourselves in and rooms for you all to rest, myself and . . ."

Erenna's voice began to fade in an out, until I could only hear mumbles. I shook my head as everyone was dancing around – their faces going blurry in my eyes. I felt pain, like burning ice throughout my veins and my own heartbeat thundered in my ears. My legs vanished from under me and I felt something hard slam into my head.

The only thing that reached my ears was dark laughter, as Crow rose to the surface.

Chapter Thirty-Three

Everyone

*C*row's piercing blue eyes flicked open; she bared her teeth as she rose, feeling a sudden pounding pain bounce in her head. She laughed – a sound dark and bitter – as her eyes absorbed the strength of the cell that held her captive, she thrummed her fingers along the bars – they were smooth and barely used, which meant she wasn't in Gatherling. She licked her fingers and raised her brow. "Titanium and iron fused into one and sealed with an enchantment . . . they've learned."

Crow flopped down on the thin bed that had been wedged into the cell and began humming to herself; her feet propped high on the wall as she roughly pulled knots out of her scraggy black hair. She smirked as Evander walked into the little prison – she knew it wouldn't take long for him to come; her eyes lazily moved to him; she whistled flirtatiously. "If these bars weren't here Evander, I think I'd have to jump you . . . have a little ride on you and see why Narrdie likes it so much. You look much better than the last time I saw you, stronger, healthier . . . less silver. One hundred percent fuckable," she teased.

Evander growled. "You're repulsive." Crow tutted as she sat up and pressed herself up against the bars; her hand snaking out in an attempt to stroke him – she licked her lips.

"Oh, come on, play with me. You seem so tense, step inside and let me relax you – I'll be gentle, well, I'll try," she purred.

"What are you doing here?"

"How many times have I almost killed you now? You're like a cockroach, don't worry next time I'll get it right and make sure I stomp on you harder." Evander's face was blank, and it annoyed her massively that he wasn't letting her have her fun with him.

"Why are you here?" He asked; his fists clenching.

"Narrdie was weak, she couldn't fight me anymore, we've been arguing a lot." Evander frowned.

"Arguing?" Crow's eyes gleamed with amusement, she gasped mockingly and giggled.

"You don't know? Narrdie hasn't told you." She teased; she was like a fisherman with a hook – just waiting for a bite.

"Told me what?"

"That we've been speaking." Evander stiffened, and Crow's menacing smirk widened – she'd just caught herself a big fish. "She can't block me out anymore, at first I couldn't figure out how I was slipping through and then it kissed me on the cheek. She doesn't know, does she?" Evander looked away from her and the cracks of guilt glowed on his face – Crow laughed. "So, why haven't you told her? Surely, if she knew she could find a way . . . unless, you don't have faith in her . . ." Crow raised her brows at him; her hand crept out once more – stroking along his arm. "Evander, why haven't you told her?" She pressed.

"I don't want to hurt her," he admitted.

"And not telling her will be better? Tsk, tsk, Evander. When she finds out and she will, she'll know that you don't believe in her and it will crush that little angelic heart of hers. She may even hate you for it, you know . . . it's much harder to block out the darkness when there's hate in your heart." He snagged her hand and threw her back, before turning away from her. She scoffed and rolled her eyes; he was always so dramatic when it came to Narrdie. "Poor Evander," she ridiculed.

"A heartless creature like you, wouldn't understand," Evander hissed.

"I've loved before," Crow snarled. Evander's head whipped around to her and his mouth gaped open slightly, his brow raising.

"You did love Dacre," he stated. "Even though he fucked you over . . . many times. You still loved him and perhaps you still do now." Crow jeered; all playfulness drained from her face – her eyes darkened.

"In the final days, I will carve your heart out make Narrdie watch."

"What's your plan Crow? Because I'll happily keep you down here." His palms began to sweat as he could feel his wolf scrap against the surface, the very sight of her made him want to shift and rip her into shreds. Crow smiled murderously – flashing her sharpened teeth, she spoke softly.

"Just surviving." Evander scoffed and turned his back on her; he was done playing this back-and-forth game, he should have known that Crow wouldn't give him any information that could have helped him – she was too smart. "This begins with a river of blood," Crow called to him – making him pause on his heels. "The blood from each group will merge into one and as it flows, I will rise. This is my world and you cannot keep it from me – not you, not your friends and not Narrdie." Evander turned to her, his head beginning to create a thunderous beat.

"What do you mean the blood from each group?"

"Their blood will fill the oceans, contaminate the air and tarnish the earth! Narrdie Moon will fall screaming for her life and this is what scares you, because you know deep down it is true! How can you convince them all that the light will triumph, if you don't believe it yourself?" Tendrils of darkness slithered around Crow; her eyes turned black as they burned into Evander. Evander couldn't move, fear wrapped around him like a spider's web. "The darkness has touched you, infected you and it claims that you will be the one who brings her down. You will tear everything inside her, crush everything good and kill her!" Evander's blood turned cold, his muscles froze in place – he couldn't run, he couldn't call for help. Crow had him where she wanted him – her eyes locking him in place. "You will kill her! You will kill Narrdie Moon! You will kill the one you love!"

"Stop," he begged, Crow released her hold and he collapsed to the floor – banging his fists into his head. A sadistic grin stretched along her lips, she stepped back from the bars and sat crossed legged on the bed.

"The world burns because of you. The moment you laid eyes on her at Gatherling, you already decided her fate," she laughed.

The cell room door erupted into small fragments as Mazruriuk raced in, followed by Nakoma and Talon. Nakoma dropped down beside Evander – who continued to bash his own head and mumble to himself.

"Evander?" Nakoma gripped his face, swearing under his breath as Evander's orange eyes turned white. "Talon, get help!"

"What's happening to him?" Mazruriuk demanded as he firmly gripped Evander's arms – Evander pushed and fought against him. Nakoma whirled on Crow – she glared at him with distaste, a Loopin, working with the light? Disgusting.

"She got into his head!" Nakoma snarled.

"He's in bad shape, we need to get him to the infirmary," Mazruriuk stated.

"You bring shame on your own, Shade," Crow snickered – spitting towards his feet. Nakoma stood in front of Crow, blocking her view of Mazruriuk – she tilted her head, this Loopin was bold – foolish.

"Don't listen to her," Nakoma grunted. "Another word and I'll cut out your tongue."

"A brave one," she whispered to Nakoma. "I'm just getting started." Her eyes shot back to Mazruriuk, the veins around her eyes almost turning black. "How's the red headed human? Rosie, is it?" Mazruriuk froze.

"Mazruriuk," Nakoma warned.

"She's a strong little one, for a human. It's a shame really, I thought she might have lasted to the end – I was wrong." The room shook as Mazruriuk stood; his odd eyes turning to a chilling black, the shadows around the room beginning to curl into him as his power awoken in his veins. Crow lifted her lip in a sneer. "That's a boy."

"Mazruriuk! Don't let her get in your head!" Nakoma hissed; his nails growing into sharp points.

"Mazruriuk? Help me Mazruriuk, where are you? I need you." Crow's voice had shifted to mimic Ray – a sound that would have convinced them both if they weren't looking directly at her.

"Mazruriuk, don't! Shut her out," Nakoma begged; he dared a step closer to the Shade, preparing to grab him in case he lunged at her.

"Don't listen to him Mazruriuk! She can show you how to save me, the Loopin doesn't want that, he wants to hurt me Mazruriuk!" Mazruriuk walked closer, Crow licked her poisoned black lips – she flashed an excitable grin to Nakoma.

"What happens to Rosie?" Mazruriuk asked through gritted teeth.

"Mazruriuk stop!"

"You see," she whispered, pushing herself from the bed and wrapping her hands around the cold bars. "He's trying to stop you. He's against you. They all are, planning to turn on you. No one here trusts Shades, it's only a matter of time until they come for you and for me!" Crow's eyes bored into Mazruriuk, the tendrils of darkness slowly began to seep towards him – Mazruriuk slowly turned to Nakoma, a feral look casting over his face. "You should kill him, kill him before he does you . . . kill him Mazruriuk, kill them all!" Nakoma hissed nervously at Crow.

"Heinous Witch!"

"Kill him!" Bloodthirst burned in Mazruriuk's eyes, his dark power wrapping around him, the black smoke that leaked from his fingers began to stretch out around Nakoma. Nakoma pleaded with him, desperately trying to snap him out of the trance she had put him under, fear crusted over his eyes – if Mazruriuk harmed him or if he harmed Mazruriuk, the oath would tear them to shreds. A serpentine smile stretched along Crow's face, darkness leaking from her – like ink in water.

"Mazruriuk, stop! Don't listen to her! She's in your head!"

"Kill them all Mazruriuk. Save Rosie, become the Shade you are meant to be!" She taunted; her face full of darkened pleasure.

A gust of wind hammered into Mazruriuk's chest – pushing him back from Nakoma, he fell back; his head smacking against the wall. Nyda burst into the room, her hair and lilac gown blowing on a non-existing wind. Audric, Talon and a handful of Monks flanking around her; her eyes dropped to Evander – who was barely maintaining his consciousness and then to Nakoma for answers.

"She got in their heads," Nakoma panted. "Take her out!" Nyda's eyes didn't shift to Crow, didn't deign to acknowledge her vicious snickering; she raised her hands, summoning that violent force to form a gust in her palm.

"I was having so much fun," Crow spat. She blew a kiss towards Audric before Nyda thrusted the angered wind towards her. Crow gasped as the cloud forced its way into her mouth and nostrils – her body turned stiff as she collapsed into the feeble bed, her fingers and toes curling up as her body seized itself and went as still as a statue.

"I fucking hate that bitch," Audric said with a low growl, his eyes the colour of slumbering flame; he shuddered feeling Crow's power on his neck, a slithering touch as it faded away.

"Nakoma, Talon, take Mazruriuk and Evander upstairs, find the Priestesses and see what they can do to sort their heads out. Make sure no one else goes near them, we don't want to start a panic, people don't know that Crow's surfaced – I think it would be too soon after the last time." Nyda ordered, sparks raining in her eyes. Nakoma and Talon nodded as they began to steer Mazruriuk and Evander away – like guide dogs leading the blind. Audric took a step closer to the cell – Nyda walked beside him; her arms folded in front of her. Disappointment, tattooed his face, Crow still remained, he'd hoped that the blast would have forced her back into the corners of Narrdie's mind, the fact that she was still lingering – unnerved him.

"She got into their heads. Two of our strongest and she got into their heads without even breaking a sweat," his voice croaked.

"She's powerful. More powerful than she's ever been, Evander and Dacre were mistaken to keep her locked away for all those years," Nyda spoke, her voice uncharacteristically solemn.

"You think?"

She nodded. "Indeed. For years she's done nothing but wait, stored up her power and Narrdie's power. She's an atomic bomb Audric, waiting for the right time to blow and when she does . . . we'll all burn." Audric snapped his head to Nyda; his eyes narrowed.

"Careful Nyda, you sound like you don't have faith in Narrdie." Nyda turned from him; her arms still folded as she headed back upstairs.

"I don't."

*R*ay wiped her mouth free of blood on the back of her sleeve; her hands gripped the sides of the sink – the basin full of crimson liquid. She'd been coughing up blood the past few nights, she was starting to worry that the sink would permanently be stained red. Her hands shook as she cupped the clear water from the tap and splashed it on her face; she gasped as someone tapped on her door.

"Ray?" She froze, her spine locking up. Talon was at her door . . . Talon . . . a Vampire . . . a Vampire that had a nose that could smell blood from miles away.

"J-Just a minute," her voice wobbled. "Are we training today?" She asked, trying to play everything off as normal, she pulled the plug – scrubbing vigorously at the ruby ring along the white edge.

"Ray, its Mazruriuk – he needs you." Her heart twanged in her chest, with a clenched jaw and a deep breath, she spoke.

"What's happened? Can it wait until later?" Talon arched a brow; this wasn't like her. Whenever it had something to do with Mazruriuk, she always came running – not matter what. Something was wrong, he tried the handle – locked, she never locked her door; she preferred to leave it open – in case Mazruriuk wanted a midnight cuddle.

"Crow got into his head, he's in bad shape. You should come and see him." Ray raised her hand to her throat; she could feel the next round of coughing rolling up her gullet; she bit her lip and swallowed – forcing down the painful lump, the taste of iron already reaching her tongue.

"I will later. I'm busy right now." Tears burned her eyes.

"Yollie, are you OK?" She winced at the nickname, the caring tone he carried in his voice; he had always treated her like one of his sisters – cared for her, loved her and protected her and here she was – keeping secrets.

"I said I'm busy," she snapped – Talon flinched back. He tilted his head as a faint hint of blood graced his nose, he scowled – not sure if it was from Ray or if he was just hungry.

"Fine, just go to him soon," he replied blankly.

The moment she could no longer hear his footsteps, the retching attacked in full swing.

Ray quietly tiptoed into Mazruriuk's room; her eyes fogging over as she saw him – lying on the bed, twitching, Talon was seated in a brown armchair beside him. "Oh Riuk," she could barely breath; she took his hand in hers and sat on the edge of the bed beside him, kissing across his knuckles. "How long has he been like this?" Talon eyed her suspiciously as he answered, his voice tight.

"A couple of hours." He rose to close the door, that familiar smell tickling him once again. "Yollie?"

"Hmm?" Ray murmured as she began dabbing a wet towel – soaked in cold water – along Mazruriuk's head, the sweat pouring from him, like a fountain; he was burning up.

"I smelt blood, outside your room and I smell it still." He watched every little movement she made; she tensed.

"Oh? I just cut my hand; I'm surprised you could smell that." His frown deepened; he could hear her heartbeat, the blood increasing as it raced around her veins. It sang to him, liar, liar, liar.

"You're lying." He growled, she slowly looked up to him and flashed him pleading panicked eyes.

"Later, please, now is not the time." His eyes glared into hers, the harshness of his glare burned down on her, her lip quivered. "Please," she begged. Talon nodded to her, she sheepishly smiled and turned back to Mazruriuk – whispering softly in his ear.

Talon stormed through the crystal white halls of the Priestesses home, he ignored the soldiers and Monks who bowed with respect to him – ignored the grand oil paintings tucked safely inside wide golden frames, engraved with swirls and other unusual patterns. The day they arrived, he'd spent hours walking through these halls – gazing at the ancient warriors that graced the oil work, some he'd heard of, one he'd even met in another life. However, today was not the time to take in more specifics – he needed advice from someone who had been on this earth for a long time. He paused outside the golden door; it swung open before he even raised his hand.

"Talon, I could smell you before you arrived, you're troubled – it's bouncing from the walls. What's wrong?" Talon rested his hands on either side of the doorframe; he lowered his head and let out one hard sigh. "Is it Illythia?"

Illythia had woken a few days after arriving, a thirst no one could describe piercing her throat, she fed and drank until her belly filled – resting for hours with no end in her room.

"No, my sister is fine. I need your help Astrid, I think Ray's in trouble," his voice was quiet, like he was about to break down – his face had paled with worry.

"You best come in then," Astrid said in her motherly tone, placing her hand on his back, a comforting gesture that he appreciated.

Talon left out no detail as he explained the situation about Ray, the blood he smelt on her, the shudder in her voice – the lies. He leaned forward; his hands cupped between his knees. "Are you sure she didn't just cut her hand?" Talon scoffed and ran a hand through his hair.

"No. She was acting weird at Gatherling as well, I never said anything to Mazruriuk because I wanted to be sure first." Astrid sighed and shook her head; she laughed bitterly.

"That is the problem, we are all keeping things secret. It haunts me, I fear that our downfall will not be Dacre or Crow – but each other." Talon nodded his agreement.

"I'll mention this to Mazruriuk. If Ray is keeping something from us, he'll find out."

*Evander felt stiff as he woke up, his limbs tender as he forced them to move, his head ached and black spots dotted in his eyes. He rose, squinting as he tried to piece together the last couple of hours, with each forced memory, his head thumped, *"you will kill Narrdie Moon."* That voice – her voice, echoed across his skull, ringing his eardrums, a cold shiver jittered along his skin – like she was here, touching him.

"No," he gasped, bile began to venture up hit throat; he jumped up, his feet carrying him into the bathroom, his limbs seething at the movement. His hands clutching the sink so tightly – his knuckles turned white, sweat beamed down his face; he looked at his reflection. His blood iced as one face stared back at him – Crow. "You're not here," he growled through clenched teeth, the wolf's claws peeking through his knuckles. Her vicious smirk turned feline, wide across her face, blood began to overflow down her black lips and trail down her chin.

"The world burns because of you, the world burns because of you, the world burns because of you." Evander roared and drove his fist into the mirror, the shards slicing up his knuckles – no, not knuckles . . . Claws. Evander shook his hand, begging the claws to go away, soothing the wolf that snarled under his skin.

"I let her get into my head! I let her get into my head," he twisted at himself. "Never. Never again, there has to be a way to stop this." He splashed his face, waiting for his healing abilities to close up the cuts that had scattered over his hand and through on a fresh shirt and jeans.

He walked down the corridor towards the dining hall, offering small greetings to those he passed, he turned the corner and paused in the doorway of the grand hall, there was no dining table, no dining chairs, all formality had been removed – replaced with giant maroon pillows and cream blankets – big enough to fit three people. Wenona, Astrid, Erenna, Aronnia and Nyda lounged across them, crystal glasses full of red wine in their hands – candles had been lit all around them as their laughter lifted in the air. Evander's stomach turned to fire and ash; his growl echoed towards them, how they all could be so calm in a time like this – pissed him off.

The cheery tone was suddenly replaced by a heavy silence, Wenona turned and gave a warning glare to him, this was not his home and she didn't care for the manners he was giving. "Forgive me," he said to them all.

"Evander, glad to see you have woken. How are you feeling?" Erenna asked as she gestured for him to sit down.

"Confused, I'm afraid I'm still piecing together what happened. Where's Narrdie?"

"Still gone. Crow is clinging onto the wheel with those filthy claws of hers," Nyda stated as she downed the rest of her wine, Astrid flashed her a look of caution.

"The Skinner's poison wreaked havoc on her, I'm not surprised she is still away – she could do with this rest," Astrid spoke, before Evander could snipe at Nyda. "Still, I wish it wasn't like this."

"Is the poison gone? From Narrdie, I mean."

"The wounds are closed; however the change took hold before I could check the poison," Wenona explained, her face softened as she took in Evander; he looked worn out, he'd slept – but it was restless, haunted even. "Your own injuries have healed well?" As if he could still feel it, Evander's hand traced the scar from the silver.

"They have, thank you."

"A wolf with all nine lives of a cat," Nyda chuckled. "Crow must be seething in her slumber to know each time, she's failed in killing you." Evander bit down on the pulsating flame, the rage he felt whenever he heard that woman's name. "How do you manage to survive her?" Nyda's eyes met his and for once they were kind, playful even – she was always nicer with wine in her hand.

"He's too stubborn to die," Astrid teased, causing them all to laugh.

". . . *T*hey all . . . fall . . . down," Crow sang as Nakoma walked towards the cell, her eyes slid towards him, her tongue scrapping the roof of her mouth; her slimy grin twitching up her lips. "You know, I can never remember the full song, it doesn't matter though – that parts always been my favourite," she admitted.

"I don't care for songs," Nakoma bit. Crow rose the grey nightgown that the healers had put Narrdie in, trailed to the floor; she tilted her head to the side as she looked him up and down.

"Do you have a name Loopin? Please tell me," she purred.

"Nakoma."

"Nakoma, Na-ko-ma," she stretched out the words, seeing how it tasted on her tongue. She bit her lip and looked over him, "Narrdie certainly surrounds herself with attractive playthings. I always thought Loopins looked like, slimy, hairless beasts, but you . . ." She growled with pleasure, her hand stroking along her breasts. "What's your secret? Bribe a witch to make you more human?" Nakoma sneered and fought down the urge to open the cage and beat her to death. "So, do you all take turns fucking Narrdie? Flip a coin? Place bids on who gets her a certain night?" Nakoma laughed, it was soft – vicious.

"You really are bored aren't you," he began. "Doing all you can to taunt anyone who comes in here. Your games are getting old."

370

"I just want some fun," her voice was innocent. *Let me out*, a voice slithered in his ears, he turned around expecting to see something behind him. "What's wrong cutie?" Crow taunted. *Let me out. Let me out of here.* The voice whispered again, it swam around his head; he smirked, and a shield shot up around his mind, a shield of black lightening that cracked like thunder as it struck her – she cringed back.

"Clever," he chuckled. "I would have thought mind tricks were below your level Crow." She shrugged and turned away – her expression now bored.

"Worth a shot. If you aren't here to entertain me, then what do you want?"

"Bring Narrdie back," Nakoma requested. Crow raised a brow, she laughed – the sound bouncing off the walls and echoing around him eerily.

"Why? Do you miss her?"

"You have two choices," he began. "One, bring Narrdie back now."

"Or you'll throw a tantrum?" She teased.

"Two, I torture you from the inside out," he continued, refusing to pay attention to her taunts.

"You'll break your oath," she warned.

"The bond is between Narrdie and me, not you. I bet if I start to burn you alive, only you will feel it." Crow stood and wrapped her fingers around the bar; her tongue snaked out and licked up the cold metal, that choking power beginning to smother the floor around her.

"I dare you."

Chapter Thirty-Four

Everyone & Narrdie

*W*enona waved her hand and more pillows decorated the dining room floor, these ones the colour of vibrant fresh daffodils. "Come sit, if we are going to have this kind of talk. I'd rather everyone be comfortable for once; I always feel so dark and gloomy being huddled around tables."

"Evander, what exactly did Crow say to you?" Sharia asked gently as she sat in front of Erenna; Erenna smiled as she began to plait Sharia's long autumn hair.

"Probably exactly what are all thinking," Nyda announced harshly – downing another glass of wine, Astrid hissed in her direction.

"I think you've had enough Nyda," Astrid warned. Nyda, dared meet her eyes – flinched as Astrid's temper flared in them; she nodded and set down her glass and bowed her head to the Priestesses – a gesture of apology. Astrid tore her gaze away from her and looked back to Evander, the fiery rage softening instantly. "She got in Mazruriuk's head as well." Evander's eyes snapped to her; his brow creased.

"Sweet mother," he breathed and rubbed the back of his neck. "She's getting stronger."

"I told you," Nyda grumbled. "She was just sitting gathering power . . . for years. Soon, she'll be too strong for any of us to control and Narrdie will just fade away." Evander's snarl rippled around the room towards Nyda, the spout of his wine glass crumbling in his hands; he sucked in air to speak, but Wenona raised her hand – silencing him.

"Unfortunately, she is right," Wenona admitted. "A better way of saying it would have been kinder," she spoke in Nyda's direction – causing the Witch to lower her head. "I was hoping we'd have a solution to this, but this goes far beyond any of our power. Narrdie and Crow were a creation that was never meant to happen, a deadly collide of dark and light. The balance was tainted and something so deadly and consumed with so much powerful energy, was created. As cruel as it sounds, Narrdie should not have been born." Audric bit the inside of his cheek as Wenona spoke; he bit down so hard that his tooth pierced his gum.

"But, how is Crow gaining more power than Narrdie?" Audric quizzed.

"Crow doesn't care what she has to do to get what she wants. She'll kill every man, woman and child if they stand in her way of standing on top. Narrdie cares too much, she'll not take a risk if it means someone gets hurt, regardless of it being a friend, family member or a stranger," Erenna added.

"As much as we all love those aspects about her, she is fighting a losing battle. She will never win, if she's not willing to lose," Fyra sniped as she glided into the room, wearing nothing but a thin piece of deep red fabric that barely covered her breasts and backside.

"How do we fix that?" Audric asked.

"Fix what?" Bayona sneered, "Fix the things that make Narrdie, Narrdie? Turn her into nothing but a weapon? No. That's not an option, she is our family!" Astrid placed her hand on Bayona's and offered her a gently squeeze. "We find more people to stand with us, take out Dacre and Crow's army until it's just them too."

"It will not work," Fyra snapped.

"Then what do you suggest?" Bayona roared at her, the venom in her voice spitting out. "Tell us, Priestess of Fire. What's your wise suggestion?" Fyra stared at her in disbelief, Bayona had never attacked the Priestesses like this before.

"Forgive me," Fyra spoke tenderly. "I should not have spoken so harshly." Bayona nodded, breathing heavily as she fought back bloodied tears.

"We have another problem," Ray announced nervously as she wandered in with Mazruriuk. Mazruriuk had a look of stone on his face, her arm gripped tightly in his hand.

Talon had told Mazruriuk everything he'd suspected, the fury on Mazruriuk's face caused the hairs on the back of his neck to stand. "Leave her to me," he'd hissed, his voice full of animalistic rage.

Ray's door was locked, a sign reading – 'do not disturb' – pinned to the soft wood. He scoffed and in one swift kick, broken through her room and sealed it shut behind him, making her scream and jump. "Riuk?" Her voice trembled. He closed the distance between them, backing her up against the wall and placing his hands on either side of her, caging her in.

"Tell me," he'd ordered.

"You're scaring me," she whimpered. She went to move under him, to push him back and demand he leaves, but his hand clamped around her throat – not enough to hurt, but enough to petrify her into talking. He hated every single moment, hated every single fear stricken look she'd given him, hated every little scared whimper she'd let out.

"Speak Rosie," he snapped, his lips pulling back in a snarl.

"OK," she breathed her voice a shuddering whisper.

Mazruriuk shoved Ray forward, staying behind her in case she bolted for the door. "Everyone who is not a member of the Pura Mensam, get out," he snarled, his voice nothing but icy, hot rage – that dark power leaking around him, just enough to make their feet move quicker. "Tell them." He bit towards Ray, as she faced those gathered on pillows.

"Back at Gatherling, when I saw the blood on the ground. After I told you about it I . . . I . . ." She bit her lip and looked down – fidgeting with the skin around her nails.

"Spit it out," Mazruriuk urged cruelly, clenching his jaw as she recoiled.

"I went back." Astrid rose, her face white with fury and shock.

"You went back?" Astrid repeated, "Rosie do you have any idea how dangerous that was?!" Ray flinched.

"I know, but I heard a voice – calling me. They whispered my name, over and over and it led me to the puddle and that's when . . . when I saw him," Ray drifted off again; not meeting anyone's eyes.

"Go on child," Wenona encouraged.

"He's a . . . Shade. The most terrifying Shade I've ever seen; he was wounded badly by Crow," she began in a rush. "He said he wanted to help us . . . that he was a white Shade like Mazruriuk, but his wound was bad, he needed blood to heal . . .so I . . ." She trailed off, not being able to say the words that quivered on her tongue and turned her insides to mush.

Astrid growled, "You, stupid girl! You gave a Shade your blood! Do you have any idea the danger you have put us all in, the danger you have put yourself in?" Her eyes snapped blood red.

"Y-Yes," Ray gulped. "I thought he was good."

"Foolish girl!" Astrid's voice shifted savagely. Mazruriuk grumbled deep in his throat as he moved to stand in front of Ray, pulling her securely behind him – the veins around his eyes darkened as he stared down the Elder Vampire.

"Do not even think to harm her," he warmed darkly.

"Astrid," Audric called, his dagger resting in his hand; he'd never kill her, but he knew how to put her down when she lost control, a lesson she had personally taught him. Astrid tore her gaze away from Ray and set upon Audric – the blade that twinkled from the light, immediately she gasped; her hand rubbed her throat as she sat down – embarrassment sweeping over her face.

"Forgive me Rosie," her voice wobbled, she met Mazruriuk's eyes. "I would never harm her."

"Did he tell you his name, Yollie?" Talon asked, he too had moved protectively towards her.

"Yes. He said his name was Ammon."

"Ammon? Ammon's alive?" Narrdie gasped as she stood in the doorway – Nakoma by her side.

"Narrdie!" Evander and Audric said as one.

Ammon.

The psychotic Shade that slaughtered my mother . . . my real mother and her people, the worst Shade that this earth could have ever spat out. Everyone looked at me with a mixture of bewilderment and I suddenly felt extremely self-conscious that I was still in the half-torn nightgown that Crow had been put in. Nakoma linked his arm through mine and lead me towards one of the ridiculously large pillows, that I hoped would be comfy and inviting – thankfully, I was not disappointed. I winced as I sat down, and Nakoma flashed me another apologetic smile, I smiled back instantly; I didn't blame him for anything.

He'd brought me back. He'd suspected a loophole in the oath and played it out, tortured and tormented Crow, broke and mended her bones, just so he could repeat it over and over, filled her head with years upon years of pain. Until she had no choice but to cower away. Thanks to him, I regained control and the only thing he wanted me to do, was keep it between me and him. Nakoma took a seat beside me and poured me a glass of water, not pulling away until I'd taken a good few sips. "Slowly," he urged, pulling the glass back when I gulped too much.

"Did you just say that Ammon is alive?" I asked again; my voice more aggravated than I anticipated. Evander was eyeing me suspiciously; his eyes surveying every ounce of me and I assumed I looked worse than I thought – I hadn't managed to locate a mirror in this maze of a house.

"Narrdie, it's good to see . . . well you again. How'd you get back?" Nyda asked – a hostile tone clinging to her tongue.

"Nakoma helped me. Tell me about Ammon," I half growled. I didn't care for this tiptoeing that people were seeming to play around me and I really didn't care for them trying to pry me away from this subject. "Ammon killed my mother. Is this the Ammon you are talking about?" My eyes must have been brutal as they burned into Ray's skull – she recoiled from me, burying her face in Mazruriuk's shoulder.

"Yes, it is," Fyra answered, before my stare could boil Ray alive.

"I thought he was dead." My hands began to shake with ire, the hatred I felt for him was like nothing I'd ever felt before and now – he was alive.

"No, he just disappeared," Evander interjected.

"How?"

"That's all I know," Evander sighed. "I do know who might be able to help fill in the gaps however, she always seems to know everything," he chuckled lightly. "Indra."

One by one our gazes landed on Aronnia; her smile turned to the excitement of a child on Christmas day.

"I'll call for her." I jumped up and immediately fell back into the red cushion - wincing and hissed through my teeth, I could feel Evander's eyes land on me, absorbing every movement I made.

"While you wait for this Indra, you need a bath and a long rest," Nakoma announced.

I'd been stuck in that cell because of Crow, for over a week - while everyone else had admired the house and gotten settled in their rooms, forgetting that this place was a ghost to me.

My room looked like it was copied and pasted straight out of a fairy-tale - bigger than my entire house had been. Tiredness had guided my eyes to the bed - my super king-sized four poster bed; my mouth almost drooled at the thought of sleeping in it. The four posts on the bed were made from dark oak, that had been embossed with Nordic symbols and ruins, white veils floated like wandering mist along the inside - offering privacy if needed. The bed was the softest thing I'd ever had the privilege to lie on, a duvet and pillows decorated the mattress - each one cased with golden mink fabric with elegant swirls. Around the room, bookcases consumed the walls, stretching up until it touched the ceiling - each one held a different set of leather-bound books and strange misshapen ornaments. I noticed that each book had been especially picked for me, as they were all subjects that I had wanted to read. I was beginning to believe that I had been given one of the royal rooms as I looked around, the silk drapes - also gold - dropped to the floor, not a single crease tarnished them.

Across the room, opposite the bed, sat a stone carved fireplace, one that reminded me of children's horror stories about cannibal Witches. Vases of freshly picked sunflowers of unusual colours graced the top - reflecting beautifully off the oval mirror that hung above. In the corner of the room sat a deep red, fan back winged chair, made from satin and had a golden trim along the top and bottom edge - a golden pillow in the centre.

I knew it wouldn't be long until he turned up, I could hear his footsteps as they thudded along the hallway, four light taps sounded from my door and a smile lifted up my cheeks. "Come in." Evander crossed the gap between us within seconds, he took me into his arms and placed a deep kiss on my lips and my nose filled with his cedarwood scent - his warm arms tightened around me.

"You scared me," he admitted. "When you went down in the forest, I was so frightened that the venom had gotten to your heart." He leaned into me, his head resting against my own; I winced as his hands hit one of the sore places that had been hurt from Nakoma. Evander paused and eyed me carefully. "Are you hurt?"

"It's nothing," I brushed off casually. Evander pulled me at arm's length; his eyes sliding over my incredulously. He spun my around and lifted my shirt, breathing in harshly as he spotted the bruises that sprinkled along my back, the ones that also matched my ribs and arms.

"Easy way or hard way?" He asked through gritted teeth, I arched my brow at him; he rolled his eyes. "You can either tell me who did this, or I can interrogate every single person in here, until I find out and kill them."

"I'll tell you, but you have to promise that you won't fly off the handle." He clenched his jaw and with a graceful flick of his wrist, motioned me to take a seat on the bed.

"Go ahead, I'll try and keep an open mind. Who?"

"Nakoma-" Before I could say another word Evander jumped up, his eyes as wild as a forest fire.

"The oath?"

"The oath is still intact!" I shouted over his hysterics, he stilled and cocked his head to the side. "Sit or I don't explain." He was hesitant but he'd sat – resting just on the edge of the bed. "The oath is fine, because Nakoma made it with me – not Crow. You and Audric have been saying that me and Crow are not the same person, Nakoma also figured that out. She couldn't break into his head, not like she did with you and Mazruriuk, he'd blocked her out." Evander frowned, he clasped his hands together and leaned forward.

"I think Nakoma, may be more than just a Loopin."

"Me too. He beat the living hell out of her, over and over, the enchantment on the bars stopped her from healing and throwing her full power at him. He said he was doing it for hours on end, until finally she ran back into the box, I keep her in and pushed me to the surface." Evander was silent for a few minutes, piecing together whatever jumbled mess was skipping along his head, finally he spoke and the anger that had laced his voice, was gone.

"Maybe Nakoma is more on our side than we believed, he brought you back and no one told him to do it and I saw him taking care of you early and I mean he generally looked like he cared." I nodded, Nakoma had been so sweet when I came back, he didn't once leave my side. "I hate to say it," Evander continued. "But, Nakoma doesn't need to be watched anymore. He got you back and I'll always be grateful for that," he admitted. Evander's eyes trailed over my face, my lips, before they slowly moved down to the curve of my breasts – I raised my brow flirtatiously, he spoke, his voice a predatory growl. "If you take off your gown, I promise to kiss all those marks better."

$$\smile$$

*M*y heart was leaping, and I could feel a lump forming in my throat as I waited on the tip of my toes for Indra. Indra had left, to return to her own realm, as she did every once in a while, so that the glamour on her would stay strong. It felt like weeks since I had seen her, maybe even months – time had seemed to slip past me, as quickly as sand through my fingers; I hadn't looked at a clock or a watch since leaving for Gatherling. I had missed Indra more than anything – her parting had felt like a piece of me had gone with her and my body jumped with excitement as I felt the ground cower under her feet.

I almost screamed with delight as the glorious glittering Dragon shook her neck; she placed her talon forward and placed her head down – bowing to us all. She nudged Aronnia's arm; her eyes smiling towards her oldest friend. Aronnia's eyes leaked softly – the wind almost wiping them away instantly, she was the first to speak. "Indra, thank the mother you are safe."

"I have missed you," Indra sang. *"I have missed all of you."* I smiled widely, I didn't know until know, how much I needed to hear her voice.

"Are you all rested?" Aronnia asked her. "I'm sorry if my calling you pulled you away from important tasks."

"I have rested well; I know why you've called and I'm afraid I may not be as useful as you are all hoping. Thus, I will tell you what I know." Indra's attention shifted towards Ray – who sheepishly kept her head down. *"Rosie, lift your head up little one. Do not let mistakes take over you, you did what you thought was right."* Her eye's smiled and held onto Ray's for a moment longer, until finally she looked towards me and I felt warmth fill me.

379

"Narrdie Moon, it is lovely seeing you again – I have worried deeply about you. But now you are in front of me, I can see there is nothing to worry about."

"I've missed you Indra, more than I ever thought I would," I admitted and laughed through my nose as she nudged me. Evander stepped forward and Indra met his eyes, they were gently but stern – Evander bowed.

"I'm glad your home safe Indra, but we need you to tell us everything you know about Ammon." Indra's face went cold, nothing but hatred, anger, murder as she heard his name.

"Aronnia filled me in on all the details that Ray has told you. I'm sorry young one, but you were tricked by him. Ammon isn't like any other Shade you've all encountered before. Killing the Mages came at a price, once he killed the lead Mage – your mother – he'd upset the balance in a way no one could have imagined. The power of the Mages backfired and sent Ammon to place, where he was neither living nor dead. He was a Capti Spirit, a creature that has been banished from the spirit world – Sulfaya's realm."

"A Capti Spirit," I repeated – making a mental note to ask the Priestesses if I could use their Library. I tried to imagine what it would have been like, to be trapped for eternity, never feeling the warm of the sun lick your cheeks – the feel of the early mornings icy wind snare at your skin or even the satisfying feeling of a full belly.

"Yes, a Capti Spirit – but with the power of over a hundred Shades, a gift his own kind had granted him for killing the Mages."

"Can someone come back from that?" Nakoma asked; his brows pulled together with worry.

"Back then Shades and Mages were like Gods to humans, they worshipped them . . . feared them and knew never to interfere with their battles. So, when Ammon turned to a Capti Spirit, the humans knew to leave him be." Indra's eyes drifted to Ray, sadness washed over them as she struggled to say the final thing – which we'd all already guessed. "The only way to bring back a Capti Spirit, is for a

human to willingly offer their blood." Ray slumped to the floor; her hand over her chest as she tried to steady her breaths – tears streamed down her face.

"Ray, you didn't?" I breathed. She tried to wipe her tears away, Mazruriuk stared forward; his jaw clenched – not once did he offer her a kind look or a calming brush of affection, I had never seen him this cold – especially with her.

"I-I didn't know who h-he was," she blubbered. "I-I thought he was a good Shade, like Mazruriuk . . . I just wanted to help him," she buried her head in between her knees and wailed. I met Mazruriuk's eyes but there was nothing – no compassion for her, it angered me. I scowled to him as I crouched next to Ray and wrapped my arms around her, she clung onto me – her hands shaking. She may have done wrong, but she was only human, still learning about this world – like I was.

"Ray said he was bleeding, which means she couldn't have brought him back, right?" I asked, Ray looked to Indra – her face full of hope. Indra's eyes flicked back and forwards, her eyes slanted slightly as they swapped looks with Aronnia.

"Narrdie, I examined the sample of blood that Nyda had taken," Aronnia announced, her face dismayed. "My sisters also looked over it, it seems that Ammon had tricked Ray into thinking he was hurt. The blood was glamoured, made to kill anyone who tried to decipher it, made to kill anyone who wasn't . . . human."

"Now that we know that you did give Ammon your blood, it creates a new problem. Ammon will be able to track you, no matter where you go." My blood froze over in my veins. Mazruriuk's hands gripped onto Ray and pulled her to him, all anger he had for her dissolved and was replaced by icy fear.

"He could find her? Now? Here?" He asked, his hands tightening on her protectively.

"No. Not here," Aronnia stated firmly. "Our home is untouchable, hidden from anyone – unless we lift the veil on it." As much as I breathed out in relief, it didn't relax me completely. Ammon the creature that murdered my mother and her people – my family, knew where we were and if we ever wanted to leave – he'd follow.

"Why now?" Evander snarled, "Why would Ammon want to come back now? He could have tried this years ago and he didn't. What makes now so important? Surely, it's not because of the war?"

"The person that Dacre's been hiding behind," I blurted; my eyes closed together as the realisation hit me, like a punch to the face. "It's Ammon. Bayona couldn't see him, because he wasn't a visible being to see." Evander's eyes locked with mine – confirming my theory.

"What does this mean for us?" Sharia whimpered.

"It means once again, we are grievously outnumbered."

'Mages are the supreme source of power in the world, as old as time itself, the Mages protect the balance of the world . . . Mages gain their power from their clan members and their supreme – the Clan leader . . . the strongest Mages reside in the most treasured and valuable clan . . . The Dai Taka clan.'

Evander rapped his fingers on my open door and smiled widely as he peered his head inside, "Good book?" I slipped a hair grip onto the page, so that I didn't lose my place, running my hand over its rough brown cover and placed it on the bedside table – right next to a huge bouquet of sunflowers and daisies.

"I like it. I woke up to these lovely flowers, your doing by any chance?" I asked as I walked over to him and kissed him lightly on the cheek.

"They might have been, I never properly apologised for being a bit of a dick while we were coming here. I asked Erenna if she could mess around with the colours for you, she was more than happy to help."

"A bit of a dick? More like a huge dick," I corrected with a playful smile. He laughed and placed his hands up in surrender.

"Fine, I was a huge dick and I'm really sorry. I really am Narrdie, forgive me?" I kissed him again and my body tingled as his hands wrapped around my waist.

"Of course, I do."

"Good, because I wanted to show you something I think you'll like. It's in my room."

"I've heard that one before," I teased.

Evander's room mimicked mine, except it was a deep orange rather than gold and he didn't have as many bookshelves, his bed was messy – the blanket spilled over onto the floor and the pillows scattered around the mattress. "Tempting isn't it," he grumbled in my ear; his breath hot as it brushed along my neck, he planted a gently kiss along my shoulder, his hand snaking along my waist – sending shivers to ripple around me. "Unfortunately, that isn't why I've brought you here." He spun me around to face his fireplace, unlike mine, there wasn't a mirror above it, but a large oil painting.

The most striking painting I'd ever seen. A woman was stood tall, her hair as white as a doves, waving down past her feet, silver jewels and spirals had been fashioned into a crown atop her head, glittering in the night sky that was painted around her. She was dressed in a faded lilac gown – tight at the waist and flowing everywhere else - revealing parts of her naked body, even in the painting I could tell that it sparkled. Her hands were raised at her sides – almost as if she was dancing when the artist decided to capture her. White tattoos grew up her arms and across her collar bone, they were of nothing in particular – just pretty patterns, making her shimmering coco skin glisten. Her eyes were a mixture of emerald, green and violet and I wondered if men and women had gone to war, just for a slim chance to be swallowed up in that stare. I was lost for words.

"That's Sulfaya," Evander whispered in my ear.

"She's . . . she . . ." I trailed off.

"I know. The mother of all, I've asked for it to be put in your room. I think you'll enjoy it more than I will." I couldn't understand why my eyes had instantly began to tear up as I looked to him. He frowned and lifted his finger to wipe away the water down my cheeks, "Why are you crying?" His face washed over with worry, worry that he'd upset me. I dived onto him and wrapped my hands around him tightly – my head resting on his chest. "Narrdie? What is it?"

"I wish we could just stay like this, normal and happy. I want nothing more than to have a life with you, be happy all the time. Whenever we are happy, I just fuck everything up." He gave me a tight squeeze and wobbled us towards his bed; he gripped onto me before diving us both onto the soft mattress.

"And how have you fucked it up?" He quizzed as he traced little circles along my arms. My heart kicked up; my stomach began dancing and thrashing around and I could feel the hair begin to stick to my neck with nerves.

"I gave my blood to Karro," I blurted.

Evander's fingers froze. I braced myself, waiting for the eruption of screams that was about to pour from him, or perhaps he'd shift into a wolf and shred me apart. Instead, he leaned up and perched next to me; he let out a long breath and slipped his hand into mine. "How'd it happen?" He asked calmly.

"When we found Demir. A Skinner got a hold of Karro and almost snapped him in half, he was going die Evander. It felt like my heart was being torn out, I saw him and then the wolves crying next to him – Oyku's howls of grief, it was unbearable. I-I had to." Evander lifted my chin, his eyes locked with mine and

I was so relieved when he smiled – not a hint of anger in that stare.

"That's understandable. I would have done the same, everyone here would, the main thing that makes you different from Crow – is your heart. However, you need to understand that because of the bond you had with him already, you and Karro are now bonded by blood. Have you read up on this at all?"

"Not yet, I know it comes with issues, but I don't know the ins and outs. Do you?" He nodded and sat up – pulling me closer to him.

"Well, it has good and bad things. The good, is that if needed, you can see through each other's eyes and no matter where you are you'll be able to find each other and sense each other. So, if one of you is scared or needs help – the other will know immediately. The bad part is also the most dangerous, you can feel each other's pain, mentally and physically."

"If I cut my hand . . ."

"His paw also cuts," Evander confirmed. My heart sank, in saving Karro's life – I had just made him number one target for the darkness.

"And if one of us dies, so does the other?" I dreaded the answer.

"No, that part is different," Evander began – the flicker of hope burning again. "If one of you dies, the other will feel the worse kind of pain ever imaginable. It would completely break you and shatter your soul. Your humanity would be lost, and you'd be left an empty shell, left to feel only one thing – pain." I opened my mouth to speak but couldn't find any words. Evander kissed the top of my head and stroked his thumb down my hand – an act of comfort. "Considering who you are Narrdie, it's important we tell only a selected few, ones we trust. Perhaps, one of them can help lower pain connection, make it a bit easier."

"Our inner circle should know," I suggested, Evander's face twisted.

"Not everyone."

Chapter Thirty–Five

I had stayed up late many nights staring at the painting of Sulfaya and wasted many mornings examining every little detail, every strand of her hair, each glimmer of her crown, the sparkles in her dress. It was comforting, it made me feel safe that she was watching over me – almost like she was my own personal guardian as I slept. Even the terror-stricken nightmares, seemed to cower and hide in her presence. Crow never seemed to whisper or even move whenever I was in my room.

I pried my eyes from the mother of all and glanced out the window, it was still pitch black, a glaze of snow had blanketed over the forest, but inside the Priestesses home, the heat never dwindled. Most of the house would still be asleep, excluding the people on watch duty and the Monks – they never closed their eyes. I however, had rested enough.

Evander's room was behind mine, he'd be in bed – lying with the covers off . . . completely naked. I bit my lip at the thought of it, the muscles on his chest – glistening in the heat, imagining his arms – wrapped around my waist, holding me against him. Heat flushed through me and my hand traced along my navel

– daring me to go further. Without another word I sprung out of bed and crept into the hallway, a breathy laugh made me freeze on my toes.

"Narrdie," Talon greeted, his mouth pulling up in a mocking smirk. I jumped and sheepishly smiled to him, could he smell how flustered I was getting. "Going somewhere?" He teased; he arched a brow and looked me up and down. My cheeks burned red – remembering I was wearing nothing but some lace underwear and a sleeveless top that revealed most of my breasts.

"I . . . I . . ." I had no words to shield the embarrassment.

"You were just going to see Evander," he finished for me. "And I, didn't see anything. Have fun," he called as he headed back down the corridor, I could still hear his snickering as I quick stepped towards Evander's room.

Pushing back the embarrassment I'd just felt; I lightly tapped on his door; his gruffly chuckle slipping through the gaps before he swung the door open. My eyes trailed over his body instantly and my knees buckled, he'd slung a sheet around his waist – just enough to cover his bottom half. "Are you aware of the time, Miss Narrdie Moon?" He teased; his voice was raspy – my insides flushed.

"I am, I could leave you, if that's what you really want," I breathed and bit my lip.

"Get in here," he ordered and yanked me inside – locking the door behind him. "Are you here for business . . . or pleasure?" He whispered as his tongue licked my neck – my body shuddered. His hands wrapped around me and began to explore underneath my shirt, I leaned my head back and breathed out hard as his lips kissed down my neck. He growled with approval – the sound rumbling in my ear, in one swift stroke, he tore my shirt clean off me and seconds later his mouth found mine. His arms gripped around me and my legs wrapped around his waist, as he led us to the bed.

Evander's mouth began to work its way down my neck, along my collar and down my chest – his hands cupped my breasts as his tongue teased them – my back arched. My nails clawed down his arms, he looked to me and grinned; his teeth roughly tearing away my thin undergarments. His arms wrapped around my legs – pulling me to him, his mouth moved down and I gasped; my hands digging into the bed sheet.

Evander tickled along my back as I lay across him; my eyes wandered to the new painting that had been placed above his fireplace. The man in the painting was haunting, something dangerous sleeping in his eyes. A steel sword held firmly in his hand – smothered in thick black blood, his mouth was open as he roared, sharp teeth extended. "Who's that?" I enquired as I gestured to the oil painting.

"Lord Kalic Ovareach, one of the strongest Vampire Elders that ever lived. That painting resembles the time he saved an entire town against a horde of Sivvs, back then Sivvs travelled in packs of fifty and they were much worse than they are now." I shivered at the thought. "They had been unleashed, tasked with wiping out the entire town and Lord Kalic lead his own to intercept them, you might know one of his strongest warriors. Astrid." I leaned up and looked at him with shock, before turning back to gape at the painting.

"She was?" I studied the art, trying to picture him fighting beside Astrid; I'd almost forgotten how vicious she could be. Evander laughed.

"Of course, she was. She wasn't going to sit at home and let her father have all the fun." My head snapped towards him – brows raising.

"Her Father?" Evander nodded, "What happened to him?"

"After they defeated the Sivvs, her father through a party in celebration; he announced that once his time reigning was over – Astrid would be his successor. Her brother was furious by this, he thought it was his right to be the next in line; he argued with Lord Kalic, but Lord Kalic called him a coward for not being a part of the battle. Later that night, her brother betrayed them – gathered up followers and slaughtered them in the night. Lady Odette – Astrid's mother – lead Astrid to a secret exit in the castle, while Lord Kalic tried to fight them off; he was beheaded. Lady Odette did what she could in order to give Astrid time to get away, but she was no warrior and he took out her heart."

"He killed his own parents out of jealousy?" Evander nodded.

"Times were different back then, it was all about power, who wants it, who has it and who will kill to take it over. Her mother had ordered Astrid to flee, but you know Astrid; she couldn't leave – not while her family were in danger. She came back for them, but her brother had put their heads on pikes; he wanted to make an example out of them. She's always sworn that she'll go back one day and tear his heart out." Evander met my eyes and sternly warned me. "Astrid has always fought herself a coward for running, even though she knows her brother has ten times the strength she has. It upsets her very deeply; it is why she has never and will never speak about her past – please never mention or ask her about it."

"Astrid is anything but a coward."

"I know, but she doesn't see it like that. Just promise to never mention this, it's why the Priestesses removed it from her room and put it in mine – the memory is too painful for her."

"Where is he now?"

"Hidden. Hidden away with his followers, makes you wonder who the actual coward is."

"I feel sorry for her brother, if she ever gets a hold of him. You don't piss off Astrid and expect a happy ending," I chuckled, and Evander laughed his agreement.

*K*ylene – one of the Priestesses warriors – knocked on my door; she was dressed in her usual white plated armour with a purple cape; her golden hair fashioned in one long neat braid. She smiled, her green eyes lifting and bowed automatically, I had to hold in my urge to beg her to not do that. "Everything alright Kylene?" I asked in a cheery tone.

"Forgive me for interrupting you, Lady Narrdie-" I held up my hand, cutting her off.

"Kylene, please just call me Narrdie."

"OK . . . Narrdie," she repeated lightly – testing how it felt. "Indra has asked me to come and find you, she would like to speak with you. However, she said you would be in your room reading," Kylene's eyes drifted to the open books that covered my bed and she half-smiled. "She wants you to know that there is no rush, come and see her after you've finished."

"Thanks, Kylene, but I don't mind going to see her now. I have plenty of time for reading, in fact I read so much that I could probably recite it all word for word. Where is she? Outside?" Kylene's cheeks lifted as her smile widened, the type of smile that was infectious.

"Indra is in her room." I stared blankly at her, not sure if I'd misheard what she'd just said. Indra was a Dragon – a big

Dragon with a long ass tail, how on earth could she have a room. "Narrdie?"

"She has a room?"

"Of course. My Lady Priestesses would never permit anyone to sleep outside, besides this is also Indra's home when she has left her realm."

"Indra?" I questioned as I squinted my eyes at her; she had to be making a joke.

"Yes."

"Indra, the Dragon?" She breathed out heavily and stifled a laugh.

"Yes, Indra the Dragon."

"Indra, with her large wings and swishy tail?" Kylene bit the inside of her cheeks, she nodded. "Aronnia's Indra?"

"Yes. Indra the Dragon. Indra, Aronnia's friend, the Indra that brought you to Gatherling." I perched my lips and arched my brow as I looked to her, her eyes were beginning to water.

"Alright, I get it. Very funny."

"Thank you, I do try," she mocked with an innocent smile.

"Where is her room?"

"You know the building behind this one? The second biggest?" I nodded. "That's her room, it's where she sleeps when she's in this realm."

Indra's room looked like a barn – only ten times bigger and there was no hay or overwhelming smell of farm animals that lingered on your clothes. The walls were painted a salmon colour, the floor covered with shiny wood flooring, the back wall had been stripped and a waterfall – spilling into a pool – was put in its place. Indra was sprawled out on a blanket of sky-blue pillows and unstained feathers; her eyes smiled at me as she looked up.

"Hello Narrdie," she greeted then shuffled her body, so I could sit beside her – the ground shaking slightly as she moved. *"The first time we spoke, you said you loved these, so I asked for some to be brought."* She flickered her tail lightly, pushing a small basket of strawberries towards me.

"Thank you," I said – trying to hide the saliva that came from my mouth as my greedy eyes slid to them. "The first time we talked, that seems like a lifetime ago." Indra laughed, the feathers wisping up as her body jittered.

"I thought you'd want to talk; you have been quiet since we learned about Ammon." Goosebumps pimpled my skin and a sudden chill captured my bones.

"Ammon," I repeated, his name tasted vile on my tongue. "The King of Shades. The most powerful Shade to every walk this earth, was brought back because he tricked a human."

"Are you angered by Rosie's actions?" I laughed sarcastically.

"No. I would be a hypocrite if I did, we've all make grave mistakes. In fact, I feel nothing but worry and sadness for her; she's being so tough on herself and Mazruriuk . . . I'd never seen his so cruel like that – especially with her." I frowned, thinking back to Ray cowering and weeping on the floor, the way Mazruriuk didn't bother to comfort her – the fury that burned in his eyes. "Promise me, that you won't think I'm a total wuss?" Indra tilted her head, inclining me to continue. "I'm frightened. More than I've ever been." Indra's eyes softened as she leaned her neck down; her eyes meeting mine.

"When we catch fear, we must face it – conquer it, before it can be released. If we don't it will swallow us up like the sea and we'd be lost forever. This life was forced upon you, it may not be what you wanted or what you asked for, but it's the life you now have to deal with. You are not alone in all of this; you have every person inside – your family. You must remember that they did not choose this path either, they are just walking it and trying to find a new one. We have lost many along the way, sorrow has washed down these walls, but so has happiness, laughter – love. We may be preparing for a war Narrdie, but we must always give ourselves the freedom to be happy and to never feel guilty for it either."

"Thank you for this Indra." She nuzzled her snout against my arm and I leaned my head against hers. "Kylene said you wanted to talk to me." Indra's eyes dropped.

"Yes. It is time that I return to my realm, permanently. I am an Elder to my own kind and have a duty to protect them, therefore I cannot join you in this battle – no matter how much I wish it." My heart dropped into my stomach, I tried to hide the devastation I felt – I didn't want her to feel as sad as she already was.

"Oh," was all I managed to say, I kicked myself for it.

"You are upset." It wasn't a question, but I answered – my voice quivered.

"Not with you, I understand completely that you have to do what's right for your own. It's just . . . I'm starting to think that we won't be able to win this," I admitted reluctantly.

"Narrdie Moon, whether I was here or not – doesn't matter. Look how far you've come; you have developed your mind so quickly to adapt in our world. Harvested so much strength, power and never let the human part in you die. You have the heart of your mother; you should wear it with pride." She batted her head against my shoulder, pushing me into the mountain of pillows, over and over until eventually – I laughed.

"I surrender," I giggled. "It would have been awesome to have a Dragon fight with us." She chuckled. I met her eyes, something glazed over them – a secret she was too heartbroken to share. My gut twanged and I felt my chest burn. "You're not coming back, are you?"

"No. Once I'm in my realm I must seal the passage – forever," she replied, her voice shaky.

"Why?" I could barely speak.

"The balance in this world is faulting, in order to protect my own, I must close it off. I will not be able to return here, and no one will be able to come to me. I have talked with the Priestesses and the Order has confirmed, once this war is done – all realms and tears will be closed." I had no words, couldn't muster up a sentence without my voice breaking and sobs streaming. Instead, I nodded and wrapped my arm around her; she leaned her head into me. *"I will miss you Narrdie Moon, you have touched my heart like no other."*

"I'm really going to miss you, Indra," I whispered through tears. A bid drop of water splashed down into my lap – completely drenching me. I glanced to her. "Are you crying?" I asked, she breathed out heavily and turned her head away – a loud sneeze rolled from her nose as the sound of more tears splashed onto the floor.

Saying goodbye to Indra was one of the worst things I'd had to do, each second felt like a dagger was slowly being plunged in my heart. I was stood outside with Erenna, Wenona and Aronnia – her hands shaking, as her eyes fought back tears. "Where is everyone else?" I asked, the yard was completely empty – even the guards had vacated.

"They've said their goodbyes," Aronnia explained softly; her voice was weepy, and I could tell she was trying not to look at any of us. Indra bowed her head to Wenona before she spoke.

"Wenona, thank you for accepting me into your home, you have been more than friends to me – you have been my family." Wenona placed her hand across her chest and bowed.

"I wish you a safe journey my friend, may the mother watch over you and guide you, until we meet in the realm of spirits," Wenona recited with a fragile smile; she stroked her hand down Indra's cheek and placed her forehead against hers. Erenna mimicked the same movement, saying her own words before they both headed back inside – arms linked around each other.

"Narrdie Moon," I stepped forward; bracing myself for the round of tears that waited in the corner of my eyes. *"Remember what I told you, be brave and always follow your heart – even if the darkness shadows over it."* I swallowed hard, the movement feeling like sharp talons scrapping down my throat and hugged her gently.

"I will." I held onto her for a few more lingering moments, which I wished would never end – before I headed back inside and gave Aronnia time to say farewell to her oldest and most loyal friend.

Chapter Thirty-Six

I sat in woolly purple PJs, with white polka dots and my favourite yellow duck slippers, admittedly they looked ridiculous, but they had always kept my toes from falling off in harsh winters. A cup of hot chocolate – with cream and a dozen tiny marshmallows – sent warmth through my chilly fingers.

Audric sprawled out beside me; he rolled around on my bed, still laughing at the dirty joke I'd just told him. "I never thought you would be the sort to tell jokes like that," he said through a muffled cough. "I almost choked on my chocolate."

"You'll choke on your chocolate, because you scoff it down like an animal!" I snapped playfully as I kicked my leg towards him; he gripped it tightly, pulled my slipper free and wiggled his fingers along the bottom of my foot. I squealed and frantically thrashed my leg around, trying to get free from his constant tickling – my hot chocolate flying out the mug. "Audric! Let go!"

"Serves you right, I'll teach you to try and kick your Watcher," he grumbled through laughter. "No one will save you now!"

"Audric, please!" I begged, my throat burned from laughing – I felt like I was hyperventilating; my hands slammed down on his back, punching and slapping. "I can't breathe," I gasped.

"This little piggy went to market ... this little piggy went, wee, wee, wee!" He sang, snagging my toes between his fingers and shaking it around.

"I surrender!" He let go and slapped my foot away from him; he raised his hands in the air as he rolled onto his back and cheered.

"That's right, Audric is the king. You don't have to admit it, I know it's true." I rolled my eyes and chucked my pillow at his head; he raised his brow. "You wanna go again?"

"Don't start with me Audric," I warned.

"Please, you bring that foot near me again and I'll break those little sausages you call toes and feed them to Karro," he cautioned as he squirmed his fingers towards me. I firmly tucked my feet under my blanket and stuck my tongue out at him – he rolled his eyes and slumped down onto the floor, observing all my books. "You know, when you read one, you could always put it back after," he suggested.

"You a librarian now? I'm comparing them all, the facts and the myths." His hand reached out and chose one at random, flipping it over and reading its description.

"Reading up on your Shades? Why don't you just go and ask Mazruriuk?" I dove underneath the covers, scooting myself around, until my head popped out beside him. "You're trying to learn about Ammon," he guessed.

"We're facing an enemy that no one knows anything about, doesn't that worry you?" Audric's lips made a grim twist, he cast the book back into the pile and leaned his head back.

"Of course, it does, but it's not like we can just walk up to him and ask." A chilling idea began to grow, an idea that could end one of two ways. I tilted my head towards him, instantly he groaned and retreated behind a pillow. "Whatever you're thinking, just stop," he mumbled through the muffle of duck feathers. I jumped on his back, wrapping my hands around his neck like a koala.

"But you haven't even heard my idea."

"Because I know you and I know it's going to be stupid and dangerous," he half chuckled as he tried to buck me off like a donkey.

"Oh, it most definitely will be," I assured him, he grimaced. "But either way I'm gonna do it and as my best friend-"

"Oh no! Don't do that, not the whole – as my best friend – thing!" He stood up and before he could move, I wrapped my arms and legs around his leg. Audric chortled, "you child, get off me!"

"Not until you listen!" He waved, shook and tossed his leg around madly, doing anything he could think to shake me off. "I'll bite you," I warned.

"No, you won't – ah!" He groaned as I sank my teeth into his calf. "Release me demon!"

"Will you listen? Or will I have to take a chunk out of your leg?" He held up his hands in surrender, smugly I opened my arms, allowing him to move; his hand rubbing the bite. "It wasn't that hard, don't be a baby."

"It was hard," he grumbled until his breath.

"Wimp. OK, just sit and listen, because once I tell you, I'm gonna need you to really help me."

"Help you with what?"

"To convince Evander."

$Evander$ was silent longer than I anticipated, I didn't know if that was better or worse than him screaming the place down. He raised a questionable brow towards Audric, who just shrugged and glared towards me. "Instead of having a private conversation with your eyebrows, say something." I urged him sternly, even if he disagreed – I was still going to do this.

"I'm just trying to figure this out. You want to go in a part of the forest, away from here and call for Dacre?" He asked, repeating what I had just told him.

"Yes."

"In the hope that he'll tell you about Ammon?"

"Yes."

"But he'll be thinking he's telling Crow?"

"Yes, because you'll both help me look like her." Evander rubbed his temples, he looked to me – hard, like he was trying to reach into my head and sift through the mess in my mind.

"You know looking like her won't work on its own. You'll have to act like her, talk like her – smell like her, otherwise he'll know. How do you expect to do that?" I chewed on my lip, this was the part I was afraid of, this was the part where his temper would burst through his skin. As if it was written in pen on my face, his nostrils flared and eyes widened. "You can't be serious? You're going to tap into the darkness's power?"

395

"Just enough to trick him. I can contain it and if I feel like it's slipping then you and Audric will be there to end the meeting. We can even put others around the area, just in case." Evander drummed his fingers on the table, he watched me for a few breaths, his eyes switched to Audric.

"What's your take on this?"

"I think she's mental," he began, I clenched my jaw. "But, I also think she's one of the bravest we have, who else here has blood oathed a creature like Nakoma and formed an alliance with Loopins, created a bond with sanctuary wolves and made our numbers rise by the hundreds? And, I've never known anyone to spit at a Shade." A proud smile pulled at my lips, remembering Egregious's fury; I looked to Audric, feeling a lump forming in the back of my throat. Evander raised his brows, amusement dancing behind those orange eyes.

"You spat at a Shade?" I perched my lips together and a laugh rumbled in my throat. "Alright. We'll do this." I blinked at him several times, bewildered.

"Really?" He nodded and I tilted my head, sensing the word on the tip of his tongue. "But?"

"But we called Dacre here. We stand outside the glamour and have the Priestesses and everyone else inside the glamour, that way if he tries any of his sneaky tactics – we'll be ready."

"How do we even summon Dacre?" Audric asked, sucking away the excitement that has burst into me. "None of us know how to even find him."

"I do." Evander and Audric both looked to me, waiting. "We need to go back to Gatherling."

*E*vander was tense, so tense that he had stayed in his own room the past few days, fearing his jerking and sleepless nights would keep me awake. I understood why, we were going back to his home, the home that now lay in ashes and debris. "You could stay here," I offered as he tightened the strap on the sheath holding one of my twin blades. "You don't have to put yourself through this." He pulled it once more, I flinched as I felt it pinch at my thigh, before he stood and cupped my face.

"I don't care about Gatherling, it's nothing but rubble and dust, you're the one I care about and I'll be damned if I watch someone else lead you away." He flicked my nose lightly and before I could say anything, his lips brushed mine. He spun me around and began to double check the buckles on my leather breastplate.

"We ready?" Audric asked as he leaned against the door, my eyes widened as I took him in. The doubled edged sword in his hand, throwing knives around his thigh, the sleek black crossbow fixed on his back and the two swords hanging from his belt.

"We're not going for a battle Audric, is all of that really necessary?" He raised his brow and lazily pointed a finger towards Evander – who was now equally armed to the teeth. "Seriously?"

"You never know what's leering around the corner, we could get there and it could be swarming," Evander argued. I rolled my eyes and signalled them outside.

"At least someone will be able to protect Audric when he sees a mouse."

"I heard that!" He shot back.

"Well, I didn't whisper it," I mocked.

Astrid and Bayona were waiting for us, along with Karro and Oyku, Astrid gave each of us a tight hug and wished us a quick and safe journey. Bayona skipped forward, a wide smile on her face. "So, thanks to the Priestesses and the Monks, if you drink this," she handed us two bottles each, of a black thick liquid. "Before you leave and before you head back, you'll be able to Lacus there, without being tracked. I'm not sure how it will taste, but careful the smell doesn't knock you sick – it has quite a stink."

Audric didn't give it a chance to reach his nose, he flicked open the cork and downed it in one; he hunched over, groaning and retching. "Fuck me, that's disgusting!"

"Language!" Astrid hissed. "Evander, Narrdie, drink up." Evander turned to me, his eyes daring me to go first. I made the mistake of letting the fumes float up and sieve into my nose, Bayona wasn't lying. It smelt of moulding food, animal waste, decaying meat and sewage – all wrapped into one tiny bottle. A wave of coughs pulled at my throat and I had to stop myself from punching Evander in the stomach, when his cackling echoed in my ears. I squeezed my nose together with my fingers and shot it into my mouth, my instant reaction would have been to spit it out and vomit all over the snow. I slammed my foot on the floor as I swallowed, joining in with Audric as I too, hunched over and fought back the sickness – Evander joining us merely seconds later.

"That's vile," I winced. "It's like medicine and mouldy juice."

"I feel like I've just drank something from the backend of a horse," Audric grumbled.

"Why is it spicy?" Evander added.

"Spicy?" Audric and I asked him at the same time, Evander gave us a confused look before shaking off the taste.

"Never mind, let's go." Karro padded beside me, his tail up and ears alert, I paused and jumped in front of him.

"Karro, na! Bon catar cema won is," I told him sternly, Karro bared his teeth in protest. *"I'm sorry Karro, you just can't this time. Wolves can't Lacus jump, do me a favour and keep an eye on everyone. Watch the forest."* I looked to Oyku for help, he whined as she brushed her head under his chin, nipping at his cheeks softly, Karro nibbled her back and sat beside her; his head lowering in a bow.

"Come on," Evander called after me.

I'd jumped us to the only place around Gatherling I knew, the spot on the hill, where Audric had brought me, Audric met my eyes – a knowing look glazing over his own. The forest had become a maze of snow and ice, sprinkling along the tree branches – dusting the leaves, it was all so pure, untouched. It seemed a shame to disturb it, to soil it with our footprints, to hear it crunching under our boots, I almost jumped us back home. As much to my displeasure, we moved forward, my heart already bracing itself for the shock and hurt I'd see when we arrived at Gatherling – no doubt we'd be visiting a ruin. "You sure it's in there?" Audric asked, as we stood outside the mound of crumbled cement, powdered ash and scorched wreckage.

"Positive, I can feel it." Even standing outside, I could hear its ghostly whispers, the thrumming of it vibrating up my feet, the dark power choking me.

"You can feel it?" Evander repeated, eyeing me carefully; I nodded, not daring to meet his stare. "When did that start happening?" He asked, his tone beginning to tighten.

"The moment I took it off."

"And you kept it from us – from me? What else are you not telling me, Narrdie?" I took a step towards the crumpled entrance. Evander's hand snatched out and wrapped around my arm, his grip was hard, I felt the pain of his fingers beginning to bruise my skin. Audric ripped my arm free and pulled me behind him, anger flared in his eyes.

"Leave her be, Evander," he warned. "She doesn't have to explain herself to you or anyone else. She's her own person."

Evander scoffed. "She may be her own person, but there is also someone else inside and they are not as separate as we think. Right, Narrdie?" My heart stung as it began to beat faster, he knew – he knew that Crow could talk to me.

"H-How?" I asked, my voice wobbling.

"How what? How do I know that you and Crow have been having little talks in your head?" Audric stilled, his breathing raspy; he tilted his head in my direction. "She didn't tell you either?"

"It doesn't matter," Audric snarled.

Rage exploded in my vision, the anger bursting in my veins – clogging up my throat, I shoved my way past Audric, until I was only inches away from Evander. "You think I wanted that? To have her swimming around in my head, whispering on how pathetic I was, how the only thing I was destined for was to die? How I had no power and could only stand by as I watch everyone, I love slaughtered?" A muscle feathered in his jaw and his eyes softened. "I couldn't stop her, I couldn't shut her out, no matter how hard I tried and believe me Evander – I tried." I pushed him hard, slamming my fists into his chest.

"Narrdie," Evander began, my voice cut through his.

"So, forgive me if I didn't rush to tell you how screwed up, I was. Typical Narrdie, right? How is she meant to fight in a war, when she can't even win the one in her head." Tears ran down my face, I didn't bother to wipe them away, I wanted him to see the pain I had endured – the never-ending torment that played in the mess, that was my mind. Audric rested his hand on my back, steading me, letting me know that he was there.

"Narrdie," Evander's voice was quiet, his eyes dropped to the floor. "Narrdie, I'm sorry."

"Let's just get what we came for."

The night had fallen over us by the time we managed to clear enough room to get inside, a lump had formed in my throat, as I took in the place, I once called home. The painted walls, were now black, charred from the fire, soot and ash covering the white tiled floor, beside me, I heard Evander's breath shudder. I took his hand in mine, yes, I was still furious with him and yes, once we'd returned to the Priestess's home, we'd have it out. However, there were times when it was important to put arguments aside and this was one of those times – he needed me. His hand squeezed mine, a way to say he was grateful. "I can't tell which way," I said, my voice a breathy whisper.

"Over here," Audric called. He'd positioned himself in front of us, his double-edged sword grasped tightly in his hand; he kicked his leg out, moving the fallen frames and art – that I used to stand and gaze at – to the one side. "Narrdie, your room. I'll go and check the rest of the place is clear," he offered, I knew he was giving me and Evander privacy; he caught eyes with Evander, a warning in his stare.

"Do you want me to go in first?" Evander asked.

My door was still closed, the door still white, immaculate. "The fire didn't touch it, it's like it just went past it. Ignored it completely." Around the outside of the door, the flames had hit, but not one spec had even dared to graze the white surface. I took a deep breath and twisted the handle, a shudder tickled up my spine. My room was still exactly how I left it, shredded apart from the dark power that had erupted from me.

"What happened?" Evander asked gently, he could see it on my face.

"Before I left," my voice was barely even a squeak, I coughed, a feeble attempt at trying to clear my throat. "Before I left, I felt it – the ring, it was trying to pull me back to it. Felt the pulse screaming in my ear, drowning out everything else and I couldn't make it stop. It was like it was forcing everything inside me to the surface, I screamed and . . ." I trailed off, my hand resting at my throat.

"It tapped into your power," Evander finished.

"Yes," I breathed. "I couldn't stop it; I closed the door because I didn't want anyone to see . . . I didn't want you to see. I was afraid that you'd lock me away." Evander spun me to face him, his hand lifting my chin until his eyes met mine.

"I would never lock you away, never. It killed me to be apart from you, I won't let that happen." I moved to pulled away, but his grip pulled me back. "I won't let that happen," he repeated softer. I nodded and moaned, as pain shot through me, like lightening under my skin, I grabbed hold of Evander's arms – using him to keep myself up. "Steady there." I winced and pointed towards the split dresser, my hands trembling.

"It's there."

"OK, sit here." He flipped over the green armchair and carefully helped me to it; I groaned and retched over, feeling like I'd been repetitively punched in the gut. Evander pulled back the dresser, he reached down; his fingers brushed the ring and a blistering wave of pain burst into me. I shrieked, collapsing from the chair and curling up on the floor.

"Stop!" I begged, my nails clawing at my chest. Evander was beside me in an instant, his hands restraining mine.

"AUDRIC! Easy, baby, easy. AUDRIC!" The pain kept coming, whipping me over and over; I thrashed and struggled against Evander's hold. "You're alright, shh, I've got you."

Audric shot into the room, breathing hard. The second he saw me, his sword dropped from his hands. "What happened?"

"Help me!" Evander yelled.

Audric dropped to his knees, his hands holding my legs still. "What the fuck happened?"

"The second I touched the ring, she started screaming. There you go," Evander soothed, as my pain began to ease. "Just breathe slowly, Audric get the ring – behind the dresser, but don't touch it. Use one of those bed scraps." Evander helped me to sit up, sweeping my hair free from my face; his eyes racked over me. He looked back to where Audric stood, the ring wrapped up in a cloth and a chilling look on his face. "Got it?"

"Yeah, fucking Dacre, piece of shit must have had it glamoured, so that only Narrdie can touch it." Audric cautiously tucked it into his pocket, "can we leave now?" He helped me to my feet and slung his arm around my waist. "Let's go home."

I paused, the thrumming leaving my ears, the sound of chittering and high-pitched tweets echoed in the air. "Birdsong?"

"Not birds," Evander whispered, signalling me to stay quiet; he pulled one of his swords into his hands – Audric freeing his own from its covering. "Nymphs."

"Skittish little things," Audric added, a sneer in his voice.

"True, but if they see we have something valuable, they'll swarm like flies," Evander said; his eyes flicking around the area.

"Whose side are they on?" I winced.

"Anyone who can offer them something shiny."

Chapter Thirty-Seven

*B*y the time we returned, the snow was falling from the sky once more – dancing and twirling in the air like pixies. "Here they come," Audric whined. Right on que, people began to spill out of the Priestesses home, a mixture of worry and unnerved expressions on their faces.

"What happened?" Astrid called over, she ran towards us and took me into her arms, guiding me over to Bayona. Her hands began to glow as she scanned them over me – searching for any lingering injuries.

"Dacre glamoured the ring," Evander growled, his eyes fixed on me, not moving until Bayona nodded that I was fine.

"Let me see it," Bayona inquired, her hand outstretched.

"Careful not to touch it," Audric advised, placing the cloth in her hand.

"Is that how Narrdie was hurt?" Fyra asked, her face was twisted in a statement I couldn't read. She leaned casually against one of the stone pillars; her arms crossed along her chest.

"Yeah, how'd you know she was hurt?" Audric asked. My head whirled in her direction; my eyes widened as I shot to my feet.

"Karro." Fyra's eyes softened as they met mine, she nodded once and offered me a gentle smile. "He felt it, where is he? Is he Ok?" Fyra pushed herself off the wall and raised her hands in a calming motion, she closed the distance between us and brushed my shoulders.

"Calm Narrdie, calm. He's alright, just a little sore. He's resting, Erenna is with him." She took my face in her hands. "I promise you, he's well." Fyra had shocked the panic out of me, she'd never shown this much kindness, this much care to anyone but her sisters. "The house knows about your link with Karro," Fyra cautioned, her Animo for my ears only. *"Proceed with care, I fear not everyone is with us. I will do what I can for you."*

"Do you think Dacre has people inside?"

"I do, but I cannot work out who. Keep your wits about you and your secrets locked away."

I wanted to throw up the minute I looked in the mirror. I had to remind myself that the icy blue eyes staring back at me, were my own and not hers, the purple veins that had stretched like cobwebs along my skin, were mine - not hers. "Well?" I was almost afraid to ask. Evander surveyed me, walking around in a circle; he laughed - a harsh bark and rubbed the back of his neck.

"It's perfect, eerily perfect," he admitted. "How do you feel?"

"Wrong." I looked towards Audric and Nakoma, they were both frozen, stunned. "Stop that," I snarled towards them. "Stop looking at me like I'm her." Audric dropped his gaze guiltily, he gave me an apologetic smile.

"You are her," Evander blurted, his face was masked in shadow and his eyes empty. "For the next hour or two, you are her. You will look like her, you will smell like her and you will speak like her. Dacre will ogle you, torment you and you will play along." Fire burned through me, almost choking as his words ignited the rage I was already beginning to feel. "You will play the part and he will believe you, because you are smarter than him Narrdie." He stopped walking as he came face to face with me, his eyes didn't falter, didn't shudder as he looked to me and I realised he wasn't seeing Crow like the others were – he was seeing me. "You've got this, don't you?" I nodded and lifted my chin, he winked and signalled in the wolves. "Have a smell."

Karro and Oyku took their time, sniffing every part of me, finally they pulled back and moved to sit beside Audric. *"She does not smell right,"* Oyku said. *"She does not smell like our Narrdie Moon."*

"Good, there's just one thing missing."

My hands were damp by my sides, I kept rubbing them on the torn grey dress – which had my breasts almost popping from the seems – to try and dry away the sweat. Bile burned my throat.

"From now on, we will only speak like this, no one is to make a sound," Evander ordered us all, he was waiting in between the trees, hidden with Audric in the shadows, while everyone else – waiting just behind the glamour. *"Whenever you're ready Narrdie."*

I took a few breaths to compose myself, ready to act into the skin I wore, I lifted my hand towards my view, the ring twinkling in the in the light. "I've got this," I told myself sternly, willing my nerves to vanish. I brushed my thumb along the knots of the ring, feeling a sudden pulse vibrate through me, almost instantly the air shifted, the forest silent and I felt like the world was changing underneath my feet.

I heard his cruel, insufferable snicker before he showed himself; his eyes rolled over me and I'd suddenly felt naked under his stare; he smiled – a smile dripping with venom. "Hello, pretty bird." I forced my own eyes to seductively gaze over him, taking in the exposed chest peeking between his black shirt, I bit my lip and tilted me head.

"Hello, my love," I purred, yet it wasn't my voice – it was feral, animalistic and dark. Black tendrils swirled around my feet, my black nails growing sharp. "How I've missed you."

"I expected to see Narrdie standing here, you can imagine my surprise." I pouted and brushed my hand up my leg, exposing my bare thigh.

"You sound disappointed, do you no longer burn for me?" Dacre arched his brow, his eyes dropping down to my breasts, my visible thigh; he growled his approval. I was definitely going to be sick.

"You know I only desire you; I'll devour you right here – if you wish me to prove it." Panic pinned my heart, I didn't want him anywhere near me, let alone touch me. "If only time was on our side, I assume you left some devastation when you took over?" A smirk pulled at my lips and a murderous cackled slipped from my tongue; I shrugged innocently.

"I was only playing with them; I didn't mean to break my toys." Dacre laughed and clapped his hands, he stepped closer to me, I had to force back the urge to recoil from him. "Will you play with me?"

"Once we get you back, I'll spend all night playing with you," he grumbled. Wrong, wrong, wrong.

Another laugh reached my ears, cold, bitter and haunting. My blood froze, my heart dropped into my stomach and the hairs on the back of my neck rose.

"Dacre, if you'd stop thinking with your member, maybe you'd be able to see when you are being made a fool." I knew that voice. I had heard it before; it had spoken to us through the shadows of a park – the same night Egregious had first attacked us.

"Narrdie, get out of there." Audric ordered me, I could hear the panic in his voice, he remembered.

He stepped into the open and I knew instantly it was him, I could feel the sudden excitement that radiated through me from Crow, her claws trying to force their way through.

Ammon.

His frightening eyes – the mixture of yellow and blood orange holding me in place, the thick white veins that spiralled and formed into strange tribal patterns and the large seven-pointed symbol that tattooed his bold head. He grinned widely, a yellow toothed smile – that looked too big for his face; he traced his black tongue along them and laughed once more. "Dacre, Dacre, Dacre, allow me to show you." He waved his hand in the air and a gust of wind blew over me, causing me to stumble back.

My glamour, Crow's glamour – was gone and once again I looked like myself. Dacre's eyes overlapped with a fiery rage; he bared his teeth. "You sneaky little bitch," he snarled.

"Narrdie Moon," Ammon sang. "You two can come out now."

Audric and Evander were instantly by my side, their weapons drawn and faces intense, Evander pulled me back, shielding me behind him and Audric. *"Karro, have the wolves fall back and surround Ray, keep her comfort and keep her safe,"* Audric ordered, not taking his eyes from Ammon.

"C-Can he . . . can he see or hear us?" Ray whimpered, I could hear the terror shaking in her voice, she was petrified. No one dared respond, not as Ammon began to circle around the glamour; his eyes tore away from me, his mouth cut a cruel line.

"What other things are you hiding, Narrdie Moon?" He asked, my voice sounding like a purr on his tongue. "You may be able to hoax Dacre, but I am far older, my sweet." Ammon's lips pulled back over his teeth, he thrust his hand out, a sound like static thundering in my ears, as his fist punctured the glamour. The veil quaked, black fire exploded along it – shattering and consuming everything in its path, until it was nothing more than ashes – crumbling to the floor like burnt paper.

Ray sucked in air and her hand covered her opened mouth; her breathe kicked up and she whimpered as she grasped onto Mazruriuk's arm. Mazruriuk pulled her behind him, blocking her from Ammon's hate filled eyes.

Talon and Illythia appeared beside them with in-human speed, their eyes the colour of rubies and bold; their fangs fully extended over their bottom lips – each tooth razor sharp. Their skin had gone as pale as a corpse, cheeks grey and thin; they looked spine chilling, the terrifying beasts they were stereotyped to be. "You do not leave our side," Illythia told Ray, her voice like a cluster of wandering whispers.

"That's better, we can see each other now. Look Dacre, the gang's all here," Ammon sang, his sinister smile spreading widely across his face – a hiss rolled from my tongue. "Narrdie Moon," he called, turning back to me. He'd turned his back on everyone, almost like he knew none of them would dare try anything, perhaps he did know – perhaps he could taste the fright in the air. Ammon looked me up and down, he rubbed his chin and scoffed. "You're the spitting double of your mother."

I lunged forward with a ferocious snarl, longing to tear that grin from his face and keep tearing until there was nothing left of him. Nakoma dropped down from the tree above me, he crashed into me; his hands pinning me tightly against him.

"Don't Narrdie," he whispered in my ear.

"Let go of me!" I demanded.

"Not like this," he breathed – hands tightening around me. "Not yet, breathe." I stopped resisting and took a second, expecting him to let me go – he didn't.

"Temper, temper Crow," Ammon hummed before laughing, Dacre smirked.

"Don't call me that!" I spat.

"Stop talking," Nakoma hissed.

"Why are you here?" Astrid snarled towards him, her hand leaning back for Bayona. "Narrdie didn't call for you."

"Ah," Ammon raised his brow, slowly tilting his head at her. "But I have come calling for her."

"Why?"

"I need to talk to her," he announced casually.

"Then talk," Sharia blurted, she was stood beside Ameer and a handful of Monks, each one with their weapons in hands. Ammon's eyes lazily swooped to her.

"What a brave little Changer," he purred. "I want to speak to Narrdie - alone. What we have to say is for her ears only."

Audric laughed humourlessly. "And we're just supposed to bow down and allow you to do that? You Capri scum." Ammon's face turned deadly as he looked to Audric; his whole hand shifting into one scaled talon.

"You're going to regret that," he promised, as he crouched low.

Something warm caressed my mind, persuading me to go, assuring me that everything would be alright. I felt the warmth pass through me again, a promise that no matter what I would be safe.

"Enough!" I yelled, my voice echoing, the power beginning to wake and rush through my body. Ammon paused. "Nakoma, let me go please."

"Narrdie," he warned.

"I'm alright," my voice was calm - steady. Slowly, he untangled his hands from me and stepped back, I moved around Audric - who instantly jumped in my way again.

"What are you doing?"

"Move out the way, Audric."

"You can't be serious," Audric bit as he gripped my forearm.

"Move out of my way. I won't ask again," my voice was dark, black tendrils wrapped around his hand, prying his fingers from me - one by one. From the corner of my eye - Ammon smirked. Evander watched me carefully.

"Audric." His voice was firm, direct - ordering Audric to his side. Audric bared his teeth and forced his legs to shift, he stood beside Evander - hands shaking violently as they held his sword.

"Ammon. You want to speak with me, then you speak here and now. Otherwise, you should really leave, we all know what can happen when I feel threatened." That warm feeling graced along my skin once more, comforting any doubt that lingered in my head – assuring me that what I was doing, was right. "Speak," I snarled, the forest shivering under the power in my voice.

"Very well," Ammon answered, his face glowing with amusement; he knew where I was calling that power from, I knew he could feel her, as she slithered around my skin – trying to claw her way to him.

"You've been busy," Dacre announced. "Who taught you to make oaths with Loopins and bonds with wolves?" My blood chilled. How on earth had he figured that out? A low snarl rippled from my tongue towards him, his mouth twitched up as he shared a looked with Ammon.

"Is that what you wanted to talk about?"

"Not at all," Dacre said blankly with a shrug. "Now that Ammon's back, he's helped me discover a way to help you," Dacre revealed – Ammon nodded as his eyes met mine – I felt the shiver of uneasiness pierce my skin. I snorted towards Dacre and turned my attention towards Ammon – the very insides of me screaming at the sight of him. I could feel Crow's longing; felt her desperately trying to tear through my mental walls.

"How can you help me?" Ammon slouched against a tree – tossing a shiny green apple up and down in the air, until finally he gripped it tightly in his hand and crushed it – the juice sliding between his fingers.

"I can separate Crow." My breath caught in my throat and for a split second – the forest stilled.

"Bullshit," Audric spat.

"You part is to be silent here!" Ammon sniped; his voice vicious.

"It appears Narrdie, is speechless for once," Dacre mocked.

The thought of having Crow, physically out of me – having my body and my mind free, being able to just be . . . me. It was overwhelming, it was what I wanted more than anything . . . but, it was also what they wanted. A chilling thought crashed into my mind – a warning. If I agreed, it would mean that Crow would be out, she'd be her own person – her own twisted psychotic person. Stronger, faster, powerful and deadlier than anything I had ever encountered – it would be a worldwide slaughter.

"We can help you be free of her," Dacre's voice turned gently, caring.

"Don't act like you're doing this for my sake, you snake in the grass! My answer is no, go fuck yourselves." Ammon cursed under his breath and pushed himself off the tree, a hissed filled the air. "I think we're done here," I stated as I turned from him.

"Oh? I don't think we are," Ammon's voice turned murderous as he stepped towards me – a dark look flashed across his face.

Ammon flicked his hand gracefully, suddenly Evander and Audric groaned, their bodies lifted up and were thrown, crashing hard into the trees. Dacre rolled forward, a crossbow appearing in his hands; his grin turned sharp as he fired a bolt straight into Nakoma's chest – Illythia screamed.

She moved to run to him, but Ammon threw another wave towards them all, closing a barrier around them, smirking as she thrashed and slammed herself into it.

"Stay back!" I warned – my Arma sprung out around me, as they both neared.

Suddenly black fire shot past me and buried itself into Ammon's chest – another immediately followed and hauled him backwards. Fyra darted forward; her black flames spiralling around her body like serpents – her hair blew furiously as her eyes locked onto Dacre. "Get away from her!" Her voice was frightening, the ground and trees around us shook as they cowered back from her. "And get away from my home!" Dacre swallowed nervous – knowing that he was no match for an Elemental Priestess; he raised his hands, his crossbow vanishing into thin air. "If I have to repeat myself – I'm going to be very displeased," she warned – the fire serpents hissed. Fyra blew one of the serpents forward, it slammed into Ammon's barrier – engulfing it in flames and releasing everyone from its hold.

"We're leaving," Dacre babbled; he gulped and slowly began to back away.

"Narrdie, we'll handle if from here," Fyra comforted as she placed her hand on my shoulder – my shield instantly dropping. Her sisters stood by her side, each one taking a stance. *"Well done, I am proud of you,"* she sang in my head.

Chapter Thirty-Eight

*W*e were all on edge, Dacre and Ammon were to thank for that – I bet they were laughing and toasting to it, I preferred to think that they were licking their wounds, trying to sooth the aching burns that Fyra had left. Most people had gone to their rooms and locked the doors after the visit, no one felt safe anymore; they all felt snared in their webs – who could blame them. Even I was beginning to doubt the power of this place; I'd watched as Ammon used only a slither of his power against the glamour – evaporating it into nothing.

I sat with some of my inner circle – we'd been unexpectedly shaken. Evander had vanished the moment Dacre and Ammon had left; he'd gathered his weapons, a few men and the wolves and left the safety of the new glamour. He'd given me a quick explanation about wanting to check they really left and make sure there wasn't another one of Dacre's small armies – waiting for us to move. He'd left before I could even beg him to reconsider – every second he was gone, was like being branded with a red-hot poker.

Nakoma had been rushed to the infirmary, Illythia not once leaving his side. The bolt had pierced his heart; almost tearing it in half. He'd survived, barely – like something was refusing to let him leave . . . or someone. He'd lost blood, too much blood, Illythia had ordered them to transfer her blood into his, threatening to tear their throats out if they'd refuse.

Mazruriuk motioned for everyone to sit down; a forced smile on his face as he softly spoke. "Dinner is ready." We'd gathered around the wide cherry wood table, piling our plates, even though none of us seemed hungry. I didn't even want to look at the food, my stomach was in knots, even the smell seemed to fill my throat with vomit. I avoided gazing at the table and turned to the grand paintings sat in golden frames, paintings of the Priestesses; their elements coming to life around them – dancing and spinning.

Mazruriuk placed a fully cooked goose with potatoes, carrots, broccoli and every other vegetable you could think of, in the centre of the table; he began pouring everyone out a glass of wine before taking his own seat beside Ray.

"Thank you, Mazruriuk, you didn't have to do this," Astrid praised, although she didn't eat – she still piled up her plate out of respect.

"It all looks delicious," Ray chimed in, she gave him a peck on the cheek and he gave her hand a gentle squeeze, she added some food to her plate, but I knew she wouldn't eat – she hadn't eaten in the past few days. She'd woken up screaming at night, shrieking that Ammon was coming for her, begging Mazruriuk to no let him take her.

"Let's all dig in, no one leaves without full bellies," Astrid said with a sweet smile. Knives and forks began to scrap along the plates, as they cut and ripped into the food, most only pushed around their food – making it look like they had eaten, while others only took a few mouthfuls before setting them down.

"When will Evander and the wolves be back do you think?" I asked Audric – he looked just as jittery as I felt.

"I'm not sure, I'm hoping soon. He's been gone a while," he replied as he gave me a sheepish smile.

"Two days," I confirmed. "I never thought Ammon would come," I said as I flattened my mashed potato. Mazruriuk hissed through his teeth towards me, a warning to keep my voice low; his eyes signalled to Ray, who had instantly paled at the mention of Ammon's name. I tilted my head, my eyes softening, I mouthed my 'sorry', he nodded and lightly placed his hand on hers – squeezing it lightly to comfort her.

"Fuck knows what goes on in that psychopaths mind," Audric spat.

"His power . . . it'll kill us all," Ray blurted. Her eyes remained on her plate, the knife and fork shaking in her hands. "We can't stop him, we can't stop him, we can't stop him!" Mazruriuk pulled her to him, whispering tenderly in her ear; she burst into loud sobs and buried her head in his chest. Mazruriuk pulled her to her feet, keeping his arm tightly around her.

"Ray, I'm sorry. I shouldn't have said anything." She met my eyes with her watery stare and nodded, forcing herself to smile.

"Screw this," Talon snarled and slammed his cutlery on the table, making us all jump. "I'm sick of this moping around. Everyone get up and follow me."

"What for?" Nyda questioned, as she stared daggered glares towards him, from the amount of wine she'd drank – it wasn't hard to see how content she was in her chair. Nyda's eyes turned to me and an uneasy feeling shot up my spine, causing the hairs on the back of my neck to spike up. Her eyes lingered with mine – a flicker of distaste glimmering over her, vanishing as quickly as it came.

"We were ready for Dacre, but Ammon caught us all off guard," Talon began; he looked to Ray. "And I'm saying his name, because we can't hide from it." Talon took her hand in his. "Yollie, I know you're scared; I know he sends waves of terror coursing through you, but you have us. We all have each other. They don't care who they sacrifice, they don't care how many of theirs are killed. We do, we watch each other's backs, we fight side by side, because we are family. We are stronger than they are." Ray wiped her eyes free of tears and nodded to him, Talon kissed her hand and smiled proudly to her. "We can't be caught off guard again. So, everyone outside – training begins now."

Demir snorted and flapped his hands around like a puppet, motioning to his leg – which had been removed from the thigh and replaced with a flexible prosthetic. Talon rolled his eyes, "you're training has improved with your new leg – more than when you had a real one. So, don't use that as an excuse."

"We train all the time," Demir whined.

"Yet, you squealed when a spider crawled up your arm," Nyda taunted.

"Why don't you have another drink Nyda," he growled. "You're good at that."

Talon had invite every member of the house to come and watch, they'd all come jumping and talking with glee, apparently, it was a rare treat to watch the Pura Mensam members fight against each other.

Mazruriuk was to lead our session, he'd been on this earth a lot longer than all of us, fought almost every being and every creature. He tied his hair back in one tight ponytail, he slipped his shirt off and flung it one side; his muscled torso was stained with scars – each one thick from deep wounds. He cleared his throat and slowly spun around – his arms raised.

"Each one of these marks on my skin, was made by the very creatures we will be fighting. The very creatures that want to kill you. This session is for the Pura Mensam members only, as they will be the first ones targeted, so, if you are here to watch – you stay silent," he barked. "This is not a show, it is not a game or a place to take bets. You make a noise or distract any members of the Pura Mensam and I will have the Priestesses lift the glamour and throw you to the mercy of the dark. Clear?" The crowd nodded; each one gulping nervously, I couldn't blame them – Mazruriuk was scary when he wanted to be. "As for you lot," he said as he turned to us. "I want no holding back – regardless of who is standing in front of you. You will fight as if you are going to kill, as if the very person in front of you, is one of Dacre's dark dwellers and you will not stop unless the other person says they give up," Mazruriuk encouraged.

"Sir, yes sir!" Audric yelled as he clicked his heels together and saluted – I stifled a laugh. Mazruriuk through an annoyed eye towards him, but I could have sworn that the corner of his mouth itched in a smirk.

"Nika?" Mazruriuk smirked as he signalled Ray forward, she smiled widely and skipped towards him. "You want me to pick?" He offered; she shook her head.

"I want a challenge," her eyes slide along us, until they landed gently upon Talon - he wiggled his eyebrows at her and laughed through his nose.

"Bring it on R-O-S-I-E," Talon teased, stretching out the word.

Part of me didn't want to watch, Ray was one of the kindest, gentlest people and had the bones and strength of a ... human, I couldn't imagine how she'd survive against a Vampire.

How wrong I was.

Ray was an animal. A ruthless, aggressive, crazed, red-headed animal. The second she'd taken that syrim; she had gone from being a gentle little bunny rabbit, to a deadly tiger

– that had been poked with a stick too many times. She had set out for blood and she'd gotten it.

Talon looked up from where Ray had pinned him – a sharp blade at his throat; he swung his claws forward, but she was fast. She flung her head back – his claws skimming just below her chin – before she pulled out another knife and rested it at his chest. "Dead," she panted.

"Nicely done," Talon said breathlessly; he winked as he brushed some dirt off her cheek. She beamed happily at him, before rolling on her back and trying to catch her breath.

"That's my girl," I heard Mazruriuk whispered under his breath. I turned my smile away from him, not wanting to intrude – he was a very private man. "Very good Nika, you've gotten faster," Mazruriuk praised. "Bayona, Nyda, you two next." A wave of gasps erupted around us, the entertained eyes, now replaced with wide anxious eyes of a doe.

"Did I hear that right?" Illythia blurted as she was guided outside. Amarlia – the head healer – linked her arm through hers, slowly helping her stand, Talon instantly jumped to his feet and ran to her side, taking her face in his hands. "I'm alright, just a little dizzy." She looked weary, her eyes glowing with a red haze, her hands shivering slightly.

"You need to feed, sister. Non avresti mai dovuto dare il tuo sangue a quella cosa," he growled fiercely. Illythia snarled towards him, she pushed him back, before stumbling back against Amarlia – who held her tightly and warned her to be careful.

"That thing, is part of our people! That thing, has proved time and time again that he stands with us and that thing, saved my life." Talon clenched his jaw. "And his fucking name is Nakoma."

"How is he?" I asked, she tore her hungered eyes from her brother and landed them on me, they softened.

"Weak, but healing."

"Thanks to you," I smiled to her, her eyes fogged up; she nodded to me. Illythia had slowly began to speak to me once more, starting with an odd conversation here and there. She'd even walked the grounds with me and talked with me in my room.

"Mazruriuk," Illythia began as she turned back to him. "A Witch on a Witch? Are you insane?"

"What's wrong with a Witch and a Witch?" I asked Astrid.

"Witches have very extraordinary powers, unique and dangerous. Each Witch is different from the other, there are no two Witches the same. Nyda and Bayona are two of the most

415

powerful Witches I've ever encountered – their magic is so different that put against each other . . . could result in a massive disaster." Astrid's faced was tainted by worry – I gulped. Illythia and Mazruriuk began to bicker, both talking over the other – Illythia's hands flew up in the air as she ranted and raved.

"Maybe those two should step into the ring," Evander breathed down my neck before gently kissing it. I spun around and wrapped my arms around his waist, squeezing so tightly he sucked in air – I didn't care that he couldn't breathe, I was never going to let him go again. I breathed him in, savouring his scent, melting into his warmth. "Miss me much?"

"I was so worried," I leaned back and slapped my hands over his shoulder. "Don't ever just leave like that!" He laughed and gripped my wrists, pulling me closer to him, he kissed me hard.

"If I stayed any longer, you would have found a way to convince me not to go. It doesn't matter now anyway, everything was fine. I'm safe and the wolves are safe," he assured as he signalled to the wolves that had joined us – Karro bowed his head and I dropped down and rubbed my hand under his chin.

"I missed you."

"We missed you, Narrdie Moon."

Evander walked past me us and I expected he was going to make a final decision about the Witch fight, instead he stood beside Audric and leaned in to speak to him. "I bet you Nyda wins," Evander mumbled with a grin – Audric scoffed.

"Bullshit, Nyda won't last five minutes against Bayona."

"You think? Fine, if Nyda wins you take my next three patrol duties and my cleaning duties for the whole week," Evander proposed as he held out his hand – his eyes daring.

"You're on," Audric sneered as he shook Evander's hand. "It's good to have you back, brother."

"Mazruriuk said no making bets," I hissed, they both half smiled.

"No, no, Narrdie – he said that the people watching couldn't make bets," Audric pointed out as he pointed to his head. "See, my smarts have found a loophole."

"You have no smarts . . . idiot," I sniped playfully.

"It's too dangerous!" Illythia snarled – drawing my attention back. Mazruriuk's eyes turned dark as he rounded on her; he gripped the hand she was waving in his face and hissed. Talon took a warning step towards him.

"What if Dacre has a Witch? A Witch equal to Bayona or Nyda's strength? Are you going to fight it?" He asked – Illythia flinched. "I didn't think so," he spat as he tossed her arm down. "The truth is, if there is a powerful Witch, none of us would even be able to get close to it!"

"That's dramatic," Demir mumbled. Mazruriuk's head whipped in his direction, a menacing smirk pulling up his lips – he exchanged a glance with Nyda.

"You think so Demir?" Demir nodded, but doubt had tainted his face. "Fine. The next fight will be between Nyda . . . and Demir," he announced – Demir's eyes widened. "Demir take out the Witch . . . if it's so easy."

"I bet you Demir doesn't even last five seconds," Audric whispered to Evander.

Nyda had her arms folded, barely looking towards Demir; her expression was exactly like every other expression she wore – uninterested with a hint of annoyance. Demir had vanished and I had a sneaky suspicion that he'd turned into a mouse and ran back inside. "Can you hear him?" I quizzed Illythia – her ears were more magnified than mine.

"No, I can't smell him either."

"If Demir shifts, what happens with his leg?" Illythia met my eyes and smiled.

"Demir lost his leg in human form and that is where it is missing. When he shifts, the leg returns – isn't magic a wonderful thing," it wasn't a question, but I nodded.

A few seconds later, Illythia nudged me and inclined her head towards the floor – a black snake was quietly making its way towards Nyda – who didn't look up from picking the dirt out her nails. Demir's snake form was only a few feet away from her before he shifted into a leopard and lunged himself forward – a snarl echoing from him. With a roll of her eyes, she unfolded her hand and flicker her fingers casually – like she was swotting a pestering fly. The leopards purple eyes enlarged as its whole body jerked backwards and flew the forest – landing roughly in a murky puddle. Demir shifted back and winced as he pulled himself up, he shook his muddy hands and glared towards Nyda. "Why the puddle?" He growled; Nyda shrugged.

"You expect to fight the Ammon's army, as a worm and a pussycat?" She mocked, Demir's face blew up like a pufferfish.

"She has a point Demir," Mazruriuk interjected, before an argument broke out. "Try again."

"Fine," Demir snapped. Demir's body shuddered and suddenly shivers crawled up my spine – a Skinner with purple eyes stood in front of Nyda. I didn't know Shifters could change into creatures of darkness and I was surprised that he'd picked the very thing that took his leg.

Nyda's brow raised – she perched her lips together; locked her eyes on him and crouched ready. Mazruriuk's eyes met Evander's, Evander grinned wickedly and nodded; he kissed me on the cheek and pressed his finger to his lips, before slumping off into the overcast of the trees.

Black sparks shot out from Nyda's fingertips, one after the other towards Demir, as a Skinner he was fast. He made it look easy as he dodged and jumped – weaving around them, each time getting closer and closer to her – those Skinner jaws widening at the sides.

Suddenly, a large grey wolf with a black ear zoomed from the trees and towards Nyda; it's paws barely even ruffling the ground – silent, deadly. Demir met Evander's eyes and they both sprinted forward. Nyda shook her head and dived up – her body was so flexible and graceful as it flipped in a clockwise circle; she shot her hands out – firing two black sparks.

One hitting Demir right in the head and the other smacking Evander in the chest – the two beasts fell backwards and shifted to their human selves . . . groaning painfully. "Fuck, they are not nice to get hit from," Evander said through clenched teeth, his body jittered uncontrollably – Nyda licked her lips.

"Childs play," she sneered.

"Still dramatic, Demir?" Mazruriuk asked, as he helped him to his feet. "No one can sneak up on a Witch. So, if Dacre and Ammon manage to recruit one, it will be Nyda or Bayona that will have to deal with it. Ladies, if you would?"

Watching Nyda and Bayona was like nothing I'd ever seen before, it was brutal, yet beautiful – scary yet, enchanting. Their level of power was astonishing, they didn't move like you would expect someone to move in a battle – there were no swords clashing together, no punches being thrown, no snarling and growling. They moved almost like they were dancing together, swaying, twirling – twisting around each other; their hands moving like they were doing the flamenco. Their powers shot out of them like shooting stars – fast and bright, they never managed to hit each other, their powers would collide and burst like fireworks. I could have and would have watched them all day and night.

Bayona tilted her head – the black sockets seemed to ripple as she sensed where Nyda was; she darted forward and flipped up high as Nyda twisted her hand and sent her sparks towards Bayona. The spark skimmed across Bayona's dangling hair – little strands flittering to the floor like falling leaves, she landed softly behind Nyda and clasped her hands on either side of Nyda's head. "My next move is to liquefy your mind . . . Dead," Bayona explained smugly.

I began to clap like a seal, ignoring the embarrassment I would no doubt begin to feel – thankfully, I wasn't the only one. "That was brilliant!" Sharia erupted excitedly. "That was the most amazing thing I've ever seen," she squealed – she was like a little girl watching a circus act. The Witches elegantly bowed and smiled – both breathing hard, as usual there was an irritated twinge in Nyda's smile; she was a graceful woman, but not a graceful loser.

"Never underestimate Bayona. Have fun doing my patrols and cleaning," Audric teased Evander.

"Now Narrdie," Nyda announced blankly; her eyes traced me up and down. "Let's see how good her training actually is."

"OK," I chimed as I popped up from the tree I had been slouched on, I skipped over to Bayona. Training had become as normal as breathing to me now, eat, sleep, train – all day every day. Evander had me train at least five times a week, sometimes he'd go as far as to surprise attack me the moment I came out of the shower, I'd gotten so used to magic and combat. "Who you putting me against?" I quizzed Mazruriuk, he didn't answer – instead he winked and took a seat beside Ray.

My blood turned to ice as Fyra took a stand opposite me and smiled darkly – her fingers flexing at her sides. "Many creatures of the dark will focus wholly on you. We are merely an annoyance to them, you are the main prey in their hunt," Fyra spoke as she began to circle me – a deadly sparkle lingered in her eyes. "They would have been ordered to capture you and if they can't . . . then they'll kill you. Either way, Crow is released. And if Crow is released, then there is no stopping her – we lose." All emotion had drained from her face; her expression turned hard, a sudden fear slammed into me – I couldn't read her, couldn't predict what she was about to do. I was in the dark. "The one thing we all must be prepared for are multiple attacks – you especially, we can't be there to watch your back all the time. You must learn to have your eyes, everywhere." I didn't like where this was going . . . I didn't like it one damned slippery, stinking bit – yet I couldn't stop my mouth from moving.

"I'll be ready. Evander, Talon and Astrid multiple attack me quite often, so I think I'm prepared." Fyra flashed me a look of distaste as she snorted; her lip lifted in a sneer before she grinned – her teeth as white as freshly picked bone.

"You're too cocky, girl. That will get you killed, and you'd deserve it." A low snarl rippled from Evander's tongue towards her – she ignored him and continued. "You may be able to take on four at once . . . possibly even five, but they will consume you in groups of ten, twenty . . . thirty even. They will swarm you as quick as the night sky swallows the sun and tear you limb from limb. Dacre and Ammon will scout every creature from the darkest corners of the world for their army, creatures you . . . even I, have not seen before. You think Sivvs are bad? They are the puppies compared to those that crawl in the cracks of the earth." My spine locked, and my throat pleaded for water. "Prepare yourself, this is about testing your physical strength – no magic. You won't always get the chance to conjure it and in my opinion, you depend on it too much." I fought back the urge to roll my eyes, I didn't feel like getting slapped from her; instead, I decided on a nod. Fyra nodded back with a raised brow; she whistled and turned around to allow Karro to take the lead.

My mouth instantly twitched up at the sight of the pack stalking towards me, Karro's eyes were focused, determined. Yet, his tail was up and waggling, Oyku and Nook moved to his flank, while the other wolves split off to surround me. *"Are you ready for this?"* Karro asked in a playful tone.

"Always." I could feel him laugh at the unconvincing tone that I couldn't seem to shift.

Karro leaned his head back and howled, distraction caught me in its' snare as I watched the other wolves howl in response – missing the moment when Karro raced for me. My eyes locked back onto him, pupils splitting as the nails on my fingers shifted into sharp talons; I could feel the blood in my veins thicken with excitement. I had never versed the wolves before. I darted forwards, my eyes snapping to Nook as he lunged for me – I kicked my heels up and forced myself to spin over him, my feet screamed in protest as they landed on the mossy floor. I whipped my head around and was met with a black furred beast pushing me back down, Karro reared up, ready to slam down onto me again. I tucked my knees into my chest and kicked him tumbling to the side.

Oyku bounded for me, Rev and a grey patched wolf called Rasha on her side, I swerved left and snagged Oyku's foot as she skidded past me – pulling her close and resting my claws against her neck. "Dead," I growled breathlessly. I had only taken out one wolf and I could feel my energy washing away, my breath was rasped, and my heart was thunderous. Oyku whined as she skipped to the side, I had barely had any time to smile at her when Nook dove onto my back – biting hard onto my shoulder. It wasn't enough to cause serious harm, but I felt the light trickle of blood sprinkle down my shoulder and the sudden stab of pain slam into me. I shrieked in rage and lifted my hands to grab Nook.

Karro yelped in agony, stopping us all dead in our tracks. Silence fell. He dropped down and whimpered – blood leaked from his shoulder and his eyes met mine. Fear, genuine fear slammed into me as I looked around and found that everyone's eyes had now set upon me. Some stared with gaped mouths, while others just stared – wide eyed.

"A blood bond?" Nyda gasped, she scoffed. "Why wasn't I told about this?"

"Narrdie was ordered by me not to discuss it," Fyra snarled towards her, Nyda dropped her head respectfully, I flashed Fyra a look of gratitude and she subtly winked back. "Narrdie, your fight with the wolves is over. Later, we will work on Karro and your, pain tolerance towards each other. Let's see how well your magic and resistance is, shall we? Nyda?" I looked to Nyda and was met with a hateful glare, her mouth lifted in a serpentine smile – the hairs on the back of my neck stood. This bitch was coming for me and she wanted it to hurt. "Begin."

Nyda raised her hand towards me, black smoke began to eerily seep from her fingers, the illuminating smell of poison filled the air. *"Wait,"* Fyra coached through my mind. *"Hold on until the last moment."* The smoke shot forward, I pulled my Arma around me and grinned as the smoke bounced from my shield and slammed into Nyda's chest. Nyda crashed onto the floor; her face dark with embarrassment and fury that I'd bested her, she gritted her teeth and winced as she hauled herself to her feet.

"Nice!" Audric burst as he clapped his hands, Nyda's head whipped in his direction and gave him a disgusted look. "To be fair, Nyda, you went for an obvious attack."

"Let's try two Witches. Bayona," Mazruriuk suggested. Bayona's smile turned to a teasing grin as she walked to stand beside Nyda; she clicked her fingers and nodded to me.

"Begin," Fyra repeated.

Nyda's poisonous black smoke entwined around the purple fire that shot out of Bayona's hand. As their powers entwined the sky grumbled, the clouds pulling together into one grey block, thunder clattered like two boulders being struck against each other, the ground trembled underneath me and a chilling frosty wind kissed at my skin. I pulled my Arma around me and felt the powers slap into it – knocking the breath right out of me.

"Steady Narrdie, store your energy – only use what you need to," Mazruriuk called as he slowly paced up and down beside us. "More," he called to the Witches. Like a hurricane tearing into a town, their powers magnified and pushed me back – I could feel the mud and moss building up behind my feet, as I slid along the ground. "More," Mazruriuk ordered.

I could feel the slow trickle of blood falling down my nose, the ringing in my ears roared and my hands shook in front of me. I opened my mouth to tell them to stop, but only a wheeze came out – all moisture was sucked out of me. My nose became a fountain, the skin on my arms began to tear, lacerations slicing along my skin. My Arma began to quiver and crack, "stop," I breathed.

"Narrdie?" I heard Audric's voice call.

"She can't handle it," Evander's voice was frantic.

"STOP!" I screamed. My Arma erupted into tiny shards and their powers shot into my chest and then I was airborne. I wasn't sure how long my body had been splitting through the air before I felt someone's arms clamp around me and pull me into them.

"Narrdie? Open your eyes, look at me," Evander was leaning over me, shaking my shoulders; he wiped a tissue over my nose and mouth. "You're alright, bit stunned. Looks like I caught you just in time," he breathed out in relief.

Bayona's hands where instantly on me – healing my wounds. "I'm so sorry Narrdie," she choked.

"It's OK," my voice croaked, I looked up and smiled to her. I tried to stand and felt the blood rush to my head, I swayed and felt Evander's arms holding me steady once again.

"I think that's enough for today," Evander announced as he scooped me up in his arms – I winced.

*E*vander carried me to his room and gently set me on his bed, apologising every time I whimpered and hissed in pain. "Wait here," he whispered, lightly brushing my ear with his mouth, before disappearing in the other room.

My body burned, ached. My fingers felt like they had been bound together whenever I tried to move them, my limbs cried out in agony and my insides felt like someone's personal punching bag. The smell of vanilla graced my nostrils, as the sound of warm running water beckoned in my ear – calling me. I almost moaned out as I imagined the hot water lapping at my fragile body – soothing my wounds.

I was half asleep on the bed when I felt Evander's warm hands curl around me and pull me to him, I tried to speak, but only short little mumbles escaped my lips. "I've got you," he murmured into my ear as he carried me to the bathroom. "Right, arms up . . . if you can." I grimaced and protested as he pulled my top over my head and wiggled me out of my jeans, before lifting me up one more time and gently lowered me into the beautiful, relaxing bath. He pulled off his own clothes and carefully climbed in behind me; he gently pulled me back, until I was leaning against him. "Just relax." He poured jugs of water over my hair, tenderly rubbing soap over my aching bones.

"Bedtime," he finally said – it was music to my ears.

Chapter Thirty- Nine

$\mathcal{E}$vander brushed my hair as I slumped down in the armchair, every part of me throbbed. It had been weeks and no matter how hard I trained, I couldn't beat Bayona and Nyda. Each time, I either ended up face down in the mud or covered in slashes and blood. "This isn't getting any easier."

"It will, just keep pushing yourself. Each time we put you against them you've lasted longer. Believe me Narrdie, you're getting better," Evander reassured.

"Getting better, but slowly – too slowly. The days are growing shorter, the wind has changed and it's like the world knows what's about to happen." Evander tied my hair into a long fishtail braid, pulled a crimson blanket over me and placed a hot water bottle at my back – I moaned as it instantly eased the pain.

"It does."

"It does?" I repeated as I nestled my cheek into the soft fabric.

"Of course, the world is a living thing. You don't think she knows when something bad is happening on her body?" I tilted my head around, just enough to catch his eyes.

"She?" He laughed, and his eyes brightened, "You think the world, is a she?"

"Don't you? She births, she protects, she watches and she's one of the most beautiful creatures ever known – no way could she, be a he." I rolled my eyes and chuckled – he had a point.

"Do you think she'll do anything to help us?"

Evander sighed, "I don't think so. She'll let us figure it out ourselves, besides, we have four of her daughters to guide us." He began to trace his fingers along my cheek, moving his fingers to caress the space between my brows.

"What happens if one of the Elemental Priestesses dies?" Evander breathed out heavily, he rose and squeezed himself behind me and wrapped his hands around my waist – I leaned my head against his shoulder.

"There are descendants of the elements all over the world, a child is born and ends up having an affinity for either earth, air, water or fire. They are normally rounded up by the Order and taken to schools – hidden far away from human eyes. These schools teach them about controlling the element, using the balance and accepting the mother's gift, each one knowing that one day, one of them will become the next Elemental.

"Our Priestesses have been around for centuries, but there are still offspring with the gifts, just not as strong. They live a normal life, the same length as humans and will do so until one of the Priestesses dies or choses to pass it on to the next one in line. Being an elemental descendent can be dangerous and can have deadly consequences, there is only one spot and everyone wants it." I shuffled in his arms, moving to hang my legs over the armchair and my head against his arm – he lifted my top up to my breast line and tickled along my stomach. His touch lighting up my skin, with warm shivers.

"You mean, they'd kill each other to move up the list?"

"Yes, however in doing that, they break the natural balance."

"Meaning that they'd never be granted the honour of becoming the next Elemental?" He nodded, the corners of his lips tweaking up in a proud smile. "And if our Elemental is killed?" Evander's jaw clenched and unclenched; he raised his brows and licked his bottom lip.

"It can be monstrous, the power of the Elemental is more than we could ever imagine, the next in line has to reach a certain age for them to be able to contain it, otherwise it will shatter them from the inside out." I shuddered. "Think of it this way, if the Priestess dies and their next in line is still a baby, that power will hunt and find them, transferring into them when they are not ready. They'll die brutally and it will keep going, all until one of age is chosen." I sucked in a breath, I never expected it would be like that, didn't think the mother would allow her gift to be so ruthless and cruel.

"They can't fight in our war, can they?" My voice was barely a sound, my very breath caught in my throat. Evander leaned down and kissed my forehead, then my nose and then both of my cheeks, before softly kissing my lips.

"No, my girl. They can't."

A loud knocked on my door, had me jumping out my skin; I winced as I rose to the side to allow Evander room to move. He unlocked the door and found Audric leaning, a tense look causing his jaw to tighten. "The Order have summoned us," he said blandly. Evander stiffened.

"Who do they want to see?"

"Me, you, Narrdie . . . and Ray." My spine locked, as I read the look on his face, it was tight and a look of dread twinkled in his eyes.

"Why do they want to see Ray?" I hissed as I rose to my feet, flinching at the pain that locked in my joints. Evander swore under his breath and slammed his hand against the doorframe.

"They are going to trial her for Ammon." It wasn't a question, but Audric nodded.

"Are they going to slot and strip her?"

"What does that mean?" I asked, my heart twanging with electric.

"They strap you down, strip you of any powers, strength, memories of our world and then banish you. You are left looking like a skeleton, wandering alone – not knowing who you are." There was no kindness in his eyes, as he spoke. Terror clawed in my throat and each breath was like swallowing glass.

"They . . . they can't," my voice shook.

"She's not a Watcher, slotting and stripping is only for rogue Watchers. They'll banish her though and could possibly remove her memories," Audric explained. There was a tightness in his jaw, he eventually looked to me; his eyes red raw like he hadn't slept in days.

"Are they coming here?" Evander asked through clenched teeth.

"No, they've sent me the location . . . Evander it's a fucking tear. They are going to find her guilty and banish her into a tear!" I couldn't breathe and I could feel the darkness roaring awake in my veins.

"We'll meet them," I snarled. "But if they think they are going to shove her in a tear and leave her to die, then I will put them in there with her. I don't care who they are, they will not touch her."

Ray trembled as she sat on her bed, the words not even being able to leave her mouth, due to the breathless sobs. Mazruriuk on the other hand, was going to burn tracks in the carpet if he continued to pace up and down. "No." He snarled over and over; Evander had asked some extra men to stand outside the room in case Mazruriuk's temper erupted. "They want her, they'll have to kill me."

"Do you really believe we'd let them harm her or send her through a tear?" Audric growled as he stood in his way, pausing his marching.

Mazruriuk scoffed. "You'd go against the Order?" Mazruriuk moved to shove Audric to the side, but Audric gripped his face.

"I would die before I'd let anyone harm her. I swear to you, she'll be safe with me, brother." Mazruriuk met his gaze, surveying him for a few breaths; he nodded, his eyes misting over as he gripped Audrics forearm.

"You bring her back to me," Mazruriuk begged him, his voice quivering.

"I swear on my life," Audric swore.

"Me too," Evander added.

"I'll rip their hearts out if they touch her," I promised.

*T*he lingering tremors had formed a line of sweat along Ray's forehead, her hand squeezed mine so tightly, the blood circulation had cut off. Audric had Lacus jumped us to a wide field, the greenery had burst into colour, as poppies had sprouted all around, the sun was burning as it beamed down and butterflies instantly took to the sky, as our presence had disturbed them. Our silence was heavy as we started forward, following behind Audric – who lead us towards eight figures waiting in tight black suits. They were stood in front of a glowing blue light, a portal – directly in the centre of the field, around it were seven statues, all of men on their knees: their swords gripping tightly in front of them.

"They're Watchers," Audric said, keeping his voice hushed.

"Like actual people?" He nodded. "How?"

"When a tear is revealed, things can slip out of them, Watchers will volunteer to guard it, contain it and this is how they do it." Ray held her hand over her mouth, stifling a gasp.

"They're alive?" She whispered.

"Yes. Preserved in stone." Audric signalled us to remain quiet as we neared the waiting men.

Instantly, Audric and Evander dropped to one knee and bowed their heads in respect – I refused; I would not bow to a group of people, who found it acceptable to banish a young girl for a mistake.

The one in the middle – who had a plain bare face and black cropped hair – eyed me as he took in my blatant disrespect, I kept my head held high – holding tightly to Ray's hand. "Let me make one thing clear," I began, before anyone had an opportunity to speak. "You make any attempt to touch this girl before we talk, I will carve your heart from your chests. You are no Order to me, I do not care for your rules, I do not care for your traditions, and I do not care how high up you think you might be; you will bleed the same."

"Miss Narrdie Moon, will all due respect-" I raised my hand, cutting him off.

"I have not finished talking," I hissed. I willed my power to me, beckoned it to come forward and wrap around the air they breathed, a subtle warning. He swallowed nervously and nodded his apology to me. "When this girl speaks, you will not undermine her, you will not patronise her, you will not interrupt her and you will not raise your voice towards her. Nod if you understand." My tendrils tightened around them, choking their words, only releasing them after they'd nodded frantically. "Good."

"That's my girl," Evander's voice brushed against my mind, rising to his feet with Audric.

"First, allow me to express the Order's condolences to you Audric, Mitchell was a good man and one of the greatest we had ever seen. I'm sure you will do him proud in his place."

"He already has," I sniped. Audric's finger brushed against mine, an act of gratitude and a warning to calm myself.

"Thank you, Lord Commander," Audric's voice had changed. He didn't sound like the jokey, potty mouthed Audric, that I was used to. "I wish that this meeting was on better circumstances, however, I must express my disagreement in the matter at hand." The Lord Commander, raised his brow, he glanced sideways towards the other members of the Order, a mocking glint in his eyes that had my blood heating.

"Noted. Rosie-Anika-Yoland, step closer," he ordered, a smirk ghosting his lips at her nervousness. She took a step, but I tightened my hold on her hand and shook my head. The Lord Commander's eyes fell on me. "Lady Moon?"

"She's fine where she is. You understand the importance of my time, I suggest you speak quickly. We know why you've called her here; she knows why you've called her here. Make your decision." I swore I was only seconds away from tearing their heads from their bodies.

"Sir Evander, please-"

"Sir Evander, does not speak for me!" I snarled, feeling the nails on my fingers shift to claws. "Perhaps you should remember who you are speaking to and show me the respect I deserve. If you fail to do so, I will happily disband your little Order." His mouth wobbled, bobbing open like a fish gasping for air, the others around him immediately dropped their eyes to the floor.

"Lord Commander?" Ray's voice squeaked. He turned towards her, making sure that every moment and every look he gave her was polite, in fear that my claws would open his belly and spill his insides over the ruby poppies. "I did not leave Gatherling that day, in the hope of seeking out and restoring Ammon. If that was the case, why would I stay in Gatherling, surely the wise thing to would be to flee?" The Lord Commander's scoff, blurted out of him, I hissed through my teeth, my eyes slitting.

"Careful," I warned darkly.

He swallowed hard. "Forgive me. Rosie, we understand accidents and mistakes can occur, however this is catastrophic. Ammon has returned and the realms, races and covens demand the consequences to be fulfilled. I am sorry, but the vote was unanimous." Ray's breath caught in her throat, she whimpered, tears strained in her eyes.

"Please," she begged. Evander linked his arm around her waist, as her knees buckled under her. "Please, don't do this."

"Rosie-Anika-Yoland, by the decision of the Order, I sentence you to be banished by tear." He nodded, signalling the men behind him to walk forward, ready to throw her through. Ray, burst into heart-retching wails, begging and pleading – screaming over and over that she was sorry.

I tutted and shot my arm out towards the Lord Commander, my twin blade materialised in my hand, the length growing until the tip rested against his throat. The other blade lying under the chin of the Watcher that neared Ray – everyone froze. "Lord Commander, surely you're not going to drag this girl in, while she's in hysterics?" I mocked, shaking my head in disappointment.

"Think very carefully about what you're doing, Miss Moon." I pressed the blade in harder, only stopping when a trickle of blood ran down his neck.

"Or what? Will you banish me? Kill me?" I laughed, the sound echoing darkly. "I'd love to see you try. Or maybe I should let Crow take the wheel, see how long you last with her?" Fear glassed over his eyes. "No? Shame. Here's our unanimous decision, you will not interfere with our people, you will not touch our people and you will not make choices about our people. You will go back to your hole and work on keeping the humans from this war. Maybe after this is all over, I might not tear you all limb from limb and feed you to my pack." The Lord Commander's eyes flicked towards Audric, who had his own blades aimed towards the other Watchers.

"Audric?"

"Sorry Vlad, but we believe you've lost sight of why we began all this. You prefer punishing and banishing, more that working on repairing this world. The Elders have been in contact and as of this morning, I am the new Commander of the Order and I am sparing Rosie-Anika-Yoland." Vlad's eyes widened so big, I thought they would pop from his skull. The other Watchers immediately dropped down to one knee. "You've been outranked."

"If you don't believe us, you can always take it up with the Elder Vampire, Lady Astrid," I offered. "I'm sure she'd happily discuss, you wanting to banish her favourite human into a tear."

"As well, as the white Shade, Mazruriuk – who's taking a liking to our Ray," Evander added as he wiped the tears from her eyes. Ray was speechless, she looked between us in pure puzzlement and threw her arms around Evander – thanking him repetitively.

My eyes snapped to Vlad and a feral snarl rippled from my throat. "Shouldn't you be bowing to your Lord Commander?" He clenched his jaw, his breath coming out in short hoarse waves, he dropped to his knees and lowered his head.

Audric crouched low, bringing his mouth to Vlad's ear. "I suggest you return to HQ and gather your belongings and I'd be quick about it. If I returned and find you still residing there, I'll do more than slot and strip you. Get the fuck, out of my sight." Like a hair in the wind, they all vanished, Audric glanced up to me – a wide victorious grin spreading wide along his face. I couldn't help but smile down to him, feeling the adrenaline vibrate throughout my body; I turned towards Evander, who shared our excitement.

"Ray?" Ray had tears streaming heavily from her eyes, her grey t-shirt now covered in dark wet patches where they'd fallen. "We were never going to let them take you," I promised her as I gently wrapped my arms around her.

"Never in a million years," Audric said as he brushed the hair from her face.

"Why didn't you tell me?" She wept.

"They would have read it on your face and rushed into something. Vlad, would do anything to hold onto power, if he read that we'd conspired against him; he would have killed every one of us. When he saw your reaction, he thought he'd won," Audric explained softly.

"However, the minute Audric announced he was the new Lord Commander – congrats by the way, brother – a shift of power had happened, the other Watchers showed their instant loyalty, dropping Vlad like the piece of shit he is." Evander finished, he offered Ray a tissue to blow her nose and kissed her on the top of her head. "I'm sorry we had to put you through this, my sweet Ray. We meant what we said, we would never let anything happen to you."

"You're family," I added. Ray burst into tears once more, but they weren't saddened sobs, or fear filled wails – they were joyful and full of relief; she jumped between us hugging us happily.

Chapter Forty

"What was it you said again?" Evander teased as he kissed down my stomach, his hands running down my thighs. We'd returned back from the meeting with the Order yesterday and Evander had left Audric to reveal the news. Evander had brushed a kiss to my neck, flung me over his shoulder and carried me to his room, only letting me go when he'd thrown me on his bed and devoured every inch of me . . . more than once. "Ah that's it, I will carve your heart from your chests." His laugh rumbled against my skin, he traced his tongue along my skin, smirking wickedly.

"Oh that? I thought you were on about the part where I said, you don't speak for me," I mocked, feeling my breath turn to soothing ice at his touch. Evander arched a brow, his hands roughly gripping my hips and pulling me closer; his lips traced along my neck, his tongue causing little tingles to goosebump along my skin.

"I may not speak for you, but I can certainly take your breath away . . . maybe even make you beg a little," he taunted. I shuddered and leaned my head back against the pillows, I pushed my hips against him, wanting more – demanding it. However, before my predatory desires could kick in, he pulled back, rolled from the bed and began slipping into his jeans, grinning smugly to himself.

"You're an ass," I hissed.

"I would give me so much pleasure, to keep you in this room and spend every second worshipping your skin," his hands braced either side of the bed beside me, he leaned in. "To have you quivering under my touch, to hear you moan for me." Teasing fucker. I leaned in to bite his ear, he laughed and pulled back, lightly throwing me, my dark grey jumper and leggings. "However, we don't have the luxury of lazy days." I whined my frustration and grudgingly forced myself from the comforting safety of the duvet and closed myself up in the clothes Evander had given me. "I have rules for today," he announced casually.

"Rules?" I asked with a raised brow. "Well, that's certainly put a damper on my mood," I joked.

"Sure, it has," he mumbled, I could hear the eye roll in his voice. "But yes, today comes with some rules," his hand slid up my leg and caressed my thigh – my breath jittered. "Only some, the first rule is there will be no training of any kind today, none whatsoever. There will be no arguments today, no talks that will lower the mood." His thumb grazed along the inside of my thigh – I couldn't help but bite my lip.

"What's special about today?" I breathed.

"It's the most important day of the year, a day which should be celebrated and worshipped by all." He pulled me into him, lifting me up into his arms and ran his fingers along the exposed part of my back. I wrapped my legs around his waist and forced myself not to melt in his orange eyes, today they were bright like burning embers. He leaned into me and kissed me gently, brushing his nose against mine. "Happy Birthday, Narrdie."

I groaned, my body flopped lazily, he laughed as he held me firmly; his arms the only thing keeping me from slumping to the floor. "Who knows?" I had never been one for celebrating my birthday – mainly because I never had anyone to celebrate it with. Audric always made sure to bring me a cake and a book each year, truthfully, that was all I needed.

"I'm afraid the whole house do."

"Great."

"Narrdie, it's time to start seeing your birthday as a positive thing. Your family want to celebrate it with you and then later tonight, me and you will go and celebrate it. I've prepared something really special for us."

"Thank you," I chimed as I kissed him on the cheek, I wiggled my eyebrows. "Can I have a birthday surprise now?" I purred, as I entwined my fingers in his hair.

"You'll get a special surprise all night, but first Audric said he's got something for you."

I dreaded leaving my room, dreaded having to endure the typical birthday nonsense, but it didn't feel like it used to. All the way to the dining hall I was stopped and wished a 'Happy Birthday', it felt nice, like they generally wanted to tell me. People gifted me with cards, flowers and other little trinkets, each one forming a lump in my throat, each one I would treasure.

Evander paused outside the dining hall and propped his ear against the frame; he frowned and shook his head, "Wait here a minute."

"Why? Is everything alright?"

"Not sure. I can hear the Priestesses in there, I don't want us to disturb them. Let me pop my head in and see if everything's alright." I nodded and fiddled with the skin around my fingers while I waited for him.

"Happy Birthday, Narrdie," Nyda wished in her usual bitter tone. I jumped on hearing her voice and turned to thank her. I paused as I opened my mouth, she seemed off – more off than normal. Her eyes were bloodshot and red, she'd either been rubbing them or crying, the skin on her wrists looked bruised and sore.

"Nyda, are you alright?" I asked as I eyed her suspiciously, looking over her wrists again – she followed my stare. "Did someone do that?" I reached for her, but she jerked back and scowled.

"It's none of your concern," she snapped.

"Narrdie?" Evander called.

"Best hurry along," she growled before storming down the hall.

"Narrdie?" Evander called again, pulling me back to his attention. I sighed and headed into the dining hall – I'd figure out Nyda's problem later.

"SURPRISE! HAPPY BIRTHDAY NARRDIE!" I was shocked that I'd managed to stay on my feet as everyone yelled happily. I was so overwhelmed, tears burst from my eyes as I began taking in hugs – I had never had a party before. Nearly the whole house was here.

"T-Thank you all," I blubbered.

The room had been done out, multicoloured balloons and banners hung along the ceiling and around the paintings, the table had been covered with a baby blue silk cloth and had been filled with so much food. In the centre of the table was a three-tiered cake, half sponge and half chocolate, decorated with buttercream swirls and patterns – my mouth began to water. "The cake looks so tasty!"

"Illythia made it," Astrid said with a smile. Illythia skipped forward and gave me a long hug and pecked me on the cheek.

"Audric helped me, it's double chocolate with a hazelnut spread in the middle and on the other side is vanilla sponge with strawberry cream. Ray, went to get the ingredients, I just really wanted to make it for you," she said sheepishly. I gave her another tight hug. "We have gifts for you too," she turned me towards another table beside the door. Another table covered with a green cloth and sparkling confetti, overflowed with presents, wrapped in elegant paper and cloth, each one with bows and ribbons – varying in all shapes and sizes.

"For me? I . . . I don't know what to say," my voice choked.

"Why not have some food first?" Illythia suggested, giving my arm a gentle squeeze.

"I can't wait to try it."

"Anyone hungry?" Audric asked; his eyes fixated on the food – he was always so greedy.

Laughter bounced from the walls and my cheeks hurt from smiling so much. I blew out my candles in one blow as everyone sang and cheered, Mazruriuk sucked in the helium from the rainbow balloons and began to mimic everyone.

Audric was the first to place a large rectangle parcel in my lap, the paper was soft and smooth. I tore into it like an animal, tossing the lid to one side.

I gasped as my eyes took in the smooth steel of the twin blades. I brushed my fingers along the handle, it had been carved to look like a rope of plaits, the bottom had been shaped into a wolf – the detail so explicit, it's eyes shaped out of amethyst. The blade was curved as it stretched to its sharp point, along the side, in elegant font, the words, we look forward, never looking back, had been engraved. "Oh, Audric," I barely breathed, my eyes glassed over as I looked to him.

"I thought it was about time you had your own . . . your own new ones." He leaned down and kissed me on the top of my head and gave me a one-armed hug. "We'll play with them later, see how sharp they really are. Do you like them?"

"They're beautiful."

"He carved it himself," Bayona added; she handed me a small present. "Mine next."

"Bayona, I love it," I told her as Evander helped me stretch out the orange tapestry. It was just like the one she kept on her wall, the hand painted symbols and patterns mimicked hers.

"Each symbol has a meaning, and if you look closely at the patterns, they represent all of us. You'd admire mine for hours, so I thought you'd want one in your room."

The lump in my throat was the size of a football, my eyes stung as they kept filling with tears. With every present I received, a new wave of tears spilled from my eyes, everyone had put so much care into everything they gave me. "I'll give you my present tonight," Evander whispered in my ear.

"I don't know what to say," I whimpered. "I've never celebrated my birthday, not properly and these gifts are more than I ever expected. I love every single one of them and I will treasure them all for, the rest of my life."

Aronnia tapped the side of her glass, "I think there's only one thing left to do. Narrdie," she began. "Cut your cake!" She squealed as she handed me a large knife and bounced on the tips of her toes.

"Wait, I want to take a picture of us all around the cake," I said.

"How?" Audric asked. I blushed with embarrassment, I didn't know why I had kept my phone, I had no need for it here – yet I still clung onto it. Audric chuckled and shook his head, "does it even work anymore? She still has her phone," he explained to the questioning looks.

"Good, I think we should start taking memories," Astrid chimed. "Hurry and get it Narrdie, I'd be quick if I was you, Karro is eyeing up your cake."

I skipped down the corridor towards my room, the grin still wide across my face; I couldn't wait to grab my phone and take pictures of everyone and everything. I hesitated outside of Nyda's room, even though she wasn't my favourite person I still wanted to invite her to come and have some cake – she was family too. I lifted my hand ready to knock, when I heard muffled, agitated voices coming from the other side.

"What do you expect me to do?" Nyda hissed.

"What you were told," a man's voice replied.

"Everyone is there!"

"I do not care for them or their whereabouts, today is the day. Make it so, Nyda," the man's voice was a calmed rage.

"It took everything I had to make that loophole for you! Why don't you do something instead of hiding!" Nyda snarled. Suddenly, I heard a sound of glass breaking and furniture rattling, and my heart thundered – was he hurting her? Nyda's frightened whimper sounded and before I could think it through, I barged into her room.

My blood turned to ice.

Ammon. He had a hold of Nyda around the throat; his eyes raised with amusement as they slunk to me, that chilling grin stretched wide along his mouth. Nyda's eyes were wide as they switched between Ammon and me, she gulped, Ammon dropped her like rubbish. "A-Ammon," I whispered, my voice timid. Ammon cracked his neck and straightened out his deep red jacket; his grin turned murderous, his eyes turned dark and filled with cruel intent.

"Well, this is an interesting turn of events. We were just taking about you, weren't we Nyda?" Nyda didn't dare make a sound, she stayed crumpled on the floor – clutching her red neck.

"How . . . What . . ." Shock and fear had captured my words; my voice had jumped out of my mouth and fled for itself – my whole-body shook.

"Nyda, is quite handy to have around . . . most of the time. She has become quite an asset of mine. Telling us where you have gone, what training you all do, your next movements and making sure we can get in here. Your Priestesses may be strong, however they focused too much on making sure we didn't break their glamour on the outside, when they should have also made sure that it wasn't broken on the inside. Nyda, managed to undo a slither, so small that they'd never notice." My eyes darted to Nyda, they flared as they met hers.

"Nyda, why?" A lump formed in my throat, another person – another betrayal and just when I was beginning to feel like we had a chance.

"Just come with us Narrdie," Nyda begged. "Don't give him a chance to hurt you . . ." Nyda's eyes widened as a furious snarl bellowed from behind me.

Astrid's eyes were as red and furious, as a burning flame. She pulled me behind her; her fangs extended to their full sharpness – ready to rip out throats. "I came to see if you needed help finding your camera. I didn't realise that there was a private party going on." Nyda flinched back, smart enough to avoid meeting Astrid's eyes. Ammon's smirk widened; his forked tongue slithered out and licked his lips.

"I'm glad you came along Astrid," his eyes turned deadly. "Now, I don't have to come looking for you." My heart kicked up as Ammons' eyes turned dark – black gunge drooped over his teeth. "Make this quick Nyda," he said testily.

I hadn't noticed that Nyda had gotten to her feet; she thrust her hand out and I felt that force she wielded smack into my chest, pushing me back until I crashed into the corridor wall – Astrid crumpled beside me. Nyda loomed over me, shame and disgust tainting her eyes; she opened her hand and blew black powder towards us. A sea of stars burst into my vision, the powder was thick, cloggy and had completely consumed me within a number of seconds, bile rose in my throat, but I couldn't cough. My nose burned, and I could feel the water streaming from my eyes. Darkness roared around me, but it wasn't mind, hands gripped me hard, painfully and I knew it was Ammon, I could feel his touch like a brand.

Then everything went silent.

Chapter Forty-One

Everyone

*A*mmon paced up and down, aggravation clinging to his brows; he had no time for patience and waiting around only fuelled his anger. His eyes didn't leave Narrdie – chained to the bed, sleeping silently, he noted every detail, every moment she made, every breath she took; the way her eyes rolled under her eyelids. He tilted his head, she was dreaming – he hoped it was traumatizing, he did love to watch people squirm. "Still out?" Dacre asked impassively as he slumped in the doorway.

"Obviously," Ammon snipped.

"You sure you gave her the right stuff?" Dacre mocked, ignoring the warning growl Ammon through his way. "Perhaps the Witch was playing you."

"Nyda assured me that this would bring her back, she knows not to cross me. If she does . . . I'll take her eyes." Ammon grinned maliciously, he could feel her, could feel her coiled up energy emerging to the surface - the excitement and bloodlust that came with it.

Dacre had ordered her to be placed in her old quarters, a four-poster double bed with a black skinned bear blanket and black drapes – it was the little things that Crow enjoyed the most. "Show time," Dacre grumbled as he signalled towards Narrdie. "Here she comes."

Narrdie's sun kissed hair began to change to the matted black; her skin from peachy to a sickly pale - the poisonous veins bulging. Narrdie's frail little fingers, shifted into the long black claws, that Crow would spend hours sharpening, her pale pink lips - stained to a deep purple. Icy blues snapped open; her sharp teeth gleaming as a wicked, vicious smile stretched along her face. "There she is," Ammon sang.

"Ammon, how I've longed to see your face again," she purred playfully.

"Have you missed me?" He teased, slowly walking towards her and unlocking the chains that kept her bound. He stretched out his hand towards her, of course, she was more than happy to accept it.

"Of course, my Lord," she replied, placing her dark lips to his cheek. "I was afraid you'd be lost to us forever."

"And your dress? I hope it's at your satisfaction, I chose it myself." He asked as he twirled her around to face the mirror. She raised her brow flirtatiously, running her hands down the corset, the netted folds of the gown, admiring the way the webbed sleeves looped over her middle finger.

"You always did have good taste," she hummed. Dacre cleared his throat and she laughed darkly. "I haven't forgotten you, my love."

"I should think not, pretty bird." The jealousy in his voice called to her, she could feel it consuming the air and biting into her skin - she adored it. She stepped towards him, her movements' feline; her hands ran up his chest. With a hungered snarl, he gripped her tightly, adding enough pain to make her hiss, before taking her lips with his own; his tongue scrapping the roof of her mouth. He pulled her back, his hand squeezing her neck. "You should not have made me wait this long."

"But it's so fun to watch you get so worked up," she taunted, her hand brushing below his belt. "However, I am curious about this valiant rescue." She stepped out of his hold and set her hollowed eyes on Ammon.

"Did you not believe me when I said I'd return for you?" Ammon circled her, his eyes running over her body - making sure everything was intact.

"I don't doubt you, my Lord. I was just concerned, Evander keeps Narrdie under constant watch."

"They're careless," Ammon spat bitterly. "I took Narrdie right under their noses, that timid Witch played her part well. I'll let you decide what to do with her later, but for now we have some work to do."

For once, Crow was speechless. Ammon's face was smug as he watched the bafflement paint across her face, he took her hand and guided her closer towards the bars, urging her to peer inside. "We already have one here." Crow moved with him, her eyes leaving his and looking to the curled-up Vampire lying on the cold floor. "Once we get all the blood groups together, they we will free you from Narrdie."

"The Witch?" Crow's voice was tight.

"Nyda will perform it and if she refuses well . . ." Dacre bared his teeth, a dark intent tattooing over his face. Crow cackled, bursting with excitement as she spun around, she'd be free, no longer would she have to endure the pining that was Narrdie. "Are you pleased, pretty bird?" Dacre asked, his breath hot against her skin.

"More than words can describe," she hummed as her tongue traced along his cheek. "Once I am freed, my power will return in full and I will crush this world into dust. When can we begin?" Ammon perched his lips together and glanced down. Crow's temper flared, a low growl sounded in her throat and her fists clenched by her sides. "Seems you aren't as prepared as you made out, how disappointing, especially for a Shade of your level. Perhaps being a Capri has tainted your powers, pity." She snarled towards him.

Ammon's anger choked in his throat, he struck out, the back of his hand whipping across her cheek – knocking her down. He gripped her throat, feeling her instantly yield to his hold as he pulled her towards him. "Remember who you are talking to," he warned, his gaze unflinching. "You are not at full power yet." Crow's breathing shuddered, her body trembling under him. "You speak to me like that again and I will crush you until you are nothing but bones and ash."

"Ah the drama," Dacre grumbled, earning himself a warning glare from Ammon.

"Forgive me, my Lord," she whimpered, a tremor of fear in her voice. He pushed her back and her hand instantly rose to rub her neck, the purple bruises already blotching to the surface. "What is needed?" She asked carefully, cowering back from him.

"We have the Vampire, the Witch, the Hybrid and the Shade, we have your blood and Narrdie, which just leaves one."

"A human," Crow finished. "There's plenty of them to go around." Ammon laughed, the sound unpleasant and sickly, his eyes grew dark.

"I know just the one."

☾

"Nyda," Evander spat – her name now causing the anger to boil in his veins. "Nyda was with them from the very beginning." He stood outside of Nyda's room, Bayona and Audric beside him. Bayona crouched down, examining the residue that remained from the black powder. "Night bloom?" Evander asked as she rubbed it between her fingers.

"Yes, enough to send a whole army to sleep. She'd need that much just to take Astrid out," her voice quivered. "The Priestesses found a tear in their veil; Nyda must have put it there during the commotion." Evander bared his teeth, the wolf's claws poking to the surface, as he clenched his fists.

"Audric, send your Watchers to gather up all Nyda's men. I fail to believe they are all innocent in this, most of them were on duty when this went down." Audric nodded, words had escaped his tongue, the prickling fear for Narrdie, had grasped him like a cold chill on a night. "Cole!" Evander called, the guard instantly running to him. "I want this room sealed off, no one enters."

"Yes Sir."

"Bayona, find what you can. Hopefully, something in here will tell us where they are or what their plan is." He caught her eye and crouched down beside her, his hand resting on her shoulder. "I'll get them both back." She nodded, and swallowed hard, her throat bobbing.

The room was still bursting with birthday decorations when they all gathered around the table, the balloons still floating high, the confetti scattered along the tabletop and the presents Narrdie had opened – all neatly organised. The silence was heavy, broken as they slumped in their chairs, their thought spiralling out of control, the hurt of Nyda's betray shadowing over their faces. "Why would she do this?" Sharia whimpered.

Evander snorted, "Fear? Cowardice? Or perhaps her heart is just black. We are all to blame, we let our guard down and we got too comfortable."

"And yet, here we are doing nothing but moping around," Sharia blurted, instantly regretting her words. Evander's eyes flared as they snapped to her, he braced his hands on the table and leaned towards her.

"What would you have me do? We have no idea where she is, do you want me to send out vast searching groups? Lower our numbers even more? We can't risk that, even for Narrdie. With or without her, there's still a war coming." Sharia bit the inside of her cheeks and nodded to him, a silent apology. He leaned back in his chair and breathed out hard from his nose.

"Everything is about to change," Illythia said blankly to no one in particular. "This isn't like before; they took her this time for a reason – Astrid too. You can all deny it, pretend to ignore it, but you can feel it in the wind, in your bones. Tell me I'm wrong?" She met each one of them, holding their stares until they nodded or looked away, she snorted. "See."

"What's your point Illythia? Spit it out," Audric growled.

"My point, is that the war isn't coming – it's here. We're out of time. Sharia is right, we are sulking around and instead we should be trying to figure out their plan. They've always tried to get their hands on Narrdie, by why now, why this day? And why take Astrid? Why not just kill her?" Nakoma's head shot up.

"Blood." Nakoma announced.

Evander straightened in his seat and met Nakoma's eyes, a knowing look residing in them. "It begins with a river of blood, the blood from each group will merge into one and as it flows, I will rise." Evander said, repeating the words that Crow had spoken; he jumped to his feet and slammed his knuckles on the table. "Crow was cocky and, in her cockiness, she was also foolish, she told us their plan." Nakoma was on his own feet now, his eyes darting around the room.

"Ammon said he could separate Crow from Narrdie, they need blood to do it. Today is a new moon, others class it as a new beginning, that's why they needed her today!" Audric swore under his breath, the others swallowing down their own gasps and outbursts as it dawned on them all.

"That's why they took Astrid," Bayona whispered, her skin had paled. "I know the enchantment they're doing; they need the blood from the head races. They have Narrdie's blood and Crow's already. They need a Vampire, a Witch, a Shade, a wolf and . . ." She trailed off, her voice sticking to her throat, her hand shook as it came up to cover her mouth.

"A human." Mazruriuk finished, his voice void of all emotion. They all turned towards Ray, who had gone as still as a deer in a wood, her skin was as pale as a ghost and a shuddering breath wisped from her lips.

Chapter Forty-Two
Narrdie, Bayona & Audric

*I*t didn't take me long to figure out where I was, déjà vu tickled across my mind as I breathed in the damp air, the cold, wet concrete floor underneath me and looked up to the cold bars that once again – had me trapped. I sat up and wished I hadn't, a thundering pain brayed against my temples, a wave of nausea laced my stomach and each swallow felt like sandpaper on my skin. With an irritated grunt I rose to my feet, feeling them wobble underneath me and called out for the creature I despised most in this world. "DACRE!"

Metal doors scrapped along the floor as they were opened and that familiar mocking laughter drifted to my ears, Dacre strutted towards me; his hands raised in surrender. "A friendly warning, try using your powers and it will bounce back onto you – curtesy of Crow." I snarled and gripped the bars tightly, begging that he'd come close enough, that my claws wound puncture his neck. "I understand you're mad, Nyda's betrayal must have hurt," he mocked. I slammed myself against the bars, thrashing and hitting them like a caged tiger. "Now, now, Narrdie."

"I swear, that I will kill you, Dacre!"

"That temper of yours is really becoming an issue."

"I will kill you!"

"Easy girl, any harm comes to me and your mothering Vampire will meet a very unfortunate end," he warned. I froze. They had Astrid, they'd brought her here with me, but why? My heart twanged with ache, was she hurt? Dacre's grin cut a cruel line, "That's better. Oh, how rude of me - Happy Birthday Narrdie." He through his head back and laughed; he gestured to the old wooden chair beside me. "Sit."

"Where is Astrid?"

"I said, sit." He ordered again, his voice stern. I lifted my lip in a sneer as I sat, hating the way my obedience made the corners of his mouth lift. "Good girl."

"What have you done to Astrid?" I asked through gritted teeth.

"Nothing, yet," he answered blandly.

"Then why have you brought her here, Dacre?" Dacre cocked his head to the side, he closed the distance between him and the bars, curling his fingers around the cold iron.

"We need her, she's to play a very important part." Chilling, was the thought that whispered in my ears, a sick feeling laced the lining of my stomach, I could feel the shakiness wrapping around my throat as I spoke.

"You're going to separate Crow." Dacre's lips pulled back over his teeth, the grin that spread along his face, had the hairs on the back of my neck standing and I was all of a sudden, happy that these bars were separating us. "You're insane," I breathed.

"I thought you'd have been pleased."

"What made you so full of hate?" Dacre's faced turned hard; a muscle feathered in his jaw. "What caused you so much pain, that you'd see the world burn?"

"We're not talking about me," Dacre growled. I rose, slowly moving towards him; my hand lifted, and I brushed my fingers against his - they tensed.

"Maybe we should." My thumb lightly traced along his knuckles. "Dacre, what happened to make you betray them, to betray Mitchell, Evander - everyone who once called you friend, family. Why?" Dacre's eyes met mine, I searched them, hoping that maybe there was a glimmer of regret – sadness. He leaned towards me, until there was nothing but the cold bar between us, he snorted; his lips widening into a twisted smile.

"Because it felt good," he whispered.

The brutality of his words burned – red tainted my vision. My hands shook as the sharp claws grew, I snarled as I thrust my hand forward – digging my talons into the side of his neck, digging further and further. Dacre groaned with pain, his blood pouring from his neck, seeping through the cracks in my fingers. His hand snagged my arm, bending it back until I heard the snap, I shrieked as the burning pain shot throughout me and cowered back towards the corner of my cell – cradling my arm against my chest.

"You vicious, bitch," Dacre hissed, his voice lethal. He wretched the door open and stepped inside, instantly closing it behind him, leaving me alone in a tight space with one of the deadliest monsters, I'd ever known.

I wiped the blood from my nose, as Dacre's fist came down on me again. I spat another chunk of clotted blood into the pool that had gathered on the damp floor and turned towards him. "Is that all?" I mocked. "Come on Dacre, I can take a lot more than a few punches." Dacre huffed a laugh and undid the top three buttons of his shirt, he crouched beside me; his hand gripping the side of my cheeks.

"I'm just getting started, did you forget how it felt last time?" He laughed darkly, "are you forgetting the broken bones? Choking on your own blood, can't breathe, can't move? I'm going to make it worse this time, I'll break every single bone, tear every bit of flesh from your skin and then, I'm going to heal you and start all over." The blow of his fist smacked into me again, until I'd lost count on how many punches had slammed into my face, something brutal brayed against my stomach, once, twice. Dacre pulled back his boot and released another seven blows into my stomach, I gasped, feeling the blood rush up my throat and cough out my mouth.

I laughed, the sound bubbling through the blood that clogged my insides. "And you say I have a temper," I taunted.

"We are feeling brave today, aren't we?" Dacre's hand snagged my neck, lifting me up and slamming me hard against the wall, my legs buckled from under me – but he didn't let me fall. "Easy there, girl." He swept the hair from my face and squeezed my throat tighter, I winced and wheezed for more air.

"I see right through you; I see the brave person you pretend to be and the scared little girl you actually are. You don't think I can't feel you trembling under me?"

"And what about you, Dacre?" He paused, his head inclining towards me. "The great Hybrid, the great follower. You cling to whoever has power, Evander, Crow and now Ammon." I laughed a humourless laugh, not caring about the blood that drooped from my mouth. "You're nothing but a power hungry, whore of a man." A flicker of rage and predatory hunger crept into his eyes, his hand snaked up and snagged a fistful of my hair; he spun me around until my face slammed hard into the rough wall – black spots dotted my vision.

"You think you're tough? I can't wait to watch you crumble into nothing, when I kill everyone, you've ever loved. All those pathetic memories you've shared, rolling around with Evander, the little family meals you'd have and my personal favourite – your little viewing with Audric." I froze. "On the hilltop? You think Crow appearing was just a coincidence?" He laughed bitterly. "Nyda knew she couldn't release me, not without drawing attention to herself; so, she followed you. She waited, waited until you and Audric let your guard down, used a glamour to make you both sleep, then she pulled Crow forward and bashed Audric's skull to make it look like you attacked him." I couldn't breathe. "Nyda has been with us from day one, ever since she led me to little Graya." Evander's sister, Nyda's best friend – she'd served her up on a plate for him. "She kept the others from finding Crow, from reaching the sanctuary in time," Dacre continued. "She even told me how broken you were, how much you blamed yourself for all those deaths, poor, poor, Narrdie." I winced, as he pressed my face harder, the stone biting hard into my cheek, I could already feel the wetness from the slit that had formed on my cheek. "I never even got to tell you the last piece of the puzzle, the final element we need to release Crow. It was so easy for Ammon to manipulate her, but I suppose their kind are the weaker race." Terror snagged my heart, as it began to take a frightening beat, my tongue went dry and heavy and before he'd even said it – I knew.

"Rosie."

Dacre snickered against my ear, his voice arrogant and proud. "Bingo. Humans should know better than to play in our world."

"You're a monster," I spat.

"Our world is filled with monsters, Narrdie. Better to become one, than die by one." His tongue traced along my neck; each touch was abhorrent, unbearable.

"Dacre," Ammon's voice echoed, amusement bold in his tone. "Having fun?" Dacre sniggered, he pulled me back and with one final ruthless blow to the stomach, he dropped me to the floor. He locked me back up and looked down at me, not a single glimmer in his eyes to even try and look like he cared.

"Just reminding her of her place," Darius chortled.

"Good. I'd love to watch you continue, however it's almost time," Ammon almost sang, excitement leaking from him like water.

"I'll get this cute little vessel ready," Dacre offered. He crouched down on the other side of the bars. "Are you ready to meet Crow?"

"Illythia!" Bayona shrieked, as she jerked up. Her cream pillow now stained red with the blood that engulfed her eyes. "Illythia!" She cried out again, knowing she was next door. Bayona felt like a sudden lightning bolt had slammed into her chest, the horror that was her vision had clogged up her throat, her head strummed with pain and even with her psychic abilities – she couldn't see. Illythia flung open her door, her teeth bare and eyes red – Talon at her side. Immediately, she retracted her fangs as she took in Bayona's curled up form, the blood that surrounded her, burning her nose.

"Bayona! I'm here," she soothed as she took her hand, allowing her to suck up any amount of strength she needed. "Talon, get a wet cloth, quick!" Bayona gasped, begging the air to fill her too tight lungs. "Breathe, take a moment," Illythia instructed her softly.

"I . . . I saw Narrdie . . ." She winced, the stinging in her eyes causing pain to ripple around her.

"Here," Talon placed the damp cloth over her eyes, taking extra care as to not harm her anymore; his hand stroking her back tenderly.

"Thank you," she breathed, feeling the cold licking away the burn flames that struck her skin. "Gather everyone," she begged as her hand gripped Illythia. "Get them all!"

"Are you sure?" Evander asked, his voice hostile, Illythia gave him a hard look and he half smiled apologetically.

"Yes," Bayona confirmed, her voice weak. "It was a tomb, they had Narrdie and Astrid. Nyda is the one who is going to separate them, I saw Narrdie on an altar made of stone, Ammon and Dacre holding her down." Audric dropped down beside her and took her hand in his, he pressed his forehead against hers.

"We'll stop them, we'll get them back and this time we'll end Dacre and Ammon for good. I promise you, sister – we'll get them back." She squeezed his hand, whimpering softly. He cleared his throat and stood to face everyone. He was the Lord Commander now and it was time to become the leader he was trained to be. "Evander, Talon, gather our people, tell Ameer to summon as many Watchers as we can. Nakoma, gather the Loopins, I want them spread around the tomb, no doubt Dacre has that place under heavy guard." Nakoma twisted where he stood, he ran his hand through his hair. "What?" Audric snapped.

"My kind are at your disposal, but there are hundreds of tombs out there. How are we going to find the right one, by then it could be too late?" He was right. That feeling of dread sat deep in Audric's stomach, cutting him hard. Think, Audric, think – he snarled to himself over and over. His jade-coloured eyes set on Karro and for once he found himself thanking the mother, for the blood bond Narrdie shared with him. "Narrdie will have to be moved to the tomb, from wherever they are hiding her. Nyda will be storing all her powers and strength for the separating, meaning we'll have a small window of opportunity to track her." Karro's ears perked up, Audric grinned to him. "When that window is open, Karro you'll be able to find out where she is. You'll be able to see where that tomb lies, then we'll move." Evander slapped him on the shoulder, praising him, before signalling to Talon to follow.

"What of Nika?" Mazruriuk asked, his voice tight and body tense.

Ray, the final key to Ammon and Dacre's plan, without her they wouldn't be able to pull out Crow. Audric's eyes rested on her, she looked more human than ever – seemed smaller in size, her body looked frail compared to everyone else. Her eyes had misted over; her breath raspy and scared, her cheeks were bony and her fingers brittle as they clung to Mazruriuk's arm. However, Audric had seen her fight, had watched this timid mouse, turn into a wildcat and tear apart anything in her way. "Ray?" He asked, he would not lock her away like a prized possession, he'd seen how it almost made Narrdie crumble. No, Ray was her own women, with her own mind and own choices. He would not dictate like Vlad; he would let her decide her own fate. "It's your decision."

Ray looked to him, shock residing on her face and he knew, she was expecting them all to keep her contained. She glanced around to the others, needing the confirmation from them – they nodded, even Mazruriuk – whose face had turned as hard as stone – nodded that it was up to her. "Narrdie and Astrid are my family too. When the Order wanted to . . . banish me to the tear," she shuddered, pushing away the chilling thought. "Narrdie was prepared to kill every one of them, to stop that happening. I know you are all hoping that I hide, but I can't sit back and do nothing. I'm going with you all." Audric clenched his jaw and nodded to her.

"Then it will be done."

Chapter Forty-Three

Everyone

*D*acre slammed me down hard on the stone slab, my back vibrating from the pain. Candles burned bright as they covered the tomb, hiding in holes where the wall had come away and gathering in corners to light up the shadows. Dacre had spent the last few hours, beating me down, keeping me weak so I couldn't fight them off. *Coward.*

"What have you done to her?" Astrid snarled, she thrashed and buckled against the chains that held her tightly to the wall. Ammon looked towards her, a look of hunger, a look so feral – every part of her went tense. A morbid grin stretched across his face, a smile as elusive and chilling as a winter storm. "Dacre, don't do this!" She pleaded, trying to contain the emotion in her voice. There was a tightness in Dacre's jaw, as he tried to block out her shouts of pleading and protesting, he looked towards Nyda, those unearthly features threatening to devour her – a silent question on his face that was waiting to be answered and he was growing impatient.

"The moon is almost up," Nyda spoke fast, her voice shaking on every word. "Go get the human." Ammon's hate filled eyes snapped to her, to the order she'd given him; he stepped closer, his body shadowing over her. A breath shuddered in her throat, "forgive me, my Lord." Ammon's lips pulled back over his yellow teeth and I thought he was going to tear her to chunks right there.

"Ammon," Dacre cautioned.

"I'll be back soon," he sang, before vanishing into nothing.

"Nyda, you don't have to do this," Astrid beseeched. "You know what will happen!" Nyda's eyes misted over, the knife in her hand quivering in her shaky hand. Dacre's eyes were on her, observing her carefully – ready to cut her down if she tried to double-cross him; he growled as Astrid continued to talk Nyda down. His hand whipped down across Astrid's cheek, before she could react – his hand gripped tightly around her throat.

"Not another word," he warned through gritted teeth.

"You pathetic pup," she snarled, baring her teeth at him. Dacre's claws poked out, his sharp nails digging into her neck, she grimaced – her blood dripping down his hand. "I will watch as they burn you," she promised. Dacre tilted his head, the claw on his thumb tracing the skin under her eye.

"Well how about I take those pretty eyes?" Dacre dragged his nail along her cheek, the crimson line forming. "Then you can compare scars with your little Witch."

"Leave her alone," I warned. Dacre rolled his eyes and leaned his head back; he sighed dramatically and turned to me.

"Suddenly, everyone's found their voice, I'll be right with you Narrdie," he mocked.

"I said leave her alone, half breed." Dacre stiffened, a low grumble slipping from his mouth; his hand dropped from Astrid.

Astrid's eyes widened, her mouth dropped open, and terror ghosted across her face. "What are you?" She gasped to him. Dacre laughed, the laugh echoed, sounding like a cluster of people – Nyda cowered back from him, as he turned towards me.

His yellow eyes slowly began to swirl, the colour changing to a chilling silver, dark veins spread around his face; his tanned skin turning to a sickly grey. He smiled, his red gums turned black and began to ooze and drip over his razor teeth.

Crippling fear choked me; it wasn't the wolf in him that made people quake with fear - it was this.

"D-Dacre?" My voice trembled.

"Nyda," Dacre snarled. "Begin."

$\mathcal{E}$vander raised his fist, stopping everyone; he could feel the darkness's presence, it was like smoke, seeping into his nose, blocking up his throat - filling his lungs. He could feel it, like spiders crawling around his skin, like food curdling in his stomach. "Slow," he whispered.

The closer they came, the more they saw the darkness taint the wood, the green of moss had turned to ash, the tree barks burned and began to wither like a struck matchstick, the fresh clean air - now foul and full of decay. Yes, this was the place. The silence was rippling throughout, it unnerved him, sent the hairs on the back of his neck to stand, the dark dwellers were never this quiet.

Oyku growled lowly, she quickstepped to catch up to him. *"Something is approaching,"* she warned him nervously. Evander nodded in her direction, he could hear the footsteps, smell the new scent that had whispered around them, whoever they were - they weren't infected by darkness.

"Be on guard, no one attacks until I give the order."

Three approached, two men and a woman in the middle of them, they dressed in thick padded leather and fur, gold and silver chains dangling from one side of their shoulder to the other. Their hair was long, and fashioned in multiple plaits, black charcoal was spread along their eyes and down their lips, red tattoos of runes and animals peeked from their skin. The woman inclined her head to the men and instantly they bowed their heads to Evander, she followed after. "I hear," she began her voice foreign and familiar - he couldn't quite put his finger on it. "That you are in need of numbers."

"Who are you," Evander asked, his voice struggling to hold the aggression.

"Lytta, of the Geirolf Clan."

"Völvas?" She nodded; Evander scoffed. "And who said I need numbers, Lytta?"

"From someone who is a friend, as well as a foe." Evander knew who she meant before the name even slipped from her lips, his smirk pulled at the corners of his mouth.

"Mara." Evander couldn't contain the laugh that burst out of him, it was sullen. Mara, a unique creature, never picking a side and always showing up when you least expected – normally during the worst times. "Ah, Mara. She has a funny sense of humour, sending me three." Lytta tilted her head towards the man on her left, she nodded once. The man grunted, lifted two fingers to his mouth and whistled. All around them, bursts of whistles, sounding like birdsong and high-pitched animalistic howls, brought the forest to life, tens – hundreds responded. "Welcome to the fight, Lytta." Lytta bowed her head to him, before vanishing in the forest fog, where she'd wait until Evander called the attack.

"Völvas?" Bayona asked, somewhat shocked. "I thought they all died."

"Apparently not, seems Mara, is full of surprises."

"What are Völvas?" Audric asked.

"Seeresses, Shamans, Witches – whatever they call themselves, they are a powerful lot. Better they are on our side than against us."

Bayona gasped as she was drawn to the sky, her hands beginning to shake at her sides, as she took in the black mist that began to take over the clouds, spiralling as they shot down towards the tomb. "Evander!" She shrieked; her hand point up. "Nyda has started."

*T*he dark dwellers descended on them, as fast as the night swallowed up the day. They worked fast, separating and isolating everyone, attacking in groups of ten. The more the dark creatures they killed – the more the dark creatures came. Mazruriuk's power surrounded him, cutting through them like a knife in butter, some fought, but most recoiled and tried to run from him.

"Nika!" A Skinner dove for him, it's jaw wide, Mazruriuk snarled his irritation and thrust his tendrils forward – it wrapped around it, squeezing until it was nothing but chunks of bone and flesh. "Nika!"

"Mazruriuk!" Illythia's voice screaming. She was pinned, held down by a Shade, wrestling to get it's knife as far from her. Mazruriuk roared, he allowed his power to swallow him – turning him into shadows and smoke. He wrapped his cloak of darkness around the Shade, forcing it down its throat, making it's veins burst, it's lungs shrivel and eyes pop; he dropped it to the floor, where it lay as nothing but a skin suit. "Thank you," Illythia said breathlessly, he helped her to her feet and quickly scanned her over.

"Are you harmed?" She shook her head. "I can't find her."

A gurgle turned their attention to the group of Skinners, Illythia shuddered. "You go," Mazruriuk ordered. "I'll deal with these; you go and find Rosie." She squeezed his hand, praying to the mother that this wouldn't be his end, before fleeing on a gust of wind.

Ray moaned, the pain splintering up her hands as she knelt on the floor, the men around her – the collectors that worked for Shades – snickered as they swarmed around her. "Lost little human," one cackled, his boot slamming into the side of her stomach. He gripped her hair, hauling her to her feet, his tongue snaked out and traced up her cheek – she grimaced at the stench of his breath. He pressed himself against her, his hand wrapping around her neck, "I think it's cute," he mocked to the others. "

Should we kill it or keep it?" Ray snagged the dagger that was tucked into her belt and thrust it deep in his thigh, smirking as his pain filled shrieks filled her ears. She kicked herself up, spinning around until her foot smashed into his face, his nose popping. She landed hard, flinching at the sting that ricocheted along the back of her legs; she gripped her dagger tightly in her hand – her knuckles turned as white as bone.

"Tough little bitch, aren't you?" One of the other two sneered, they began to circle her, predators watching their preys, final fight. "Can you handle two at the same time," his grin was slimy. They lunged for her, she ducked as one made an attempt, to grab her, she tossed her knife to her other hand and stabbed it hard in his chest, dragging it all the way down, until his insides splattered on the ashen ground. The other moved before she had a chance to look up from the core, he stuck her face hard with the palm of his hand, he gripped her hair and dragged her along the floor, before lifting her off her feet and sending her crashing into a boulder. Ray leaned over, coughing out thickets of blood, she cried out as she reached for her dagger, screaming as his foot brayed down on her hand, until she felt her fingers break.

"I'm going to show you the meaning of pain," he spat.

"Enough," Ammon snarled; he waved his hand, dismissing him.

"My Lord," he greeted, his voice trembling.

"Leave."

Ray stared in horror as Ammon strutted towards her, he tilted his head and laughed darkly – brushing away the hair that was glued to her face, from sweat and blood. "Hello again, my sweet Rosie." She stuck him hard across the face and forced herself to her feet, snatching up her knife and holding it on its side – perfect for slashing. Ammon snickered and brushed the mark where her hand had hit; he'd been hoping for a fight. "I do love humans for their courage . . . and stupidity. Would you like to play? You can barely stand, my dear."

"You used me," she growled.

"Poor little Rosie, fucking white Shades has made you naïve. Did I hurt you feelings?" An angered scream bellowed out of her, she ran at him, slashing her dagger crazily, but each move she made; he dodged – not even breaking a sweat. He grabbed her arms and flipped them behind her, pinning her up against a tree. He smiled, a haunting look and breathed her in, smelling along the crook of her neck. "Is that all you've got?" He whispered in her ear,

"Let her go!" A voice filled with fury snarled. Ammon rolled his eyes and groaned in annoyance; he arched his head to the side – at the foolish Vampire.

"Run along, before I snap your little fangs," he warned.

"Illythia, don't," Ray begged.

"Let. Her. Go." Ammon spun Ray around and drove his fist hard into her stomach, she dropped to the floor – gasping and groaning in pain.

Illythia shrieked with rage and ran at him, she veered to the side – dodging his fist and slashed her claws across his eye, taking a protective stance in front of Ray. Ammon nodded as he felt the marks her nails had left, surprise filling his eyes as his thick blue blood lingered on his fingertips. "You made me bleed, girl. No one has ever been able to go that," he praised.

"Come near her and I'd do more than scratch you." Illythia knew all too well, that he could wipe her out with his power, all he'd need to do was wave a finger, but he was arrogant and liked to make everything a show.

"I would really love to stay and play, but unfortunately . . ." He trailed off and looked up to the sky, the ever-growing dark mist, was now fierce and sparks began to shock the ground around it. "It seems we are pressed for time."

Illythia gasped as something behind her ripped through her back and clenched tightly around her heart. Ammon leaned his face close to her ear, "you lose." The Ammon she stared at, the one across from her vanished like mist – a mirage, trickery, a glamour she failed to see. "You want to scream? But you can't, not unless I allow it. I can make you feel years' worth of pain, or none at all."

"You kill her, you lose everything." Ray's voice quivered; she stood on her feet, holding her dagger to her own throat. "Let her go and I'll come with you." Illythia wanted to shriek at her, to shake her and tell her not to do this, but her body had become a statue of fear, frozen on the brink of death.

"You're bluffing," Ammon snapped, his voice tense. Ray clenched her jaw; with shaking hands she dug the knife in her neck and slit enough to make the blood dribble down her collarbone. "Stop!" Ammon snarled, his eyes wide with panic. "Stop." Ammon carefully pulled his hand from Illythia's chest, gently lowering her to the floor; he turned to Ray, his hands outstretched. "Put it down," he begged her. "Rosie, put it down." The knife slipped from her fingers and clattered to the floor, Ammon breathed out in relief and waited; his hand still outstretched for her. "Time to go."

Nakoma could smell her, she was close and she was hurt. The fire in him burned, burned to find her, it scorched its way through the creatures that launched for him, never giving them a chance to skim even a hair on his head. He froze, the toxic blood that flowed through his veins – iced over. His swords slid from his hands, his heart beginning to shrivel in his chest, he ran to her and pulled her to him. "Illythia?" His voice croaked; her back was bleeding – claw marks lingering on her pale skin. "Illythia." He held his hands over her eyes, waiting to feel that familiar pulse of life, seconds passed – minutes. Nakoma ripped into his wrist, not caring to be gentle, he let his blood pour over her mouth, knowing that it wouldn't poison her, fore her blood also ran in his veins. "I will not lose you."

Talon emerged on them, Mazruriuk close on his heels. "Nakoma?" Talon asked, seeing his sister cradled like a newborn babe, in his hands. "No," he breathed. He moved to go to her, but Mazruriuk's hand on his shoulder had him halting.

"Look."

Illythia's eyes snapped open, she jerked up – retching and gasping. She looked to Nakoma, her eyes turning as black as his, her hand reached up to cup his cheek. "Nakoma," she breathed. She leaned up, her lips meeting his, they held each other fiercely, possessively.

"Illythia," Talon spoke softly, shock sparked through him, setting his feet moving until he dropped beside her, he was relieved that she was alive – that relief suddenly turning into dread as he examined her face. "Your eyes, they're like . . . his."

"You've both shared blood," Mazruriuk began, his voice was tense, rushed. "Offered it up to save each other's lives, I believe that makes Illythia a half breed and Nakoma, will have some of your Vampire abilities." Talon's face pulled tight, his eyes scrutinizing over Nakoma and Illythia, he was surprised; she looked unbothered by this.

"You love him." Talon spoke, it wasn't a question, but Illythia's smile was answer enough. Her smile faded, as quickly as it had come.

"Rose," she gasped; her eyes flooding with tears.

"You saw her?"

"A-Ammon had her, I tried to stop him and he . . . he was going to tear my heart out. She made him spare me, gave herself up in exchange." She sobbed, Nakoma pulled her into him, whispering soothingly in her ear. Mazruriuk dropped to his knees.

"Ammon has Rosie," Mazruriuk said, his voice barely a whisper. "We're too late."

☾

*N*yda's body was vibrating, swaying from side to side; her lips moving so fast, I couldn't make out what she was staying. Astrid continued to pull, thrash, do everything she could to free herself - each attempt failed. The moment Nyda has begun her chant, my body had surrendered, my limbs felt like they were weighed down by chains, nails pinning my hands and I could feel Crow, clawing her way towards the surface – gutting me from the inside. "Dacre," Nyda called. Her voice was chilling, consumed by shadowed whispers.

Dacre rolled up his sleeve, holding his wrist over the wooden bowl, he winked towards me – arrogant bastard. Nyda raised a dagger with a stained bone handle, towards the ceiling, her eyes rolling back in her head, as blood trickled from her nose. In one fast movement, she slash the blade across his skin – twisting his hand, so not one drop was wasted, once she was done, she returned to her, zombie-like stance.

"Look who I found," Ammon sang, as he dragged Ray into the tomb.

"No!" Astrid shrieked. "Let her be!"

Dacre grinned wickedly and gripped Ray's face. "Hello Rosie." She bared her teeth and spat in his face; she lunged for him, but Ammon swooped his hand around her and pinned her to the wall.

"She's a feisty one," he mocked, pinning her hands above her.

"Get the fuck off me!" She growled, Ammon struck her with a quick backhand and a ripple of snarls, echoed as Astrid lunged against the chains. Dacre wiped the spit from his cheek and looked to Ray, his eyes looking her up and down like a piece of meat he wanted to demolish.

"Such brave spirits humans have."

Nyda fell backwards, falling into Dacre's arms; she sucked in the air and winced as she spoke – her voice frail. "The spell is done, we just need to mix the bloods, the moon is almost high."

"Let's not waste time then."

Ray's screams shook the tomb, her screams splintering into terrified wails, Ammon gripped her by her hair and dragged her towards Nyda – her dagger reflecting in the candlelight. Dacre held Astrid in a vice grip, one hand around her hands – the other around her throat; she struggled against him; every movement useless. "Nyda, please stop!" She begged. Nyda's lip quivered, she couldn't meet her eyes; she couldn't meet Ray's either, even if she was rethinking her choices – she knew it was too late. The fear she felt towards Dacre and Ammon, dominated over everything else.

"Hold her here," Nyda ordered. Ammon forced Ray's head down, pulling her hair to one side.

"Nyda, you don't have to do this," I pleaded. Nyda's eyes met mine, she blinked several times, trying to remove the tears that threatened to spill over.

"Hold her still," Nyda said, her voice suddenly empty of emotion.

"Ray, close your eyes," Astrid begged. "Close your eyes, sweet girl. Narrdie, look away."

I couldn't.

I was powerless, all I could do was watch in horror. Nyda didn't hesitate as she slid the blade along Ray's throat, slowly. I screamed, I screamed as her blood erupted; I screamed as I saw the light leave her eyes and her body sag to the floor. Ammon tossed Ray's body aside like a crumpled-up piece of paper – not a shade of shame darkening his face. "That was intense," Ammon snickered. "Dacre, your turn."

My blood pounded in my ears, I could feel my heart shattering to pieces, as Dacre towed Astrid forward, pushing her head down. The smouldering fire that burned in her eyes, was now vacant – reduced to defeated tears. She looked to me, that mothering smile gracing her lips once more.

"Be brave, Narrdie Moon. Do not let the darkness, stop the light from coming through." I heard her voice sooth my mind, I clung to it – begging her not to go, pleading with the mother to save her. She closed her eyes, as Nyda slit across her skin, tossing her beside Ray once her blood ran dry. I shrieked.

Nyda clasped the bowl in her hands, carefully swilling it until the bloods were mixed. "Open her mouth." Dacre gripped the sides of my cheeks, squeezing painfully until my lips parted, Nyda wasn't gentle as she poured the blood into my mouth. Dacre's hand covered over me, digging in, until the liquid ran down my throat.

Then I heard her laughing.

Fire ignited in my veins, scrapping and burning every part of me, my skin felt like it was being stripped off – slowly. Needles pricked my heart, over and over and the drumming in my head, swelled against my temples. I could feel her, she lingered on the brink of my skin, peeling herself forward; savouring every bit of agony I was feeling – she wanted me to hurt. Darkness erupted around us, swallowing the tomb, blowing out the candles; eerie whispers bouncing along the walls. I couldn't scream, I couldn't move, I couldn't feel anything but pain.

My world vanished.

⟨

Crow moaned in pleasure, she ran her hands over her body – her body, not Narrdie's. She could feel it, feel all the darkness absorbing into her, feel all her power finally returning. The candlelight flickered as they came back to life and she turned to face her loyal subjects. She tutted, looking down to the wasted corpses of a human and Vampire, ones she knew would haunt Narrdie forever.

"I had my doubts on you," she hissed towards Nyda – who had her head bowed, fear licking at her insides. "I thought you'd be too spineless, too pitiful to perform such a task. However, I was mistaken. You have earned you place amongst us, at least for a little while longer." Crow's face lifted as she turned to Dacre and Ammon, a cruel grin spreading wide. "My Lord, my love," she greeted them. Dacre growled with lust, his eyes slowly devouring her; he gripped her throat and pulled her towards him – her tongue licked along his lips. "Later, my love," she teased; her hands trailing along his stomach. "We have work to do, but later I'm all yours," she promised.

Ammon snatched the dagger from Nyda's hand, he moved towards Narrdie; raising it high – ready to plunge into her chest. "NO!" Crow snarled, her icy eyes flaring wide.

"If we don't kill her, she could be our undoing!"

"I said, no." Pain shot through him, threatening to rip him from the inside out. "She will not die like this. If anyone is to kill her, it will be me, by my hand." The bone in his wrist snapped, poking from his skin; he hissed his pain, but bowed his head to her.

"Yes, my Queen."

"Good." She released her hold on him, smirking as he cradled his bone. "I want her to suffer first, let her friends find her; let them think she is safe. Then and only then, will we destroy them all."

Chapter Forty-Four
Narrdie

*W*e'd lost.

Crow was free and I could feel deaths hold on me, in fact, I invited it – begged it to take me. Crow had been torn from my body, made into her own person – her own terrifyingly power person. Did I even have any power left? Nyda had willingly released Crow, knowing the havoc and slaughter she'd take out on the world, reducing humans to nothing but slaves or bones.

I was useless. My heart had been left in pieces; my soul was shredded – I was nothing but a shell, I didn't stop the tears that dripped from my eyes. The darkness had won, taken everything from me, I didn't know if there was anyone left alive.

I could feel my body dying, but even that was dragging out – Crow, was this her way of making me suffer? My impending torment. "Why can't I just die already?" I asked to no one in particular, my voice sounding hollow and dull in my ears.

"Because I will not allow it. Your spirit is not ready for me, my daughter. It is not your time." Her voice was like a melody, exactly what I'd imagine angels to sound like. It was comforting, soothing, like finding a light in the distance, after being stuck in the

frightening dark. The bitter cold of the tomb, the crushing silence – vanished, I felt the warmth on my skin, and it felt, safe.

"Hello?" I called out desperately, fearing that I was once again alone.

"You are never alone." Her hand rested against my cheek, it was comforting; she moved into my vision and tears burned my eyes for a whole new reason.

The most alluring, breath-taking women stood before me, smiling down at me – light glowing behind her. Her hair waved over her shoulder, glittering like diamonds had been veiled over her; silver and emerald eyes looked down to me, full of kindness and love. Her skin sparkled as it peeked from her lilac wrap and even in the dim light of the tomb, her silver jewels glistened. I knew who she was, I had spent hours, days, getting lost in her painting. The mother of all, Sulfaya. I was sure I must have been dead.

"You are not dead, my child." She assured me, her hand softly brushing my hair.

"Your painting doesn't do you justice," I almost wept. "Why have you come, if not to take me?" Her fingers tenderly brushed away the tears that trickled down my cheeks.

"Your spirit is broken; your light has been dimmed. My daughter, you have lost and given so much, it has caused you to fade; I am not here to take you – but to fix you." Her hand lightly rested behind my head, her other taking my hand, carefully she pulled me up, I braced myself – expecting to feel the overwhelming pain, of my broken bones and battered limbs. There was no pain, no stinging, not even a dull ache – no lingering symptoms that Dacre had even touched me.

"Narrdie Moon, let the path of light guide you, let it show you the path to follow. Do not let the pain taint you, pain is just that, it does not command you." I couldn't stop myself from looking to them, their bodies still curled on the floor; smothered in blood. Sulfaya followed my eyes, to Ray and Astrid; her brows knotted, she breathed out – a gusting of white wind, floated over them, removing the blood, cleansing the cuts on their throats. She'd made them look pure again, the bruises along their cheeks, now rosy and warm, their hair contained and resting elegantly around them, she'd made them look at peace.

"Thank you," my voice barely a breath.

"Take comfort in knowing, that they are with me; they are proud of you and will watch over you. They are not gone, my sweet child You will see them again. Take my words to your

heart, Narrdie Moon. You must rise, protect this world from those that seek to burn it, help guide those that fight with you."

I whimpered and tore my gaze from her. "I can't, I can't do it anymore. Crow, she's so powerful, more powerful than ever and I have nothing. I have failed you; I have failed this world." To my surprised, she laughed and tilted my chin up, until I met her eyes.

"You could never fail me. Crow was never stronger than you, she uses her power without balance, without thinking of the cost. You have your own strength, you understand the natural collide of the light and dark, you can overcome her. Believe in yourself, my daughter – find the light." Sulfaya leaned over me and placed her soft lips to my forehead. I felt it, felt the purity of her burst over me, felt the strength – my strength speed through my veins and pull the shattered pieces of my heart and soul, back together. She stroked my cheek once more, the light around her brightening. *"Release your spirit."*

$$\smile$$

$\mathcal{K}$arro had found me though our bond, he looked exhausted, beaten down and I knew why, he'd felt every fist, every kick and every broken bone, that Dacre had given me. He'd felt Crow, tearing and splitting me apart, as she'd brutalised her way to the surface, Sulfaya may have healed us, but it had still taken its toll on him. I moved to drop to Karro, but felt strong hands pull me into a tight embrace, the smell of cedarwood and jasmine filled my nose. My body eased, falling into him and I felt the prick of tears fog over my eyes, as Evander kissed me hard. "Narrdie," he breathed against my skin. I buckled in his hands.

"Crow's free," I sobbed into him, my legs buckled. "They killed Astrid and Rosie." Evander pulled me into him, shushing and making calming noises in my ear.

"I know, I know my girl." His jaw clenched as he looked down to them, they looked peaceful – thanks to Sulfaya.

A retching scream, filled the tomb – making us all fall into heavy silence, silence laced with pain and sorrow. Mazruriuk had fallen to his knees, clutching Ray's tiny body into him, his hand shook as he brushed it over her face. I stepped from Evander's arms and crouched beside him, placing my hand on his shoulder – the only comfort he'd allow. "I'm sorry, I'm so sorry," my voice quivered.

"How?" My lip trembled at his question; the memory still fresh in my mind.

"Nyda." Her name, was like fire on my tongue. I could feel Mazruriuk's energy darken the room, the pain he felt, turning vicious as his eyes ignited.

"We will mourn them both, but first, we tear them all apart." Mazruriuk growled, his words shocking me. His voice was raw, unsteady with rage, I could see the urge for revenge shadow across his face and I was more than happy, to give it to him. Mazruriuk's eyes fell on me, he felt my cheek and shook his head. "Not today. You have been weakened and these two deserve to be returned home."

"I can do this," I protested.

"Mazruriuk's right. A lot of our own were harmed trying to get to you. The war has changed, now that Crow has awaked her powers, the best option is to get back and regroup. If we push forward now, we are sure to lose." Evander pulled me to my feet, catching me as I swayed; he gave me a knowing look. "Narrdie, you can barely stand."

"Getting out of here, won't be easy," Karro blurted, it pained me to hear the strain in his voice.

"We stay together."

Audric clasped me against him, squeezing me so tightly I had to plead with him to let me go, his eyes were red, his face like marble. "I heard," his voice was tight. "About Rosie and . . . Astrid."

"Our family keeps getting smaller." Audric gripped my chin in his fingers and shook his head.

"Our family, remains in all us, no matter where they are." His eyes darkened as they looked past me, he pulled me behind him, his shoulder's seeming to grow wider, his muscles bigger and his doubled edged sword held firm in his hand. "Evander," he called through clenched teeth and nodded towards a hill stop.

There she was, Crow.

She stood tall, the moon high above her; she raised her hands high, as if they cupped the silver glow and a malicious smirk stretched wide along her cheeks. Her hair had been pulled back into a high ponytail, a horned crown with golden chains and a deep ruby gemstone; sat perfectly on her head.

Her icy eyes were chilling, they burned with the desire of fresh blood – yes, the Queen of darkness was finally here. She laughed, the sound slimy and cruel, she tilted her head to the side, as Dacre and Ammon flanked to her side.

"Narrdie Moon," she sang, stretching out my name.

I snarled and took a step forward, Audric shot his arm out, blocking my path. "Don't fall for her taunts," Audric shot back to me, keeping his voice low. The wolves circled around us; I could feel Mazruriuk's shadows form a shield across our people, he stood behind us – holding Ray close to him; Astrid held carefully in Evander's arms.

"Where's Nyda," I hissed under my breath. "Where's their creatures?" I couldn't feel them, couldn't hear them, the area around the tomb was bare. Something wasn't right.

"This is an ambush," Evander said, his tone had shifted to worry. "Karro, fall back, call the signal to round up and retreat." Karro's teeth were bare, slowly he padded back, keeping his eyes firmly on Crow, he nipped Oyku and instantly she dropped back with him.

"Make them bow to me," Crow purred. A mound of black smoke – as big as a tidal wave – spilled from the trees, causing everything in its path to wither and turn to dust, trees groaned as they shrivelled and decayed, the forest floor burned like lava and the earth began to crack under our feet.

"Run."

We'd fallen straight into Crow's trap.

The smoke descended on us fast, consuming every path we'd tried to take, steering us towards the awaiting horde. The horde had already began their attack, on the other half of our group, thunderous booms rippled throughout the forest, as Bayona forced them back – a stream of sweat lacing her forehead.

Her face dropped as she turned to Evander, to Astrid's body in his arms, her eyes glassed over, her face changed into something horrifying; her lips pulled back over her teeth and the air around her, thickened with fury. She roared, the sound as piercing as a banshee, her hands thrusted forward, her usually bright white light – now dark, furious and full of devastating power.

"Down!" Audric shouted.

Bayona's blast shot all around us, my breath sucked out of me, my body retched up on a fantom wind and was pushed back – branches and leaves, whipped at my face viciously. My head slammed hard against a rock and stars danced in my eyes, bile and blood filled my mouth and my bones rattled under my skin. I leaned over, vomiting onto the burned ground, my limbs screamed with each movement, nauseating dizziness choked around me and my eyelids became a dead weight.

Chapter Forty-Five
Crow

Crow licked the blood on her fingers, she crouched beside the young Watcher, savouring each moment of his death, taking pleasure, as she watched him choke on his own blood. A blast in the sky pulled her attention from Ameer, it was strong, strong enough to vanquish the black smoke she had unleashed on Narrdie. "That Witch will be a problem," she hissed towards Nyda – who trembled and dared not meet Crow's piercing eyes. She felt the twang in her chest, a sudden feeling of guilt, as she looked to Ameer, someone she had once called friend.

"Her name is Bayona," Nyda breathed. Crow snarled and whirled on her; her bloodied hand gripped her throat.

"Did I ask for her name? Did I ask for you to speak?" Nyda gulped, wincing as Crow's claws poked into her skin.

"Crow, let her be. We may need her still," Dacre said, his voice amused. Blood had splattered his face, his shirt torn and hands coated in crimson. Crow ran her eyes over me, taking devilish pleasure in the exposed skin, feeling the heat between her legs burn. She dropped Nyda – who instantly recoiled back – and swayed towards Dacre; her tongue gliding along the blood that prickled his face. Dacre growled his approval. "Are you having fun?" Dacre asked, his hands snaking around her waist, she pressed herself against him.

"Tons," she breathed into his ear, snagging it with her teeth. Another boom rippled around them, and Crow snarled, she turned back to Nyda. "Go and kill her." Nyda bowed her head. "Oh, and Nyda, if you fail, I'll flail you alive and feed you to a pack of Sivvs." Nyda's breath caught in her throat, she repressed a shudder and bowed low to the pair. "Did you find her?"

"Not yet, however Bayona's outburst has separated them all, I believe it'll be easy to pick them off." Crow smiled and ran her hand over his chest, Dacre leaned into her, but she pulled back.

"Soon, there's just one more thing I want to do."

$$\smile$$

*C*row managed to keep as much out the fight, as she needed, she felt untouchable; those that did dare to tackle her – ended up as another corpse for the worms to feast on. She was beginning to get bored, she longed for a worthy partner to play with, most however, cowered and ran as she danced her way through the forest, going deeper and deeper than most dared to follow. Hunger drove her forward, searching for her target and just as her patience dwindled, she caught his scent.

Crow's haunting eyes locked onto Audric, she stalked along the cliff top, watching him like a vicious animal waiting to strike. He was strong, a wealthy warrior for her to practice with, the dark dwellers that rushed him, failed and were reduced to puddles. He was good, exceptionally good; his speed, his senses, had been trained to their best ability. Yes, he would do perfectly.

With a playful rumble, she backflipped from the edge; landing gracefully in front of him. She hissed, a warning command for those around to flee, he was hers and she would not have anyone interrupt. Audric whirled around to face her, his shoulders puffed up and face crumpled into hatred; he snarled. "Crow."

"I was hoping to find you. Tell me, what kind of Watcher, allows his charge to be taken, beaten, tormented and then left a broken shell?" She laughed heinously. "Not only have you failed to protect her, but you also let your surrogate Vampire mother – die. How ashamed your brother would be." Audric flicked out his blades and lunged forward, Crow's grin turned dark, murderous. "Good, little Watcher." She mocked, as she launched herself towards him.

Audric groaned, wiping his mouth free of blood, he rose from where she had knocked him down – for the third time. She was fast, much faster than a Vampire and she used it to her advantage, waiting until the last second; she was strong, stronger than any creature he had ever fought. She sighed and picked at the crusted flesh under her nail. "Ah, Audric, you aren't making this very entertaining for me. The so called, Lord Commander of the Order."

"You're holding back, Crow. Why?" Audric quizzed breathlessly. The minute he was stable on his feet, Crow's palm struck his chest; the hit, backed up by a wave of dark power, that hurtled his body back into the cliff wall. Audric swerved, dodging the blade, that she swung down towards him; she hissed her annoyance, as the blade wedged in the cliff crack. Audric skidded forward, slamming himself into her and pinning her by her throat, she perched her lips – gesturing for a kiss. "You could have killed me a few times over. You're waiting for something."

"I will kill you, Audric." He snarled, lifting her forward, before brutally banging her head hard against the sharp rocks. Black blood oozed from her skull and her teasing grin dropped, fury burned in her eyes. "You messed up my hair," she growled. His hand tightened, crushing into her windpipe, on a regular person – the pressure would choke them. However, he knew that Crow couldn't be killed as easily as anyone else, at least now; he didn't have to worry about it impacting Narrdie.

"Leaving Narrdie, has made you vulnerable. Now there is nothing protecting you." Crow's eyes looked past him – to where Narrdie and Evander stood, with wide eyes, a deep rumble sounding in her throat; she smirked proudly.

"Don't worry, I won't hold back anymore." She raised her hand and a sharp painful spark, ripped into his chest, he fell back; his hands lifting to the wound – feeling the thick dark blood, which gushed from it.

Crow swooped down, scrapping Audric's double sided blade, into her hands; she didn't face him as he ran for her, she kept her eyes on Narrdie, soaking up the fear in her stare. She dropped low and skidded through his legs, her elbow striking the back of his knee, dropping him to the floor.

Crow's foot slammed down hard over his chest, Audric groaned as the ball of her heel, dug hard into his wound. He tried to rise, to flip her off, but felt a sudden force pinning down his arms – a force that felt like slime and death. "I win," she sang, before spinning the blade in her hand and driving it down hard into his heart.

Narrdie's scream was like music to her ears.

Crow flashed her a wicked smirk – her pointed teeth winking in the moonlight – she twisted the blade in his chest, his screeches echoing and blood gargling from his mouth. "Audric!" Narrdie wailed, rushing towards him, only to be stopped as Evander's hands wrapped around her.

Crow crouched beside him, gently wiping the blood from his mouth. "Take a deep breath," she warned, retching the blade from his body. "Have you tasted death enough?"

"Get away from him!" Narrdie snarled.

"I'm not going to kill you just yet, Audric. No, you have a much bigger part to play." Crow caught Narrdie's burning glare, as she leaned down and placed her lips to his.

Audric's body tensed, vibrating, as blood curdling screams and screeches ripped from his mouth. His hands clawed at the ground, mud and dirty digging underneath his nails. Crow's smirk was triumphant, she watched with wicked glee, as Audric's sun kissed, tanned skin, turned grey – his blue veins, changing into a darkened purple. The tips of his fingers turned black, like ink had been painted over them and his jade eyes, fading as the darkness consumed. "Stand," she ordered. He breathed heavy; his body grew taller, stronger – deadlier. She circled him, running her finger along his chest and shoulders. "Very impressive."

"Audric?" Narrdie's voice shuddered. Crow turned to her and laughed cruelly. "What have you done to him?" Narrdie's eyes were filled with horror, tears streamed down her face.

"I fixed him." Crow moaned, as she could feel the darkness's hold circling around him, the power in his veins, now hers to command. "Audric?"

"My Queen," his snarl replied.

"Kill her."

Chapter Forty-Six
Narrdie

*A*udric.

I couldn't see him, not the Audric I knew, my Watcher, the person who had risked his life to save me, who'd had been there for me when I had no one.

My best friend.

I could feel the hatred; feel it in his eyes as he looked to me. The darkness that Crow had tainted him with, leaked from his skin, clogging the air – choking me. "Kill her," Crow commanded him; her face lighting up like a Christmas tree.

"Narrdie, we have to go," Evander's voice rang in my ears, it was faint – muffled by the shock that had gripped me hard. "Narrdie!" Evander's hands gripped my shoulders, shaking me until I looked to him. "We need to go."

"We can't leave him," I whimpered.

"It's not Audric anymore!" I tore my gaze back to Audric, who was now heading straight for me, mist gathered in his palms, igniting with fire; he threw one forward, the flames barely skimming the top of my head.

A golden Arma burst forward, thrusting Audric back until he landed at Crow's feet. Bayona ran for us, her hand outstretched; her lip quivered as she took Audric and the dark energy that had tainted him. "Audric, no," her voice trembled.

"Evander, most of our people have fallen back," Talon announced as he ran to join us, he was breathless, his eyes burned a hungered red; Rev and a small group of wolves ran at his flank.

"Run away, little Narrdie!" Crow taunted; anger had creased he face.

Evander's fingers tightened on my arm. "Now's not the time."

"I'll kill her."

"I know, but that day isn't today. Think of our people, they need you." I nodded and Evander pulled me back towards Talon. He cupped his hand over his mouth and released three, high-pitched calls, within seconds, the forest came alive with whistles. "Lytta will cover us."

"Who's Lytta?"

"I made some new friends."

$\mathcal{W}$e'd barely made it back alive and if it wasn't for Lytta and her clan – we'd all be dead. Lytta and her people had formed a line, separating us and Crow's army. Their powers moved as one, creating a light so bright and powerful – it was like the sun itself, had exploded. The dark dwellers cowered back, dissolving into northing but dust if they came to close. The Priestesses had invited them inside, but the Völvas, preferred the outdoors.

I'd went straight to my room, shook off the healers, ignored Evander as he called my name – even ordered Karro to stay away. I wanted to be alone, I wanted the crushing silence, wanted to feel the heavy pain that laced the air. Crow had won tonight, in more ways that she'd hoped.

It had been two days since the battle, two days since the darkness had dug its claws into Audric and ripped him from me. I had been a mouse in this home, barely speaking to anyone, couldn't stand the taste of food and whenever laughing reached my ears, anger would ripple inside of me.

I had taken to sitting outside most hours, staring into the emptiness of the forest, it was quiet, almost like there hadn't just been a battle – like the blood hadn't stained the mossy floor. I tucked my knees into my chest and wrapped my arms around them, I'd come out here to be alone, but the crunching of boots on stone, had me groaning.

Nakoma dropped down beside me, bracing his arms across his knees. "You know, as the days grow, so does the oath and I can feel your sadness in it – it's loud," he said, trying to lighten my mood. "I guess I don't have to ask what's on your mind." I snorted and shuffled my head away his from his prying eyes.

"She set out to find him, because she knew that infecting him with the darkness, was like killing him to me. I've lost him." Nakoma clicked his tongue and let out a long huff.

"You haven't lost him; you know where he is – you know he's alive. He's just . . . different. You can still get him back – we can still get him back. Mazruriuk can't get Rosie back, she's lost, as well as Astrid. Illythia is just as broken, she blames herself for Ammon taking Rosie and I may not have come here on good graces in the beginning, but I've grow to care for everyone; I feel there loses as well," Nakoma admitted. "And Evander is losing someone now."

"Who?"

"You." The word hit me like a ton of bricks – smashing into my chest and burying me under rubble. I turned to him, searching his face for the predatory creature we'd caught, but there was genuine grief in his eyes, sadness tainting his face. "What I'm trying to say is . . ." he trailed off, his breath shuddering in his throat. "We are all broken. We are all wounded and feel the heaviness of failure and we all need each other. Stop feeling sorry for yourself alone, come inside and let us share it, let us pick you up." The pit in my stomach ripped open again and the tears gathered in my hands, as I sobbed into them. Nakoma put his arm around me and pulled me into him, his hand rubbing my back.

"I couldn't stop her, the moment she was ripped from me – I felt her take every bit of power in me. I'm useless now, I have nothing." My sobs turned to wails and my tears began to stain his t-shirt.

"You're wrong, Narrdie. She can't take what is yours; what runs in your blood. Find it, find it and unleash it."

"I don't know how."

"It starts with you letting us in." Nakoma tilted his head behind him, as more crunching boots approached us. "Come inside soon," he said, as he rose to his feet.

I knew who lingered behind me, waiting for an invitation; I nodded to the space beside me. "You can sit." Evander was still in the same bloodied clothes from the battle, he caught my eyes looking them over, my jaw clenching at the stains.

"I haven't had time to change," he explained anxiously. "Narrdie, about Audric I-"

"Don't say his name," I snarled. "Don't *you* say his name, you stopped me. I could have done something!"

"Done what?" He snapped. "All you would have done, is die. You would have died and then it would have all been over. Narrdie, you couldn't have stopped her," his voice softened. "Not like this." I looked to him, aware that my face was stained with tears.

"I should have done something," my voice broke. Evander rested his hand on my cheek, he kissed the top of my head and pulled me to him.

"There are ways, ways to get him back and I promise; I will do everything in my power to bring him home." I wrapped my arms around him and he pulled me onto his lap. "Don't ever shut me out," he breathed, brushing his lips against mine. "We will face the darkness together."

Shrill calls and high bird echoes, bellowed around us, Evander shot to his feet and pulled me up with him – my heart immediately jumping to a frantic beat. "What is that?" Fear spiked into me, scared that it was Crow's army, coming to finish us off while we were all vulnerable.

"It's Lytta. Get the Priestesses."

Lytta was breathing hard as she stood just beyond the veil of the Priestesses home, an angered look residing on her face. "We found someone," she announced to us. She turned her head back and hooted like an owl.

Mazruriuk snarled and I could feel the ripple of anger leaking off him, like the heat from a bonfire. My own fury began to bubble to the surface, two of Lytta's people – Shakti and Bjorgan – roughly dragged along Nyda, dropping her to her knees in front of us. "We found her wondering the forest, alone." I wanted to kill her; to tear her skin off and burn her insides. "What do you wish of her?"

"Kill her," Mazruriuk snarled, his voice sounding like eerie whispers on a dark night. "Kill her like she killed Rosie and Astrid."

"Kill the traitor," voices began to burst behind us.

"Enough!" Evander commanded, his voice drawing everyone to silence. He walked forward and perched down beside her, the tip of his knife lifting her chin. Her eyes were wide, her cheeks were scrawny, and her skin was as pale as the moon. "Was it worth it?" He asked, his voice was quiet, scarily calm. "Was it worth betraying everyone who called you friend?" Her eyes watered, and her breath was pitchy as she tried to gather her words. Evander's hand snagged around her throat, his blade cutting her neck. "Was it fucking worth is Nyda?"

"I'm sorry," she whispered.

"You're sorry?" I blurted, wrath sparked through me, setting my feet moving towards her. "You expect to come here, give us a pathetic apology and then all would be forgiven?" I struck her hard with the back of my hand. "Did Crow kick you out? Realise you were worthless to her? Is that why you're back?"

"I couldn't say no, I couldn't cross her, or Dacre, or Ammon. They would have killed me in worst ways than you could imagine." Her voice was weepy, the water leaked from her eyes. "I didn't want it to get this far."

"Worse ways than having your throat slid and blood drained?" I bit, forcing away the images that played in my mind. "You've double crossed everyone for years Nyda. You biggest mistake, was coming back her and hoping for forgiveness. Dacre told me what you did all those years ago." Nyda's eyes turned panicked. "You didn't just cause Rosie and Astrid's deaths, did you?"

"Narrdie, please."

"Talon, Illythia, the day Adelina died – Nyda was the one who brought Crow to the surface." Their angered hisses, sent shivered up my spine, I looked to Evander. "That wasn't her first betrayal." I saw the realisation shadow across his face; his eyes flaring.

"Graya." It wasn't a question, but I nodded. Evander raised his sword and marched towards her; I flung my arm out – blocking his path.

"You deserve your death; Nyda and you will get it. I'm going to make sure that, Evander, Illythia, Talon, Mazruriuk and every other person you've wronged gets a change. Each time you are on the brink of death, I will have you healed. So that the next person can have their revenge. You will spend the rest of your life, feeling nothing but torture and pain." The words fell out of me like venom. Nyda's face was a mask of unwavering terror; her body shook and her breathing came out in shuddering gasps. "Karro, tear her to shreds." Karro lunged for her, his teeth bare, but her next words had me ordering him to stop.

"I can bring one back!" She shrieked, recoiling from the saliva and heckles of Karro's jaws. A heavy silence filled the air, as we all felt the weight of her words, felt the pain it plunged into our hearts and it was Bayona, who cut into the silence.

"You lie. Death can't be erased, only the mother of all, holds that power."

"No, she doesn't," Fyra interrupted. "There is a way, but in order to bring one back, another must pay the cost."

"I am happy to pay the cost," Nyda's voice trembled. "I want to make it right; I know the mother has turned her back on me." Mazruriuk's fist slammed into her cheek, knocking her back down; his hand gripped her throat and hauled her to her feet.

"You expect us to choose? After we have lost so many?"

"You don't choose," Nyda whimpered.

"Then who?" He asked, dropping her to the floor; her hand rubbed at her raw throat.

"Those that have fallen."

To be continued . . .

Acknowledgements

This book has been years in the making, and without the support of all my family and friends – I would have not had the will and confidence to go on with it.

To my mum and grandad, throughout the years, you have
both been there, supporting me through my hard times and encouraging me to follow my goals. Words cannot describe how much love I have for you both.

To my best friend and my rock. Who has always come calling, whenever I need him, who took care of me and cheered me
up on my dark days. Not only are you my best friend, but you are my family, my brother.

Special Thanks To
Howy White, for allowing me to use, the amazing photography for me cover.
www.howywhite.com

Lauren Rennie, for allowing me to use her, beautiful face on my cover.

And

Ethan Grey, for helping me with my editing and grammar.

Look out for BOOK TWO

ERUPT

The Bringer of Darkness

By Taara Petts

Coming Soon

Printed in Great Britain
by Amazon

77315760R00275